# Blood Shot Eyes

## By Patrick W. Picciarelli

*To Susan, whose love and devotion made this book possible.*

Chapter One

The black Mercedes limousine turned down a darkened path in the park and slid to a stop on a sheet of thin ice. The park was a deserted oasis of unkempt, litter-strewn lawns, chipped concrete walkways, and moss-covered statues. The well-dressed, heavyset man in the car's backseat wiped his sweaty palms on his trousers and stared out the window.

"What happens if the cops see us?"

The brunette sitting across from him said, "Don't worry, I know this place. It's not going to happen. Does your driver know enough not to bother us?"

"He'll leave us alone. He's done this before, honey."

"Helga. The name is Helga."

A young blonde sitting next to Helga happily downed champagne straight from the bottle. The girl, who looked to be about nineteen years old, was beginning to suffer the ravages of a night of marathon drinking. Her hair, which at the beginning of the evening had been shining and alive, had lost its curl. Her makeup appeared pasty, and the whites of her eyes had changed to a bloodshot red; a gray wool skirt that originally ended at the knee was now hiked up to thigh level.

"You promised us some goodies, Herman," the blonde slurred a moment before emitting a volcanic burp. "Oh, excuuuse me." She threw back her head amidst gales of laughter.

"Ah, youth," the fat man said. He shifted his weight and produced a plastic bag from his pocket. "This shit's the best available."

As the two women watched, Herman Zoltag dumped an ounce of barely stepped-on cocaine onto a black, book-sized tray. Like an artist sculpting his latest creation, he used a business card to fashion cigarette-thick lines. The younger woman squealed with delight. Helga yawned.

After making certain the lines were neat, Zoltag pushed the remaining mound of cocaine to the right of his creation. He looked at both women and extended the tray. "Who's first?"

The blonde snatched the tray, put the straw in her left nostril, and vacuumed the entire first line. "Fantastic." She grabbed the bottle of champagne and took a long gulp.

Helga leaned forward, straw in hand, and inhaled a conservative quarter inch. As she bent over the tray, her breasts became partially exposed beneath a silk blouse that had the top three buttons undone. She rubbed her nose and handed the straw to Zoltag, who ogled her cleavage.

He maneuvered his three-hundred-pound girth to the edge of the leather seat, carefully accepted the tray from Helga, and sucked down half a line. He sneezed and seemed to feel the drug's effect immediately.

"Good shit," he said, sliding back and scooping up the Dom Perignon. He poured the bubbly liquid into a champagne glass and sipped it like a lord in the presence of his minions.

The three continued drinking and snorting, each taking a turn, or so it seemed. Helga had taken only the first sampling. Her shoulder-length wig hid her sweeping the powder to the floor.

#

Zoltag looked at his watch. Eleven p.m. They'd been in the park for more than three hours.

He turned his attention to the two women who were still attacking his supply of coke and champagne. As usual, the drug was going straight to his groin, and he felt the familiar pulsating of his penis. Zoltag thought it was a good time to make his move. He could see Kathy, the younger one, was stoned. She could barely form a simple sentence.

Helga, if that were her real name, seemed more in control. She wasn't much older than Kathy, twenty-five or six, he thought, but she handled her cocaine and alcohol much better. He had picked up the right two this time. A rare double-header.

As he talked to Kathy at the bar in the Village earlier that evening, he had been surprised when Helga wandered over from a table. She had been sitting alone, ignoring men who were coming onto her. Helga immediately became warm and friendly, and Zoltag figured she sensed he had drugs. Some broads have a sixth sense when it comes to coke; they always seem to know who has it. It was usually easy for him. Dangle a bag of whatever illegal substance they were looking for under their noses, and in two hours they'd be naked. Helga, he figured, was probably married and out to raise a little hell while her husband stayed home and watched the kids. What bullshit. Zoltag was happy he'd stayed a bachelor.

Now the two women seemed ready. He kicked his shoes off and extended his legs, one toward each woman. He nudged each with his feet. Helga stopped talking, and Kathy stared at him cross-eyed.

"Time to play," he said.

Both women sat motionless as he eased his feet under their skirts. Neither protested. He caressed their inner thighs with his feet. He found the warm area between their legs and began rubbing. Kathy moaned softly. She spread her legs wider and tilted her head back, closing her eyes in a

7

drug-induced euphoria. Helga stared at him. She licked her lips and squeezed her legs together.

Nice firm thighs.

Helga whispered, "I have a surprise for you."

Zoltag loved innovative women. "What could you have planned I haven't already thought of?"

Helga flashed a lusty smile. "Kathy and I thought up something you might like. Interested?"

Zoltag looked at Kathy, who by this time had taken to grabbing his foot and rubbing it furiously against her crotch. She didn't look like she could conjure up a way to take a piss, he thought, let alone devise a kinky way to get him off, if that's what she had in mind. He looked in Helga's hungry eyes and knew that was *exactly* what she had in mind.

"What do you want me to do?" He was dry-mouthed and hoarse, the result of a combination of desire and too much cocaine.

"Wait outside," she said. "Kathy and I have to talk."

He considered what she had said. While he would have liked to pounce on the two of them now, he was up for a game, thinking that Helga might have some sex toys in the oversized bag she had with her. Besides, he felt like stretching.

He removed his feet from the girls' respective crotches. Kathy whimpered and continued to rub herself, now using both hands to masturbate. He wondered whom she was fantasizing about.

His shoes back on, fat Herman Zoltag hit the evening air. The car door slammed behind him. It had to be thirty degrees, and he had left his jacket in the car. Even though he was fueled on drugs and champagne, the artificial heat source wasn't sufficient to keep him comfortable. The last thing he wanted to do, however, was get back in the limo, at least not yet. He would give the girls a reasonable length of time to prepare for whatever it was they had planned.

He could see headlights on a distant highway. Other than that, he guessed the only people in the area were probably in his car.

He walked to the front of the limousine. Bruno, his driver, was asleep, his head resting against the window and a small rivulet of saliva at the corner of his mouth. Bruno was a good chauffeur and even better at keeping his mouth shut. Zoltag couldn't think of better qualities.

He wondered if he was supposed to get back in the car or wait to be summoned. He strained to look through the tinted glass. All he could see was a distorted reflection of himself.

At last, the power window opened a fraction, and he heard Helga's voice call out. "Come in now…hurry."

Zoltag leaped in the car and swallowed hard when he saw Kathy's blouse open and Helga licking the girl's exposed right nipple. Kathy lay facing away from the aroused fat man, her pantyhose tangled on the floor. Zoltag thought he could kick a field goal between the spread legs of the nubile Kathy. Another ten degrees, and they would be at right angles. Helga grabbed his turgid penis through his pants and began stroking.

"Take off your clothes," she said in a sultry voice.

"What about you?"

"You first. It's part of the surprise."

The fat man could barely contain himself. He tore at his clothes, all the while staring transfixed at Helga. She straddled Kathy, facing her while sensuously rubbing herself against the younger woman. Helga's skirt was above her hips and climbing. Her arms encircled Kathy, her head buried in the nape of the unmoving woman's neck. The kid hadn't stirred, probably expended after her ninth orgasm of the evening, Zoltag figured.

He booted the last of his clothes across the carpeted floor. "Ready."

Helga turned slowly, removing her right hand from behind Kathy's back to reveal a bulky CO2-powered gas gun. She punched the long barrel between Zoltag's eyes, breaking his skin and propelling him backward.

He clutched his head, stunned, his eyes wide in shock. He stared at his hands and saw his own blood.

"The fuck...?" he said, searching Helga's face for an answer.

"Surprise, dickhead." Helga backhanded Zoltag across the cheekbone with the breech of the Crossman pistol.

Zoltag tried to scream, but the pain was so intense, the attempt produced no sound. When he sucked in his breath for a second try, Helga was ready with a fistful of pantyhose, and in went a ball of nylon.

She grinned and said, "Nothing beats a great pair of legs." She tied his hands with his sweat-coated T-shirt and laboriously flipped him over on his back. His dashboard-sized buttocks were on the floor, and his back rested against the supple leather seat.

Helga had one hand on his testicles and slowly twisted while the gas gun in her other hand played a melody on the bridge of his nose. Beads of sweat rose from every pore of Zoltag's flabby body. Where the fuck is Bruno when he needed him? Blood ran into his eyes, blurring his vision. *What the fuck was this about?*

She removed the gag and said, "Don't make a sound." Helga stuck the thick barrel of the gun in Zoltag's nose to make her point. He sucked in air and tried to blink away the coagulating blood from his eyes.

Helga literally had him by the balls, and in a move that surprised him, she relaxed her grip.

"Do you like your balls?" she asked, her face less than an inch from his doughy features.

Zoltag nodded vigorously, knowing that she had not asked the question rhetorically.

She kneeled in front of him and asked, "Where's the tape?"

Through pained and bloody lips, Zoltag said, "What tape?"

Helga shoved the pantyhose back into his mouth and whacked his left knee full force with her heavy gun. Zoltag let out a muffled scream, and then he defecated on the floor.

She moved backward, wrinkling her nose.

"You want to end up like her?" she said. She grabbed Kathy's hair and lifted the young girl's head off the seat, revealing a hole where Kathy's left eye had been. A whitish-yellow fluid oozed down the girl's cheek.

Zoltag stared at her, his eyes bulging.

The sight of the dead girl's hollow eye socket revolted him, and Zoltag proceeded to eject his last meal with the fury of an erupting artillery piece. Except the bursting projectile hadn't anywhere to travel because his mouth was plugged with a dead girl's pantyhose. He began to drown in his own vomitus.

Helga yanked the pantyhose free, releasing a torrent of odorous liquid, which narrowly missed her and landed on an uncaring Kathy. Zoltag keeled over on his side, slipping from the relative splendor of the leather seat to the soaked rug of his $95,000 automobile. Helga stuck the barrel of the gun under his testicles.

In a controlled voice, she said, "Now, I'm going to ask you for the last time, where the fuck is the tape?"

His voice barely audible, Zoltag spit out, "Dropped ceiling…office…both copies."

She placed her face next to his ear and asked softly, "Are you telling me the tape is in the ceiling in your office?"

Zoltag, in immense pain and thoroughly exhausted, nodded.

She screwed the barrel into the recess between his testicles and his anus. He let out a whimper, and she backed off the gun.

11

Zoltag swallowed hard.

"Please don't hurt me anymore," he pleaded. He now knew who had sent her, and he understood if he didn't cooperate, the pain he had just experienced would be like cutting himself shaving.

Helga grabbed one of the fat man's shoes and shoved it in his mouth. She put the gun against his left kneecap and fired, sending a .177-caliber brass pellet traveling at 560 feet per second through flesh and bone.

Zoltag's world exploded into a ball of fire, igniting at the base of his skull. He begged for his life through a size twelve Gucci loafer.

Helga smiled. "You aren't lying to me are you, Herman?"

Zoltag had lost any ability to speak or gesture. He simply lay in a puddle of his bodily fluids, hoping the pain would go away. He made gulping noises in response to her question.

Helga smiled and reloaded the single-shot gas gun as Zoltag's eyes widened in panic. She turned on the radio and raised the volume. Zoltag kicked at the floor in a vain attempt to alert his driver. There was no response.

She tried to place the gun's muzzle against his left eye, but he knew what was coming and would have none of it. He shook his head violently from side to side, spraying sweat and blood, trying to forestall the inevitable. Finally, the gunmetal came to rest in an eye recess, and she squeezed the trigger. Within seconds, Herman Zoltag, man about town, stopped struggling. A warm feeling slowly enveloped his body. He felt the gun barrel enter his ear. The last thing he recalled thinking was that it tickled.

## Chapter Two

Ray Yale had walked to within fifty yards of the old man on the park bench when he stopped. To reach him, Yale had to walk through ankle-deep grass yellowed by the November chill.

Overcoming his fear of treading through grass high enough to conceal his feet, Yale took a few steps closer to the man. He shuddered. Almost thirty years since his Vietnam experience, Yale still marveled at the way his palms moistened when he walked through tall grass. He thought of the possible tripwires that might be lying beneath the surface, hastening his journey to hell. He smiled wistfully. Why would the Viet Cong plant booby traps in Flushing Meadow Park?

Yale glanced at his watch. Not bad, only twenty minutes late. He'd brought back many quirks from Vietnam, but a military man's penchant for punctuality was not one of them.

The old man was very thin and appeared to be short. He wore a long brown overcoat and a wide-brimmed Stetson that Yale's father would have called a "Spencer Tracy hat." Even though Yale had approached from the front, the old man gave no outward sign he was aware of anyone's presence. Quite the contrary, he stared straight ahead, almost as if looking through Yale.

13

Yale peered under the brim of the hat and said, "Mr. Carpenter? My name's Ray Yale. Sorry I'm a little late." He held out his hand.

Arnold Carpenter looked up slowly, his watery eyes focusing on the younger man. He was back from wherever his thoughts had taken him.

"I'm sorry, Mr. Yale, I was lost in thought. Sit down, please." They shook hands and Carpenter shifted to make room on the bench.

Yale settled on the splintery wood, lifted the collar of his nylon aviator jacket, and buried his hands in his pockets in an attempt to protect himself from the chill of the late autumn afternoon. "You always ask for meetings in the middle of nowhere, Mr. Carpenter?"

Carpenter smiled sadly, avoiding eye contact.

"Ah, a Manhattanite," he said. "Totally lost outside the big city, Mr. Yale?"

"Actually, I live here in Queens, but this has got to be one of the strangest places I've had to meet a potential client."

The old man turned to look at him. "Oh, I'm not *potential*, Mr. Yale. I'm going to hire you, for reasons I shall explain. Let me first tell you that I wanted to meet you here because this is the place where my daughter, and a man she was with, were murdered nine years ago."

Ray Yale looked around at the deteriorating city park, a big park by anyone's standards. This was the site of two World's Fairs, a mecca for millions of tourists during those happier times. He hadn't been here since he was a kid, but he had read, and was now seeing firsthand, that years of neglect and the clumsy scrawls of graffiti artists were leading to the park's demise. He did recall a double homicide had occurred in the park.

"I'm sorry about your daughter. I was a cop back then, but I was working in Manhattan, and I don't remember the case very well. I'm sorry."

"Don't feel bad for not remembering my daughter's murder, Mr.

Yale. The case has become a distant memory for most, especially the police department. That is why I called you." Carpenter had resumed staring straight ahead. "I would like you to find out who killed her."

Yale cleared his throat. "Mr. Carpenter, I don't know how you found me, but—"

"The stories in the paper…about you and your wife."

"Murder cases are usually best handled by the police. They've got manpower, a crime lab. Besides—"

Carpenter interrupted him with a raised hand. "How old do I look, Mr. Yale? Seventy? Seventy-five? I'm fifty-nine years old. My daughter's killing is now slowly killing *me*. My wife, Sarah, died two years ago. I'm surprised she lasted that long. Her daughter was her life, as she was mine." With the help of a hand on Yale's shoulder, he got to his feet. "Come, walk with me."

Yale was at least six inches taller than Carpenter, who walked slowly. Yale found himself taking half-steps as he once did when walking with his elderly mother. The two men covered about thirty yards in silence, following a concrete path that curved around a pair of dead elm trees. Carpenter gripped Yale's elbow, and they came to a halt.

They stood in front of two flagpoles. Both poles were in varying stages of decay, with chipped paint exposing rusted metal. Ropes hung the length of each pole and flapped in the wind. Kids must use them to swing on, Yale thought. The ropes beat against the poles, creating a hollow, metallic sound.

Carpenter gestured with both hands. "These flagpoles are a disgrace."

The entire park is a disgrace, Yale felt like saying. "Yes, but what—?"

"Look up, Mr. Yale, at the very top," Carpenter said, his gaze wandering upward.

Yale could see a swastika mounted on German iron eagles at the top of each pole.

"These flagpoles were part of the German exhibition during the 1939 World's Fair," Carpenter said. "I'm a Jew, Mr. Yale. My real name is Karpinski. My entire family—my parents, my older sister, God rest their souls—and me, the youngest, escaped from hiding in Poland and came to America in 1943. Do you find it ironic that after my family escaped the tyranny of the Nazis, my only child should die near the emblem of the Reich?" The old man raised his hands to his face and began to cry softly.

Yale put his arm around Carpenter's shoulder but kept silent. *What words of condolence hasn't this man already heard? Let him cry.* Yale also figured that this wasn't the time to compare name changes. Yale's real last name had originally been Iallicci, but by the time his grandfather had settled on Elizabeth Street in New York's Little Italy, it had morphed to Yale.

Carpenter composed himself and started back toward the bench. "I must sit down."

They fought the wind back to the bench and sat in silence for a minute.

"Wouldn't it be something, Mr. Yale, if New York Jews came to this place and tore down those hateful things?"

"You mean Jews with influence in this town don't know these things exist?"

"Surely you are joking. Do you think I'm the only Jew in New York who knows these poles are here? Jews are very politically astute, here as elsewhere. If anyone, Jews or otherwise, really cared about those flagpoles, they would be gone. I just don't think anyone cares anymore."

"But you care, Mr. Carpenter."

"I care about one thing, Mr. Yale, finding out who murdered my

Katherine and bringing that person to justice."

It was getting late. In the distance, traffic was beginning to back up on the elevated portion of the Van Wyck Expressway with commuters on their way home to their fortresses in suburbia. How did they do this every day and keep their sanity? Yale tugged at his collar to ward off the increasing chill. "Like I said, you'd best let the cops handle this. I don't think I—"

Carpenter held up his hand. "The police aren't doing anything. In the last nine years, there have been six different detectives assigned to my daughter's case. In the beginning, they were always calling me, just to let me know what they were doing, and if they were making any progress. Then the calls began to dwindle. I would occasionally hear from a detective who said that there was nothing new, but they were hoping for a break. The last detective called about a year ago, and she called my daughter *Caroline*. That doesn't give me much confidence in the police."

"No, I suppose not."

"I still call them now and then, but they think I'm an old fool. I can tell it in their voices; they just want to get me off the phone. 'Nothing new,' they say. 'When we hear something, we'll call you.' I was just about to give up when I saw the story about you and your wife in the newspaper. I followed all the stories very carefully and with great interest. I said: now there's a man who won't give up, who *didn't* give up. Then I called your police headquarters, and they said that you left the police department to become a private investigator. That's when I knew I had to contact you. I know you won't give up."

Yale thought about the not-too-distant past while he was still on The Job and had pleaded for help from the police department and was turned down. He was reminded that his superiors in the NYPD had totally disregarded his loyalty and reputation as a good detective just because he

17

tried to fight the system. He empathized with Carpenter.

His forced retirement had been, perhaps, a blessing in disguise. At least now he didn't have to deal with the pettiness endemic to any big city police department, but he wanted to tell Carpenter that he was carrying around too much emotional baggage to be of any help. At this time in his life, Yale didn't think he could detect an egg roll in a Chinese restaurant, let alone solve a homicide. But he also knew that Carpenter didn't care about any of this. The old man saw him as his white knight. Carpenter was dangling from a cliff and was certain Yale had the rope to pull him to safety. Yale knew what it was like to plead to the deaf.

What the hell, he thought, it couldn't hurt to get some more information. "Tell me about your daughter, Mr. Carpenter."

"She was a good girl," he began, and then added, "basically."

Yale raised an eyebrow.

"I can't see very far these days," Carpenter said, "but my peripheral vision is still very good. Your expression tells me that you think I'm about to qualify my daughter's conduct. Not so. I will tell you, however, that she was a product of the world we live in. At home, she adhered to our dictates. She lived in our house, we set the rules, and for the most part, she obeyed them. We even taught her to speak Yiddish, which we often spoke at home. At her studies, she excelled, but in her sixteenth year, she became her own person, at her mother's and my expense."

"Drugs?"

Carpenter nodded. "Drugs, drinking, the wrong friends, late nights, all of it. We believed it was a phase she was passing through, and we were partially correct. We didn't love her any less. We were more disappointed and frightened than angry, actually. She was our only child, and we were perhaps a little more protective of her when she was growing up, and we were afraid of losing her to her new lifestyle. However, by the time she reached college age, she was accepted to the Columbia School of Journalism and had returned to her normal self, except for occasional lapses."

"What kind of lapses?"

"She would come home every now and then smelling of alcohol and suffering the effects of drug abuse. Those times were rare, but they happened more than I would like to admit. She didn't think we knew what she was doing, but we did. During those times, she would often sleep for twenty-four hours. She never, however, missed school. Once in college, her lapses occurred only on the occasional Friday night or during a school holiday."

A straight-A junkie, Yale thought, but kept it to himself.

"In totality," Carpenter continued, "she was a good girl and treated us with respect."

"Tell me about the day your daughter was killed," Yale said, hoping the question wouldn't cause a flood of tears.

Carpenter sighed. "She was with two other people, a man named Zoltag and a woman whom the police never identified. This Zoltag was much older than my Katherine, and from what the police have told me, all three of them met for the first time the night of the murders in a bar in Greenwich Village. I don't recall its name. The police told me that the three of them got into Zoltag's limousine and came to this place, where we are right now. They came here to drink champagne and take drugs. This is where Zoltag and my Katherine were murdered."

"Where was your daughter found?"

"Both Zoltag and my daughter were in the backseat of the car. As I said, the other woman was never found. The police and the newspapers speculated that she was the killer."

Yale kicked into cop mode. "How were they killed? Was there a

19

driver? What happened to him?"

"They were both shot in the head. I think the man had other wounds elsewhere on his body, but I'm not certain." Carpenter put his elbows on his knees and placed his face in his hands. "The chauffeur slept through the whole thing, I was told."

"Two people shot in the head in the backseat of his car and he slept through it?" Maybe Carpenter had his facts confused. "Did the police say anything about the caliber of weapon that was used? Did they say anything about a suppressor...silencer? Did you read anything about that in the papers?"

The old man thought for a moment.

"I don't know about such things, Mr. Yale. I suggest you ask the police. I really don't recall."

"Do you know if any of your daughter's friends were interviewed?"

"I didn't know any of Katherine's friends, but I don't think so. The police said Zoltag was the object of the killing."

"Target, you mean."

"Yes, target. My daughter was in the wrong place at the wrong time. Do you think the police should have questioned Katherine's friends?"

"Well, we don't know for sure that they didn't. I'll have to check."

"Does this mean you'll look into Katherine's murder, Mr. Yale?" Carpenter asked, hope straining his voice.

Yale shifted to face Carpenter. "You've got to understand something, Mr. Carpenter. This case is very old. By police department standards, it's downright ancient. There's a rule in homicide investigations that says if you're not well on your way to a suspect within twenty-four hours, the trail begins to get cold. After nine years, the trail is positively frigid. I'll check around to see what I come up with, though." Yale felt

20

sorry for the old man; he knew what it felt like to have nowhere to turn.

"Is it customary at this time for me to give you a retainer?"

"It's my practice to get a rather large retainer, yes, but let me see if I can do anything for you first. I just hate to return money." He smiled, but the old man just nodded.

"I understand. Thank you very much, Mr. Yale." He reached into his overcoat pocket. "Here is a card with my home number on it. I'm retired now, you know. Jewelry business." Carpenter stood, handed over the card, and shook Yale's hand feebly. He took out his wallet and removed a picture. "And this is Katherine."

Yale looked at the photo but didn't touch it. For reasons he couldn't explain, he felt it wasn't the right thing to do. It was a head shot of a teenager, all smiles, long blonde hair and the innocence of youth. "She looks very happy."

Carpenter compressed his lips. "She was." He carefully put the picture back in his wallet, as if trying not to inflict discomfort on his daughter. "You are giving me hope."

Yale rose, pocketing the card. "There will be some hope only if there's some new information. I'll be in touch." Yale squeezed the old man's shoulder and began to walk the mile to the street where he had parked his car. There was a strict 'no vehicle' rule in the park, and he wondered how a limousine had gotten this far without being challenged. Too many questions left unanswered, but right now Yale's first priority was getting to his car and turning on the heat.

Yale looked over his shoulder and watched Carpenter set out in another direction. He saw from the card that the old guy lived in Forest Hills, quite a hike, even for a younger man. He stopped and called to Carpenter.

"Do you have a car? I could give you a ride home."

21

Carpenter turned. "Thank you, Mr. Yale, but I feel like walking. It helps me forget."

He started to wave when he heard the old man's voice over a sudden gust of wind.

"Forgive my manners, Mr. Yale, but how is your wife feeling these days? I've seen nothing in the newspapers."

Yale turned and began to walk away.

In a voice barely audible to himself he said, "She died, Mr. Carpenter, about a year ago."

The old man called after him, repeating the same question. Yale didn't answer. He felt tears run down his face, the taste of salt tingling his lips as he avoided the grassy areas on the way to his car.

## Chapter Three

Yale had gone straight home after his meeting with Arnold Carpenter. There were times when he staggered into his house rubbery-legged drunk at three a.m., collapsing fully clothed on his bed. He had quite a few of those nights since Vivian died, and waking up with a hangover was now the rule rather than the exception.

Last night, however, was different. Instead of burying himself in a bottle, he chose a book, which failed to facilitate his escape. Television was no help either, he found most shows boring. He managed to get to sleep after some fitful tossing and turning.

His eyes popped open at eight a.m. He swung out of bed, surprisingly well rested, before he had a chance to realize that he was still in a depressed mood.

His best time of the day was that first five seconds after waking, when he still had a clear mind and no recollection of his recent past. Yale's first thoughts were of Vivian, always Vivian. On his way to the bathroom, he smiled when he thought of how she would kid him about the speed in which he was able to get out of bed, even after a session of love-making and many hours of deep slumber. She had said he got up so fast that if he looked quick enough he would still be able to see himself in bed.

The place certainly felt empty without her.

He padded naked to the bathroom and into the shower and was once again reminded of odd habits he had brought back with him from Vietnam. He still felt compelled to take quickie showers, a throwback to when he was in that armpit of a country and water was a precious commodity.

Yale dressed and went downstairs past the empty basement apartment of his two-family house, removed the three locks that secured the door to the one-car garage, and backed out his newly purchased Jaguar S-Type.

Yale caressed the steering wheel of the car he likened to the Starship Enterprise. He was wrapped in close luxury, surrounded by leather, facing an array of dials and gauges. He drove in the nearly soundproof cockpit like an astronaut weaving through an asteroid shower, losing himself momentarily to a Captain Kirk fantasy. Today, the heavenly bodies he dodged were gypsy cabs speeding to their next radio-dispatched fare. He knew a neighborhood had seen better days when yellow cabs were nowhere to be found.

He arrived at the Omega Racquet Ball and Health Club, or just plain 'gym' as he called it, in ten minutes and was pleased to see the parking lot nearly empty. He had chosen this particular gym because it was open around the clock, affording him the opportunity to use the weight room whenever the notion struck. Normally mobbed from late afternoon until midnight, the early morning hours were pleasantly devoid of the craziness that late crowds bring.

He began his routine with a gut-busting ride to nowhere on a stationary recumbent bike. He hated this portion of his regimen, but he figured for each mile he went a minute particle of fat dissolved in his forty-seven-year-old aorta. The push-ups, sit-ups, free weights, and machines

24

were actually enjoyable, and he was able to envision his body transforming into a finely honed instrument.

Yale paid virtually no attention to the other people in the workout area. He cruised from one station to another, lost in thought. While a million miles away on a triceps machine, he heard someone calling his name.

"Hey, Ray, you don't answer me when I call you?"

Yale turned and saw Sal Bertuna, who he would best describe as the closest one could get to the legal definition of a dwarf without actually being one. Bertuna was a burned-out Vietnam veteran who felt a kinship with Yale because of their mutual war-time experiences. As usual, Bertuna was festooned with gold neck chains and wore a black T-shirt and white spandex workout pants. Resembling a gangster penguin, Bertuna made a second home out of the Omega, mainly because he had never married, lived alone, and could find a friendly ear among the gym rats and business people who often humored the lonely man. He had been after Yale to hire him for surveillance work since Yale had gone into the private investigation business.

Yale wiped his forehead with a sleeve. "I get lost when I'm working out, you should know that by now, Sal," he said, hoping Bertuna would take the hint and get lost.

Oblivious to the implication, Sal said, "Hey, Ray, ya know I'm still lookin' for a little extra work on the side, like maybe I could follow somebody around for ya or somethin'."

Yale held up a finger and grunted through another set of triceps extensions before replying. "Come on, Sal, you already have a job, or are you saving for that dream yacht? Besides, that Mr. T starter-set you're wearing wouldn't exactly make you inconspicuous."

"Man, I'm like a little bored. Bellevue can get tedious, you know what I'm sayin'?" He fingered his chains. "I could always wear a shirt buttoned at the collar to hide these."

Yale knew Bertuna's regular line of employment was in the Bellevue Hospital morgue; it was his responsibility to prepare the bodies for autopsy and clean up the mess afterwards. Bertuna worked at what the Army had trained him to do. During the Vietnam War, he'd been assigned to Graves Registration. Thirty-five years ago, it was his job to clean, catalogue, and ship dead soldiers back home.

"Well, I wish I could help you out, buddy," Yale said, "but business is a little slow."

"If you could keep me in mind, I'd really appreciate it. I'd do a real good job."

"When something comes up, I'll let you know," Yale said as he began his third set of triceps extensions. He didn't like cutting him off, but unless he did just that Bertuna would bend his ear forever. Yale doubted the veteran could handle the tedium of surveillance. He struck Yale as being too manic, even though today he seemed calm. The man was burned out after hauling bodies in Vietnam, and now, after too many years of doing almost the same thing in a hospital, he didn't know anything else.

Before Yale had realized how starved for friendship Bertuna was, he would often tease him good naturedly about his height and the reason he had survived Vietnam without a scratch was that bullets probably flew over his head. Yale now regretted throwing those barbs, however good intentioned, at a man who had lost his sense of humor in a rice paddy.

After a quick shower, he drove home and went to his office in the spare bedroom at the back of his apartment. One quick call would help him decide if getting involved in the Carpenter case was worth his trouble and his client's money.

Yale dialed Lieutenant Michael Sheehan's private number at the

One-Ten Precinct Detective Squad. The phone was picked up on the first ring.

"Lieutenant Sheehan, One-Ten Squad." Sheehan's voice was crisp and authoritative.

"Michael, Ray Yale."

There was a moment's hesitation.

"Ray. Long time. Jesus Christ, I haven't seen you since…."

"Yeah, I know."

"Listen, I'm awfully sorry about your wife. I never expected you to drop out of sight like that. I called you after the funeral, but I never heard from you."

Yale remembered Lt. Mike Sheehan to be one of the few bosses on The Job who stood up for him at his department insubordination trial. Sheehan had missed the funeral because he was hospitalized with a back problem.

"I guess I needed some time to get my head straight. Everything came all at once, the cancer, the forced retirement. I know I owed you more than most anyone else, but I just wasn't up to socializing."

"Your wife was a helluva cop," Sheehan said. "The Job shouldn't have tried to force her out over the cancer. And they damn sure shouldn't have made you retire because you tried to save her job."

"Those were the rules, Michael. She was out on extended sick leave and had to retire. I just knew it would kill her if she couldn't work at the job she loved."

"So you think it was smart to go to the media to change the rules?" Sheehan said. "Look where it got you."

"The desk jockeys at the Puzzle Palace wouldn't listen. I had to do something. But hey, I was able to save her job and the jobs of who knows how many other hapless cops in the same position *because* of the media."

And one reporter in particular, Yale thought.

"But she died anyway."

"Yeah, but at least she was a cop 'til the end." He wanted to get off the subject. "My head's screwed on a little straighter now," he lied. "How's the back?"

"Okay. Maybe I'll put in for the three-quarters and run." Sheehan had been threatening to retire on a disability pension for years, but three young Sheehans in need of college educations kept any ideas of leaving the department out of consideration.

"Busy for lunch?" Yale asked.

"Can't really get away, I've got monthly reports. Maybe some other time." Translation: I'm available, name a place. The Job has a long memory, and each was aware that any superior officer being seen with Yale might have a career reversal, and department phones are always subject to taps.

They agreed on a restaurant through generalities and street jargon.

"By the way," Sheehan asked, "how long you been off The Job now?"

"Almost three years," Yale said. He had actually been retired for eleven months.

They would meet at three o'clock.

Chapter Four

Skylights Cafe was located on a side street in an area consisting
mostly of abandoned warehouses in western Queens. It survived as a
watering hole because it was situated off the heavily trafficked service road
where the Long Island Expressway emerged from the Queens Midtown
Tunnel. Yale liked it because the only vehicles parked anywhere near it
were tractor trailers and other big rigs. A lone passenger car or small van
would stick out, making it easier to spot Internal Affairs or some other
local or federal snoop. Yale had used the bar on many occasions when he
held clandestine meetings with reporters during his days of fighting with
the brass. He felt safe there and knew Mike Sheehan would, too. The
owner had become an ally during those turbulent times, allowing Yale and
whomever he was meeting to use his office on the second floor. He
waived to the big Irishman behind the bar and made his way toward the
back.

Yale navigated through the crowd of drinking men and made his
way up a rickety staircase to the office, barely big enough to hold a
battered desk, two wooden chairs, and a filing cabinet that appeared to
have had the lock shot off. Yale sat down, opened the desk drawer, and
retrieved a bottle of Johnnie Walker Red Label, with the seal intact. He

debated having a drink before Sheehan arrived, but the dilemma became moot because he couldn't find a glass.

Someone kicked the door. Yale sat up, alert.

"What?" Yale said, suddenly wishing he hadn't given up carrying a gun.

"It's Mike, open up, my arms are full."

"Stand back a little, the door swings out." He opened the door carefully to see Lt. Michael Sheehan holding a pizza box, a bottle of vodka, and two water glasses, all carefully balanced.

Yale grabbed the bottle and glasses. "You come prepared."

Sheehan put the pizza on top of the desk. He had gained weight since Yale had last seen him. His stomach strained at his belt, and he had added another chin to his rugged Irish face. "Your friend downstairs asked me what I was drinking and gave me the glasses. The pizza I bought at Domino's. I ate lunch here once, about three years ago, and my gut still hasn't recovered." He shook Yale's hand and tossed his raincoat on top of the filing cabinet. "How the hell've you been?"

They exchanged the pleasantries old friends are obligated to trade, and Yale did the honors by pouring the first round of drinks while Sheehan folded back the top of the pizza box and pulled out two slices. He plopped down a greasy slice of Sicilian in front of Yale. They ate, making small talk about the state of pizza making in contemporary America for five minutes before Sheehan opened up.

"So what's going on?" he asked, reaching for a second slice. "An old friend doesn't materialize out of nowhere and ask for a sit-down unless it's important."

"What's going on," Yale said, "is Katherine Carpenter."

Mike Sheehan looked over the rim of his glass. "Are you working that case?"

30

"I may be. The girl's father asked me to look into it. If I take it, it's only because I feel sorry for him. Sounds like he's getting a royal screwing by The Job. Looks like the case just went away. Is there something to look into?"

Sheehan poured himself another drink, this time a double. Yale could see why his friend had put on weight. Drinking like this and sitting around the squad room all day while your detectives go out and make you look good was bound to add on a few pounds. Kojak notwithstanding, most detective lieutenants led rather sedentary lives.

"It's been a lot of years, people lose interest," Sheehan said. "It's a shame, but that's the way it is. I was just getting to the One-Ten when it happened. Both the Carpenter kid and the fat guy were shot in the eyes. He took another round in the knee and one through the ear into the brain, but you could see he was tortured before he died. About a quarter ounce of coke and four empty Dom Perignon bottles were laying around. Party time, I would say. It was a mess."

"Like how?"

"He vomited and crapped himself. For chrissakes, Ray, I'm eating over here."

"I thought it was your back that was bad, not your stomach."

"Now it's both. I'm getting old."

"What else?"

Sheehan tossed what remained of the second slice of pizza back into the box, apparently resigned to the fact murder and his belly didn't mix. He didn't give up his drink, though.

"The fat guy," Sheehan said. "Zoltag, I believe was his name."

"Yeah, Zoltag."

"He was a mutt. Full-time photographer, part-time drug dealer." Sheehan explained where the women were picked up in Greenwich Village and the drug angle. "Then they drove to the park."

"Tell me about the chauffeur. How come he didn't hear the shots? Or did he?"

Sheehan took a long gulp of straight vodka. "Gas gun, no sound. Slept through the whole thing."

"Gas gun?"

"They both were shot with a CO2 gun, a gas gun, the kind you can buy in any sporting goods store. They're making them real powerful now. The kind of gun it was, we're not sure, but it was definitely a CO2 gun. There were traces of the gas on their faces. The fucking thing is quieter than a fart and doesn't have barrel riflings. No ballistics. We didn't release the part about what kind of weapon was used to the press; with them, we called it a shooting, period. Even with that we had the usual number of crazies confessing."

"Sexual activity?" Yale asked.

"We got a blood type from saliva on the Carpenter girl's breasts. It wasn't Zoltag's. Must have been the other girl's. No semen in her mouth or vagina. Both bodies loaded to the *kishka* with blow."

Yale was curious about the murder weapon. "What do those gas guns shoot, BB's?"

"This one fired brass pellets. It had a caliber, something like a twenty-two, only a little smaller, I think. We found a number of gas guns that would do the trick, but a person doesn't have to ID themselves when they buy one of them." He poured his third drink. "The fucking things should be outlawed."

Yale was still hungry, but he closed the lid on the pizza box. Out of sight, out of mind, he reasoned. "Where was the sector when all this was going on?" he asked, referring to the patrol car that would have been assigned to the park that night.

32

Sheehan sighed. "Is there ever a cop around when you need one? Supposedly they were patrolling the park. It's a big park."

"They were elsewhere and busy the entire time the limo was in the park? How long would that've been?"

"Zoltag's driver said they were in the park a good five hours. The precinct roll call for that night indicates the car was a Conditions Car, meaning they didn't handle any regular radio runs; they patrolled on their own keeping the park safe for the citizens." He smirked. "My guess is they were cooping, probably sleeping somewhere on the south end in a bunch of trees. The coop is located way at the other end of the park by the lake. Cops use it because they can see anyone who approaches."

"What'd the cops say when you interviewed them?"

"What else? They insisted they were patrolling all night. It's bullshit, but they stuck to their story, and we couldn't disprove it."

"So maybe they're telling the truth and the killer was just lucky."

"We had no choice but to call it luck. Look, there's no cars allowed in the park. This limo sails in, stays for half the night, and no one sees a thing. What would you call it?"

Yale let it go for now. He could interview the cops, but all that would accomplish was maybe proving that they were fucking off. "Aren't we talking two cars here? The four to twelve and the midnight to eight, right?"

Sheehan shook his head. "Nope. The park Conditions Car was a six to two. Just the one car." He was close to finishing his third drink. Damp stains had appeared under his arms, and his breathing was audible in the tiny office.

"Maybe you should go easy on the booze," Yale said.

"You sound like my wife."

"A wise woman."

"How could she be? She married me."

Yale laughed. "Whose idea was it to go to the park?"

"The driver said he thought they would be going back to Zoltag's apartment. That's where they usually went, but he said Zoltag told him to go to the park. He lowered the partition every now and then to give the driver directions. So I guess it was Zoltag's idea. Maybe he was into snorting in the great outdoors." He chuckled at his own stab at humor.

Yale was still nursing his first drink. "Who was the second woman?"

Sheehan burped. "Excuse me. Don't know, looked like a setup. From what the bartender said, it appeared that the second broad walked over to the two victims and started a conversation. They all left together about an hour later."

Yale poured an inch of scotch into his glass. "Description?"

"Vague. Even the chauffeur didn't get a good look at her. White, maybe middle twenties, long straight brown hair, about five-six, dressed well. That's about it."

"Can I see the DD5's?" Yale asked, hoping the case follow-ups would have more details.

Sheehan leaned over the desk. "Ray, if I give you copies of those Fives or even let you look at them and someone finds out, I'm fucked. In case you've forgotten, you're not the most popular guy at One PP."

The last thing Yale needed or wanted was to get a friend in a jam; he had so few friends left on The Job. "I had to ask, pal. Forget it. Tell me more about the mystery woman."

"The shooter? And we're sure she was the shooter. No prints in the car other than both victims. She probably didn't touch much, and what she did touch she remembered to wipe clean. A pro."

"You think she was hired?"

"Unless she has an unusual hobby. We hit Zoltag's brownstone five hours after the chauffeur woke up and found the bodies. The place was tossed, expertly, mind you, tossed real good."

Yale lingered over a slow swallow. The Scotch was going down real smooth. "So why were they killed?"

Sheehan shrugged. "First we thought drugs, but we found half a key of marching powder in the apartment. If it was a drug hit, the coke would be gone. We really haven't got a fucking clue. As for the Carpenter girl, she was in the proverbial wrong place at the wrong time. The killer was after him, and she just happened to be there."

"After nine years, you've got nothing?"

Sheehan twirled his drink, staring at it as if a genie had emerged from the bottom of the glass. "I hate to admit it, but we've got less than nothing, if that's possible. We did an extensive background on each of them, and we came up with zero. We discounted the drug theory because he wasn't dealing with the Colombians; his connection was some kid in the Village. We squeezed him, and he told us that Zoltag was the salt of the earth. He paid his bills, never bought on credit. Drug Dealer of the Year. As for the hitter, she might as well have been a ghost. She walked away from that car and vanished. No trace, not even footprints. She must have stuck to the paved walkway. At the beginning, the press played it up because of the girl. It was the standard 'Young Beautiful Co-Ed Killing' headline. Is there ever a young broad in this town who's whacked that's not young and beautiful?"

Sheehan continued without waiting for a reply, years of cynicism dominating his monologue. "I don't have to tell you, once the press starts playing up a killing, we're under a lot of pressure to come up with something. Everything was checked—his legitimate photography customers, his illegitimate drug customers, his business and personal relationships. Everything. Zero. After a while, the papers found another grizzly murder to break balls with, and the hullabaloo died."

"Which detective caught the case originally?"

"Charlie Wright."

"'Pun' Wright?"

"One and the same. Know him?"

"Only by reputation," Yale said.

"Well, he worked for me for years. Quite a character. Ever hear the story about him and the arrest he made on the subway?"

"A Pun Wright story I missed? Hard to believe. Thought I heard 'em all."

"One night he got involved on the up-town 'E' train."

"What happened?"

"He's off-duty, riding home on the train, and he hears screaming coming from the next car. In he goes and catches two mooks trying to rape some young girl. She was fifteen, I think."

"Nobody tried to stop it?"

"Six people in the car. Everybody sat there staring into space. Typical."

"So what happened?"

"Our hero identifies himself, and one of the skells pulls out a thirty-two and lets two go. Missed Wright by a hair. Wright was carrying a Glock nine and emptied the whole clip into the guy. Fourteen rounds. Kills him dead. Collared the other guy."

"Jesus."

"A few days later, a TV reporter asks Wright why he shot the guy

36

fourteen times. You know what he says?"

"What?"

"He says because he only had fourteen bullets."

Yale nodded but didn't smile. "Sounds grim."

"The best detective that ever worked for me," Sheehan said. "Got dumped to my squad because he insulted some boss, but the quality of his work more than made up for the stunts he used to pull."

"What did he get on the Zoltag thing?"

Sheehan grabbed the bottle of Scotch and poured another two inches in Yale's empty glass. "You're slowing down."

"I try experimenting with moderation every now and then. I guess this isn't going to be one of those times."

"Doesn't sound like much fun. Anyway, Wright had a snitch who gave him the name of someone who may have been involved in the park killings. The name's in the DD5's, but it doesn't much matter."

Yale was beginning to feel lightheaded from the booze. "Why the hell not?"

"Because one day Wright goes out looking for the guy, the next day he comes in, tosses his shield on my desk and retires. Just like that." Sheehan made three attempts at snapping his fingers then gave up.

Yale wasn't certain he heard correctly. "You say retired?"

"Retired. Out the fucking door, down to One PP, put in his papers, never saw him again. First, I thought he was drunk or something, but he was dead serious sober. I called him—shit, everybody called. Never returned anybody's calls. It was like he said 'Fuck you,' and vanished. Real strange because he loved The Job and was real good at it."

"You think his pulling the pin had something to do with the case?"

"Who the hell knows? I don't even have a gut feeling on this one." He patted his ample stomach. "A verifiable mystery."

"What about the name his snitch gave him?"

"We went looking for the guy—some ginzo name—no offense."

"None taken."

"Without Wright's connections, we got nowhere. Couldn't find him."

"Who's had the case after Wright?"

"Five other guys—or should I say detectives. I don't want to piss off the female contingent."

"You mean to tell me that in nine years there's been nothing?"

"Other than the possibility that Wright came up with, no. The DD5's are submitted every thirty days like the book says on a homicide, but no, zero."

"How can I find Charlie Wright?"

Sheehan shook his head. "Don't really know. He doesn't even have a phone. He took his pension in a lump sum so he doesn't get a monthly check. Couldn't trace him that way. No credit cards either. Can you believe it?"

"Does he keep in touch with anyone?"

"I hear Nick Abrutti; they used to be partners. I ran into Nick at a retirement racket, and he said he saw Wright a few years back. Nick's in your business now. I've got his number in my book." Sheehan dug into his jacket pocket.

Yale waived an unsteady arm. "Forget it. Nick and I go back a long way. I know where to find him." He stood up and staggered, catching himself on the desk. "I shoulda had another slice of that pie to soak up summa this booze."

Sheehan smirked. "You should drink more—builds tolerance." He poured another two fingers for himself, spilling more than what made it into the glass. "Listen, Ray, if you can't find Wright, call me at home, and

I'll get you the name he came up with from the Five's. We couldn't find the guy, but maybe you can."

Yale shook his head. "You're the only friend I've got left on The Job, Michael. Hate to see you get jammed up because of me. I'll find Wright—ask him myself."

Sheehan nodded drunkenly. "Okay, buddy. Hey, do me a favor— sit back down and have just one for the road, okay?"

Yale rubbed his chin. "Just one, okay." He sat down.

#

Four hours later, Yale and Sheehan staggered out of the bar. Yale watched as Sheehan got into his department auto and weaved his way onto the expressway. It had rained, and the deserted street smelled of damp cement and garbage. The wind swept up the empty avenue as Yale buttoned his coat and hiked up his collar. He had to look neat for the other drunks he might run into. He walked to his car with his hands in his pockets and the deliberate, unsteady gait of a man trying to appear sober.

## Chapter Five

Ray Yale rolled over in bed one revolution too many and crashed to the floor. He was naked. As the blood rushed from his head, he staggered and crashed face-first into a dresser, cutting his forehead. His heart pounded, and pain ran from head to toe. He had a hangover of monumental proportions.

Yale gently touched his throbbing forehead. The blood was less than he expected from such a sharp blow. Seeing his underwear on the floor next to the bed, he bent down as fast as his headache would allow, scooped them up, and applied them to his wound.

He dove for the bed and looked at the clock. Seven-fifteen. He guessed it was morning, even though the drapes were pulled and the room was dark. He had to reconstruct the previous night. Ever since he'd begun to drink in earnest, recalling reality had become a hobby.

Images came to him in jerky, stop-action frames. Mike Sheehan, Scotch, lots of Scotch, the one for the road that had become quite a few. He remembered leaving Skylights. He shouldn't feel this bad; he hadn't had all that much. A drinker's dread came over him. Had he gone straight home or stopped somewhere along the way? He couldn't remember and checked to his clothes to find a clue.

40

His pants, jacket, shoes, and shirt were strewn on the floor in a trail that led from his bed and out the bedroom door. Considering the clothes, he imagined a living being had lain down and melted out of them. It reminded him of the Wicked Witch of the North (or was it the West?) in *The Wizard of Oz.*

He searched his jacket and pants, but he came up with nothing to indicate he had visited another bar. He must have, though, because his money was out of its clip, and the bills were bunched into balls. He remembered tipping the bartender at Skylights with a ten-spot from a neatly clipped stack of money on the way out.

He recalled something Mickey Mantle had said as he checked himself into rehab: if he knew he was going to live this long, he would have taken better care of himself. The Mick was very profound.

Yale had an overwhelming desire to spend the rest of the day in bed watching old movies and reintroducing his body to solid nourishment, but he was obligated to track down Charlie Wright to see if anything could be done on the Carpenter case. He knew he couldn't function in his present condition, and he tried to jumpstart his body by taking an unusually long and cold shower. The water hammered him like bullets.

Yale scored his hangovers on a scale of one to ten, one being mild and ten being when he was near death. Prior to entering his shower, he fixed his hangover at eight on the Johnnie Walker Red Scale. When he emerged from the numbing blast of cold water, he was hovering at a 5.5, which was certainly better, but a long way from being able to hold a coherent conversation. What he needed was a good snort from his private stash.

He donned a white terry-cloth robe and padded to the rear of his house where a second bedroom doubled as an office. Digging through the back of his 'A' through 'G' file drawer, he found the cardboard box he wanted.

He carried the box to his paper-strewn desk (someone had once told him an orderly desk is a sign of a diseased mind). He lowered his window shade, opened the cardboard box, and buried his nose in its contents, inhaling deeply.

Crayons. A genuine three-tiered box of Crayolas, never used, their blunted points arranged like impeccable little toy soldiers.

The recollections came fast and hit hard. He was instantly transported to his youth when his biggest responsibility was getting home on time for his father's pasta and gravy. No Italian family ever called it sauce. Recollections came in a series of brief vignettes: Rockaway Beach on a summer weekday afternoon, Christmas holidays at his aunt's house in New Jersey (the first relative to escape the congestion of Manhattan), his first day of school. He was transported back to the family restaurant, where he helped his chef dad prepare the night's special. His job required him to sit on a stool with a giant ladle and stay out of his father's way. He remembered the walk from the restaurant to the subway bound for Ebbets Field holding his father's hand and skipping clumsily to keep up with New York's number one Dodger fan. Pez, Duncan Yo-Yos, and Slinkies flooded through his bruised brain at lightning speed.

Burnt Sienna and its colored cohorts brought him down to a four on the hangover graph. A breakfast of scrambled egg whites, skim milk, and throat-closing dry toast had a fractional positive effect, but at least he was doing something right for his body. The price of pushing fifty, he thought. It was at least good for some psychological improvement in his condition. Getting dressed in decent clothes would help, too.

Yale called Nick Abrutti's office to see if he were available. A secretary informed him Mr. Abrutti could see him at 11:30. Yale smiled, thinking that now it took an appointment to see Nick. A few years ago, when he'd started out, Nick Abrutti could be found camped out on attorneys' doorsteps, hawking business.

Yale chose his wardrobe carefully. He had strayed away from style shortly after his wife died, but he knew looking good made him feel better. It was worth the extra effort to bring himself up one rung on the ladder of depression. Today he selected a dark green double-breasted suit, white shirt, paisley tie, Gucci belt, and highly polished Ferragamo shoes.

Looking good and feeling like shit was how he was conducting his life of late, but he knew that an ounce of image was worth a pound of performance. If you looked the part, people didn't scrutinize you very closely. He examined himself in a full-length mirror before leaving. He could bullshit his way through the day.

Yale went down the sloping driveway to the garage and walked around the perimeter of the Bimmer to check for damage, a ritual after each blackout. Not a scratch, but he wondered how many accidents he had caused as he careened home on automatic pilot. His coordination was a bit off, and he drove extra carefully the short distance to Nick Abrutti's office.

The building was located a Frisbee throw from Manhattan on the Queens side of the East River in Maspeth. Nick Abrutti Security & Investigations, Inc., was situated on the top floor rear of a three-story office building adjacent to the Long Island Expressway.

Abrutti's empire took up the entire floor. A receptionist and two secretaries were busy at their jobs when Yale walked into the office. There were a dozen small cubicles with shirt-sleeved men talking on telephones. A number of photographs featuring Nick with every celebrity known to man hung on each available square inch of wall space throughout the office. There were also pictures of Nick with people Yale didn't recognize but who looked important in tuxedos. The receptionist announced him, and he went into Abrutti's private office.

43

Nick Abrutti's eyes lit up, and he broke into a broad grin when he saw Yale. He was seated at his desk, an oversized mahogany behemoth Yale thought could substitute as a landing deck on an aircraft carrier. Even this enormous office lacked enough wall space to hang all of the departmental awards and news stories detailing the exploits of Nick Abrutti, Master Detective.

Abrutti came from around his desk where he had been reading the latest issue of Penthouse and embraced Yale, firmly planting a kiss on his cheek and pumping his hand enthusiastically. He held Yale at arm's length and looked at his head. "Nasty cut, Ray, but a nice suit."

"Cut myself shaving," Yale said, suddenly feeling ashamed of his wound. Abrutti knew clothes, Yale remembered, especially Italian designers. He wore a grey silk suit and a white shirt with monogrammed French cuffs. His tie matched a pocket silk in his jacket. Abrutti's diamond pinky ring shone like a thousand suns, and his gold and diamond ID bracelet, if attached as an anchor, could secure the Queen Mary. His shoes were some kind of black leather weave that Yale surmised might be made out of the skins of loan shark victims. Yale called the look part of the Wise Guy Collection. Abrutti had an affinity for gangsters. He associated with them, frequented their hangouts, talked like them, dressed the dress, and walked the walk.

"What do you shave with?" Abrutti said. "Scotch? It's comin' out of your pores. I got somethin' will straighten your ass right out. Sit." Abrutti went to his desk and produced a bottle of amber liquid in a cut-glass decanter. "My agent gave this to me." Abrutti was the only PI in New York with a press agent. "Single malt, whatever the fuck that is." He rummaged through another drawer for glasses.

Yale waved him off. "I'll pass, Nicky." Abrutti liked to be called "Nicky" because it sounded like a mobster's name. Abrutti's two kids were

Paulie and Frankie.

Abrutti sat down in his swivel chair. At 5'8", he was dwarfed by his desk. He raised the bottle. "Sure?"

"Positive." Yale never understood how anyone could stomach alcohol while in the throes of a hangover. He wanted to ask Abrutti about Charlie Wright straightaway, but he knew Abrutti and his warped sense of Italian respect might be insulted if he got right down to business without delving into the social amenities.

They talked about the old days for a while, which morphed into Abrutti saying how good things were and how much money he was making. He asked Yale more than once to consider going into partnership with him. Yale wondered why, if he was doing so well, he needed a partner. Probably gambling, he thought, answering his own question since Abrutti, who would bet on which ice cube would melt faster, probably needed money. Yale didn't even consider going in with him because Abrutti had built his business on his ability to keep himself in the spotlight. After Vivian's death, Yale made every effort to avoid the glare of publicity. He respectfully declined Nick's offer.

"I came to ask you about Charlie Wright," Yale said when he thought the obligatory small talk had run its course. "Know where he is?"

"Humph, Charlie Wright. There's a name out of the past. Last I heard he bought a pet store in Manhattan. Hold on, I got an address." He went through the address book on his phone. "Here it is." He scribbled on a Post-It square and handed it to Yale. "I remember me and Wright used to stop by an Irish joint up from the One-Ten for lunch. You been there?"

"Not yet."

"Maybe he still stops in the joint. Let's hit it for lunch, maybe you'll get lucky. You up for it?"

"Yeah, sure, but no stops at the bar."

"Too early for me anyway. What do you need Wright for?"

"He was the last detective who came up with anything on a homicide I'm looking into. Killing in Flushing Meadow Park."

"Oh, yeah. Guy and a girl got it in the head, right? Coke all over the place, right? I left the job about a month before it happened. Worked with Wright for a while. What a fuckin' nut."

"So I heard," Yale said, looking at the address of the pet store Nick had given him. *"Chez Pup,* what the hell is that?"

"It's like a health food store for dogs."

"Dogs?"

"Yeah, on the Upper East Side. Those yuppie fuck-ups will go for anything. *Chez Pup* is like 'shape up.' Get it? That fuckin' whacko Wright thought it up. Kinda catchy, ya gotta admit."

"Yeah, real catchy. Guess that's why they call him 'Pun.'"

"Well, that's the last address I got for him and that's gotta be seven…eight years old."

"Pretty good detective I heard. I found out that he was the only cop out of a roomful of detectives who came up with anything on the killings."

Nick leaned back in his chair and put his feet on the desk. "A very good detective. Not as good as me, of course."

"Of course." Yale recalled Nick informing the press he had captured an elusive urban terrorist called 'Carlos the Jackal,' who was actually a brain-damaged street mugger called Carlos the Jackass. "You were the best."

"Wright liked to work alone. Good-looking guy, tall, blonde, well built, worked out every day. The broads loved him, but he didn't love the broads."

"What's that mean?"

"Ran home to the wife every night. Guy could get more pussy accidentally than me and you could get on purpose. Wasn't interested. Rarely even stopped after work for a cocktail with the guys. Straight home." Nick made a gesture with his arm like a plane taking off.

"Why'd he retire so fast?" Yale asked. "He started handling the park thing and then he was gone. From what I heard, he loved the job. Hear anything?"

"Really strange. Like you said, the guy loved the job. All's he ever talked about, then all of a sudden….""You think it had something to do with the case?"

"A lousy double homicide? The guy musta handled a million homicides. Nah, I don't think so. I never heard nothin' other than the guy just dropped outta sight. You're gonna have to ask him yourself."

Yale stood to up. "I think I'll do just that. Ready?"

Nick swung around, grabbed a black raincoat from a rack, and they left the building.

Yale settled comfortably in Abrutti's new Mercedes sedan and exchanged war stories for the ten-minute ride to the Woodside Inn. The bar was sprinkled with a few hardcore neighborhood drinkers and, as he expected, no one had seen Charlie Wright in years. Yale thought that the only reason they were there was that Abrutti was lonely and wanted company for lunch. Abrutti had a thousand acquaintances and no real friends. They had lunch, with soft drinks, and were on the way back to Abrutti's office within an hour.

They drove about a block in silence when Abrutti punched a button on the steering wheel and the radio came alive.

"You ever listen to this guy?" He raised the volume. "He's a pisser. Wolfgang Steiner."

Yale had tuned in the Wolfmeister, as he was known, on one

occasion and didn't like his humor. As far as Yale could determine, Steiner's whole act was taking listener phone calls and talking about the size of his penis.

"To tell you the truth," Yale said, "I don't listen to much radio, and when I do, I like the guy opposite him."

"Danny Doremus? Where've you been? They threw him off the air after they found a pile of coke and kiddy porn in his apartment. Shithead."

"I guess I've got better things to do. This guy, though," he pointed to the radio, "I can live without."

Nick guided the car into an empty space by a fire hydrant in front of his office. "The Wolfmeister has to grow on you. He's the biggest thing in radio. I know him, ya know. Met him at a party on the East Side. Nice guy. They're even making a movie about him. That I gotta see."

Yale had the door open. "Is there anyone you don't know? Thanks for lunch." Nick lowered the window when Yale got out of the car, and they shook hands. Yale was glad he didn't get kissed again.

He watched Nick turn the corner before thrusting his hands into his pockets and walking the short distance to his car. He felt slightly more clear-headed than he did when he got up, but he would need a good night's sleep before returning to normal.

# Chapter Six

Yale cruised the side streets of the Upper East Side of Manhattan trying to find a safe parking space close to *Chez Pup,* located on Third Avenue between 84th and 85th Streets. Yale found a spot about three blocks away on a street whose three-hour street cleaning restrictions had just finished. Timing was everything in this town. A brisk autumn breeze from the west had blown the city's pollution-ravaged air to the towns and villages of Long Island, where Yale thought it belonged. His hangover was mostly history. He was now bone-weary, his body craving a peaceful night's sleep. He made his way down Third Avenue, leaning into the wind, which normally wouldn't have bothered him. The way he felt, a slightly stiffer breeze would probably have knocked him over. Yale was daydreaming about soft sheets before realizing *Chez Pup* took up four storefronts, and he almost walked right by them. The place was huge. A glass window showcased stacks of bottles and cans billed as vitamin supplements for dogs. Another window contained canine exercise equipment, including a treadmill Yale thought looked more professional and sturdy than what he had been using in the gym. There was a stacked display of spring water for the family pet called *Puppier.* Yale laughed. Didn't these people know dogs would rather drink out of toilet bowls? The next window contained books and magazines, most dealing with the psychological well-being of man's best friend. One was titled *I'm OK, You're a Mutt.* There was even a magazine for the single pooch looking for a mate.

Only in New York.

The store was crowded. Yale looked around for someone in charge. By eliminating dog-accompanied adults and disregarding the young salespeople, he spotted a short, heavyset man about sixty-five with bifocals perched on the end of his nose and carrying a case of dog food. Yale made his way past the customers and their charges and stepped in front of the man as he was entering an alcove that had a sign marked EMPLOYEES ONLY.

"Excuse me, are you the owner?"

The man peered over his glasses in the general direction of Yale's feet. No dog. His face was deeply tanned. "Bob Zanichelli. You are?"

"Ray Yale. I'm looking for Charlie Wright." He offered a hand but withdrew it when he realized Zanichelli was still gripping the bulky box.

"Cop?"

"Used to be. Currently a private investigator."

"Currently?"

Yale gestured toward the crowd. "I may open one of these somewhere. Business looks good."

Zanichelli smiled. "Follow me to my office. We can hear each other in there." He led the way down a narrow corridor, kicking an already partially opened door wide open. He put the box in a corner of the small office, sat behind a metal desk, and pointed to the only other chair in the room. "Have a seat."

"You sell dog food here, too?" Yale said, attempting humor. It fell flat. He nodded at the box.

Zanichelli laughed. "Only organic. Got a dog?"

"I have a hard enough time taking care of myself."

"You and me both. I don't have one either, but don't tell anybody. You a friend of Charlie's? Want some coffee or something stronger?"

"No thanks. No, I'm not a friend of Charlie's. I'm working on a case he handled when he was on the Job. I asked around and was told he owned this place."

Zanichelli's voice softened. "We were partners until about seven years ago, maybe a little longer."

"Were?"

Zanichelli leaned back in his chair, barely able to fold his arms across his broad chest. "Yeah, *were.* 'Bout that time he waltzed in here and said he wanted out. Just like that." He snapped his fingers. "We were doing real good, even then. I asked him, how come? He got a little belligerent, so I backed off. We worked out a money deal, and he was gone. The whole thing took maybe a week. Never saw him again. I send him a check once a month to some dump he lives in on Ninety-seventh Street."

"Was he still a cop when he left?"

Zanichelli hesitated. "What did you say your name was?"

Yale told him again and handed him a business card.

"Got something that says you're retired?" Zanichelli said as he perused the card.

Yale showed him his NYPD ID card, now perforated with the word RETIRED.

"Sorry, but I wanted to make sure who I was talking to." Zanichelli fingered the laminated card. He turned it over, read the back, and returned it to Yale. "He retired the same week he walked out of here."

"Any clue as to why?"

He shook his head. "To this day I can't figure it out. Thought maybe I'd hear something from the neighborhood. I live on Ninety-fifth Street, you know. Up there the city's still pretty much a neighborhood. Didn't hear bupkis." His eyes went wide. "Well, I did hear that he divorced his wife about the same time. Strange. Him and his wife got along, as far as I knew."

"Did he ever mention a case he was working on, a double killing in Queens?"

"The one in the park?"

"Yeah. What'd he say about it?"

"All I remember was he mentioned it about the time he quit here. Don't remember what he said though." His face turned sour. "Can't figure out how a guy like that could just drop out the way he did. He was always so full of life. Loved to kid around." Zanichelli looked to Yale, hoping for an answer.

Yale had none. "Could you give me Wright's address?"

Zanichelli rattled off the address from memory. "I tried calling him. He had his phone disconnected."

"Ever try to go up there to see him?"

"I went a few times. No answer at his door. You know, I think he was home at least some of those times, but he just wouldn't answer the door. You talk to him, tell him to give me a call, he used to be my best friend." There was a sadness in the man's eyes.

Yale got up and shook Zanichelli's hand. "Sure."

"If you know anybody has an extra fifty G's laying around wants a percentage of a dog health store, tell them to call me. After all these years, I know Wright's not coming back, and this place is getting too much for one guy, especially an old fart like me."

Yale nodded and left him to his canine customers, deciding to walk the twelve blocks uptown to the address Zanichelli gave for Wright rather than lose his parking place. As Yale walked north between Eighty-fifth and Ninety-sixth Streets, he marveled at the number of adults of working age who were strolling the avenues enjoying the brisk fall afternoon. He wondered how many seemingly unemployed people could afford the inflated rents of the swank Upper East Side. Truly a Manhattan mystery, he thought.

New York was a city of well-defined socio-economic neighborhoods where a person could go from where the streets were paved with gold to where the streets weren't paved at all. North of Ninety-sixth Street, urban blight sat squalid and ominous.

What a difference crossing one street made, Yale mused as he made his way to Ninety-seventh. While white faces were not all that rare this far south on the fringes of Spanish Harlem, Yale still stood out as an outsider and absorbed the glares of the neighborhood residents.

Wright's building was an attached pre-war brownstone that resembled all the others on the block. The building's facade was rubbed raw by the relentless pounding of pollutants that could reduce stone to dust faster than Niagara Falls could shape a boulder in its path. The reddish-chipped cement of the stoop abutted a wooden door, warped from New York's brutal winters and scorching summers. The minuscule foyer, which smelled of urine and dust, contained eight mailboxes, all forced open, with no names. The tenant directory had two listings, one being, C. WRIGHT 8A.

Yale took the steps two at a time for the first three flights then yielded to Scotch-induced exhaustion and dragged himself up one more landing to the top floor. Wright's apartment faced the front of the building, commanding that all important view of Ninety-seventh Street that Yale was sure came at a premium.

Yale cocked his head to listen for signs of life coming from inside

8A. He was able to discern the faint sound of a television. He knocked. No response. He knocked harder. Still no reply.

Yale kicked the bottom of the door. "Charles Wright? It's the police, open up."

No answer.

Yale tried a different approach. "Mr. Wright, This is…," he muffled his mouth with a clenched fist, "…Detective Ballbag, Twenty-Third Squad." Loud and clear he said, "We've got something to tell you regarding a Mr. Robert Zanichelli. Could you open the door, please?"

The television died, feet shuffled to the door. Yale waited. Nothing happened.

A few seconds later, Yale heard the unmistakable sounds of locks being thrown. After a crescendo of metallic bangs and booms, the door opened about four inches. It was secured by a chain.

The hallway light was dim, but the interior of the apartment was dark. Yale heard the sound of labored breathing. He had an uncomfortable feeling that a gun was pressed against the back of the door.

A gravelly voice asked, "Who are you?"

Yale got a strong whiff of stale tobacco, coffee, and cheap rye. He held up his double-window ID case at eye level, one side showing his New York State private investigator's license, the other displaying his NYPD retired ID card. He thrust the ID card forward to show that he was not the enemy.

"My name's Ray Yale. I'm retired from The Job. Bob Zanichelli gave me your address. I need some help on something I'm working on."

The voice from the blackness said, "So you're not on The Job. You bullshitted me." The door started to close.

A shoe between the door and the frame, Yale asked himself, or a hand against the door? Yale chose the hand as less likely to evoke a violent reaction. "Please, hold it a second. Yeah, I bullshitted you, but I heard you inside, and you didn't answer my knock. Come on, I'm working on a case you handled when you were in the One-Ten Squad, and I need a couple of questions answered. You *are* Charlie Wright?"

After a while the deep, hoarse voice said, "I am." A distinct, hollow echo emanated from the flat.

"Just a few minutes of your time is all I ask...please."

"PI now, huh?"

"Yeah, working on the Zoltag/Carpenter homicide in the park. Could I come in?"

The door didn't budge. "Who you working for?"

Yale squinted, trying to adjust to the blackness inside the apartment. "The father of the girl who was killed."

Ten seconds of total silence passed, then the door swung open. Yale was immediately hit with a blast of hot, dry air. In all his years of police work, he had never found a tenement to be comfortable during the cold weather. They were either freezing or like saunas, usually the former.

Yale stepped into the apartment, and his eyes began to revert to night vision. The only illumination, a pulsating bluish hue, came from a television set with the volume turned off. Wright walked toward the TV and said, "Lock the top lock on the door and follow me." Wright hit a switch on a floor lamp, and light from a weak bulb filled the room like a slow-moving fog.

The apartment was of the railroad variety, long and narrow, popular in the years preceding World War II. Heavy wool blankets hung from the windows, ensuring privacy and blocking out any available light. Yale kicked up dust from a threadbare area rug. A well-worn recliner, greasy and battered, stood a few feet in front of the television. The walls were paneled with dark wood, and the furnishings consisted of a broken coffee table, two end tables, and a sagging couch. Nothing matched. Two soiled cartons of Chinese food were opened on one of the end tables with the menu being used as a placemat. Be it ever so crumbled, there's no place like home.

In one corner of the living room stood a fully decorated, artificial Christmas tree, complete with brightly colored balls, garland, and extinguished lights. Yale thought he saw a fine layer of *faux* snow, but soon realized it was a coating of dust.

"Getting into the spirit a little early?" Yale said at the man who had now turned to face him.

"That's from three years ago, never took it down." Yale looked at what appeared to be a sixty-year-old-man dressed in soiled flannel pajama bottoms and a stained T-shirt. He had matted gray receding hair, badly in need of a trim. Wright's pasty skin stretched tightly over his skull, making him look like a walking cadaver. His sunken eyes were lost in their sockets. He appeared to be about six feet tall and weigh perhaps a hundred and fifty pounds. He had a moustache, which hadn't seen scissors in months, and at least a five-day growth of beard. A burning cigarette dangled from the corner of his mouth. He scraped backward in a pair of tattered slippers, flopped into the recliner, and without looking down grabbed a glass filled with a dark-colored liquid from the floor. He took a sip and gaped at the silent television. Yale figured if Wright had a gun, he'd ditched it in the pocket of his robe.

"You *are* Charlie Wright?" Yale asked again.

"How many times you gonna ask me?" Wright took another pull on the drink without removing the cigarette from his mouth.

Yale still wasn't convinced. "You used to work in the One-Ten Squad? You handled the park killings?"

The man's eyes met Yale's. They were hollow, moist, and dead.

56

"I get the impression I'm not what you expected." Wright laughed mirthlessly. "Pull up a couch. Want a drink? Feel flattered, I don't usually give any away."

Yale looked for a clean spot on the couch, gave up, and sat on the end closest to the door. "I just expected someone—"

"Less fucked-up looking?"

"You were described…differently to me."

"My tux is in the cleaners. Look, you wanted to know about the park murders, ask away, while I'm still in a good mood." He smiled, revealing a mouthful of tobacco-stained teeth. "Want that drink?"

"No thanks." Yale said. "Bob Zanichelli wants you to call him."

"What are you, my fucking social director?" His voice was high-pitched and strained. "You got murder questions, ask. If not, kindly find your way the fuck out." Another sip.

This was Mr. Personality? The guy loved by all who knew him? What happened to the good-looking guy in great shape who had women falling all over him? Yale thought the only thing this guy ever worked out with was a corkscrew.

Yale cleared his throat, holding a rapidly rising temper. "Yeah, I understand you caught the case."

"Got there ten minutes after the sector called. Fucking mess." He turned to look at Yale. "You know about the murder weapon?"

"Uh huh."

"What was it?"

"Gas gun, fired at close range."

"Well, now you know as much as I do." He reached behind the recliner and produced a bottle of Four Roses with about three inches of whiskey remaining. He filled his glass.

"Not really," Yale said. "I understand you came up with a name, a possible suspect. That I don't have."

Wright gave him another comforting stare. "Didn't you see the Fives?"

"No."

"How'd you know about the murder weapon then?"

"Got it from a friend, verbally."

"I've got the solution to your problem: Look at the Fives."

With those words of wisdom behind him, Wright stirred in his chair. Yale thought the interview might be over.

Yale said, "Wait a minute, I can't see the Fives. I don't have access." He felt silly saying it.

Wright slithered back in his chair. "What Job are you retired from, the Wichita P.D.? Any cop can get a DD5. Call in a contract, for fuck's sake."

Yale was silent while he searched for an answer. Wright leaned closer to Yale, studying his face through bleary eyes.

"Say, I know you. You're that lieutenant with the sick wife, right?"

Yale glared at him. "That's me. You going to tell me about the suspect?"

Wright ignored the question. "How is she?"

"Dead," Yale said softly.

Wright blinked, assimilating the information. "Yeah, so's mine."

Yale almost told him he heard he got divorced but thought better of it. "My condolences."

"Yeah, mine too."

There was a brief moment of awkward silence. Yale asked, "The name of the suspect?"

Wright had his own agenda. "Bosses really broke your balls, huh?"

"With baseball bats."

"I know the feeling. Been through a little of that myself." He brought his glass up and took a long gulp, as if celebrating a pleasant reminiscence.

*This was the guy that didn't drink much?* "Could I have that name?"

Wright wiped his mouth with a hairy arm and belched. "Tony Cippolone."

"Tony who?" Yale didn't dare take out anything to write on for fear Wright would clam up.

"Cippolone. Something I do a lot of lately."

"Do what?"

"Sip-alone. I do a lot of that." He took another sip.

Yale smiled. "Still have your sense of humor, I see." Yale sensed immediately that he said the wrong thing.

Wright turned from Yale and stared at the TV. Through clenched teeth, he said, "I lost my ability to laugh eight years ago."

An opening, Yale thought. "That when you left The Job?"

Wright sat transfixed, eyes glued to the silent television set. "Yeah."

"Did your retiring have anything to do with the park killings?" Yale asked, almost anticipating a negative response.

"None of your fucking business. Interview's over." Wright started to get up. It was an effort.

Yale knew he didn't have much more time. "Spell Cippolone."

Wright spelled the name as he walked toward the door. "Let's go, Sherlock, you gotta go. Every day I make an effort to know one less person. Today, you're it. Out." He didn't look back at Yale.

Yale followed dutifully. "Tell me this before you throw me out: how'd you come up with this Cippolone's name? Was he supposed to be the shooter? I heard it was a woman."

Wright swung the door open. He turned to Yale. "Got his name from a snitch. He said Cippolone bragged he knew about the killings when he was fried on coke. He got talky."

Yale asked, "Any idea where Cippolone is now?"

"Last I heard he was on the street doing scams. The day I retired, I stopped caring."

"What about whoever caught the case after you? They couldn't find him?"

Wright snorted. Yale got the brunt of bad booze. "Detectives these days couldn't find pus in a pimple. My snitches only talked to me. He's probably still out there. Seek and ye shall find."

Yale stepped into the hallway. He shuddered from the sudden chilliness. "Listen, I've got a paying client. Want to earn a few extra dollars helping me track this guy down?"

Wright began closing the door. "Do I look like I need money? I'm independently wealthy. Now go, it's been nice meeting you. Bye."

Yale jammed the door with his shoe. He wondered for a moment why Wright would be living like this. Zanichelli was probably sending him a few thousand dollars a month. Was he blowing it all on booze? Maybe his wife took him for everything before she died. He may have a bunch of kids in college, like Sheehan. "Is there anything you need?"

Wright came to within three inches of Yale's face. "Yeah, for you to get your foot out of the way and to leave me the fuck alone."

Yale moved his foot, and the door slammed. He suppressed an urge to throw up. Of all the days to have a drunk breathe on him, this was not it. He regained his composure, slipped a business card under the door, and left the building. He had a feeling he had just gotten all the help he was ever going to get from retired Detective Charles Wright, but he knew he was better off without his help. Wright was a speedbump; he'd only slow him down.

Yale stood on the street and raised his collar against an increasing wind. He hadn't eaten anything since his lunch with Nick Abrutti, and his booze-ravaged belly demanded food. He found a small Japanese restaurant just south of the DMZ and settled in to enjoy a double order of sushi along with two glasses of club soda. Yale cabbed it back down to where he had parked his car, relieved to find it still there. The rush hour had ended a few hours ago, and the ride to Queens was quick and uneventful. He thought about Charlie Wright for most of the thirty-minute trip, trying to fathom what had become of the man described by various people in terms directly contradictory to what he had just seen. Aside from his confrontational attitude, Wright's appearance was very upsetting. He couldn't be any older than Yale, probably a little younger. Had alcohol done that to him? What had embittered him toward life? Yale still wasn't convinced the park killings weren't partially to blame. At least Yale now had a name, a possible suspect: Anthony Cippolone. He was surprised The Job hadn't put in more of an effort to try to find him. With cynicism rearing its ugly head, he figured that once the case no longer made headlines, no one really cared. Maybe Arnold Carpenter was right: no one really cared about anything anymore.

Yale left his car in the driveway. He entered his empty apartment and was immediately reminded of the previous night's drunken adventure. His clothes were thrown haphazardly across the unmade bed, and dirty dishes lay in the sink.

Yale showered quickly, donned a robe, and called Carpenter. He leveled with his client, explaining that getting anywhere in his daughter's murder case would depend on finding Tony Cippolone, a slim prospect at best. Yale now felt justified in putting himself on the clock, and he and Carpenter agreed on a retainer to work against his hourly rate.

"A check will be in the mail tomorrow, Mr. Yale."

"I'll be in touch," Yale said. He felt sorry for his client. The only thing he had left were memories of his daughter, and the frustration of not having been able to see her killer brought to justice. He wondered if he missed Katherine as much as Yale missed Vivian. He realized how much anguish the man must be enduring. He felt his client's pain and his own loneliness.

No matter how tired he was, Yale still dreaded getting into bed without Vivian's body heat radiating next to him, even after a year without her. Drinking dulled that pain, but he was sober now, and the loneliness was intense. Tomorrow, he hoped, the loneliness would diminish slightly. He had great faith in his tomorrows.

Yale crawled beneath the covers and decided to read to bring himself to the brink of sleep. He didn't want to lay awake thinking of his wife even for an instant. Why was it, he wondered, that L.A. cops wanted to be actors and N.Y. cops aspired to be writers? His one aspiration after the job entailed getting out of the city with his wife and raising a kid, maybe two. Now all he wanted was to be left alone.

## Chapter Seven

Yale knew his computer, and one of the several proprietary databases he subscribed to, would be the quickest and easiest way to locate Tony Cippolone.

Even though he didn't have a social security number or date of birth, the uncommon last name should be easy to track; there were only thirty-three matches in the entire state. Of those hits, twenty-two were over sixty-years-old. Yale had gotten the bum's rush by Charlie Wright before he could get Cippolone's approximate age, but he assumed that he was dealing with a younger man. Of the eleven that remained, five lived upstate with no history of ever residing in New York City. The last six were all possibilities. To further narrow the field, Yale ran a credit header history on each man, entering social security numbers and dates of birth supplied by the DMV database.

The credit information on his list of Anthony Cippolones came back in five minutes. Of the six, five were married, had established credit, and paid their bills on time. Number six was a thirty-eight-year-old who never had a credit card in his life. There were no judgments or liens against his salary because he had never held a job.

Bingo.

He ran a New York State criminal record check on this last prospect and found his target resided on Manhattan's Upper West Side at 444 West 50th Street. He had four convictions dating back to 1998, one for drug possession and three for larceny. He served two years for the last larceny conviction, having been released on parole in April of 2008.

He called the New York State Parole Board and found that Cippolone had not been to see his parole officer since November of that year, about the time of the park killings. Coincidence?

Cippolone was officially a parole violator. Yale figured Charlie Wright had probably gotten this far using official police methods, which were as efficient as Yale's only more time consuming. If Cippolone wasn't picked up that probably meant that he was not at the address supplied by the credit bureau. Still, Yale was obligated to check the address. People tend to be creatures of habit, and no one had looked for Cippolone in years.

Yale signed off the computer when his stomach told him it was lunch time. As he sat down in his neat kitchen with a steaming bowl of linguine under his nose loosening his sinuses, he encountered a beverage dilemma. A crisp chardonnay would go so well with the meal, but he wanted to stay away from alcohol, at least for a few days until his latest guilt trip with the bottle retreated from memory. He glanced longingly at the refrigerator, where an unopened bottle of the dry white lay on a shelf. He had once seen a bad movie in which the hero struggled with his demons, grabbed a bottle of booze, and dramatically poured its contents down the kitchen sink. Unfortunately, this was real life, so Yale chose the less dramatic method. He didn't open the refrigerator. As he sipped tap water with his meal, he thought he may have a problem the next time he needed a bottle of ketchup.

Yale dressed to blend into the West Side neighborhood: baggy jeans, boots, and a hooded sweatshirt beneath a leather jacket. He decided to take a train rather than risk having his car vandalized.

Anthony Cippolone's listed address was in the heart of Hell's Kitchen, now called "Clinton" by the small enclave of the upwardly mobile who lived there. Yale guessed that the name had a certain amount of snob appeal. It was still a tough, high-crime neighborhood of working Irish who were slowly being pushed out by a new wave of Hispanics and a smattering of pioneering yuppies.

Yale emerged from the subway at 50th Street and Eighth Avenue and walked the one block to number four-forty-four. It was a row tenement, similar to Charlie Wright's building, only much better maintained. The steps were swept and the front door glass was actually clean enough to allow sunlight to spill onto the spotless tile floor. The mailboxes were made of polished brass. There was no Cippolone listed.

He was contemplating his next move when two young Latino boys opened the inner door and jostled each other as they reached for the door leading to the street. They were energized kids, speaking a combination of Spanish and English. Yale guessed that they were about fourteen years old, too involved with their own banter to be concerned about the stranger who was temporarily sharing the small foyer with them.

"Hey, guys, what's goin' on?" Yale said, smiling at the two boys. Both youths, already sophisticated in the ways of the world, turned and eyed Yale warily.

"Listen, I'm trying to find a friend of mine, maybe lives here. Name's Tony." He tried for his most sincere expression.

One of the boys, the more aggressive of the two, elbowed his way in front of his friend. "Don't know no Tony," but then added, "Tony who?"

"Cippolone, Tony Cippolone. Know him?"

The boys looked at each other and giggled. The same kid said. "Maybe. What's in it for me?"

The other boy chimed in, "For us," and gave his friend a dirty look and a poke in the side. They exchanged tough guy glances.

The talker turned back to Yale. "Yeah, for us."

Both kids were wearing the latest in baggy designer jeans and sneakers that cost more than Yale's boots. They might be kids, but either they dressed well enough to have parents who held good jobs or both boys knew the art of the street hustle. Yale thought the latter.

He reached into his pocket. "How's about a pound each?" He pulled two fives from the bottom of a neatly folded roll of bills and held them out. The one with the smart mouth said, "Man, that won't even get me a blow job on Eleventh Avenue." They both laughed and gave each other high-fives.

So much for the innocence of youth. "Okay, there's a dime in it for each of you." He peeled off two tens.

The kids looked at each other and turned to Yale. In unison they said, "Cool."

"You know who I'm talking about? Tony Cippolone?" Yale showed them Cippolone's head-shot picture from his driver's license and rattled off a description based on DMV data. "About my height, maybe a little shorter, but real skinny, about a hundred and fifty pounds, thirty-eight years old."

The quiet one said, "Yeah, we know him. Used to live upstairs with his mom."

"'Used to'?"

"Don't live there no more," he said, "not for years. His moms died about two years ago."

"When'd you see him last?"

The same kid said, "Dunno, maybe a cupla months."

"How long's that? Two months…more?"

The quiet one was getting braver now that he had Yale's attention. "The fuck I'm supposed to know, man? Cupla months, maybe five or six." He was showing off for his friend's benefit.

"Where?"

"Seen him go into a bar up on Amsterdam Avenue."

"Which one?"

"Dunno. Somewheres in the Seventies. I was comin' from my aunt's house."

"How about you?" Yale said to the other boy. The kid shook his head.

"Know where he hangs?" Yale asked.

Both boys shook their heads.

"Did he work when he was living here?"

"Did the same thing most everybody else does around here, sell drugs," the Mouth said.

"Where around here?"

Both kids pointed outside.

"On this block?"

They both nodded.

Yale gave the kids the money. They ran out of the building, down the stairs, and onto the mean streets. He looked after them, shaking his head.

Yale took Cippolone's picture and went to a storefront photographer on Ninth Avenue, giving the smiling proprietor a hundred-dollar bill to make fifty copies.

Yale distributed the pictures throughout Hell's Kitchen, giving them to every hooker and street person he could find. Within two hours, the pictures were gone, along with his business cards and a promise of two-hundred dollars to the person who could lead him to Anthony Cippolone. He decided not to ask the beat cops, they looked too young to be familiar with the neighborhood. Besides, if he brought up a reward to any of these teenybopper cops, they would probably lock him up for offering an unlawful gratuity.

Yale feared he had reached a dead end. The pictures were his only hope, and he knew it was a stretch. Yale's best bet would have been the uncooperative Charlie Wright. He wondered why such a good detective would stand by and let someone get away with murder.

## Chapter Eight

"Yale Investigations," the female voice said.

"Jackie, it's me, Ray."

"Hey, honey, how y'all doing?" Jackie Randall was one of the operators at his answering service.

"Couldn't be better," Yale said, not without sarcasm. "Holding any calls for me?"

"Not a one, honey. If there was anything important, I'd call you and a message. You should know that by now."

"Just checking. Thought maybe it slipped your mind."

"Slipped my mind? Never happen." She laughed heartily.

Jackie had been his regular operator since he had gotten the service. They talked often but had never met. "How foolish of me. If I get any calls about a picture, let me be the first to know, okay?"

"A picture, got it."

Two days passed and no one had called about Cippolone. He decided giving Charlie Wright one last shot, not ready to resign himself to the fact that maybe the case was just too old and couldn't be solved, at least not by someone with his limited resources.

#

An unshaven, potbellied man was dragging garbage cans to the curb in front of Wright's building. Despite the chill, he was wearing knee-length shorts and a dirty T-shirt. Yale stepped around him and started up the stairs.

"Yo, mister," the man said.

Yale turned. "Me?"

"Yeah, you. You lookin' for Charlie Wright?" He had a slight Latino accent.

Yale came back down the stairs. "Yeah, how'd you know?"

The man smiled. His remaining teeth were stained and chipped. "You got those cop eyes, believe me, I know. I also know Wright used to be a hot-shot dick. All's he ever had come over to see him were other cops. After a while, all youse guys look alike. The eyes, they're like dead, ya know?"

I've got to work on that stare, Yale thought. "Yeah, I know. Wright get many visitors?"

"Not for a long time. Never talks to nobody, neither. Never says much of anything. Christmas time he's good though." He rubbed two fingers together and smiled.

"You the super?"

"Yeah, the name's Armand, but my friends call me Moldy."

I can see why, Yale thought. "So, is our boy home?"

Moldy looked at his watch. "Bars opened a little while ago. He definitely ain't home."

"Which joint does he go to?"

"Give me a second, I gotta think." He put his hand to his head for effect.

Another entrepreneur. Yale took out his money clip and peeled off a ten. He wasn't in the negotiating mood. "Going once…going twice…." He waved the bill in the air.

Moldy snatched the money. He smelled of coffee, toast, and cheap booze. "A joint on Third, corner of Ninety-fifth. Ginmill called Tierney's." He jammed the ten in his pocket.

Five minutes later, Yale stood in front of the bar. Just on the friendly side of 96th Street, Tierney's appeared to be one of the few remaining old Irish saloons in the neighborhood. The rest of the area's drinking emporiums were places frequented by the upwardly mobile. Tierney's facade was dirty glass and rotting wood, painted over so many times with the same dark green paint that it had acquired a sizable thickness. Three steps down, both physically and socially, led Yale to the door.

He stood just within the threshold for a minute to get used to the diffused light from dirty light bulbs. Six men of indeterminate age sat at the bar, each separated by at least two barstools, all silently concentrating on their drinks. No friendly neighborhood tavern here, only serious drinkers need attend. The bartender was draped across the bar, reading a racing form. No one looked up. A cloud of smoke hung like fog. Yale's eyes began to burn almost immediately, but not from the smoke. Stale beer had congealed in the S-pipes connecting to the kegs, and the odor was overpowering.

Charlie Wright sat at the end of the bar facing the door. He was hunched over a glass like a vulture over carrion. A cigarette dangled from one corner of his mouth. Yale purposely banged into a stool as he approached the slouched figure so as to alert Wright to his presence. The former detective remained motionless.

Yale sidled up to Wright. "Remember me?"

71

Wright kept his head down. "The bullshit artist, sure."

Yale looked into the mirror over the bar. There was enough kitchen grease on it to lubricate a tank. He wondered what person in their right mind would eat in a place like this.

Wright hadn't shaved. He smelled from stale sweat. He picked up his drink with a trembling hand and took a short swallow. The cigarette never moved. He swung his body on the stool to face Yale. The whites of Wright's eyes were yellow. "I thought I asked you to leave me alone."

The bartender came over. "Want somethin'?"

Yale shook his head. The bartender looked relieved. He walked back to the end of the bar and his racing form. "I need help finding Anthony Cippolone. I want you to do some work for me, help me find this guy."

Wright removed the cigarette from his mouth with a bony hand. "I told you, I don't need to work anymore."

"What I got is a father who wants the person or persons who killed his daughter. The case is nine years old. You were the only detective that came up with anything." Yale gave Wright the once-over. He was wearing a threadbare white dress shirt with a frayed collar buttoned at the neck. There was enough room between the collar and his neck to jam a salami. His chinos were held up with a belt that had extra holes punched in it to fit around his thin waist. Wright appeared even skinnier than the last time Yale had seen him. "That is, if you're physically able to help me. Everyone tells me you were a good cop once."

That got a rise out of Wright. He got off the stool and stood nose to nose with Yale. "Listen, asshole, I'm not on The Job anymore. I'm tired of dealing with cops. I'm tired of you, and I'm tired of life." His voice was slurred but strong. He teetered backward, stopped by the chipped mahogany bar. "Now get the fuck out of here and leave me be…please."

Yale thought he saw tears in the man's eyes. Wright glanced down quickly, whirled, and climbed back on his stool.

Yale grabbed a jutting shoulder, spinning him around. "Listen, I'm tired of this shit. All I'm asking is that you point me in the right direction. If you don't want to help me, think of Katherine Carpenter's father. He's been living in hell for nine years. You're sitting here wallowing in self-pity when you could be doing something useful." Yale's voice grew louder. "Something happened to you, right? Something bad? Well, straighten-the-fuck-up and get on with your life." Yale was shouting now and even had the attention of the *Walking Dead* extras sitting at the bar. The bartender stopped working on his second million and listened intently. His hand dropped under the bar.

Yale caught the sudden movement and whirled, pointing with his finger. "Don't even think about it, shithead." The barkeep's hand made a slow retreat and rested on the bar.

Wright stared straight through Yale, saying nothing. This aggravated Yale even more. "We all got problems, wise guy. You know some of mine, you know what I've been through. I'm almost to the edge, but I survive every day, some days better than others, but Jesus Christ, I'm not going to let myself turn into a lump of useless shit."

Charlie Wright blinked once, turned, and resumed drinking.

Yale knew that if he stayed any longer he would either have a stroke or punch Wright and probably kill him. He turned to leave. He was almost to the door when he spun around. "And another fucking thing...I don't want your goddamn help. Your brain is sloshing around in that cheap crap you're drinking. I don't need you. I need a cop...a real cop." He lowered his voice. "Someone told me that was you."

Wright never moved, just continued to stare silently at the filthy mirror. With a wave of dismissal, Yale was gone.

73

The fresh air on the street hit Yale like an ocean surge. He gulped the coolness of it, expelling the dank aroma of the bar. He walked away without looking back, stopping briefly at a coffee shop on Third Avenue to wolf down a tuna sandwich and guzzle two glasses of club soda from a filmy glass. His stomach was in knots and his hands were trembling. He was disappointed with his inability to convince Wright to help him and angry with the former detective for his surly attitude. That son-of-a-bitch ruined his day.

Even during his worst bouts with alcohol and depression, Yale couldn't recall being like Charlie Wright. He'd seen cops like Wright before—burned-out, hopeless drunks—falling over the edge when they were at the peak of their careers. He wondered what gave him the push. The next step for Wright would be a fast self-inflicted gunshot to the head, providing he could hold the gun steady.

During the subway ride home, Yale contemplated his future course of action. He knew that without Wright's help, he was at a dead end. He would like nothing better than to pay a visit to the One-Ten Squad and light a fire under the detective currently handling the case, but given his reputation within The Job, he doubted anyone would cooperate. He was cynical enough to understand that his motivation in the case was not catching a murderer so much as it was relieving Arnold Carpenter's considerable pain. Yale knew all about pain. The old man had put a lot of faith in Yale's abilities, and he was about to be let down hard. Yale knew he had to talk to his client as soon as possible and tell him the bad news.

He checked his answering machine as soon as he got home. Nothing new. Reluctantly, he called Carpenter, arranging to meet the old man at his Forest Hills apartment in two hours. Carpenter wanted to talk and sounded anticipatory at the sound of Yale's voice. Yale put him off until the face-to-face meeting. Hey, who knows, maybe within the next several hours Cippolone would turn himself in, Yale thought. One could always hope.

\#

Arnold Carpenter's ivy-covered apartment house was located on a tree-lined street in Forest Hills, an old-money section of Queens. Close to Manhattan, it afforded the well-heeled the opportunity to live in the city but not be a part of the decay. Yale fearlessly parked his car in the first spot he found without regard to street light location or proximity to the local foot cop. If his car wasn't safe in Forest Hills, it wasn't safe anywhere.

Yale was buzzed in, and his client met him at the door of the fifth-floor apartment.

"You have news?" Carpenter asked expectantly as he ushered Yale into his tidy home.

They faced each other in the foyer. "Yes, sir, but none of it promising."

The old man's face sagged noticeably. He was wearing a burgundy cardigan sweater, a white shirt, and gray slacks. His floppy slippers shuffled as he led Yale by the arm into a living room that was a throwback to World War II. The furniture was at least fifty years old but appeared reupholstered and looked good. The floors were wooden and highly polished, and a small upright piano stood against one wall, an array of silver-framed pictures atop its polished lid. Yale noticed a fine layer of dust on the wood surfaces. The lack of a woman's hand, he thought.

They seated themselves on a velvet, bolstered couch. The old man offered Yale a cup of coffee. Yale politely refused.

"What happened?" Carpenter asked.

Yale told him about trying to run down a slim lead through Charlie Wright and about the lack of cooperation he received from the retired detective. He told him about the visit to Cippolone's former address. "So you see, Mr. Carpenter," Yale said, "without me being able to locate Cippolone, we've come to a dead end."

Carpenter wrung his hands. "There must be something else you can do, perhaps something you've overlooked."

"Believe me, sir, without Cippolone we've got nothing. And even if he should miraculously reappear, we don't know what he has to contribute. All we've got is a detective's informant coming up with his name. Sometimes these guys'll give up anybody for money or to make the police think they're valuable."

Carpenter lowered his eyes. "So there's nothing?"

"I feel he's still in New York, possibly somewhere on the West Side of Manhattan. But finding him, particularly by myself, would be almost impossible. Maybe you should hire another investigator who has better police contacts."

"I wanted you because you have it here." He touched the center of his chest with a slender finger. "What good would a new investigator do if he has to deal with the police? They've had the case for nine years and are getting nowhere."

Yale didn't want to sound like he was defending the police, but said, "That's part of the problem…nine years. Maybe if they'd been a little more thorough in the beginning…well, we can't worry about what could have been. We've got to be concerned with today, and today we're just fresh out of leads. I'm sorry."

There was an awkward silence. Carpenter said, "I know you've done your best, Mr. Yale—"

But my best wasn't good enough, Yale thought.

76

"—and I thank you for your efforts." He rose with great difficulty.

Yale remained seated, trying to think of a way to comfort his client.

"You know, there's a possibility that this Cippolone may pop up somewhere." He felt the need to give the old man some hope. "He's probably still out there doing things he shouldn't be doing. It's just a matter of time before he gets locked up on an unrelated charge."

Carpenter looked at him and smiled. "I don't know if I can wait that long, Mr. Yale. Thank you for taking the time to talk to me in person about this."

Yale stood up and shook his client's hand. "I haven't gotten your check in the mail as yet, but when I do, I'll return it." They walked toward the door.

Arnold Carpenter shook his head. "Please keep it, Mr. Yale. It sounds as if you've been quite busy on my behalf. I insist you keep it."

"I couldn't."

"You'll make me feel much better if you do."

Yale had no intention of keeping the check but agreed to the request. He would tear it up when it arrived and let Carpenter find the extra money when he got his bank statement. He left Arnold Carpenter standing at the threshold of his apartment, a look of utter hopelessness in his eyes.

A cop is taught not to react to people's problems. Become personally involved, and sooner or later objective investigations become impossible. They rammed that into your head in *How to Be a Detective 101*.

As a young detective Yale had worked in Brownsville, Brooklyn, in a precinct that had the highest homicide rate in the city. Two or three murders a week were not uncommon, and after a while, the faces of the victims and the circumstances surrounding their killings became blurred. Most of the dead were poor, disenfranchised, or homeless, cut down over a joint or a $5 bag of heroin. It was easy to lose sight of the fact that these victims were human beings and not just numbers. While some cops thought the community was better off without some of the dead, Yale took a different approach. He saw every twisted, bloody body as a mother, father, sister, or brother. A sign over his desk read: JUSTICE FOR THE DEAD. Every case got a fair, objective shake.

But try being objective when you know what the loss of a loved-one is like, how the pain invades every nerve and fiber in your body and doesn't shake loose no matter what you do. The rule book doesn't count on empathy.

Yale, feeling tears coming to his eyes, swallowed hard, turned, and left Carpenter standing in his apartment alone with his thoughts.

Yale had a few of his own to contend with.

Chapter Nine

At midmorning, the doorbell rang.

Yale never answered the door unless he was expecting someone. Unexpected visitors were invariably sales people or religious fanatics on a conversion crusade. He ignored the bell and continued to work at his computer. The bell rang again. Yale kept typing. After two minutes of silence, the bell began chiming steadily as if someone were leaning on it. Yale, a little peeved, went into the living room, opened the window, and stuck his head out. An overhang above the front door prevented him from seeing his visitor.

"Who is it?" he hollered.

A man's voice shot back. "Police, I'm looking for Ray Yale."

Yale's first thought was that he had mowed down an innocent bystander after his drunken meeting with Mike Sheehan. Then he remembered that he had checked his car after his blackout and found no damage. Maybe he had punched someone in a bar who had asked him for the time. He tried to remember but came up blank.

"Just a minute." Yale took a deep breath and ventured downstairs to confront his recent past. When he opened the door, he saw a man in an ill-fitting suit. It took him a few seconds to realize that he was looking at a

79

cleaned-up Charlie Wright. Words failed him. He just stared, open mouthed. Finally he said, "Police, huh?"

Wright smiled thinly. "Hey, it worked for you." He looked past Yale. "You going to invite me in or what?"

Wright wasn't wearing a coat despite the chilly morning air. Yale, stepping aside, wondered if he owned one. "Yeah, sure."

Wright entered the vestibule and pointed up the flight of stairs leading to the top floor apartment. "Where...up there?"

"Uh, yeah, go ahead." He followed Wright up the stairs. "Go in the living room." He pointed the way. Wright sat on a beige leather couch, and Yale took a seat opposite him in a recliner.

"How'd you find out where I live?" Yale asked.

Wright smiled, lips tight, concealing what was left of his teeth. "I had your card, you left it, remember?"

"I don't have this address on it."

"Didn't have to, phone company sources. They still remember me. I told you I was a pretty good detective once."

"I'm impressed."

Wright patted his shirt pocket. "Can I smoke?"

Yale said, "No."

Wright looked surprised. "That's usually a rhetorical question."

Yale shrugged. "Not around here. I don't even own an ashtray."

"It's your house." He settled back into the folds of the leather.

"Why are you here?" Yale said. After the way Wright had treated him, he felt getting directly to the point wouldn't be impolite.

Wright's eyes shifted from the carpet to the walls. "I came to apologize. I acted like a shithead, and I know you don't deserve that, no one does." He cleared his throat. "After you left the bar, I went back home—if you could call it that—and I dug out a copy of the Carpenter

80

file. I saw the kid's picture, and then I thought of the old man. A nice guy. He deserves a shot at a decent investigation. I guess I'm not as bitter as I thought I was. The thing is, I just want you to know that if you still want some help on the case, I'll give you a hand."

Yale felt Wright was being sincere. He appeared sober, too, and he certainly looked a lot better that he did on the last two occasions Yale had seen him. He had shaved, and even though in need of a haircut, he had at least washed what was left of it and slicked it back. He wore a gray Brooks Brothers conservative suit, pants pressed to a fine edge. The white shirt still fit loose around the collar, but it was clean. The striped tie was neatly knotted and stain free.

Yale said, "I appreciate the change of heart."

Wright began fidgeting. He rubbed his nose and ran a hand through his hair. "Before we get into that, there's something I gotta tell you."

"Go on," Yale said cautiously.

Wright stopped his nervous movements and looked Yale straight in the face. In a strong voice, he said, "I've got AIDS."

Yale held his gaze. A jumble of colliding thoughts ran through his mind as they tried to emerge as a coherent sentence. "Huh? Wha…you…but…." He shook his head, trying to rid himself of the memory he had of a doctor telling him for the first time that his wife had cancer.

Wright held up both hands. "Stop a minute. You sound worse than I look."

"I'm sorry…my mind was…I mean I was trying to say something that made sense, but…."

"You were thinking of your wife?"

Yale massaged his eyelids. "Yeah." Suddenly, he felt very tired.

81

"I told you I recognized you when you came to my apartment. I followed your story in the papers after I left The Job. I didn't know she died, though."

"I wanted to keep it quiet. Toward the end, we both had enough notoriety."

"They forced you out?"

"You might say that. I got department charges of insubordination. They told me to stay away from reporters. I wouldn't. It was the reporters that publicized Vivian's case after The Job was going to force her to retire with a disability."

"Stupid rule," Wright said.

"You're out sick one year, and they force you out. In Vivian's case, it would have killed her quicker than the natural progression of the disease."

"She loved The Job?"

Yale smiled, his eyes becoming unfocused. "She used to say that next to me, The Job was her only love. A good detective, too, worked Queens Robbery." An awkward silence followed. To break it, Yale said, "You want something to drink?" He started to get up.

Wright shook his head. "I'm going to try to cut back on that, too."

Yale said, "I mean tea or soda or something. There's no booze in this house." He thought of the bottle of table wine in the refrigerator, but it didn't count.

"Reformed drinker?"

Yale was on his way to the kitchen. "Let's just say I'm undergoing a renovation. What'll it be?"

"Coffee."

Yale turned. "Just tea or soda, never drank coffee, don't keep it in the house. I don't get very many visitors."

Wright's eyebrows shot up. "A cop who doesn't drink coffee? I suppose you don't like doughnuts or play golf."

"Can't stand either one. I'm a regular rebel."

"That's the good thing about having AIDS. You can start a bunch of bad habits without worrying too much about the consequences. I once considered becoming a crackhead, but I figured I'd already lost enough weight. Whaddaya think?"

Yale thought Wright was strange, but he kept his opinion to himself. "You want to tell me about your illness?"

Wright's eyes softened. "AIDS. I've got AIDS. You can say it, go ahead."

Now he was sounding like Mr. Rogers, Yale thought. "Okay, AIDS. I'm sorry if I sounded condescending."

"No problem, man. Get me some tea with lemon, then we'll talk."

Yale busied himself in the kitchen, not looking forward to a discussion on disease. Still, he had Charlie Wright sitting in his living room, and if he had to listen to his story to get some cooperation, he would.

Yale came back to find Wright holding a framed picture of Vivian. He replaced it gently on the coffee table.

"Beautiful woman. From the newspaper accounts of what you did for her, you must have loved her very much."

Yale put a steaming cup in front of Wright.

Wright sipped his tea. "I loved my wife, too," then added nonchalantly, "she's the one gave me AIDS."

Yale choked on his tea. His eyes teared, and he coughed as he pointed to the cup. "Hot stuff." He wiped his mouth with the back of his hand. "What the hell happened?"

Wright smirked. "What usually happens on The Job, only most of the time it's the cop who fucks around. We have all the time we need.

How many guys you know told their wives about midnight grand jury appearances or the ordered overtime?"

Yale nodded, trying unsuccessfully to recall even one cop he knew that hadn't cheated on his wife at least once.

"With me it was the other way around," Wright said. "I was so busy being a super cop that I never knew what was going on at home. My wife wound up having an affair. I never knew." He wrung his hands.

Yale didn't know what to say. "I'm sorry."

"Don't be. I should've known. The fucking Job came between us. She asked me to get off the street a hundred times, to grow up. In the beginning, we had plenty of time for each other, it was great. After a while, I was never home, and she went her own way. I was too self-absorbed to see what was happening."

"How'd you find out?"

"About the HIV? You said you met Bobby Zanichelli, right?"

"Yeah."

"About three months after we opened the doggy store, we decided to insure ourselves, leaving each other as beneficiaries. It's a standard business practice. If one partner dies, the survivor buys out the dead guy's wife. Key man insurance they call it. Well, I hadda take a physical for the policy and they caught it in my blood test."

"What'd you do?"

"First, I got re-tested, then I cried. I didn't know how the hell I got it. My first concern was for Sheila, my wife. Never in my wildest thoughts did I think she gave it to me. I thought it was the other way around. We were together for six years, but before that I was a typical single guy, if it moved and was female, I screwed it. My doctor told me the virus could incubate for years before becoming symptomatic. I was nuts with worry. I hadn't cheated on my wife, I loved her. I figured it had to be some slut I picked up in Studio 54 or somewhere before I was married."

"How did you find out she gave it to you?"

"I had to tell her I had it, and she took it surprisingly well. That got me to thinking, if she was so pure, why wasn't she giving me hell or throwing me out of the house? She had a feeling something was wrong with her, but never went to a doctor 'til after my test came back. Anyway, she tested positive. She was full-blown and was just beginning to get sick. I never knew. She confessed to the boyfriend—said it was a brief fling—but blamed it on me. She said because I hadn't paid any attention to her, she decided to find someone who would." Tears welled in his eyes. He wiped them away. "We used to be inseparable, you know, then The Job drove the wedge between us."

"You can't blame The Job for what she was doing, it was part of her character," Yale said, wondering if he had gone too far.

Wright nodded. "Maybe you're right, but The Job certainly didn't help."

"Did you ever find out who it was?"

"The boyfriend? Some musician. Friend of a girlfriend of hers. Never even found out his name, didn't really wanna know."

"That why you retired so quickly?"

"Yeah. My wife left me two days after her test came back. I couldn't face anybody. I just dropped out. No one knows about the AIDS." He swallowed hard. "Except you."

"What became of your wife?"

"Dead, three years. I divorced her a year after we split."

"Kids?"

Wright smiled, shaking his head. "We were classic DINKS."

Yale had to ask. "What's a DINK?"

"Dual income, no kids. After I got diagnosed, I just wanted to be alone. I can't remember the last time I said more than ten words to anybody."

"Your super—"

"Moldy? That nosey bastard."

"—says you used to have people over your place, said they were cops."

Wright thought for a few seconds, then laughed. "Oh, that was my AIDS support group. We'd meet once a week. Once every month or so it was my turn to have them over to my palatial digs. You know, come to think of it, they did look like cops. It was the dead eyes."

"The eyes are a giveaway."

"Anyway, I gave up with them. It must have taken them forty-five minutes to climb the stairs to my apartment. Besides, after a while, I found them too depressing, particularly when they started dying off. Makes you think you're gonna be next."

"How're you feeling?"

"Right this minute? Great. With this thing, you've got good and bad days. Today's a good one. Don't know when my 'use by' date's gonna come around."

There was another uncomfortable silence. Yale wished the cups were empty so he could start clearing them.

Wright broke the stillness. "I'm full-blown now, been full-blown for three years, but I've been pretty lucky. I've only been real sick twice; both times with pneumonia. Considering the abuse I put my body through, I'd say I'm doing okay. I take life one day at a time. How about you?"

"Yeah, me too."

Wright slid to the edge of the couch and took a notepad from his jacket pocket. He tossed it on the coffee table. "Everything you've always wanted to know about Anthony Cippolone."

86

Yale flipped through the pages of the well-worn book. Cippolone's personal statistics were there, as well as his known haunts, friends, and jailhouse buddies. As he perused the pages, it became evident to Yale that Wright was a meticulous notetaker. All his inquiries into Cippolone were in chronological order, written in a neat legible script. Wright had scoured all of Cippolone's hangouts, talking to everyone who knew him, with negative results.

"What kind of a person're we dealing with here?" Yale asked.

"My informant said our boy Tony's a big cokehead. According to my source, about three weeks after the killings, Cippolone was bragging that he had information about the job in the park. Those were his exact words, 'the job in the park.'"

"Your snitch didn't get any more out of him?"

"At the time, he didn't know what the hell Cippolone was talking about, so he let it drop. But it was the Carpenter case."

"But you don't know for sure."

Wright's eyes came alive. He grinned. "I know. I got a feeling."

Yale believed Wright's intuition was right on the money. He went from doubting the ex-detective's stability when he walked in the door to realizing that Wright retained a good deal of his instinct.

Wright beamed, then quickly compressed his lips. "I've been kind of neglecting my appearance lately, especially my teeth. I'm a little self-conscious about them."

"I think your teeth are the least of your problems. What do you think?"

Wright broke into a broad grin, baring a worn smile. "I can still chew a steak, that's all I should really give a shit about."

"Well put," Yale said. He pointed to the notepad. "Now, let's get back to this asshole."

"Cippolone's still around. I can feel it. He's on the con is what I hear."

"You keeping up with this guy's career?"

"The case's always interested me, mainly because I couldn't find the mook. Besides, his name was the only lead I ever came up with. I'd ask in the bars every now and then if anyone's seen him. Sometimes I'd get a positive response, but I was just too fucked-up to do anything about it. That, and if no one else was looking for him, why the hell should I? I'm not on The Job anymore."

But the predisposition for the hunt still remains, Yale thought. No matter what Wright was going through, he was still a New York City detective, and they take The Job to the grave. "You said he was doing a con. What kind?"

"Dunno. That was the word on the street, but it has to be a bit more sophisticated than what he went away for."

"Which was?"

"Cippolone would go to wakes and steal the corpse's jewelry. You believe that?"

"You're bullshitting me."

Wright held up his right hand. "I kid you not. He had a junkie accomplice who would create a diversion in the back of a funeral home while Cippolone kneeled at the coffin of some bejeweled stiff. When the time was right, he'd snatch a ring or a necklace. I heard he did it for years, never hitting the same funeral home twice. Most of the time no one even noticed anything missing from the body until the coffin was being closed for the last time, by then he was long gone. Some set of balls, huh?"

Yale thought he had heard of every scam imaginable, but this one was new. "How'd he get burned?"

Wright grinned. "He pulled his shit at a cop's mother's funeral.

88

There were fifty cops in the viewing room. Surprise! He should have done his homework."

Yale chuckled. "That's the bit he was paroled on?"

"Yep. Stopped seeing his P.O. right after the park shootings."

"What a coincidence."

"You believe in coincidence?"

"Nope."

"Me neither, but I don't think he's the killer type."

"I don't either."

"You got a current picture of him?"

"Follow me." Yale led him to his office.

Wright examined the computer with interest while Yale shuffled papers on his desk. "Nice setup."

Yale handed him an envelope. "Beats having to drive to the office. There's about a dozen five-by-sevens in there. It's a DMV photo, but it's okay."

"I had a mugshot of him, but this one's a little better. When do we start?"

"Tomorrow night. I doubt this guy's a morning person. A kid I interviewed at his old address said he saw him a few months ago on Amsterdam in the Seventies. Maybe we should start around there. Go back to your place and familiarize yourself with the case folder again and maybe reach out to some of your old snitches."

Wright put the pictures in his jacket pocket. "Sounds good to me." He turned to leave. Yale thought he was going back to the living room, but he turned for the stairs.

"Hey, hold it a second," Yale said. "Where're you going?"

Wright appeared surprised. "To solve the crime of the century. See ya."

Yale grabbed his arm. "Don't you want to know how much I'm paying you?"

"You mean I'm gonna get paid? You don't have to pay me, it'll be good just to get back into it again. If it'll make you happy, cover my expenses."

Yale continued to hold his arm. "Go back inside for a minute, okay?" He steered Wright into the living room. When they were seated, Yale said, "If I'm getting paid, you're getting paid."

"You really don't have to. I'm just glad for the opportunity. It's good therapy."

"I know, you're independently wealthy."

"Sort of. Bobby sends me three large a month as part of the *Chez Pup* buyout. When the note expires, so will I."

Yale ignored the remark. "Well, I have a client who'll be tickled to know his case has legs again. He gave me a retainer. I'll give you twenty an hour, plus expenses."

"What's the rate?"

"I'm getting sixty-five."

"In that case I'll take thirty." Both men laughed. Wright asked, "Can I go now?"

"Wait here a second." Yale went to his office, emerging seconds later with a spare pager. He tossed it to Wright. "Take the beeper in case I need to reach you. My beeper number's on the back."

"Gee, how high-tech," Wright said, mockingly. "No cell phone?"

"That comes later with the two-way wrist radio. There any particular reason you don't have a phone in your apartment?"

"You have a phone, you gotta talk to people. You beep me, there's a payphone in front of the building." Wright attached the beeper to his belt and held out his hand. "Thanks for giving me a shot, Ray. You won't be sorry."

Yale was surprised at the frail man's strong grip. "That's why I looked you up, remember? Keep track of your hours and expenses. Come on, I'll walk you downstairs. You have a car?"

"Nope. Gave up driving when I gave up on life."

"You may need one before this case is over. Still got your license?"

"Sure."

"Then lease a car. I'll pay for it. It's a business expense."

Wright was in front of Yale, taking the steps slowly. "I used to date her."

"Who? What're you talking about?"

"Lisa Carr. I used to date a Lisa Carr in high school." Wright was laughing hysterically. His ailing body shook, and Yale was afraid he would take a header down the stairs.

Yale had to laugh. He wondered if he would be able to crack jokes if he was as sick as Wright.

When they reached the landing, Wright said, "I'll use cabs. Don't worry, I'll get receipts." He was still laughing when he left the house. There's nothing like being your own best audience, Yale thought.

He began closing the door when he heard the retired detective call his name from the street. "Yo, Ray!"

Yale swung open the door.

Wright was on the sidewalk, back toward traffic. "I almost forgot to tell you, I called Bobby Zanichelli last night. I'm meeting him for lunch tomorrow. I think me and him are long overdue for a talk." Then he turned and walked away.

Yale smiled and closed the door. He had to call an old man in Forest Hills.

*Blood Shot Eyes*

Chapter Ten

Charlie Wright was already seated in the West Side coffee shop, studying a table strewn with police reports and notes, when Yale arrived.

Yale slid across the seat facing him. "Doing your homework?"

Wright looked up. "I've been calling snitches I haven't spoken to in nine years. Our boy Tony's been busy. Got the Carpenter case folder here, too"

Yale ordered tea. The first sip warmed him immediately. November had made a chilly debut. "What did you find out?" He noticed Wright was dressed a little more to suit the weather with an Army fatigue jacket and boots.

"Well, he's definitely still in the area, working scams as far as I can tell."

"Does this help us find him?"

"It could, he's doing his cons on the East Side. He probably won't be shitting where he dines." He grinned. "He seems to have become a little more sophisticated in his old age."

"How so?"

"He's got one scam where he rents an apartment in a swank building and then sublets it to twenty or so marks for about half of what

92

it's worth. He gets a pile in security deposits and advance rent. He's long gone when a convoy of moving vans show up on the first of the month."

"What else?"

Wright dug into a sheaf of paper and extracted a police complaint report. "This one's cool." He passed it to Yale. "He takes out a one-nine-hundred phone number and creates a phony business. Each call costs twenty-nine ninety-five a minute. Then he goes around to companies in office buildings, mostly on Park and Madison Avenues, dressed as a delivery boy. He asks for a non-existent person then asks to use the phone when he's told no such person works there. He's supposedly calling his boss to ask for further instructions, but he's really calling the nine-hundred number. He stays on the phone long enough to have the charge count, I think it's eighteen seconds, makes some excuse, then splits. The business automatically gets charged on their phone bill, and he collects a check from the phone company. For thirty or sixty bucks, the businesses don't complain, probably don't even notice the charge. He only cons big companies, hits an entire building, makes over a grand easy."

Yale hated to admit it, but he admired Cippolone's ingenuity. "He never got caught?"

Wright shook his head. "This complaint is the only one I've been able to find. I've got a snitch on the East Side says Cippolone's been doing it for years."

They decided to concentrate their efforts on the West Side of Manhattan, figuring Cippolone lived in the neighborhood for years, was familiar with it, and he wouldn't want to spend any more time around his victims on the East Side than he had to.

Yale paid the check, and they stepped out into the cold. It was almost 9:30, and the wind whipped off the Hudson River with a fury. Yale was concerned about his new employee's ability to withstand the weather.

93

"You okay for this? If it gets too much, we'll take a break, okay?"

Wright clapped Yale on the back. "Ray, my boy, I may be in questionable shape, but going after bad guys somehow makes me feel good. Let's get to it."

Yale gave him a stack of newly copied pictures of their quarry. They decided to concentrate on the single bars on Broadway, Amsterdam, and Columbus Avenues, figuring Cippolone, all-American boy that he was, might want to connect with a woman.

"We'll work the same street on opposite sides. Offer the bartenders a deuce if they spot him and you make it back in time to nab him. An ace just for information. Give your beeper number"

"Do I get the two hundred if I spot him?" Wright winked.

"I'll give you tomorrow off. C'mon, Watson, the game's afoot."

By two in the morning, Yale realized there were more bars in the neighborhood than there were probably in the Casbah. The cold had taken its toll on him; he was exhausted, and he had ceased feeling his toes around midnight. If he felt like this, he wondered how Wright felt. Surprisingly, Wright still seemed bright-eyed and eager to continue, although Yale began to notice a wheeze in his voice. They took periodic breaks in diners and pizza joints.

Wright warmed his hands over a table candle in an upscale diner on Broadway during one of their breaks. "Man, I could use a drink."

Yale was still on the wagon and had no desire to fall off. "When we call it a night, you can suck down a quart of Rye. For now, we stay sober."

They hit the street again after a twenty-minute respite, calling it quits at 4:00 a.m. They kept up the pace for two more nights. On the third night, they got a bite.

Yale was just coming out of a bar on Amsterdam and 92nd when he saw Wright frantically waving his arms on the other side of the street.

94

Yale dodged traffic and was at his side in a flash.

"What?" he said, breathlessly.

"Bartender in Steve McGraw's Cabaret on Seventy-second Street. Says Cippolone's there now." Wright stood on his toes, looking up Amsterdam Avenue. "We need a cab." He walked into the gutter and waved. Empty taxis cruised right past the two men.

Yale looked at his watch. "Theater's letting out. All the cabs are going downtown. Forget it, we'll walk."

Wright looked at him like he were crazy. "You've gotta be kidding. We're talking over a mile here." He jumped out in front of a moving taxi. A cab screeched to a halt, the front bumper just three inches from his shins. He smiled at an astonished Yale. "That's how you do it."

Steve McGraw's Cabaret was a magnet for actors, mostly the unemployed variety. Yale knew that Cippolone would stand out like a Klan member at a gospel meeting amongst the young thespians who frequented the place drinking cheap beer and bragging about the part they almost got. The former cops agreed on a game plan. They would be a couple of guys out on the town, not much of a stretch, and would try to engage Cippolone in conversation.

Yale spotted him immediately and jabbed Wright in the side. "Over there." Cippolone was in the middle of a crowded bar, and he wore a leather bomber jacket, tight-fitting black jeans, and a white silk shirt open to mid-chest. Around his neck was a small gold-colored razor blade supported by a thin gold chain. He sported a ninety-mile-an-hour hair style popular with the wanna-be wise guys from Hell's Kitchen.

"Looks like Teen Angel," Wright said.

Cippolone was trying to talk to a sweet-looking young yuppie blonde who made Doris Day in her prime look like a slut. The blonde gave Cippolone her back. He shrugged, glancing around the bar for other

95

prospects. He changed stools to be seated next to two young women and immediately interrupted their conversation. Yale couldn't hear what was said, but the women ignored the interloper.

Yale leaned into Wright. "Follow my lead."

"You da man," Wright said between clenched teeth.

Cippolone succeeded in annoying the two women to the point where they picked up their drinks and moved to the other end of the bar. The ex-detectives slid into their warm vacant seats. Timing, Yale thought, is still everything in this town. They ordered drinks: Wright a Rye and soda, Yale a Scotch to give a nice warm glow to his thawing ass. He would re-mount the wagon tomorrow. When the drinks arrived, Wright slid two one-hundred-dollar bills across the bar. The bartender smiled, scooped up the money and walked away.

Yale stole a glance at Cippolone. He was sure Teen Angel saw the pass. He decided to get bold. He looked Cippolone in the eye and winked. Cippolone seemed confused for a moment, and then he smiled and nodded. It worked, Yale thought, Cippolone figured he had just seen two guys score a drug deal. Now, Yale figured, they had something in common.

"Not going too well with the ladies?" Yale asked Cippolone. Wright just smiled and went back to his drink.

The con man's face was fidgety and animated. "This ain't my kinda place." His voice was strained and high pitched. "broads have their noses stuck so far in the air, I'm surprised they ain't bleedin'."

I bet you know all about bleeding noses, Yale thought. Wright jumped in. "Me and my friend ain't lookin' for pussy, we're just out partyin' for the night."

"What's the occasion?" Cippolone asked.

"Wednesday," Yale said. "Me and Charlie only party on days ending in 'Y'."

It took a few seconds to register. Cippolone let out a weak laugh. In the few minutes they had been talking, Cippolone had finished two drinks and was ordering a third. Yale knew that he was blasted on coke and was looking for that happy medium between wound too tight and dead. Cippolone didn't give the glass from his next drink a chance to form a wet halo on the bar before he killed it.

"Got the thirsties?" Wright asked.

"You know how it is," Cippolone said from the corner of his mouth. "My heart's poundin' like a fuckin' jackhammer."

"Smoke a joint," Yale said. "Works for me."

Cippolone shook his head rapidly. "Don't have any. I'm waitin' on another cocktail." He signaled the bartender, this time ordering a double.

Wright extended his hand past Yale. "Say, man, what's your name? I'm Charlie Knapp. My friends call me Whitey." He pointed to Yale. "This here's Eddie Norton. You don't wanna know what his friends call him." The three men laughed.

Cippolone pumped their hands while nervously looking down the bar, waiting for his drink to appear. "They're slower than shit around here." He practically snatched the drink from the bartender's hand when it arrived, and half of it was gone in seconds. It was the magic bullet. Yale saw him calm down almost immediately.

"Feelin' better?" Yale said.

"Yeah, feelin' fine." Cippolone smiled. "The name's Lindberg, Doug Lindberg."

"Pleased to meet you, Doug," Yale said. Wright made a mock toast with his glass.

"I'll be right back, okay?" Cippolone said. "Don't let anyone take my seat." He slid off the stool and made a beeline for the men's room.

"Must be Miller time," Wright said. "Time for another hit."

Yale was on his second drink and was starting to feel the effects. He would have to slow down.

"Now that we're old buddies, where do you suggest we go from here?" Wright said.

"Haven't got the slightest. Let's play it by ear."

When Cippolone got back, he was in a talky mood. "So, whaddaya do?"

"We're postal workers," Yale said. "What about you?"

He ignored the question. "Oh, yeah? Hey, I got one for ya…what's it mean when the flag in front of the post office is at half-mast?"

"Got me, what?"

"It means they're hiring! Get it?" Cippolone emitted a screech that could pass for a laugh.

Wright smiled. "That one I haven't heard. Most of the crazy-post-office-guy jokes I heard before. That's a good one."

"Yeah," Yale said. "Great."

Cippolone leaned over Yale and whispered, "Say, I saw you make a buy from the bartender. He deliver your shit?"

Wright lowered his head. "Naw, I owed him that money. He don't have anything tonight. You got something?"

Cippolone straightened up, shooting a quick glance around the bar. On a conspiratorial level, he said, "Got me an eight-ball, want some?"

Wright feigned interest. "Yeah." He reached into his back pocket.

Cippolone grabbed his arm. "Forget it. Have a hit on me." He passed Wright a tall amber vial filled to the top with white powder. "You can't be a cop. You look worse than I do."

Wright smiled, revealing his stained teeth. He palmed the drug and mumbled, "Fuck you very much," as he made his way to the men's room.

"I'll pass," Yale said. "Been drinking a little too much. All I need's

98

a DWI bust." The bar was emptying out. The acting crowd needed its beauty rest, and half the kids would be sleeping with Preparation H smeared under their eyes tonight to prevent looking bagged-out for their big auditions tomorrow.

Yale tried his hardest to extract personal information from Cippolone during Wright's trip to the bathroom. He tried to find out where Cippolone lived, who he hung out with, and what he did for a living.

No matter how high and talkative Cippolone was, he continued to keep the conversation general, if not slurred.

Wright came back and passed the vial to Cippolone. "Thanks. Good shit."

Cippolone said, "My turn." He spun off the stool, staggering slightly as he weaved toward the bathroom.

"He doesn't waste much time, does he?" Wright said.

"I'm sure he's just getting warmed up."

"Find out anything? I figured I'd leave you two alone. Didn't want to spook him with too

many questions."

"Nada. He's a clam, been in the game too long. It's second nature for a guy like him to keep his mouth shut. Hey, how was the blow?" Yale smiled.

"Yeah, just what I need. I'm skinny enough. I don't want to be skinny and impotent. I dumped a little down the commode. Quiet, here he comes.

Cippolone perched himself on his stool and began talking like a machinegun. For the next few hours, the former cops listened to the ramblings of a junkie.

Finally, at 1:00 a.m., Yale had enough. It was time to get the hell out of there. "I'm calling it a night. I can't believe I gotta go to work in the morning. You sticking around, Charlie?" He pushed away from the bar, zipping up his jacket.

"Nah. I got a closet full of mail at home I gotta throw down a sewer."

Cippolone thought that was hysterical and laughed loud enough to make Yale's head pound. The coked-out con man didn't look ready to go anywhere, though. "I think maybe I'll hang out for a while, then maybe see Leah. She's a broad I know. She lives around."

Spoken like a true cokehead, Yale thought, no concept of time. It was a little after one in the morning, and this guy probably thought it was around nine o'clock. His girlfriend would love a visit from a wound-up junkie at 2:00 a.m. They shook hands, each promising to meet again and talk about old times. On the way out, Wright whispered something to the bartender.

Outside, Yale and Wright walked across the street and stepped into the shadow of a storefront. Yale was cold, tired, and his joints ached. Wright began to shiver.

"What did you say to the bartender?" Yale asked through chattering teeth.

"I told him to tell Cippolone he was shutting down in thirty minutes. Maybe that'll get the human vacuum out the door and on his way home. I don't think I can stand out here for another two plus hours until four a.m. I don't feel so good." Wright was very pale as he stood hunched over against the cold.

"You take off," Yale said, "I got it from here."

"No, man, I'm in for the duration. I'll stay just...."

"Charlie, you're no good to me if you collapse," Yale said. "Without you I would never have gotten this far. Go home. I'll beep you tomorrow. You did real good...now go." He put his hand on Wright's

100

shoulder.

Wright didn't protest. His labored breathing was audible above the intensity of the wind. "You need me before that, beep, okay?" He stepped into the middle of 72nd Street and got the first cab that came along.

Yale shivered for fifteen minutes before Cippolone came out of the bar. Bless the bartender's heart, Yale said to himself, he had another few bucks coming.

He followed the slight man east on 72nd Street, then south on Columbus Avenue. He was an easy tail, looking back only occasionally to eyeball passing women. At 69th Street, Cippolone made a left and walked up the stairs to a brownstone near the end of the block.

Downstairs, Yale huddled against a tree for ten minutes. When he saw Cippolone leave the building, he ducked low behind a car. As the little man staggered toward Columbus Avenue, Yale double-timed it across the street, perusing the names on the mailboxes in the vestibule of the brownstone. There were six apartments, and the name on one of them read, 'L. Porter'. Teen Angel had struck out in the love department again, Yale surmised. The former lieutenant reached street level in time to see Cippolone turn south on Columbus Avenue.

He ran to catch up to his prey, arriving at the corner out of breath and sweating, despite the frigid night air. He saw the black leather jacket navigate through a crowd of drunks leaving another bar. Yale followed at a discreet distance on the opposite side of the street.

Cippolone had the energy of a cocaine addict, walking briskly for ten blocks to the Wilshire Hotel off Columbus Circle. Yale had a difficult time keeping up but managed to catch a glimpse of Cippolone as he rounded Broadway and entered the hotel.

Yale knew the Wilshire to be a former single-room occupancy hotel, recently renovated and doing a good trade with out-of-town business people on a limited budget. He decided to march into the building like he was a guest there.

At the entrance, a gorilla in a doorman's uniform eyed Yale suspiciously but said nothing as Yale smiled and entered the lobby. A desk clerk to the right of the lone elevator was engrossed in a magazine and failed to look up as Yale walked deliberately past him, standing impassive in front of the steel elevator door. The car was ascending, and Yale watched the digital number stop at nine. At this hour, Yale figured, Cippolone was probably the only passenger.

Yale entered the elevator when it returned, pressed nine, and removed his house key from his pocket. A closed-circuit camera was trained directly on him, and if someone was monitoring it, he wanted it to appear that he was going to his room. When he exited the car on nine, he faced a dilemma. Left or right?

There was thirty feet of hallway in either direction. Two cameras panned the corridor from either end. He chose his political affiliation and turned right, walking slowly, examining door numbers. He hadn't the slightest idea what he was looking for, but he knew he would know when he found it.

He reached the end of the hallway, waving drunkenly at the camera before turning and walking in the opposite direction. The floor was heavily carpeted, and Yale was only able to hear the sound of his own breathing. He had nearly traversed the length of the corridor when he heard music coming from Room 904. If I was strung out on coke and couldn't sleep, Yale asked himself, what would I be doing? Listening to rock music, of course. I'm a regular Sherlock-fucking-Holmes, Yale thought, as he congratulated himself on finding Cippolone's room. Now if he could only get out of there without being locked up for criminal trespass.

Leaving the building was a snap. He should have realized that the hotel couldn't afford to have someone stare at a security monitor on a twenty-four basis. He strode out unchallenged, his first stop a payphone. He called the hotel and asked for Mr. Lindberg in Room 904, hanging up before the clerk could make the connection. Yale would pat himself on the back sometime tomorrow after a good night's sleep. Right now, all he could think of was getting lucky like Charlie Wright and finding a suicidal cabbie who would pick up a lone male at this hour and take him home. He would call Wright when he regained consciousness.

#

Leah Porter fastened the two bolt locks and slid the police bar against the door after Tony Cippolone had left. She turned around and walked directly into Wolfgang Steiner. He stood in the foyer, naked, arms folded across his chest.

"Who was that?" he asked.

She tightened her robe and swallowed hard, trying to buy time. "Uh…some drunk. Got the wrong apartment." She couldn't meet his eyes and tried to step around him. A muscular arm encircled her waist.

"It took you five minutes to get rid of him?"

She laughed nervously. "You know, some drunks, they can't—"

Steiner backhanded her across the face. Spittle sprayed from her mouth, and she bounced off the wall. He pressed his naked body against her. "I heard you say 'Tony.' Who's Tony? Don't lie to me, Leah."

Porter brought her hand away from her mouth. No blood. She looked at the rug. Almost inaudibly, she said, "Tony Cippolone." She covered her head with both hands, expecting blows that never came. When she looked up, Steiner was striding away.

"Jesus Christ! Cippolone! I haven't heard that name in nine years."

103

He disappeared into the bedroom, coming out seconds later in black jeans. He was struggling into a shirt. "You told me you haven't heard from him since the park. You fucking lied to me, didn't you?" His eyes were wide and he clenched his right fist.

Porter raised her hands, defensively. "Wolf, I'm sorry, I didn't think I had to bring his name up. He stops by maybe once or twice a year. He's harmless, really."

Steiner was breathing heavily. "Harmless? He can destroy me. Don't you see that? All these years and you chose not to tell me he was still around? You told me he jumped parole and vanished after he drove you that night. You said—"

Porter took a step toward him. She put her arms around him, burying her face in his chest. His hand fell to his side. She felt herself quivering and tried to contain it. She looked up at him. "I didn't want to worry you. I didn't think I was doing anything wrong. He doesn't even know you exist. He hasn't said anything in all these years. He won't say anything now." She tried to sound convincing, but she wasn't sure she even believed what she was saying.

Steiner pushed her away. "He shows up in the middle of the night, and from what I heard he sounded pretty wound up. Probably strung out on blow, right?"

"Well, yeah, but—"

"Jesus Christ! How can you trust a junkie, a cokehead no less, to keep his mouth shut?" Steiner whirled and strode back into the bedroom. Porter followed.

Steiner sat on the edge of the bed, putting on a pair of cowboy boots. "What the fuck were you thinking? You know what I've got to lose? Nine years ago no one knew my name. Now…." His voice trailed off, and he ran his hands through his shoulder-length hair. He looked up. His eyes narrowed. "You're not lying to me about anything else, are you, Leah?"

She shook her head. "No, Wolf, I didn't lie to you about him. I just never told you because I didn't think it was important." Her excuse sounded feeble, even to her.

He walked to the door, mumbling something she couldn't hear. "I gotta do some thinking." He turned to her as she stood in the entrance to the bedroom and softened his tone. "This isn't nine years ago, honey. We got rid of one blackmailer, I'm not about to give someone another opportunity." He was gone before she had a chance to respond.

In the bedroom now, alone, she fell to her knees and cried. My God, she thought, will I lose him over this? After all we've been through?

Stuffed animals, piled high against one wall in the bedroom, was her solace. She went to them and lay amongst her massive collection of the fuzzy toys, hoping they would bring her some comfort. She cuddled the animals she had collected since her youth and put a ten-inch bear against her swelling cheekbone. Within minutes, she was asleep.

## Chapter Eleven

The discomfort Yale felt the next morning from a slight hangover paled next to the exuberance he was experiencing because of last night's turn of events. At least some headway was being made in the case. Finding Cippolone was a step in the right direction, albeit a small one.

He waited until late afternoon before calling Charlie Wright, thinking the former detective needed as much rest as he could get. Wright returned his beep within fifteen minutes.

"You feeling okay?" Yale asked.

"Could be worse. I think I'm coming down with a cold. No big deal."

It could be a very big deal in his condition, Yale thought, but let it go. "Thanks for the help last night. We got our man." He told Wright about finding Cippolone's hotel and the brief stop on 69th Street.

"Great, what do we do next?"

"Did you originally interview Zoltag's chauffeur?"

"No, Queens Homicide did. We were backed up, and the boss sent one of their detectives."

"I'd like the chauffeur to take a look at a picture of this Porter dame to see if she looks like his third passenger that night."

"Wouldn't you call her a long shot? All Cippolone did was mention her name, maybe she's just a good piece of ass."

"You got somewhere else we could go with this? We might as well check everything before we lean on Cippolone. I doubt he's going anywhere; he doesn't think anyone is on to him."

"We haven't got a picture of Porter."

"I can get one when she leaves her building." Yale was mentally planning his strategy, trying to recall the physical layout of the block and if there was a good place to conceal himself with a camera.

"You get the picture," Wright said, "and I'll check the old DD5's for the chauffeur's address." They agreed to talk later and compare notes.

Back in his office, Yale began the well-practiced routine of exposing a life via computer. Within ten minutes, he had completed the preliminary inquiry, establishing a date of birth and social security number for Leah Porter.

She was thirty-seven and lived at the address on 69th Street where he had followed Cippolone. He fed this information to a large credit bureau under the guise of checking Porter's credit history for a mortgage loan application. Within seconds, a lengthy credit report was being printed out. His trained eyes skimmed over the computerese on the credit report. His eyes bulged. "Jesus Christ, she's a cop!" He tore the page from the printer and reviewed the information, carefully concentrating on the codes and credit industry-speak with which he was not totally familiar.

She was a former cop. Her credit record indicated she had been hired by the NYPD in 1981 and had left in 1985. Prior to her coming on The Job, she had held a variety of retail sales positions, all for short durations. She hadn't worked since 1985.

An ex-cop. Yale knew that many inferences could be made from someone who had spent only four years on The Job. Generally, no one quits the NYPD except to move on to a better position, and that wasn't the case here. That only left termination for cause, and a credit report wouldn't list something like that. He looked further.

Leah Porter had twenty-two credit cards, and she used every one of them. The cards were everything from gas cards to the best department stores in Manhattan, including Bergdorf Goodman, Bloomingdale's, Saks, and Chanel. Yale made a quick calculation and saw that she had spent over thirty thousand dollars on clothes in the last twelve months. Her payments were always on time. Nothing can compare to throwing on a dress from Saks when looking for a job to show a potential employer that you're broke and hungry for work, Yale thought.

He was intrigued. There was the absence of the usual car loan, and her DMV report indicated she didn't own a car. No mortgage, either. The apartment on the West Side was a rental. How was she paying all her bills if she didn't work? Why did she leave The Job? Or was it The Job that had left her?

He grabbed the phone and dialed a familiar number.

"One-Ten Squad. Detective Hans."

"Lieutenant Sheehan, please," Yale said. He heard the rustle of paper.

"Ah…Lt. Sheehan is on his swing. Chart says he'll be in tomorrow. Wanna leave a message?"

Yale hung up without replying. I can't wait until tomorrow, he thought, sifting through a pile of business cards he had secured with a rubber band. Sheehan's NYPD card was located near the bottom of the pile. Yale said a silent prayer and flipped it over. Sheehan's home phone number was on the back.

A woman answered and called Sheehan to the phone after giving Yale the third degree. A typical police wife, Yale thought, not admitting that her husband was home until she was sure the caller wasn't about to drag him out of the house for no good reason.

"Ray," Mike Sheehan said, "either I don't hear from you in a year or I can't get rid of you. What's up?"

"It's business, Mike, and I wouldn't be calling you at home unless it was important. I need a favor."

"For you, anything, as long as it doesn't get me indicted."

"Remember what we were talking about the other day?" Yale said, not wanting to be specific. Yale hadn't trusted telephones since he was a rookie. The less said, the better.

"Yeah."

"I need a blood type. I should have asked when I saw you, but I never thought I'd get this far."

"You got something?"

"What I got you'll get, as soon as it makes sense. So far it's just a good hunch. I need the blood type to move it along. When and if things fall into place, you'll be the first to know."

"Where are you?"

"Home. You got my number?"

"I got it. It'll take about an hour. Stay there." He hung up.

Yale knew the scenario even as he was replacing the receiver. Sheehan was calling his squad and getting a detective to go to an outside phone and call him back. After getting instructions, the detective would go back to the squad room, get the blood type that was found in the saliva left on Katherine Carpenter's breast from a DD5, go back to the outside phone, and call his boss with the information.

Ninety minutes later, Yale's phone rang. "Yeah."

"Ray?" Sheehan said in a harsh whisper. He was making a poor attempt at disguising his voice.

"It's me, want my social security number?"

"Wise guy. Took me a half hour to find a goddamn working phone."

"Well?"

"'A' positive."

The phone went dead.

'A' positive, the most common blood type in the world. He shrugged. It was better than nothing.

He looked up Nick Abrutti's pager number and called it, knowing better than to try his house on a weekday night or any other night for that matter. Yale's phone rang within three minutes.

"Who wants Nicky?" Yale heard the sounds of merrymaking. Abrutti's speech was slightly slurred. He usually referred to himself in the third person when he was drunk.

"The IRS," Yale said and thought he heard the unmistakable sound of a jaw hitting the floor.

"Who the hell is this?"

"Ray Yale."

"Hey, man, don't go doin' that shit. Nicky's heart ain't what it used to be. What's happenin'?"

"Tomorrow, or first chance you get, could you find out a certain cop's blood type? Actually, she's a former cop, been off The Job since eighty-five."

"What did ya do, meet some broad and you wanna run an AIDS test on her first?" Abrutti thought this was hilarious. "Nicky'll have her pee in a jar, too, if you want."

"Nick, this is important, real important. Can you do it? You got more contacts on The Job than me."

Abrutti got serious. "Real important, huh? Where are you?"

"Home." He gave him the number.

"Gimme the cop's name—"

"Ex-cop."

"Whatever. What's her name?"

"The name's Leah Porter." He spelled it. "I haven't got a shield or tax number. Problem?"

"Don't think so. Hey…Porter…that sounds familiar."

"You know her?"

"Maybe. Give me some time, things are kinda fuzzy."

Yale picked at some ancient Chinese food he found in the refrigerator and waited for the phone to ring. When it rang, he knew who it was before he picked it up. "Who wants Ray?" he said, doing his best to sound like an inebriated Nick Abrutti.

Nick sounded stone-cold sober. "It's Nicky. What's the matter with you? You sound like you got a mouth full of pussy."

"Chinese food. Speak to me."

Abrutti lowered his voice. "We gotta talk."

"So, talk."

"Not on the phone, numb-nuts. Somewhere private."

He had something hot, Yale knew, which required a face-to-face meeting. "Pick a place where I can hear myself talk."

"Okay," Abrutti said. "You remember where I used to meet my clients when I first started out? That restaurant in the Doral Hotel on Lexington Avenue?"

"Uh-huh."

"I'll be there in a half hour."

"I may be a little—"

The line went dead.

Yale had tried to tell Nick that he might be a little late. He knew

111

Abrutti had a short attention span, and if he had to wait more than fifteen minutes for Yale he might get involved with a visiting transsexual from New Zealand and decide to show her the town, at which point Yale would be a memory. Yale dressed and was out the door before his belt was threaded all the way through his pants.

He took the upper roadway of the Queensborough Bridge. The rush hour just over, there were only a handful of cars on the span, and he floored the Lexus, covering the distance between Queens and Manhattan in less than three minutes. Yale turned onto Lexington Avenue running ten minutes late.

Nick Abrutti's Mercedes was triple parked near the hotel's canopy. At the first sign of a tow truck, the doorman would drive the car around the block, returning after the truck hooked some other hapless New Yorker. Yale pulled his car behind the Mercedes. He tossed the keys to the doorman, pointed to Abrutti's car and said, "I'm with him."

It took a few seconds for his eyes to adjust to the dim light in the restaurant. Abrutti was seated on a stool at the corner of the bar, facing the door. A few bored hotel guests hunched over small tables in the cocktail lounge, but Abrutti had the bar all to himself. When he saw Yale, he hopped off the stool. He was wearing a burgundy, double-breasted suit, white-on-white shirt, green and white tie with matching pocket square, and highly polished boots that Yale thought had at least two-inch heels. The latest in mob wear.

"Let's get a table in the corner," Abrutti said, leading Yale to a tiny table just big enough to hold two drinks and a potato chip.

Yale waved away an approaching waitress. "What've you got?"

Abrutti leaned across the table. He didn't have far to go. "After you mentioned that broad's name, all of aa sudden I remembered her. She got fired from The Job in eighty-five or eighty-six. I remember 'cause I was

112

just goin' into business, and I ran into her at a racket in Brooklyn."

"Why was she fired?"

"Brutality. She beat a prisoner to death on the street, said the guy tried to kill her. The court believed her, The Job didn't. It was in all the papers. The Policewoman's Dyke Association, or whatever the fuck you call it, tried to save her job. No good, off she went. You don't remember hearing all this?"

Yale vaguely recalled the case, but not the name. He was involved with his wife's illness around that time and wasn't keeping current with Job gossip. Drinking a half bottle of Scotch a day didn't help his memory either. "It's not real clear."

"Well, it was a pretty big deal at the time. She was on all the talk shows with her union rep. They said it was sexual recrimination."

"Discrimination, Nick."

Abrutti looked indignant. "That's what I said."

Yale rolled his eyes. "You couldn't tell me this on the phone?"

"No, man, 'cause I hired her as one of my operatives. She lasted one case. I almost lost my friggin' license because of her."

"What happened?"

"Like I said, I ran into her at some party. Not a bad lookin' broad. I figured I'd get me a little police pussy, ya know? Uh, no offense intended to your dead wife."

"None taken." *How do I meet these people?* "Go on."

"So, she was lookin' for work. I ask her if she wants to do a fidelity surveillance, you know, a cheatin' husband case. She says okay, so I give her this guy's picture and tell her where he hangs out. I tell her to watch the asshole and follow him if he leaves. Simple enough?"

"Sounds simple to me."

"She's a smart broad, but she did something pretty dumb."

113

"What?"

"She goes in the bar and starts talkin' to the guy, which is okay, because after three hours in the gin mill, she knew he wasn't goin' nowhere. If he tried to pick her up, we could report that back to the guy's wife."

"I take it she was wired."

Nick had a pained look on his face. "She was wired, alright, with the latest and most sensitive recorder I had. The mike could pick up the sound of a nipple getting' hard."

"You have a way with words, Nick."

Abrutti beamed. "Don't I though? Anyway, they get to talkin' and the guy's a little drunk and asks her to go out to his car."

"What for?"

"To give him some head. It's right on the tape, I swear to God." He held up his right hand. "Even I wouldn't do that. I mean, they were talkin' about the goddamn weather or somethin' and then all of a sudden he's asking for a blowjob. So they go out to the car, and you can hear on the tape where he whips it out and asks her to stroke it."

"All this is a little above and beyond, no?"

"No shit. Just listen to the rest of the story. She grabs him by the old love lance with one hand—he starts moanin' and shit—and with the other hand she proceeds to beat the crap out of him with a collapsible steel night stick, the kind the Feds use. You flick your wrist, and the thing extends like a seventeen-year-old's hard-on. She beat this poor schmuck to a bloody friggin' pulp."

"You think she planned the whole thing?"

"I can't imagine anyone carryin' one of those things around unless they plan on usin' it. I think maybe she just wanted to beat the shit out of someone that day, and this guy was handy."

114

"How'd she almost make you lose your license?"

"Would you believe she dropped the goddamn recorder in the car before she split? The first cops on the scene found shithead unconscious and vouchered the recorder. You believe it? The new breed. I would have stolen the fuckin' thing. You?"

"That and the car." Yale was beginning to get a headache. "Then?"

"I was truly fucked."

"Sounds like it. How'd you beat it?"

"Believe me, Ray, if the guy'd died, I'd be workin' for you."

"Perish the thought," Yale mumbled.

"Turns out he was in the hospital for five weeks with a skull fracture. I called in every favor owed to me and killed the beef. I even gave the guy's wife her money back, and you know that ain't me."

"What happened with Porter, she get locked up?" That could explain the lack of employment history after her NYPD career had ended, Yale thought, chastising himself for not running a criminal check on her.

Abrutti shook his head. "You ain't thinkin'. If I skated, so did she. How could they lock her up without involving me?"

"Makes sense. Know what she's doing now?"

"Haven't heard shit, and I don't want to hear shit. The broad's a fuckin' nutcase." He tapped a manicured index finger against his head.

"What does she look like?"

Abrutti was deep in thought. "From what I remember, a nice lookin' broad. Tall…tallern' me, about five-nine or ten, long blonde hair, slim…not much in the tit department, but solid. You could see the way she walked she worked out a lot. She was wearing a short skirt at that party. Legs up to her arm pits."

"Eyes?"

"Blue. She had some freckles across here." He pointed to the bridge of his nose.

Yale recalled the description of the shooter as having long brown hair, but she could have been wearing a wig or had a dye job. The age was about right. He'd have to see if he could get a better description from the chauffeur.

"You get her blood type for me?" Yale asked.

"'A' positive."

Yale's brain churned. Could it be falling into place after nine years? Was Leah Porter the shooter? If she was, what was the motive? Spurned lover? Was Zoltag really the intended victim? After listening to Abrutti, he thought Porter could have killed Zoltag and Carpenter because she had a hangnail and was pissed off. But if that were the case, Yale thought, why didn't she kill the driver, too?

He reached across the table and pumped Nick's hand. "Nick, I owe you one."

"Want to tell me what's goin' on? This have somethin' to do with Charlie Wright and the park killings?"

Yale got up. "I can't go into it now, Nick. As soon as I'm sure I'm not tripping over my own dick, I'll tell you the whole story." He squeezed Abrutti's shoulder. "See you around."

"Trippin' over your dick's okay, just don't stand on it." The gospel according to Abrutti. "All this stuff has gotta be tied in."

Yale turned around. "Why? What makes you say that?"

"Because the crazy cop, that Porter broad," Abrutti said. "When she was fired, she was working in QTF."

Yale was unfamiliar with the term. "What the hell is QTF?"

Nick smiled. "I keep forgettin', you worked in Manhattan your whole career, Queens is like another world. QTF's the Queens Task Force. They run out of Flushing Park."

116

## Chapter Twelve

During a commercial break on his radio show, Wolfgang Steiner was contemplating spending the rest of his life in prison. The reemergence of Anthony Cippolone in his life had so upset him that he committed what can only be considered a major faux pas in the radio business: he failed to hear the cue from his engineer that the commercial was over and he was back on the air. He was first aware of his mistake when, through his earphones, he heard the panicky voice of his assistant, Quiana Tompkins.

"Wolf! Are you awake in there? We've got ten seconds of dead air." Tompkins was in a glass booth outside the studio where Steiner sat, alone. She couldn't see him and neither could the half dozen other technicians and production staff whose offices and work areas were scattered around the Madison Avenue offices of WROK Radio.

Steiner snapped out of his reverie. My God, he thought, an amateur wouldn't leave dead air. He quickly regained control. "Just making sure America was on the ball, Quiana." What the hell was he supposed to do next? He had forgotten. "What are we up for, Quiana?"

"We were going to take some calls before we went to break, Wolfmeister."

She sounded her usual self, cool and professional, Steiner thought. For a broad named after a synthetic fabric, she ain't bad, but this was his show and he had to be in control. "I think we should do the news. What's going on in this cesspool of a city?" He fad to force himself to concentrate on his patter. He looked at his gold Rolex. If he rushed the remaining commercials, he could be off the air in fifteen minutes. He had to talk to Leah about Cippolone. Steiner couldn't afford to have that loose cannon bring him down.

"Well, Wolfmeister, the new mayor is cracking down on those squeegee guys you find all over town."

"Hey," Steiner said, "let me tell you about those guys. They're ruining the, um…the um…what's the term I'm looking for here, Quiana? Help me out."

"The quality of life, Wolfmeister, the quality of life."

"Thank you, Quiana…the quality of life. You know, I'm glad to see there's more to you than just a huge pair of knockers." He was settling back in now, doing what he did best.

Quiana's sensual laugh filled the studio. "Oh, Wolfmeister!"

"Well, it's true, you've got the largest breasts I've ever seen. Isn't it true that most women with large breasts aren't very smart?"

"Oh, Wolfmeister!" Quiana let go with a well-rehearsed giggle.

"Anyway, if it was up to me," Steiner said, "I'd execute all those squeegee guys. What right do they have to bother me and clean my car with a filthy rag?" Most of the thirty-eight phone lines in front of him lit up.

"Wolfmeister, we've got some reactions from callers. Want to take some now?"

"Okay, we'll take one call about the squeegee bums. Janet, give me one at random." Janet Romano, Steiner's studio engineer, was a statuesque redhead, nicknamed Janet-From-Another-Planet. She was a former listener whom he had hired because of her belief that she had been kidnapped and sexually assaulted by aliens from outer space when she was a teenager. She was passable as an engineer, but Steiner liked to exploit her eccentricities on the show. Today, however, he was more concerned with getting the hell off the air.

"Okay, loser, you're on the air," Steiner said.

"Hey, man," the irate caller said, "I'm a mobile window cleanliness technician, and I take personal offense at you callin' me a bum."

"You're a mobile window cleanliness technician? Everybody's got a title. I know what you are, you're a black brother that likes to intimidate white people into giving you money. Why don't you get a real job and stop panhandling? That's what it is, you know, panhandling." To Steiner, this was schtick at its best. He believed he was the consummate actor and could get people to believe anything he said.

"Yeah, I'm an Af-ri-can Amer-i-can. What are you, a Jew boy?"

Steiner was enjoying baiting the guy. "Yeah, I'm a Jew and proud of it. Let me ask you something, how old are you?"

"I'm twenny-three."

"You miserable low-life! I accomplished more before I was six years old than you have up to now. You're nothing but a pothole on the highway of life." *I can't go too over-the-top with this guy,* he thought, *it's not politically correct to beat up the disadvantaged these days. Better end this quickly.*

Quiana giggled. "Oh, Wolfmeister!"

*Must she laugh at every goddamn thing I say? It's her job, but enough already.* He looked at his watch again. Two minutes after the last time he had looked.

"You know what you are?" the caller screamed. "You're a bigot, that's what you are, a bigot!"

Now for the coup d' grace, Steiner thought, gleefully. "Your mama's a bigot." That gets them every time.

"You white motherfucker! I'm going to come up there and kick your white ass!"

Steiner cut him off by hitting the seven-second delay button, sending him into electronic limbo. The listeners never heard his diatribe. He was glad all callers were put on a lag to deal with such outbursts, less to worry about from the FCC. "I guess he decided he couldn't match wits with the Emperor of the Airwaves, huh, Quiana?"

"You're a genius, Wolfmeister."

They went to a commercial.

He heard the door open behind him and turned to see Eugene Hochendoner hurriedly grab a pair of earphones and roll up a swivel chair next to Steiner's.

"Where the fuck've you been?" Steiner said calmly. He had learned a long time ago that controlling people was easy if you didn't intimidate them. If you did, eventually they rebelled. He was smarter than most people; he didn't have to raise his voice.

"Had to use the can, boss," Hochendoner said, averting his eyes from Steiner's penetrating gaze.

Steiner grabbed the man's chair and spun it around. Eugene Hochendoner was a professional stand-up comic who sat next to Steiner during the show and anonymously fed him funny lines, which he scribbled on a legal pad. The world thought the jokes were adlibbed by Steiner. The comedian's eyes were bloodshot. "You're fucked up, aren't you?" Steiner said. "You smoked a joint in the john, didn't you?"

"Aw, c'mon, Wolf." He grinned. "A joint takes the edge off; the shit make me funnier."

120

"No, my man, it makes me funnier, and when you get fucked up, I look like an asshole because you're too wasted to function." Steiner immediately thought of Tony Cippolone and his drug problem. If he gets too fucked up and talks….

"Yeah, man, I'm sorry, I won't do it anymore."

Steiner clapped him on the back. "At least not at work, right?" They both laughed. Now we're buddies again, he thought. *He idolizes me, the poor prick. Show a little appreciation and it'll save me from having to give him a big raise.*

He got the five-second signal from Quiana through the earphones. This one he heard loud and clear. They were back on the air.

"So what else is new, Quiana?" Steiner said, slipping back into his radio persona.

"There's a story in the *Post* about a group of gay cops who are suing the NYPD for sex discrimination."

"What do they want to do, " Steiner asked, "have the right to play drop the soap in the precinct shower?"

Quiana said, "Oh, Wolfmeister!"

Steiner closed his eyes and slowly shook his head. Let this day end, he prayed.

"No, Wolfmeister, it says here they want the right to bring their same-sex-partners to official police department functions."

Hochendoner busily scribbled on his pad and help it in front of Steiner.

In a falsetto voice Steiner said, "Is that your nightstick, Officer Bruce, or are you just glad to see me?" Janet and Quiana broke up. Maybe Eugene is better stoned, Steiner thought.

"What they want, Wolfmeister, is to be able to go to official ceremonies, like Medal Day, it says here, and have their lovers recognized as family."

"Oh, Christ!" Steiner bellowed. "Isn't this city screwed up enough? Do we really need a bunch of fairy cops with flowers sticking out of their gun barrels pirouetting on their beats? Quiana, would you trust a cop who has lipstick in his handcuff case?"

"Well, what about policewomen, Wolf? What do you think of gay policewomen?"

"I would trust them with my life sooner than I would limp-wristed guy cop. You ever seen one of those dyke cops, Quiana?"

"Well…how would I know if I saw a lesbian cop or for that matter a gay male cop?"

"I had a run-in a few weeks ago with a gay cop over on Madison Avenue here that had a great impact on me."

"Would you like to tell our listeners about it, Wolfmeister?"

*That's it bitch, keep feeding me those lines.* "Well, I wasn't going to, but since you insist.

"I'm leaving the studio after the show, and I see this cop standing on Madison and 62nd Street. Must have weighed two-fifty and ugly as a hyena. Very out of shape, needed a shave, too. So I walk over to complain. I was going to say, 'Hey, I'm a taxpayer in this town, and I don't expect to see one of New York's Finest looking like a bag of dirt.' The thing was, the closer I got, the more I realized that it was a policewoman! I wasn't about to complain about her appearance; she'd kick my ass! She may have been big and ugly, but if it came to two out of three falls, I'd bet everything I had on her…or it…whatever" He switched off his microphone for a second and said to Hochendoner, "Tell me I'm not the best."

Hochendoner nodded vigorously.

"Wolfmeister," Quiana said, "it sounds like you hate gays."

"Who, me? I just don't think they should be cops." Steiner didn't, in fact, hate gays, but he distrusted them as much as he distrusted members of most minority groups.

Janet told Steiner that a lot of calls were coming in.

"What's up, Janet, we got people out there who disagree with the Emperor of the Airwaves?"

"Numerous, Wolf, numerous."

"Hard to believe. Guys or girls?"

"About equally divided," Janet said. "I've got a guy on line seven who says he's a cop and a member of GOAL."

"GOAL?" Steiner asked. "What the hell is that?"

Quiana cut in. "That's the gay cop's fraternal organization, Wolfmeister."

"Hey, I knew that," Steiner said in mock defense. "Let me talk to him." Janet transferred the call.

"Is this Wolf?" the caller asked.

"This is the Emperor of the Airwaves. You're on the air."

"My name is Paul Peters, and I'm a New York City Police Officer and member of GOAL. I don't think—"

"Hold it a second,' Steiner said. "What does GOAL stand for?"

"Gay Officer's Action League. We're a group of gay cops, men and women, who want to educate the public and the New York City Police Department about the positive contributions gay people are making to the force."

Hochendoner shoved the pad under Steiner's nose.

"What did you say your name was?" Steiner asked. He wanted to work his faux ad-lib into the conversation.

"Peters, Paul Peters."

"You must like being associated with a peter all the time, am I right?" Steiner said. Quiana guffawed.

"Listen, I called to have an intelligent conversation with you, to try to tell your audience we're like everybody else. You're just too ignorant to listen."

"I'm ignorant?" Steiner said, taking another page from Hochendoner. "Tell me, is it true the real name of your organization is Policeman's Urban Society for Sexual Indiscretions?"

"What?"

Steiner repeated the name. "PUSSI for short, right?"

"I'm sorry I wasted my time with an obviously homophobic moron," Peters said.

Steiner didn't want the cop to hang up. Baiting a gay cop was great radio as far as he was concerned. "How long you been a cop?"

"Six years," Peters said.

"Ever had another male cop as a lover?"

"Of course, but what does that have to do—"

"Because while you're playing find the salami with your buddy," Steiner said, "my ass, pardon the pun, is unprotected on the street."

"That's the dumbest statement I ever heard. What do you think we do, have sex during working hours?"

"Why not? I do, right, Quiana?"

His sidekick chuckled. "Oh, Wolfmeister! You know that's not true! Your wife may be listening."

"Screw her," Steiner said, then added, "just kidding, dear."

"I called to tell you about our suit," Peters said.

"Your suit's probably lavender with a flap in the back," Steiner said.

Hochendoner stifled a laugh and wrote GOOD ONE! on the pad.

"Our lawsuit, our lawsuit!" Peters said. "Are you gonna listen, or what?"

"Yeah, yeah, spread some propaganda, go ahead."

Peters rambled for three minutes about the gay community's inalienable right to congregate wherever they pleased, while Steiner either talked over him or interrupted with Hochendoner's crude jokes.

"Are you through?" Steiner asked when the crusading cop paused to gather his thoughts.

"Well, yes...just about."

"Don't ever let it be said that the Emperor of the Airwaves doesn't let the opposition speak their mind, even if they are perverted and spread disease." Steiner waited for the explosion.

"You stupid bastard!"

But Steiner had already hit the seven-second delay, depriving America of hearing the cop's last remark. "Thank you for calling. Anything else, Quiana?

"That's about it for the news, Wolfmeister."

"Okay, then let's wrap it up." Steiner read his usual list of plugs and signed off. He had gone five minutes past his allotted time. Usually, he went at least twenty minutes past the official end of his show, but he knew if he wanted to go on all day, the station manager would let him. His popularity was such that the rest of the day's programming would be preempted had he chosen to read from the Manhattan phone directory. He was exhausted. He must be getting old, he thought.

He took the private elevator one flight to his office on the third floor to avoid contact with station employees. He passed through the plush executive reception area of WROK, New York's premier rock radio station, and punched the three-digit combination lock on his office door. He shut it behind him, sitting down hard on the leather modular sofa located next to a wall mural depicting a robed Steiner standing before a throng of admirers. The painting was a gift from grateful station officials when WROK went from the basement in the Arbitron ratings to number one a year after Steiner's arrival. He knew that his show had a trickle-down effect for the rest of the day's programming. Listeners tended to keep their dials on WROK-FM after he signed off.

He removed his John Lennon-style shades and clumsy engineer boots. His slight paunch was straining at the snug jeans. He unbuttoned the pants and tossed his leather vest across the room, where it landed in a heap against a wall. He stretched out, his six-foot-five-inch frame dwarfing the supple leather couch. He let out an audible sigh, relaxing for the first time since he had arrived at the studio before dawn.

He knew he was the very definition of the word *star*, but he felt it could all come crashing down quickly. With his freedom depending on Tony Cippolone's ability to keep his mouth shut, he didn't feel as if he were in control. My God, he had so much to lose.

On the wall directly opposite him was a poster-sized enlargement of the cover from his autobiography, *Bite Me*, which had been published five months ago and was still on the *New York Times* best seller list. He laughed. He had not only failed to write the book, but he still hadn't read it. His editor, an up-and-comer in the publishing industry, wrote the entire thing herself from taped interviews. He had her twisted around his little finger, too. Steiner had come a long way from his first job in radio.

He remembered the early years, the small radio station in Gary, Indiana, his firing for being too risqué for the straight-laced station owners, and his eventual hiring in New York where the station manager at WROK was willing to take a chance on him. His irreverent style and uncanny ability to know what big-city audiences wanted propelled him to the number one slot in New York radio.

With the fame, he recalled, came scrutiny, both from the press and from less reputable sources, most notably in the form of Herman Zoltag.

126

That prick Zoltag saw a way to get rich from Stein's success by blackmailing him over an episode in their shared past, an episode so lurid that public knowledge would certainly lead to jail and ruination. We were friends once, for Christ's sake, he thought. Steiner at once began to consider reverting to his former intense lifestyle to rid himself of Zoltag, but he hesitated to get involved due to his current celebrity. Today, he cursed the improprieties of his youth, as many do in retrospect. He knew he had too much to lose by getting involved with Zoltag on a personal level. Then, salvation appeared in the form of Leah Porter. How well he remembered the day he met her.

He had been told of the violent policewoman by a member of his staff, and he booked her on his show to conduct one of his typically tasteless interviews. From the outset of their discussion, however, he realized that Porter possessed not the slightest iota of conscience. She had bludgeoned a defenseless old man to death and tried to beat the charge by using a sexual harassment defense. Steiner set out to exploit that character flaw by having her become totally dependent on him. He saw in her the potential to do his bidding without questions of morality or ethics coming into play. After the show, they began a sexual and co-dependent relationship that endured. How many times had he banged her right here on this couch, he asked himself. Too numerous to remember.

He kept Porter supplied with enough money and material playthings to keep her happy. There was no need for her to work, and he preferred to have her available when he needed her. He never discussed his past, but he confided in her the need to dispatch Zoltag and recover a damning videotape that his former friend was utilizing to extort money from him. She had been a good soldier. He told her that after the deed was done, she was to deliver the tape to him immediately.

He stressed that she was not to look at the tape and trusted her blind devotion to comply with his orders. And just like a good soldier, she had obeyed. In fact, her only mistake was involving that loser Tony Cippolone in the operation. He cursed that decision, but he knew nothing about it in advance. She had gone on her own to get a ride from the park that night. Porter had told him that Cippolone was on the periphery that night and didn't know that his help had resulted in a double homicide. The story was in all the newspapers the next day; how could Cippolone not have realized what he had been involved in the previous night? Steiner had asked himself that question many times during these nine years, although Porter's reassurances that Cippolone had vanished, probably dead from a drug overdose, he thought, had allayed any fears he had. As the years passed, he almost forgot about Cippolone, except for the occasional feeling of helplessness regarding not knowing positively what had happened to him.

Now, all of a sudden, Cippolone had come knocking on Porter's door, and Steiner once again felt the gnawing dread of discovery. Cippolone's drug use scared him. He was now worried that Cippolone might run off at the mouth one day and bring Leah Porter down. If she got arrested, he asked himself, was he far behind? Porter had told him on many occasions that Cippolone knew nothing of their relationship, and he had kept his concubine as much a secret as possible, but he knew that in this town, someone besides the two of them had to know of their arrangement. Yes, the future of Tony Cippolone would have to be discussed with Leah immediately. He knew she would forgive him the slap he had given her the previous night. She always did.

He got up and went to the window that overlooked Madison Avenue. His gaze was on people in the next office building, but he wasn't seeing them. He was thinking about how, after Zoltag, the next killing had been much easier to plan and execute. He had sweated the park shooting, particularly after hearing that a woman Zoltag had picked up that night was also killed. He had read somewhere that soldiers in combat killed more easily with each successive killing, and now he could see why. He hadn't perspired a drop over the next one.

With Zoltag out of the way, he had begun to feel more confident about his future. His ratings were soaring, and his show was going into syndication. There were, he recalled, two blights on the horizon. The first one was Marvin Tavlin, a right-wing religious fanatic who had vowed to get him thrown off the air because of what he called 'blasphemous immorality.' At first, Tavlin was a mild nuisance, then his holy crusade began to get results. He was a real pain in the ass. A few sponsors began dropping Steiner's show. This sent some potential affiliates, particularly in the Midwest, to their own sponsors, asking them to scrutinize his audio-tapes to see if he was too objectionable for middle America. Because of the scrutiny, he was told to clean up his act, at least until the syndication deal was signed. He had no choice but to comply, and this led to a drastic dip in ratings. He saw his career going into free-fall when he was censored by the station. Those were bad times.

Without giving it too much thought, he had once again called upon Leah Porter to salvage his future. He had told her to make it look like an accident. She did the second-best thing: she made it look like a street mugging gone bad. Tavlin was dead, and Steiner was off the hook, once again thanks to the brutal efficiency of Leah Porter. The syndication deal went through. The second problem was Dan Doremus, his morning drive-time competition on an AM station.

Steiner still didn't like to admit it, but he was jealous of Danny 'D', as he was known to his radio audience. Doremus' show was something new in the world of morning radio: an original program with talented, supporting staff and the best writers in the business. Doremus played to an older audience from a different social strata, a group that spent the most money for advertised products. While his own show may have had more listeners, Doremus' audience made more money for the station. Steiner felt he had to get his competitor's listeners to corner the New York market and become the self-proclaimed Emperor of the Airwaves.

He had toyed with the idea of killing Doremus but decided his death would garner too much publicity. Instead, he had elected to destroy his opposition's reputation, unleashing Leah Porter to help him salvage his career.

The newspaper accounts stated the police had received an anonymous 911 phone call that there was a burglary in progress in Doremus' East Village cooperative apartment. The arriving officers had found an empty apartment with the front door hanging from a hinge, easily spotting a pile of coke and enough child pornography to make John Wayne Gacy blush. Doremus yelled frame, and the case was eventually dismissed, but not without enough adverse publicity to ruin his career. Steiner thought it was a nice touch that Porter had enrolled Doremus in an organization that advocates sexual relationships with underage boys. The last he heard, his former rival was the morning jock in a small city down south, his principal audience being farmers who liked company while milking their cows. Steiner's ratings had almost doubled.

Steiner sat down at his desk and thumbed through a newly signed contract. The deal called for him to star in three movies and a weekly syndicated cable television talk show. Yesterday, he had learned from his agent that a pay-per-view New Year's Eve special was a done deal. His various projects would bring him over nine million dollars in gross earnings this year. So why, he asked himself, was he so worried? Why couldn't he trust Leah's judgement? Because he was smarter than most people, and he knew their weaknesses. He also wondered how long he would put up with Leah. The phone rang. He considered not answering it but thought it might be Porter.

"Hello," he said.

"I know you don't like to be disturbed after the show, Wolf, but it's your broker," his secretary said. "Shall I put her through?"

Steiner had left explicit instructions that if his "stockbroker" called, he was to be told immediately.

"Yeah, there's always time to talk to my money." Always ready with a good line. His secretary laughed and connected him.

"Hi, honey," Leah Porter said.

"I was hoping you would call. Are you mad at me?" Steiner would have her on his side in a minute, if she weren't already.

"Why should I be?"

Total denial. "You know, last night."

"Oh, that. Forget about it. I was wrong. I should have told you about Tony. I'm sorry. Are you coming over tonight? I'll send out to that Japanese place you like."

"I don't think so, not tonight. I'm beat. Besides, we saw each other twice this week. How many times can I tell Stephanie I've got to stay in Manhattan for a late meeting? The last thing I need is a suspicious wife." He really didn't think his wife had the mental capacity to be suspicious, but he didn't feel like seeing Leah again tonight. He thought more than twice a week was spoiling her.

"How about a little afternoon romp then?" she said. "I just got back from the gym, and the shower made me all warm and tingly. We could fuck our brains out and then I'll throw you out." A throaty laugh.

He imagined her slipping a hand beneath her robe and rubbing a nipple between two fingers. He was tempted to see her. "Believe me, it sounds inviting, and if that friend of yours didn't decide to visit in the middle of the night, I'd have the energy, but not today. Okay?"

"If you say so." She sounded disappointed.

"Have you heard from him?"

"No. And stop worrying. He was high and wanted some company, no big deal."

"Him being high is what I'm worried about. What happens if he talks? Cokeheads love to babble."

"He won't talk. What can he say, that I needed a ride from Queens? He didn't drop me anywhere near Zol...the guy's apartment. He was nowhere near the park. Believe me, if there was a subway anywhere around there, I would have taken it."

"Don't you think the asshole can read?" Steiner was aware of his rising voice, and even though he had his office soundproofed two years ago, he saw no sense in testing its effectiveness. "It was in all the papers for days. Don't you think he could figure out what you were doing in Flushing Meadow Park in the middle of the night?"

"It's been nine years, for chrissake! He'd have said something already."

"Drugs make for loose lips. Besides, that's not all I'm worried about."

"What else?"

"What if he gets locked up? He might talk to save his ass, or there's blackmail. " He didn't want another Zoltag on his hands.

"Who's he gonna blackmail? Me?"

"No, me."

"He doesn't know about you."

"You know about me."

"You think I'd turn you in?"

"To save your cute little ass? Maybe."

"Please," Porter said, "don't say that. I love you."

He didn't want her to think he didn't trust her. "Just kidding, dear. So forget the blackmail, what about the cops?"

"He's been sharp enough to stay out of trouble all these years. That's why I never mentioned him again. He's a nonentity; he's out of our lives. He's got a whole new identity, a new name. Relax."

"Leah," Steiner said, "I'm sitting on top of the world right now, and the only way to go is down. I just don't want that asshole giving me a push."

"Wolf, I take personal responsibility for him. He likes me, the poor schmuck. The last person he'd rat on is me, that's if he even suspects anything."

"He likes you? Isn't that sweet." Always get them on the defensive. "I'm jealous."

She sighed. "You know there's only you."

"I know that," he said, hoping she heard the wariness in his voice. "Anyway, you'd better be right about him. Our future depends on it."

"My future depends on you loving me. You love me, don't you?"

"Of course I do," Steiner said. He knew that as long as he tossed her a few I love yous every now and then, she would jump off a bridge for him. Or take a life. "Listen, I gotta go. We'll talk tomorrow, okay?"

"Okay, sweetheart, until tomorrow."

Wolfgang Steiner hung up, gripped the phone in its cradle, and wondered if he would still be the Emperor of the Airwaves this time next year.

#

Ten blocks away, Leah Porter stared at the phone she held in a

133

white-knuckled fist. She had done his bidding because she loved him and would gladly do what he asked again and again to prove her love. What bothered her was that she knew Steiner was trying to manipulate her.

She released her death grip on the phone, went to the kitchen, and poured a glass of apple juice. After she had framed Dan Doremus, Steiner became detached from her, more distant and less available emotionally. That attitude had lasted until he needed another 'favor.' The same thing had happened when she killed that religious nut in Brooklyn. He was always so solicitous when he wanted something and so remote after she delivered.

What worried her was that Steiner's fame and wealth would become so great that he would leave her. What recourse would she have? She couldn't very well contact the police, even anonymously, and tell them all she knew about the crimes for which he had been responsible. She might have her revenge, but she would also be residing in a penitentiary for the rest of her life. *But I have my insurance, don't I?* She stood in front of the foyer mirror. "Our Wolf isn't going anywhere is he, Leah?" she asked her image.

She finished her drink and then carefully rinsed and dried the glass. She went to her horde of stuffed animals and selected the panda. It was her biggest and most prized creature. At about fifty inches tall, the panda provided a lot to cuddle. She brought it to the window facing 69th Street. The glass filtering the afternoon sun, she settled into the window seat and watched the passing parade of people as they went about their lives. She basked in the warmth, hugging her fuzzy friend.

She knew wolf thought of her as completely subservient and pliable. Maybe she was, where he was concerned. The police department, she recalled, had thought she was crazy, and maybe she might be that, too. What she wasn't, however, was stupid.

134

Yeah, she had her insurance. She moved quietly to her bedroom closet, opened the door, and knelt on the bare wood floor. Scattering a mountain of boots and shoes, most of which she hadn't worn in years, she uncovered a small square safe bolted to the floor by the rear wall. She twirled the combination dial, and the door swung open.

One item lay inside: a VHS videotape inside a Winnie the Pooh cardboard slipcase. Before he died, Zoltag had told her, under extreme duress, that the videotape she wanted had been copied. He told her of the second tape's location, expecting the information would make her spare his life. She smiled, thinking it was always nice to cling to hope, to have something to live for. Unfortunately, Zoltag had given up the information too quickly, thereby forfeiting the only bargaining chip he had. Men had such a low tolerance for pain, she mused. He should have tried binding arbitration. Hey, it works for the police union at contract time, doesn't it?

She removed the slipcase and fondled the tape in her hands before inserting it into the VCR at the foot of her bed. The video never failed to captivate her. Wolf had asked her if she had looked at the tape after she returned with it from Zoltag's apartment. No, she had told him, and in fact she hadn't. She would never lie to Wolf. He had failed to inquire about a copy, however, and she just never brought it up.

When she got home, she had immediately hid the copy behind her dresser and, for reasons she never quite understood, hadn't looked at it, at least not until after she had killed Marvin Tavlin and Wolf started acting coolly toward her. If the tape was so important to him, she surmised, it might also be important to her.

Leah watched with fascination as the images on her television screen spoke a language she understood. She saw, for the hundredth time, a woman being murdered on a deserted street in Queens. There was blood, plenty of blood. It pooled around her head as the camera zoomed in for a

135

close-up. Leah felt herself becoming aroused and slipped her hand between her legs.

She smiled. No, you're not going anywhere Wolf, she thought, because I possess the terrible secret that could ruin your life and surprise the hell out of the New York City Police Department.

Chapter Thirteen

Yale went through the now routine paging procedure for reaching out to Charlie Wright. The former detective called back in ten minutes.

"You've gotta get a phone," Yale said.

"Tomorrow. What's up?"

Yale explained what he had found out about Leah Porter.

"You know," Wright said, "I remember the Porter case from about ten years ago. Too common a name to make a connection with our Porter when I talked to you yesterday, though. A real headcase, if I remember correctly."

"So I'm beginning to find out. You know anybody in QTF?"

"Queens Task Force? Sure."

"Think we could get a paper on her? I want to know more than the war stories I've been hearing. If she's the shooter, I'd like something official on her background. We should know who we're dealing with."

Yale heard the wind rushing around Wright's phone.

"I've gotta do some digging and some major calling in of favors. It's been a few years. Her jacket could be anywhere."

"You've got the contacts, I don't."

"You gonna be home most of the day?"

"I've got some paperwork to catch up on, so I should be. Call me later." Yale hung up and busied himself with what he hated most: writing reports and balancing his checkbook. At 3 p.m., the doorbell rang. A uniformed police officer was standing under the overhang with a large manila envelope against his chest.

"You Lieutenant Yale?" the young cop asked.

Yale nodded, not wanting to verbally commit a felony by stating he was an active-duty officer. He noticed the cop wasn't wearing a shield or nametag. No radio car.

The officer shoved the envelope against Yale's chest. "I wasn't here." He turned and walked away.

Yale heard the phone ring. He took the stairs three at a time and reached it, breathless, on the fourth ring. "Yale," he said.

It was Wright. "You get my gift?"

"Just arrived. You remembered my birthday."

"It wasn't easy to get, but it's your size. Exactly what you wanted. I'll talk to you later." The line went dead.

Yale got a cup of tea and settled into the recliner in the living room before tearing away the masking tape that sealed the bulky package, which contained two inter-departmental reports on Police Officer Leah Porter, written on standard UF49 forms. The first one was from the Commanding Officer, Internal Affairs Division, and it concerned the investigation that had led to Officer Porter's arrest in 1984. The second report was from the Commanding Officer, Psychological Services, Health Services Division, regarding Porter's background and psychological profile compiled just after her arrest. Both reports were addressed to the Police Commissioner, with copies going to other concerned commands. Yale noted that the information in the Psych Services file was garnered from sources other than Police Officer Porter. She had refused to cooperate.

Yale flipped through the forty-plus pages. He went to the kitchen and brought back a pitcher of hot tea. This was going to take a while.

Leah Porter's upbringing had been turbulent and unpredictable, even given the routine beatings that her father inflicted on herself, her mother, and her two brothers. While violence was the norm, young Leah never knew in what form her family's pain would arrive. Her father was a right-wing fanatic, an uneducated man, loutish in demeanor and brutal in his actions. He reigned supreme in his home, beating and verbally abusing Leah, her mother, and her younger brothers whenever the whim struck him.

Bart Porter had married Leah's mother in their last year of high school because she had gotten pregnant. Bart's father threatened to castrate his son unless he 'did the right thing.' Desiring to retain his testicles, young Bart quickly married the nubile, yet markedly stupid, Sharon Ann Hislop. The year was 1963, and the Porters became parents two days after President John F. Kennedy was assassinated in Dallas.

The new father was a card-carrying member of the Ku Klux Klan and a new inductee in the John Birch Society. He had an abiding hatred for all liberals in general and John Kennedy in particular. Praying for a boy, but not totally disappointed in his first arrival, he proudly named the child Leah, a name he always pronounced 'Lee.' Needless to say, his next two children were named Harvey and Oswald. Fortunately for them, they were both boys, but to Bart's way of thinking, it hardly mattered.

As his sons grew older, they rebelled against their father's tyranny, and Bart found he had less and less control over them. Unlike the rest of the family, the boys' beatings ceased when they became too much of a match physically for their father. A habitual truant, Harvey had started a criminal career as a teenager and was spending his adult life in and out of jail. Ozzie, a bit smarter, but just as feral, managed to avoid prison, and Bart, when commenting on his sons, would say that Harvey was in jail and

Ozzie ought to be. The apple of his eye was Leah, and in his own oafish way, he doted on her.

Leah had yearned for her father's approval and did everything she could to please him, despite the cuffing she would receive when she didn't curry his favor. She began her young life not with dolls but with guns. Barbie, much to her dismay, was not armed with an M-16. Her father introduced her to hunting at an early age and berated her if she missed her target or didn't kill an animal with one shot. Soon, young Leah became fascinated with weapons of all kinds.

At age twelve, while other girls' interests turned to boys, Leah's turned to knives. She had a collection of fighting blades that would make a Turk proud. She favored edged weapons, once slashing the face of a male bully in school with a sharpened credit card. No one messed with Leah Porter, in or out of school. She had no friends and spent her time with her father or practicing with some new exotic killing implement she had made or bought. No stray dog or cat was safe from little Rambette. She sliced, diced, and blow-gunned every furry little creature whose misfortune it was to cross her bloody path.

In her nineteenth year, Leah Porter began to contemplate her future. Her primary goal was to get out of her house, closely followed by a burning desire to be associated with weapons. She had recently acquired her first boyfriend, a Neanderthal who had just been accepted into the Nassau County Police Academy. Between bouts of rough sex, which always left both parties bruised but satisfied, young Officer Moose convinced Leah that police work was the way to go. You could beat the shit out of anyone you liked and get paid for it, he had told her. She had asked if she could carry a gun off-duty. You bet your sweet young ass you can, her brain-damaged lover had told her. Look no further, Leah Porter decided, I'm gonna be a cop!

While Nassau County wasn't hiring at the time, New York City was. She took the written test and scored high. Because of an affirmative-action ruling, women and minorities were pushed to the top of the civil service list, and she found herself in the six-month academy course in record time, commencing her training in 1981.

The physical training portion of the academy curriculum suited her. She was long and lean and in excellent shape. She neither smoked nor drank, and drugs were something that other people did. The daily gym classes were a breeze, but she worried about the academic part of her studies. She was bright, but sitting in one place in front of a book for an extended period of time tended to make her eyes glaze over. She needed a 70% average to graduate and was in serious jeopardy of not making the grade. This was easily rectified by initiating a wild sexual relationship with one of her instructors. She gave him oral sex in a utility closet on an almost daily basis. Her exams were failures when she submitted them, yet they miraculously turned to passing grades when they made a brief stop on her lover's desk.

She was initially assigned to a Harlem precinct. Within months, she was the most active cop in her command. Her arrest record, to be fair, was admirable, although she brought most of her prisoners to Central Booking in need of medical attention. She needed no reason to beat a prisoner senseless. "Could I have a cigarette, officer?" Wham! "You can't hold a smoke between those lips anymore, can you dickhead?" "What's that, you want to take a piss?" A fast steel-toed shoe to the testicles made that difficult. A real humanitarian was Police Officer Leah Porter.

Even as her reputation spread as a heavy-handed cop, she was in no real danger of getting into trouble. After all, this was Harlem; she was beating black people, and no one really cared. Leah was able to blend into a violent world quite nicely, thank you. After two years on patrol, she was

141

transferred to the Street Crime Unit, an elite command of professionals who ferreted out the worst violent offenders New York City had to offer. She worked with the same small team every day, and eventually, familiarity bred contempt.

There were two other female officers on Leah's team who were hard-working, fair-minded cops. They objected to Leah using prisoners as punching bags, and after repeated futile attempts to make her stop the abuse, they had no other recourse than to inform their boss of her violent behavior. After being dressed down by her lieutenant and knowing exactly where he had gotten his information, Leah went searching for the two rats.

She ambushed the first woman in the ladies room at work, and after beating her silly with a nightstick, attempted to drown her by stuffing her head into a commode. As the drowning cop's life was flashing in front of her eyes, the second policewoman wandered in. Leah, not totally out of control and thinking the first cop dead, sprang for the second victim. The newcomer fought like a caged animal. With the hair-pulling, face-punching, and groin-kneeing not doing the job, Leah pulled her service revolver, and the struggle over the gun continued until a round was discharged, fortunately missing both combatants but bringing a phalanx of pistol-waving male cops to the rescue Both cops survived their injuries, but for the first, and definitely not the last time in her short police career, Police Officer Leah Porter was in trouble.

The New York City Police Department, being the closed society it is, immediately put a clamp on the incident and quietly transferred her to the Queens Task Force, a unit whose sole mission was to patrol the entire borough, often not where they were needed, but in white, highly-taxed neighborhoods whose residents had effective political clout.

Not one to learn a well-deserved lesson, Leah continued her vicious ways, albeit not as often, considering the ethnic makeup of the area where she patrolled, and was soon making frequent trips to the Civilian Complaint Review Board, where it was said she was on a first name basis with everyone, including the janitorial staff.

Porter was an equal opportunity psychopath, assaulting people without regard to race or ethnic origin. She should have known that white taxpayers believed in the system and knew how to write letters and that smacking around a white, middle-class yuppie on the way to synagogue would make her a familiar visitor to the Review Board, whose mandate it was to investigate charges of brutality or verbal abuse. But Leah was a female, and at the time, they were untouchable in fear someone would cry sexual discrimination.

All the charges against her were deemed 'unsubstantiated,' and after her thirty-third and record-breaking appearance at CCRB, someone placed her smiling picture above the front door. While her job seemed secure, her career came to a crashing halt when she killed Jubilation Q. Hargrove in the summer of 1984.

J.Q., as he was known to his friends, was a sixty-two year old black janitor who toiled evenings in an office building in the all-white neighborhood of Forest Hills. On the last night of his life, J.Q. decided to take a smoke break in front of the building where he worked. Before venturing out into the warm summer night, he polished off what remained of his second pint of cheap wine.

The building where J.Q. worked was on Austin Street, located in a business district typically crowded with parked cars, and a slightly drunk J.Q. chose to lean against an empty marked police car while he sucked on a Marlboro.

Inside a restaurant, about a block away, Police Officer Porter and her partner were just settling down for their meal break when she discovered that she had left the portable radio in full view on the front seat

143

of the radio car. Not desiring to lose five days' pay for a stolen radio, she interrupted her steak and eggs for the short walk to the car and its retrieval. Seeing J.Q. Hargrove leaning against her clean radio car did nothing to lift her spirits.

J.Q., lost in thought, either failed to hear Porter order him off the car or didn't move fast enough to suit her. With the good old days of beating blacks still fresh in her mind and the thought of eating tepid eggs fueling her fury, Leah laid a nightstick across J.Q.'s right shoulder. Numbed by cheap alcohol, J.Q. hardly felt the blow and barely moved. He blinked once at the enraged cop but said nothing.

Infuriated, the policewoman began pummeling the old black man with a pent-up rage. After a minute of body and head blows, she looked down to discover a dead man at her feet. One blow to the head too many. She quickly surveyed the street for possible witnesses but didn't see any. With a magician's dexterity, she reached into her back pocket and removed a .25-caliber automatic pistol wrapped in plastic. This was a "drop weapon," carried by many cops, that could be planted on someone living or dead to justify using force. Leah knew to swath it in plastic so the lab couldn't find traces of police issue pants fabric in its crevices.

She removed the protective covering and placed the pistol in the late J.Q. Hargrove's right hand, the one that held the cigarette, and tossed the butt into the gutter. After mussing her clothes and hair, she ran back to the restaurant and told her partner of a crazed African American who was leaning against their car waving a gun in her face and hollering, "I'm gonna kill me a white bitch." Leah, being the humanitarian she was, said she didn't want to draw her revolver for fear of hitting an innocent bystander, choosing instead to defend her life with a nightstick. Through tears, she pushed her partner into the street with instructions to secure the crime scene while she went to the ladies room and bashed her head against the steel sink. Satisfied with the resulting bruises, she called 911 on a payphone and requested a supervisor and an ambulance. She used the payphone rather than a radio because she knew reporters monitor police radios, and she didn't need the extra scrutiny of the media.

The three hours of intensive interrogation following the killing went well. All the responding brass seemed to be on her side. A sweep of the immediate area produced no witnesses. Her head was bandaged, and she was given a tetanus shot. The Duty Captain prepared his report, and notifications were made to the dead man's family. For the first time since she had killed Hargrove, Leah began to relax.

Six hours after the incident, the Borough Commander strode into the squad room where Leah was being questioned. He told her he had spoken personally to the family of the deceased and apologized for being late. Smiling, he asked if she would mind repeating the story once again for his benefit. Leah played the poor, distraught cop and recounted her confrontation with the dangerous and out-of-control black man who was ranting about killing a 'white bitch.' She also told the inspector that she had desperately tried to keep the black man from grabbing her gun from its holster and that he had kept screaming that he wanted to die.

The Borough Commander nodded sympathetically and asked the Duty Captain if Porter had signed a statement swearing to her story. The signed paper was produced (Yale had a copy of it in front of hm), and Police Officer Leah Porter was placed under arrest for the murder of J.Q. Hargrove. J.Q., it seemed, had a laryngectomy four years prior due to throat cancer brought on by heavy smoking. The man had no voice box and couldn't utter a sound.

The indictment was swift and pointed: murder in the second degree, noting that Police Officer Porter had displayed a depraved indifference to human life and had killed poor J.Q. Hargrove by beating him to death with a nightstick. The press had a field day. Porter was the first female cop ever to be charged with such an abhorrent crime. Once her prior record became public knowledge, the media dubbed her "The Maniac Cop." A long jail sentence seemed a virtual certainty until an organization of militant policewomen got involved.

The Policewoman's Defense League (PDL) was an offshoot of the recognized, conservative policewoman's fraternal organization. Formed by a small group of radical female cops, PDL sought to right the wrongs, real or imagined, dealt to policewomen in the NYPD by a male-dominated job. This was the first time that PDL had the opportunity to display its clout in such a public forum. They bombarded the media with images of Leah being the victim of discrimination. They shouted to anyone who would listen that Porter would never have been indicted had she been a man. Her detractors brought up the fact that Porter had lied regarding Hargrove's ability to speak. Simple, PDL said, she was forced to lie by the responding detectives, all of them male, who told the impressionable Porter that no one would believe her if she said the victim was just waving a gun around without saying anything. It wasn't Porter's fault, they said, it was the big, bad male detectives who coerced her into lying. They said that the killing was justified based on what had happened, forget about what Porter was forced to say about the verbal threats.

The media blitz then began in earnest. Leah appeared on every morning television and radio show that would have her and granted an interview to every print reporter whose newspaper or magazine had a circulation of more than a dozen. There were ten news stories in the package Wright had sent Yale. A few has-been celebrities had taken time off from guesting on Hollywood Squares and jumped on the Leah Porter bandwagon and began championing her cause. By the time the case got to court, a jury of her peers chose to believe that every male in the police department forced Leah to lie about a minor portion of the killing scenario and acquitted her.

The New York City Police Department, however, found her guilty in their Trial Room of "conduct unbecoming a police officer" and promptly fired her. Porter's supporters swore to fight on and eventually got her job back, but Leah chose to leave the job she said had ruined her life.

Two hours later, Yale rubbed his temples and stared at the pile of papers he had discarded on the rug as he read them. In his gut, he knew Leah Porter was the Flushing Meadow Park shooter. But the case was just beginning. Why did she do it? Without a motive, he had nothing. He also needed real evidence to get a conviction. His tightening belly wouldn't convince a prosecutor that Porter was a double-murderer.

With these thoughts running through his mind, he checked his answering service for the calls he had ignored while reading the NYPD reports. He got a real easy case from a man who wanted his thirty-year-old son located. The old man was sick and wanted to contact the boy to make amends. Yale considered blowing him off, but he was still in business, and the case appeared simple. The old man supplied Yale with his son's vital statistics: Social Security number and date of birth. Yale's new client sent him a $1,500 retainer via messenger, and Yale used his computer to find the kid in less time than it took for his remaining tea to get cold. When Daddy's check cleared, he would call him with the joyous news.

With next month's expenses covered, and the prospect of solving the Carpenter case becoming more of a reality, Yale beeped Charlie Wright. This time he waited half an hour for a reply.

"What'd you think?" Wright asked.

"I think you have a lot of friends. Fast work."

"Someone owed me. Now what?"

"You read the reports?"

"I got a summary over the phone."

"I think we got us a killer. The question is why did she do it?"

"Maybe that's how she gets her jollies," Wright said. "It doesn't take much to set her off. I've seen a lot of blood-thirsty cops in my time, but she takes first prize."

The most violent person Yale had ever known was an eighteen-year-old infantryman in Vietnam who wanted to guarantee his survival. "I guess you could say that, but this seems too organized for a thrill killing. She's in the park, whacks two people, and strolls away? She was taking a helluva chance not being seen, wouldn't you think? And how'd she get away?"

"Not a clue."

"Well, we have to start somewhere. I'm gonna get that picture of her. I thought of The Job ID shot, but no one looks real in those things."

"Where you gonna get a picture, then?"

"I'll take it myself." Yale looked at the time. "Probably tomorrow, bright and early."

"You gonna call her? You got her number?"

"It's unlisted, but I'll have it within an hour. Friends in Ma Bell. After you get the chauffeur's address, give it to—"

"I've already got it."

"No shit?"

"It took one phone call. I also got the names of the cops who had the park sector on the night of the murders."

"Any problems getting the information?

Wright chuckled. "I told a clerk I was writing my memoirs. She remembered me. No problem."

"Great. Who were the cops?"

"This might sound stupid, but the Task Force, which turns out of the park, doesn't patrol it. The One-Ten does." Yale heard paper rustling above the noise of traffic. "One cop I know, Arlo Moran. The other one died about three years ago."

Yale was immediately suspicious. "How?"

Wright hesitated. "Man, you're a paranoid bastard, aren't you?"

"I don't believe in coincidences. How'd he die?"

"Liver failure. Big drinker." Wright laughed. "The clerk called it ferocious of the liver. Sounds like something I'd say, huh?"

"I'm sure you'll make a note of it." Yale reached for a pen. "Give me the cop's name again, for the report. The name of the game in this business is justifying your time to the client."

"Arlo Moran. Dumb as a basketball, totally useless. He's had the park sector for years. The park's a dumping ground for dead wood, like being put out to pasture. But The Job says he's supposed to keep a memo book, though. I'll see what he has to say."

"You want to talk to him? I was gonna do it."

"I know the guy, I'll interview him. He won't be straight with someone he doesn't know."

"I want you to be up front with the guy. If they were cooping or goofing off that night I want him to know we're not going anywhere with the information. Be frank. We want to know if he saw anything."

"No problem, Ray, Frank's my middle name."

"No really," Yale said. "This cop might have held something back from the detectives for fear of getting jammed up."

"No, I mean Frank really is my middle name. Charles Franklin Wright."

Yale sighed. He asked himself why he kept setting himself up for Shecky Wright. "Okay, I'll see the chauffeur. What's his name?"

"Bruno Tartaglia." Wright rattled off a Brooklyn address.

Yale scribbled down the information. "I'll get Porter's picture to you ASAP. In the meantime, can you get to Moran today?"

"How about tomorrow? I've got a doctor's appointment today."

Yale had almost forgotten about Wright's illness. "Is everything okay?"

"Just a normal T-cell count test and some pokes and probes. I'm used to it."

Yale thought Wright's voice sounded anything but acclimated. "Okay, I'll call you when I get Porter's picture. Take care."

After he hung up. Yale realized how futile those words must have sounded to Wright.

Chapter Fourteen

Yale sat on the edge of his bed with his head resting in his hands. He had been entertaining thoughts of suicide ever since the death of his wife. For this reason, he had given up carrying a gun. But now, he knew he had reached a point in the Carpenter case that might prove dangerous. If Leah Porter had killed Katherine Carpenter and Herman Zoltag, she could easily kill again. Hell, Yale thought, she had murdered that helpless old man when she was still on The Job, why wouldn't she kill him if he got too close?

He let out a deep sigh and, with some determination, set out for the basement to confront one of his many demons.

Yale pulled a chain on a bare bulb and illuminated a small area behind the boiler. Against the rear wall was a dust-laden steel safe. He twirled the combination dial, opening the door wide to reveal two shelves stuffed with yellowing envelopes and small jewelry boxes. He reached past the house deed, his will, assorted military decorations, and his wife's jewelry and grasped an object wrapped in an oil-soaked cloth.

He carefully placed it on top of the safe, laying back the corners of the cloth as if unveiling a priceless work of art. Yale stared down at his service revolver. He picked it up gingerly with both hands, keeping the gun

151

at arm's length and examining its oily finish.

Yale was never what he would call a gun nut. He knew most cops came on The Job with a firearm fetish or soon developed one, even if for a short period of time. Because of his Vietnam experiences Yale never fancied guns. He had his fill of them during the war. He remembered dreading going to the NYPD range to qualify twice a year, and he only looked forward to the meatball sandwiches that were offered in the on-site cafeteria. He had never even bought a smaller off-duty revolver, which was the first thing most cops did when they got off probation. He figured one gun was enough.

Yale had scrupulously avoided carrying his gun since Vivian died, even though as a retired member of The Job he was duly licensed to carry a pistol anywhere in New York State. Thoughts of suicide had danced through his head on many occasions, and he had fantasized about placing the gun barrel in his mouth and pulling the trigger. He was always afraid that one night during a bender he would impulsively kill himself. After the big bang, it's difficult to say, "Oops, I'd like to take that back; I really didn't mean to do it." A gun combined with booze, a bad day, and a cop in a foul mood could do in a fraction of a second what every bad guy in New York had dreamed about his whole life.

Now, he was determined to put at least this demon behind him.

He turned the pistol over in his hands and looked down the barrel into the six loaded chambers Not that scary. Letting out a deep breath, he felt in control, maybe for the first time in a year. He knew that if he was going to get on with his life, re-arming himself would be an important part of the process.

Yale closed the safe and carried the gun by the trigger guard back to his apartment. He felt lightheaded as he took a bath towel and removed the excess oil from the gun's blued finish. He swung open the cylinder and examined the bullets. They felt oily. He knew that the waterproof bullets were, oddly enough, subject to oil penetration. He made a mental note to buy more ammunition.

Yale dressed quickly in black jeans, a grey sweatshirt, and a nylon aviator jacket. He searched a carton of old police equipment and retrieved a Galco speed holster and threaded it through his belt, tucking the holster's end into his left rear pocket so it wouldn't be seen below the waist-length jacket. He jammed the empty revolver into the holster, and it immediately felt foreign to him, but he became used to it by the time he left the house. Like riding a bike, he thought.

Yale took the subway to the West Side of Manhattan to begin the surveillance of Leah Porter's building. He stopped at a sporting goods store on the way and purchased a box of .38 Special ammunition and loaded his revolver in front of a nervous store clerk.

A black barrel bag containing a Nikon 35mm camera equipped with a telephoto lens was slung over his left shoulder as he strolled down West 69th Street in search of Leah Porter's apartment building. The camera rested on a bed of plastic bubble-wrap, lens protruding slightly from the front of the bag. Yale inserted his hand through a concealed opening, ready to immortalize the former policewoman on film.

Porter's brownstone looked like all the other buildings on the block: attached, three stories tall with thirteen steps leading to a glass and wood front door. Yale leaned against a tree on the opposite side of the street, plotting his next move. Pedestrian traffic on the block was brisk, as cars made the turn from Central Park West onto the westbound street.

Yale spotted a nosey neighbor poised at her second-floor apartment window surveying the block through a pair of miniature binoculars. He had seen two signs posted on lampposts informing all ne'er-do-wells that the block was under constant surveillance by block

153

watchers. Yale thought that the old woman in the window was taking her job a bit too seriously. He knew he couldn't stay on the street too long before she called the local precinct to report a suspicious man.

Yale strolled casually across the street and entered Porter's building as if he lived there. One mailbox read L. PORTER. There were three other boxes, ergo only four apartments in the building. He looked out to the street and saw that his line of sight went directly to the front stairs of the building directly across the street. About seventy feet, he figured, as the flea-infested, diseased New York City pigeon flies.

Yale left the building with a definite plan in mind. He walked west, into the wind, and turned onto Columbus Avenue, scanning both sides of the street looking for a card store. Yale knew he wouldn't have far to look. All that was left of the once cohesive, ethnic neighborhood were restaurants, boutiques, and card stores, all run by young entrepreneurs satisfied if they milked three years out of their businesses before moving to the next trendy neighborhood.

He entered the first card store he came to and picked out a card, not for its clever prose but for its garish envelope, in this case an orange iridescent number that Yale thought was bright enough to signal a Coast Guard rescue plane. On the street, he removed the envelope from the paper bag and threw the card in the nearest trash basket. From a payphone, he called Leah Porter's unlisted number, which he had gotten from a phone company source. He hung up when a female answered. She was home.

Yale jammed the gaudy envelope into Porter's mailbox, leaving about three inches exposed, and quickly left the building. He sat on the stairs of the building across the street and waited. He could see directly into Porter's narrow foyer and easily spotted the orange envelope jutting from the mailbox. If Porter left the building, he figured she would see the envelope, remove it, and Yale would have a positive ID. He was congratulating himself on his ingenuity when he saw the old lady with the binoculars giving him the once-over. He wondered how much time he had left before he would be challenged by the local precinct's sector car.

Yale's toes were beginning to get numb from the cold when he saw a figure pull the orange envelope from the mailbox. The front door opened, and he got his first look at Leah Porter, psycho cop. She was dressed in a purple jogging suit with a white sweatband around her shoulder-length blonde hair. Yale noticed that she was also wearing small wrist and ankle weights. He watched Porter pause momentarily at the top of the stairs and open the envelope. She ran her fingers inside and turned it upside down, giving it a brief shake. She quickly surveyed the street in both directions before folding the envelope and putting it in her jacket pocket. Yale was looking toward Columbus Avenue but snapping pictures of Porter, who was standing directly in front of him. He guided the camera after her as she walked down the stairs and stood in front of her building, stretching.

Yale had no idea whether his camera was capturing his subject in center frame because he couldn't very well lift the bag to eye level to take careful aim. He decided to follow her and use up all his film, just to be certain he got at least one good picture. He stood up slowly, stiff from the cold and from sitting in one position for ninety minutes. He was doing his own form of stretching when he saw the radio car make a slow turn into the block from Central Park West and glide to a stop in front of his building. The young cop in the passenger seat lowered the window about three inches and wiggled a finger at Yale. Yale smiled and waved, hoping he could waste enough time for Porter to be on her way. The cop rolled down the window another few inches. He was letting precious heat escape, and he looked pissed, Yale thought.

155

"Excuse me, sir," the officer said, "could you come over here for a second?"

"Who, me?" Yale had one eye on the cop and the other on Porter, who all of a sudden had taken a keen interest in the events unfolding on her street.

The young cop lowered the window all the way. "Yeah, you, come over here."

Yale kept his head down and descended the stairs. Christ, he thought, in this day and age of cop killers and psychos, you'd think these guys would get out of the goddamn radio car to have a fighting advantage in case things went bad. He knelt down to the cop's level and said, as quietly as possible, "I'm retired from The Job. I'm a PI working a case." He peered through the car's windows past the two cops and saw Porter watching the scenario intently. Yale dug his wallet from his back pocket and handed his retired NYPD ID and a business card through the open passenger window. Both cops examined them like they were winning lottery tickets.

Leah Porter was starting across the street toward the radio car.

Yale said, "Quick, let me in the car."

The cops looked at each other a moment before the operator finally woke up and reached over his partner's shoulder to unlock the back door. "Hop in, Lou," he said. Yale hadn't been addressed with the diminutive for Lieutenant in quite a while, and for a second he felt like he was on The Job again.

Once safely in the car, Yale said, "Now take off." He lowered himself in the backseat and, as the radio car pulled away, slowly turned to see Leah Porter staring at the vehicle as it sped down the block. He recognized the familiar expression of someone who had seen too much death.

Before Yale could board a Queens-bound subway, he had to sit through ten minutes of apologies from the two sector cops and, once accepted, another twenty minutes of war stories. When the enthusiastic young officers dropped Yale off at 72nd Street and Broadway, he felt strangely sorry for them and thought of a young cop who many years ago had their same passion for The Job before it was dashed by the reality of politics.

There was a one-hour film processing booth in the Roosevelt Avenue subway station in Queens. While his film was being developed, he ate lunch at an Indian restaurant, dosing the fire in his gut with a few beers.

Yale examined the pictures during the short cab ride to his house. Out of thirty-six exposures, he found two that were crystal clear and centered. The first was a head shot of Porter walking down her front stairs, and the other was a full body shot of her as she stretched in front of her building. Yale put her between five-eight and five-ten, which would fit the park shooter. The closeup showed a very pretty face with expressive lips and some pale freckles across the bridge of her nose. It was her eyes that drew his attention, the same dead thousand-mile stare that he had seen so often in Vietnam.

Yale went to his office with a steaming cup of tea to catch up on reports and expenses relating to the case. He hated paperwork, but it had to be done expeditiously before he forget any facts. In an hour, Yale was just about finished running the spellcheck on the computer when the phone rang. It was Charlie Wright trying to talk above traffic.

"Get any pictures?" Wright asked.

"Couple good ones. Not a bad looking girl."

"Gonna ask her out?"

"From what I know about Porter," Yale said, "I'd probably have to wear body armor."

"How do I get the pictures? I want to get to that cop Moran tomorrow. He might know her. I called the One-Ten, he's got the parade. I'll catch him after he signs out."

"What parade?"

"The Thanksgiving Day Parade. Tomorrow's Thanksgiving."

Am I so self-absorbed, Yale thought, that I forgot tomorrow is Thanksgiving? The irony was that it was one of his favorite holidays. Both he and his wife had no close family, so they would gather all their single or otherwise disengaged friends and have a large, raucous celebration that would include a huge feast. "Jesus, I can't believe I forgot. You doing anything tomorrow? You have a family dinner or something?"

"Family? Me? Nah. I've got a sister in Western Pennsylvania somewhere, but the commute's a bitch, besides, I haven't seen her in years. I'll be home relaxing in the splendor of my surroundings. You?"

"Nothing. Listen, pick up the pictures here, say about noon, then after you talk to the cop, why don't you come back here for dinner? My wife and I always said no one should be alone on Thanksgiving. Now I'm by myself, and so are you. To my way of thinking, I'd rather be alone on Christmas."

"Sounds good. I'll bring a bottle of vino."

"And bring a record of your expenses to date so I can pay you." Yale hated owing money.

He hung up and went back to the book he had started last week, but he couldn't concentrate. He tried television with the usual results. Seventy-two channels and not a damn thing interesting on any of them. He thought a hot shower would help him relax so he could fall asleep, but the soothing effects of the water hadn't helped. He was still restless and tense. Something was telling him to have another look at those Leah Porter

158

pictures.

He went to his office and examined the photos, holding them at arm's length, shifting them from left to right, then up and down. No matter which way he angled the pictures, Porter seemed to be staring at him. He put them against his computer and paced slowly around the tiny office, never diverting his gaze from them. Porter's eyes still followed him around the room. Yeah, Yale thought, I'm losing it.

Was Porter suspicious about what had happened in front of her building? Was she savvy enough to realize that she was under surveillance? Yale hoped not. It would only make his job tougher. But then she had been a cop, and cops were always wary.

Chapter Fifteen

Charlie Wright sat in an idling gypsy cab parked up the street from the One-Ten Police Precinct station house. The beat-up cab's heater was going full blast, but Wright still felt a chill. He hoped to God he wasn't coming down with something. For him, a cold could be fatal.

He watched as cops in civilian clothes spilled from the station house and scattered like roaches fleeing a kitchen after the light had been turned on. It was Thanksgiving, and the cops had worked the Macy's parade in Manhattan, most of them on overtime, and now it was their turn to be with their families and forget about the mayhem of police work, at least for one day. The cops, most of them rookies, scrambled to their cars, honked good wishes to each other, and started quickly on their way east to escape the city, lest dawdling could somehow involve them in police work. All seemed to have a definite destination in mind, all, that is, except for Police Officer Arlo Moran.

Wright observed Moran standing on the top step of the entrance to the station house and lighting a cigarette with the glowing end of one he had just smoked. Wright knew a little of Moran's background. He was fifty-two years old and had never married. His one and only friend, Dick Emery, his partner, had drunk himself to death a few years back, and these

160

days Arlo spent most of his time in the Donegal, the local cop watering hole just up the street. No one particularly cared for him there either, but he always had a pocketful of cash acquired from shaking down the unlicensed vendors in Flushing Meadow Park, and he was also known to buy a round every now and then.

When Moran began walking up the street toward the Donegal Bar, Wright paid the cab fare and double-timed to catch up to him. Winded, he made certain he was abreast of Moran before he said anything. He knew most cops disliked being tapped on the shoulder from behind. Sometimes they turned ready for combat. Wright didn't want to see if Moran fell into that category.

"Hey, Arlo," Wright wheezed, "how're you doing?"

Moran wasn't one to talk and walk at the same time. He stopped, eyeing Wright suspiciously. "I know you?"

Wright extended his hand. "Sure. Don't you remember me? Charlie Wright…from the Squad."

Most detectives had as little to do with the uniformed contingent of the precinct as possible, but Wright knew the value of maintaining a good relationship with the patrol force. Treated as equals, most cops would go out of their way to help Wright with his cases. The detectives who looked down on the uniforms would find themselves up against a brick wall when they needed help in locating witnesses or performing other tedious work they thought beneath them. Wright had been one of the few people to acknowledge Moran's existence.

The cop's face lit up with recognition. "Hey, yeah! Charlie Wright! Howz it goin'?"

"Not bad, Arlo, not bad. Just in the neighborhood, thought I'd stop by and see some of the guys."

"You ain't been around for a while. Cupla years, right?"

Wright noticed that Moran was even in worse shape than the last time he had seen him. The top of his baggy jeans were below his ample belly, and there wasn't enough of his flannel shirt to reach his pants. A soiled ski jacket draped his sloping shoulders and was unzipped, despite the chilling breeze. As misshapen as his body was, Moran's face stood out as his most unattractive feature. At least a dozen craters littered his face from hairline to chin, each deep enough, Wright thought, to hold a commuter's toll change.

"Yeah, it's been a while. Say, Arlo, you doing anything now? Want to join me for a drink? I'm working on a case; I'm a PI now, and maybe you can help me. I was gonna ask the guys in the Squad, but I figured you'll be just as much help."

Moran looked thrilled. Wright figured flattery would get him everywhere.

"Yeah, sure, Charlie. Howz about the Donegal?"

Wright didn't want to see anyone else he knew. "Nah, you got a car?"

"Me? Sure!" Moran pointed to a rust-encrusted Dodge Dart parked next to a fire hydrant. "Where we gonna go?"

"The Mark Twain Diner on Northern Boulevard. I'll buy you dinner. They got a liquor license." The diner was a short distance from Yale's house, his next stop.

Moran's car stunk of stale beer and rotten tuna fish. It was only a ten-minute ride to the diner, and Wright took shallow breaths all the way. He kept the conversation general because he didn't think Moran could talk and concentrate on driving at the same time. When Wright got out of the car, he sucked in gulps of what passed for fresh air in New York.

Moran had a problem sliding his girth into a naugahyde booth but managed to squeeze in after removing his jacket and sucking in his

162

stomach. When Wright took off his coat, Moran said, "Jesus, Charlie, you lost a lot of fuckin' weight."

Subtle, Wright thought. "I'm sick, Arlo," he said. "Real sick.

Moran drew back in the booth as much as he could. "Is it catching?"

Wright shrugged. "I don't think so." He looked around and lowered his voice. "You ever hear of Arterial Monochromia?"

Moran was wide-eyed. "You got that?"

Wright lowered his eyes. "Yeah."

"What is it?"

"A blood disease. Ralph Kramden had it."

"Ralph Kramden...from The Honeymooners?" Moran took this information in with a tightly knit brow. "I remember him, but he was fat."

"You saw him in the last stages, when you put on weight. I just got it. In about three months, I'll be two hundred and fifty pounds."

"I can't catch it?"

Wright scratched his head. "Nah, I'm on my way to being cured."

The diner was empty except for a few old people huddled over hot turkey sandwiches. Wright wondered where their families were. A bored waitress materialized by their booth.

"Youse want menus?"

"I'll just have coffee and a cheese Danish," Wright said, saving himself for whatever Yale would spring on him for dinner. Moran ordered a triple Manhattan with four cherries. The drink arrived in a water glass along with Wright's coffee and pastry. Moran downed half his drink by the time Wright got the cup to his lips. The cop lit an unfiltered Camel with yellow-stained fingers. Wright watched, fascinated, as Moran stuck two of those fingers in the remaining liquid and fished out two maraschino cherries. The slovenly cop tilted his head to one side, dangled the fruit by the stems, and lowered them into his mouth. He chewed happily. "So, what is it you wanna talk about?"

"I'm working on a murder case," Wright said. "You remember the two killings in the park in eighty-six? In October?"

Wright knew that despite Moran's reputation for being a dunce, he had a remarkable memory. He remembered things that he chose to remember. Wright knew he would be able to recall, for example, exactly how much money he extorted from the vendors in the park, and he probably kept a running mental tabulation as to how much each of them owed him for his "park tax."

"Yeah, sure I remember. What about 'em?"

"You had the park that night?"

"Yeah, it was a Friday. Me and Dickie did a six by two. Didn't see shit. I told all this to the detectives from Queens Homicide. Why didn't I talk to you? It was your case, wasn't it?"

"I started with it, but I retired."

"I'm gonna do that someday. Who you workin' for?"

"The family of the girl who was murdered."

"Oh, yeah. A real shame. Well, I don't know nuttin. Say, mind if I have another drink?"

Wright signaled the waitress and pointed to Moran. "That limo was there for hours. You didn't go past those flagpoles for your whole tour?"

"Nope. Chased kids out of the park, around the zoo, that kinda shit. Didn't go near the poles." He avoided Wright's eyes. "If I seen somethin', I woulda said."

"Maybe you saw something and you didn't realize what you saw."

"Huh?"

Wright put two pictures of Leah Porter side by side in front of Moran. "Did you see her that night?"

Arlo looked quickly at the pictures and pushed them back to Wright. He kept his eyes down. "Nope, don't know her."

Wright knew he was lying. Simple detective logic: the averted eyes, not answering a direct question. He pushed the pictures back. "I didn't ask if you knew her. Look at 'em again. Did you see her that night?"

Moran ignored the photos and looked toward the bar. "Hey, where's the broad with my drink?"

"It takes time to mix a quart of that stuff, Arlo." He left the pictures in front of the cop and lit a cigarette.

Moran looked relieved when he saw the waitress approaching with the cocktail.

"Thirsty, huh, Arlo?" Wright said.

"Yeah, look, I'll finish this, then I gotta go." He downed it in one gulp. Wright noticed beads of sweat on the cop's brow. Moran had also begun to lick his lips excessively.

"Just a few more minutes of your precious time, okay, Arlo?"

"No, really, I gotta go." He wiped his mouth with his sleeve. "Thanks. And Happy Thanksgiving." He struggled to get out of the booth, but Wright grabbed his arm.

"I'm afraid I can't let you go until I get some honest answers."

Moran stared at Wright's bony hand. "I don't remember nuttin, honest. Leggo!"

Wright released his hold, and Moran began to get up.

"How's business in the park, Arlo?"

Moran slid back into the booth. "Whaddaya mean?"

"You know, the shakedowns. Business must be pretty good this time of year, what with the holidays approaching and all. All the dough you're making there, you could buy enough of that shit you're drinking to float a battleship."

165

Moran looked around frantically. One old lady was staring at them over her turkey special. A crooked cop was paranoid about everybody, Wright knew. Right now, Moran was probably thinking the old lady was from Internal Affairs.

"Keep your fuckin' voice down," Arlo said. It sounded more like a plea than a command.

"I'll keep my voice down when you get straight with me."

"I been straight. I don't know shit." His gaze darted around the diner like a spectator at a tennis match.

Wright pointed to the pictures of Porter. "If you know about this broad or anything else, it's not goin' any further than me. If you didn't see anything because you were in the coop, tell me that too." Wright put out his cigarette. He leaned across that table. "Now, I asked you if you saw this person, and you said you didn't know her, but I didn't ask you that. But you do know her, don't you?"

Moran swallowed hard. "Yeah, I know her. Everybody knew her. I used to see her all the time in the park. She was in QTF."

"We know that Arlo. Why didn't you just say you knew her?"

"I knew she was fired from The Job. If she's doin' somethin' now she ain't supposed to be doin', I didn't wanna get her in trouble."

"That's exactly it, Arlo. She's not on The Job anymore, so who gives a shit, right?"

Wright watched Moran digest this information.

"Yeah, I suppose."

"Now, let's start over," Wright said. "Did you see her in the park that night?"

Moran was quick to answer. "No, I didn't see her in the park that night. Definitely."

Now Wright understood. "But you did see her that night,

166

somewhere…right?"

Moran shifted his gaze to the clock above Wright's head. He licked his lips. "No."

Bullshit, Wright thought. He can only be protecting her because if he gives her up, he'll be giving himself up in the process. In a voice loud enough for all the lost souls in the diner to hear, he said, "So, you're making how much extorting money from those Columbians?"

Moran's face turned as red as his neck. "Shhh! For chrissakes! If I tell you anything, I'm gonna get jammed." He looked around the room like a junkie waiting for the midnight delivery.

"Arlo, you've got my word. This conversation never happened. However, if you don't tell me where you saw her, I'm gonna drop a quarter on you and your park thing. I swear on my dead mother." Wright looked at the diner's greasy ceiling. Cops knew from mothers, he reasoned, and never swore on them, especially dead ones, unless they were serious.

"Can I have another drink?" Moran asked, his hands trembling.

"Arlo, you can have an open tab in this joint if you just tell me the truth." He waved to the waitress for another Manhattan. They sat in silence until it arrived and Moran took a healthy slug.

"Okay," he said, "I seen her that night."

Wright's stomach churned. "Where?".

"Fifty-fifth Avenue, off One Hundred and Eleventh Street."

Wright thought for a moment. "That's outside the park. What the hell were you doing these?"

Moran lowered his voice. "We had a coop on Fifty-Fifth Avenue, me and Dickie."

"Outside the park?"

"Yeah, in Dickie's broad's house."

"You mean you parked a radio car on the street and went to some woman's house? Wasn't that taking a helluva chance?"

Moran shook his head. "Nope. We'd pull the sector car into the broad's garage. Backed it right in. Dickie got laid, and I watched TV and had a few drinks." He had lowered his voice and was talking through the side of his mouth. "We was the Park Conditions Car. No jobs, just ride around the park. Good deal, huh?" Moran smiled, sheepishly. He lit another cigarette. "Nobody ever bothered us."

Wright tapped the pictures. "Tell me about this cop."

"We got to Dickie's girl's house about nine, maybe a little later, like usual. So we're in the house, and Dickie and his girl, they go in the bedroom and—"

"What was her name?"

"Who the hell remembers. Elsie something…no, Elsa, yeah, that was it, Elsa."

"You remember the address?"

"Wouldn't do you no good. She went back to fuckin' Bolivia or wherever she come from after Dickie died." Moran sounded sad. "She really loved Dickie."

"Yeah, yeah, get back to that night."

"I fell asleep in the living room. Dickie and the broad was sleepin' in the bedroom. We were supposed to be signed out at two-fifteen in the mornin'. Dickie wakes me up at two-thirty. We run outta there like we was on fire."

And nobody was looking for them. Real popular team, Wright thought. "Go on. Tell me when you saw the girl cop."

"There was a door from the house right to the garage, we didn't have to go outside to get I the car, ya know? Dickie's girl opens the garage door, and I start to drive outta there. No lights, ya know? I ever put the lights on 'til we're down the street. Neighbors might see."

"The cop, Arlo, the cop."

"Oh, yeah. She was walkin' past the house when I pulled out. Damn near hit her."

"You're sure it was her?"

"Yeah, sure. It was her alright."

"She say anything?" Wright's palms were sweaty, just like in the old days when he was moving to make a big arrest.

"She started to. She looked pissed, but she kept on walkin'."

"Anything unusual about her?"

"Whaddaya mean, unusual?"

"Like was she carrying anything? Did you notice what she was wearing? Were her clothes torn or messed up? Stuff like that."

Moran went into his think mode. His eyes narrowed, and his lips pursed. "Ya know, I really hadn't seen her in a while—"

"That's because she wasn't on The Job anymore, Arlo."

"—so I didn't remember her too good. She looked okay to me. She was off The Job then?"

"Yeah, cupla months."

"Oh," Moran said. "That prob'ly explains the hair then."

"What about the hair?"

"I remember seein' her goin' and comin' from work. Her hair was short, and it was blonde."

"How was that different from what you saw that night?"

"Her hair was longer," Moran said. "About down to here." He pointed to his shoulder. "And it was dark, maybe brown or black."

Wright smiled. That's enough for me, he thought. We've got ourselves a murderer.

#

169

Ray Yale stirred a massive pot of chicken cacciatore with a long-handled wooden spoon. He had learned how to cook from his father, and each recipe was proportioned to serve a small army, with enough left over to keep the family in dinners for a week.

It was a pleasure to prepare a meal again. The aromas coming from the kitchen filled the apartment, bringing back memories from his youth, perhaps not with the rush of his crayon fix but with a gradual immersion into a comfortable and secure time in his life. He was lowering the burner under the pot when the doorbell rang. He saw Charlie Wright's balding pate from the living-room window

Wright was grinning when Yale opened the door.

"Hit the lottery?" Yale asked.

Wright shoved two bottles of Chianti against Yale's chest. "I got things you wanna hear."

Yale opened a bottle of wine in the kitchen and smelled the cork. Chianti Classico; it would go well with dinner, he thought. He poured two glasses. He'd consider cutting down on his consumption tomorrow.

Wright was busy on the couch in the living room, scribbling something on a small pad. He tore off a sheet and handed it to Yale. "My hours and expenses. Now for the good news. Moran remembers seeing Porter the night of the killings."

Yale stuffed the paper in his shirt. "Tell me."

Wright related the story about the coop, the Porter sighting, and how he extracted the information. "What's the next step, boss?"

Yale stretched out on a recliner and sipped his wine. "Well, what've we got? Porter walking down a street in Corona in the middle of the night about the time of the murders. If she gets locked up, her lawyer will say she's an exercise nut, likes to take midnight strolls, walked all the way from

Manhattan, does it all the time. At least now we know why she chose the park for the kill. Your boy Moran went into the coop every night at around the same time. He'd been doing it for so long, probably every cop in the area knew him and his partner weren't going to be around. She had the whole park to herself. She could have blown the damn limo up, and no one would have been around to see or hear it. It convinces me she's the shooter, but it wouldn't convince a jury."

"She was probably wearing a wig," Wright said. "The Five's said the shooter had dark hair."

"And as for this Moran character, he'd make some lousy witness. Even if he proved reliable, it's not enough. We gotta know why she did it. I'll tell you one thing, though—she had to have a car stashed somewhere. She wasn't anywhere near a train, and I'm sure she wouldn't take a cab. There would be a record of the trip. Maybe she had a driver."

"Cippolone?"

"Maybe, but that still doesn't give us motive."

"Like I said, what's next, boss?"

"I don't know." He pushed himself up and out of the chair. "I think better on a full stomach. Follow me."

Yale led Wright to a small dining area in the kitchen and told him to take a seat at the table while Yale did the honors. He also poured more Chianti. Wright dug in. Maybe it was the effects of the wine, but Yale thought Wright had put on a few pounds. Now maybe he could only put a pepperoni between his neck and shirt collar instead of a salami. Or maybe, Yale deduced, he was wearing a tighter collar.

"Hey, Ray, this shit is great," Wright said, after polishing off two helpings of chicken.

"A fitting testimonial." Yale was impressed with Wright's appetite. "You're feeling pretty good?"

"Strange, but I can't remember when I felt better. A little cold coming on, but pretty good." He sighed. "But that could change at any time. I'm one of the lucky few who has survived as long as I have without becoming really sick a lot. I'm a survivor."

Aren't we all, Yale thought. He speared more chicken. The two of them had just about wiped it out. He only thing he would have left for future meals were a few wings. Sorry, Dad, he thought to himself. He wiped his hands on a paper napkin.

"Okay, your belly's full," Wright said. "Any revelations?"

"We have to establish motive. That means we could follow Porter around, but I don't think my client can afford an extended surveillance. Of course, we could do it for free."

"Not a good idea."

"That's why I think we should fracture the law a little bit."

"Tap it?"

"I'm not crazy about the term," Yale said, "but yeah, tap it."

"How're you gonna get into the apartment?"

"Charlie, technology has come a long way since Watergate. I may not have to get into the apartment."

"Meaning?"

"A friend of mine owns one of those spy stores in midtown. He's got more gadgets than James Bond. I'll see him tomorrow."

"What do you want me to do?"

"Hang loose until we see what I come up with." Yale cleared the table of dirty dishes and brought a bowl of three-bean salad to center table. They picked on that and toasted Katherine Carpenter with what remained of the Chianti. Afterwards, Yale went to the office and wrote Wright two checks; one for the hours he had put in on the case and the other for expenses.

172

When Yale got back to the kitchen, he saw Wright staring at his own belly.

"I don't think I've eaten this much in five years. I actually think I've eaten myself sober." He got up, waddled to the phone on the kitchen wall, and called a car service.

Yale walked his guest to the door, and they shook hands. The wine had given him a warm glow. "The management thanks you for not smoking."

"I smoke too much, anyway," Wright said, smiling through clenched lips. "Oh yeah, before I forget, I want to thank you for giving me a shot at this case. Not too many people would have believed in me with my attitude."

Yale held onto Wright's hand. "I wouldn't have either, my friend. You've changed."

"I guess I have, haven't I?" A gypsy cab pulled in front of the house. "My ride. Talk to you tomorrow."

Yale watched Wright stagger slightly descending the stairs and looked forward to a good night's sleep, comforted in knowing that they were making some headway. He had seen a remarkable change in Wright's attitude, but he could also see a big change in his own. He had originally taken on the Carpenter case to get back at The Job for what he considered a gross mishandling of the investigation, to seek revenge on an organization that had given his wife so much grief as she fought for her life. And because he felt Carpenter had gotten a similar screwing by The Job.

But now, it was all about Katherine Carpenter. She was the only victim here. A homicide victim. He would find her killer because that was The Job. The real job. He was leaving his hate and bitterness behind him.

He had changed, too.

Chapter Sixteen

Another day, another hangover. Yale entered Manhattan through the Midtown Tunnel and wondered if that would be his epitaph. Traffic was light this day after Thanksgiving. He figured that people who weren't legitimately off from work had either decided to take a sick day or were in some hospital having their stomachs pumped.

The spy store was located on East 31st Street, between Lexington and Park Avenues, a block of mostly residential buildings and brownstones. As he crossed the nearly deserted street, he saw a large red and white canvas flag fighting the wind above a storefront. It read: ProTech, Inc. Sounds more like a condom, Yale thought. The front window housed an array of electronic gadgets, bulletproof vests, and books relating to the spook trade. A small sign advertised: Pistol Licenses Secured. The tinted glass on the front door obscured the store's interior. The door was locked. He pressed a bell. An intercom speaker emitted a garbled message. He leaned against the talk button.

"It's Ray Yale. My business is with Ralph Nieves."

The door clicked, and Yale walked out of the cold November air into a small showroom. The room was fitted with glass display cases, wood shelves, and a desk partly hidden behind a smoked-glass partition. Yale

174

knew that the glass was bulletproof. Two panoramic security cameras did their thing on opposite walls. On the rear wall was a large mirror, which Yale knew to be two-way bulletproof glass. He also knew that behind that wall, over two dozen people were working in a soundproofed and near sterile environment to protect fragile computer components.

A man sat behind the desk and peered over the top of reading glasses. One hand held a pen, the other was hidden beneath the desk.

"You can put the gun down, Ralph. It's me, Ray Yale."

The man at the desk broke into a wide grin. "Ray, long time, bro! You remember my little pistol stash, eh?" Ralph Nieves was a wiry man of medium height with an overabundance of nervous energy. He was fifty-two years old but looked ten years younger and wore his graying hair short. His moustache was pencil thin and made Yale think of Caesar Romero. He hugged Yale and stepped back. "Man, how long's it been? Three years?"

"More like four."

He gave Yale the onceover. "Wow, four years. You're lookin' good…in shape. Hey, bro, sorry about the wife. I found out about it after the funeral. Sorry I wasn't there."

Yale nodded. "Thanks, anyway." He leaned on a glass display case. "Keeping busy?" It was a rhetorical question. Yale had known Nieves for fifteen years, from the time they had worked together in a joint city-federal drug task force. He was always busy.

"Picking up, bro, picking up."

Yale laughed. "Show me around the place. Ever since I realized I could work a computer, I've had the urge to buy more gadgets."

"Then follow me. . .and get out your checkbook." He started the tour at the display cases, which contained miniature transmitters lined up in neat rows. Another case held tape recorders, and Nieves gave Yale a demonstration of the more sophisticated devices. Nieves' inventory of

175

countermeasure equipment detected anything from phone taps to hidden tape recorders, and they were custom built into everything from brief cases to rolls of toilet paper.

"Come over here," Ralph said. He led Yale to a six-foot glass display case that contained a coatrack supporting a herringbone sports jacket. He opened the case with a key and handed Yale the jacket. "Go ahead, bro, try it on."

The coat was a little tight around the shoulders, but otherwise it fit Yale fairly well.

"What does it do," Yale asked, "explode?"

"No, bro, it takes pictures, with sound. Want a dozen wallet sized of the front door?" He turned Yale toward the door.

"This thing's a camera?"

"Video or thirty-five millimeter with a tape recorder. I designed it myself."

Yale patted down the coat, trying to find the camera. "How does it work?"

"Take it off, I'll show you." Nieves pointed to a button hole that contained a tiny fish-eye lens. Sewn into the rear vent was a compartment that contained a miniature camera and tape recorder.

"This does video, too? They make camcorders that small?"

Nieves put the coat back in the case. "They don't, bro, but I do. With the technology today, I can miniaturize anything. . .except my alimony payments." He laughed at his own joke. "C'mon, let's sit down and catch up. You want some coffee or something?"

Yale declined, and they sat on opposite sides of the desk, Nieves' gaze darting to the door occasionally. An occupational habit, Yale thought. They talked about old cases and cops they'd known who had retired, died, or went to jail.

"So tell me, my friend, after four years what brings you here to see me? Can it be my sparkling personality?"

"I need your expertise, Ralph. I'm working on a case that requires a little discreet technological investigation."

"Hey, I like that, bro, *technological investigation.* Suppose you get caught doing this technological investigation, what would happen?"

"About ten years."

"At least now I know where we stand. It's good to be up front. What've you got?"

Yale didn't get into details about the Carpenter case. He told Ralph he needed to conduct an electronic surveillance from a remote location if possible. "These conversations," Ralph said, "you'll be privy to them, right?"

"Of course." Yale knew Ralph was covering his ass. Legally, Yale could only record a conversation he was part of.

"Describe where the equipment is going to be used."

Yale gave a detailed description of Leah Porter's brownstone.

"Does the apartment face the street?"

"Yeah, there's only three apartments, and there's three floors. The apartments go from the front to the back of the building. There's at least one window facing the street."

"How far's the building across the street?"

"I dunno, maybe seventy-five feet."

"So you would be on the roof?"

Yale nodded.

"Is it a horizontal line from point A to point B?"

"It can't be straight," Yale said. "I'll be on the roof, she's on the top floor across the street. I'd say about a five degree angle to her window, maybe less."

"Does the window have a covering? Blinds or shades?"

Yale tried to remember. "If there is a covering, it was up the last time I was these. It's probably just lowered at night."

Nieves got up. "Follow me in the back, I've got just the thing for you." He selected a key from a massive ring and opened a steel door. The room was long and narrow, with six desks on one side where women sat talking on phones in hushed tones. The phone receivers had scrambler units attached to them with elastic bands. On the left were steel tables, each manned by a technician in a white coat, hair netting, latex gloves, and masks. All were busy assembling electronic devices, some staring through illuminated magnifying glasses. Yale counted five men in the back loading equipment into wooden crates. All were armed with semi-automatic pistols. He figured Ralph's operation stretched all the way to the next block.

"Wait here a second." He left Yale standing by the door while he went to the back and talked to one of the packers. The man looked over his boss's shoulder and gave Yale a quick onceover. He nodded to Ralph, turned a corner, and vanished from sight. Nieves returned, smiling. "Follow me."

Yale did as directed and walked with his friend up to a solid wallpapered wall. Nieves reached into his pocket and produced a small black plastic box. He held it to the wall and squeezed a button. A portion of the wall swung inward and Ralph moved to one side. "My office, bro. Step inside."

The office was plush with deep pile carpet against mahogany paneling. The desk looked to Yale as if it had been carved from a block of granite. The man whom Nieves had spoken to in the packing area entered the office soundlessly, lugging a canvas duffle bag. He placed it gently in the center of the room and left without saying anything. Ralph opened the bag and assembled a strange device that looked like a small metal box with a six-inch barrel sitting on a VCR, both mounted on a tripod.

"I give up," Yale said. "What is it? Let me guess, another one of your inventions?"

"You got it, bro. Come over here, I'll show you how it works. This thing is going to solve your technological investigation problem." Ralph cleared his throat in preparation for his presentation. "I call this my Super Bug. It uses an infrared laser tube. This here." He indicated the barrel-like protrusion. "It produces a beam of light that aims the device. You ever see those cop shows where the SWAT guys have a bad guy in their sights and you see a little red dot on the guy's chest?"

Yale nodded.

"Well, that's why you can't keep it on too long. It's okay for sniping because the target's in sight for only a short period of time, but if you kept this laser on for the duration of a surveillance, your subject would be sure to spot it."

"Okay, so you aim it at what?"

"In your case, the window. If the window is open, you'd aim it at a wall, something immobile. A window is better because it vibrates, like the skin on a drum. Whenever someone speaks in the room, the window vibrates slightly. Got it so far?"

"Hanging on your every word."

"Now, once you have a point of aim, you shut the laser off." Nieves flipped a toggle switch on top of the metal box. "And you come down to this thing that looks like a VCR and punch this button."

"Which does…?"

"Which turns on an invisible infrared beam. We call it an IR beam. It can't be seen, so it can be trained on the window for as long as the battery lasts."

"How long would that be, Mr. Tool Man?"

"In this kind of cold weather, not long, about five hours, wise guy. I'll throw in some extra batteries."

"Looks pretty easy."

"Well, it ain't, bro, and I'll tell you why. The IR beam I told you about is good because the target can't see it, but it has one major drawback—you have to align it almost perfectly at a ninety-degree angle to the window, like straight on. That's why I asked you if you were going to be level with the window. Just to stay on the safe side, I suggest you lay it flat on the roof to limit the angle. Then there's the other problem of ambient noise, weather, wind, and all that shit. Try to use this on a calm day."

Yale walked around the device. "Is there anything else I need to know?"

"Just a couple of things, but they're important. First, if the window is open, even partially, and the laser goes through the open part and hits something that's not flat—"

"Like a curtain?"

"Yeah, like a curtain, the beam will scatter, and it'll leave a glow on the curtain that could be spotted. Also, don't look down the barrel to see if the laser's on. At that distance you'll burn a hole in your head. Questions?"

"Can I record off this thing?"

Nieves showed him where to plug in a recorder.

"So, the bottom line is I can only hear one side of a conversation if someone's talking on the phone, right?"

"Right, but of course you'll hear everything if two or more people are talking in the same room. It beats getting caught burglarizing someone's house."

Yale thought that someone with Porter's police experience would talk as little as possible on the phone. Maybe she'll get some visitors, he hoped.

"Okay, I've got it. Now, how much is this thing gonna cost me?"

Nieves smiled. "Bro, believe me when I tell you that you can't afford to buy it, but I'll tell you what. I just built two of them, and they haven't been field tested yet, so why don't we consider this a field test? I'll bill the DEA. They're buying a shitload of these things, and they pay us to run them through actual field conditions. Take it and play with it, just don't get busted. Deal?"

Yale extended his hand. "Deal."

He hoisted the duffle bag onto his shoulder and was off to commit his first felony since retiring from the New York City Police Department. He wondered what other laws he would be breaking before this case was over.

## Chapter Seventeen

After leaving the spy shop, Yale decided to make a cold call on Zoltag's chauffeur. Advance notice gave witnesses time to embellish their stories and bolster their importance to a case. In this instance, Zoltag's chauffeur could be privy to illegal activities by his deceased boss, and given lag time, might change his story to make him or his dead employer look good. The worst case scenario was that the driver might bolt. The cold call was always best.

Not knowing whether the chauffeur, Bruno Tartaglia, would be cooperative, Yale wanted to ensure cooperation and make certain his trip to the far reaches of Brooklyn, a city unto itself as far as Yale was concerned, wasn't for naught.

He made a short stop at his home for two reasons: to call Tartaglia and ascertain that he was home and to get his duplicate lieutenant's shield, which was given to him by his squad when he retired. A man answered at Tartaglia's number. Yale hung up and was on his way.

Tartaglia lived on a tree-lined street in Bensonhurst. Yale always liked the neighborhood, a tight-knit, mostly Italian area, with children playing on neatly trimmed front lawns and clean streets. The homes were old but well maintained, with the exception of an occasional ultra-modern brick and glass fortress—a mobster's dream house.

Bruno Tartaglia's modest one-family home was aluminum sided and had a tiny front yard and a driveway that led to a detached one-car garage. Yale parked at a meter between two identical black Cadillacs a short block away.

The man who came to the door was heavy, short, barrel-chested and had a puffy face that made him look like a Basset Hound. He looked about fifty years old. An unlit six-inch cigar protruded from his full lips, and he wore jeans that looked ready to fall around his ankles. His arms were unusually long and extended well past the cuffs of his Free John Gotti sweatshirt.

"Yeah?" His voice was raspy.

"Bruno Tartaglia?"

The man looked at him suspiciously. "Yeah."

"My name's Ray Yale. I'm a detective assigned to the murder of Herman Zoltag and Katherine Carpenter." No lie there, Yale thought. Maybe he would get through the day with only committing one felony. "I need to ask you a few questions." Yale saw no need to produce his knock-off shield unless asked.

"Jesus," Tartaglia said, "you guys still workin' on that thing? C'mon in." He held open the door and led Yale into the living room, where they sat on a plastic-covered couch.

"I'm havin' a little guinea red. Want some?" He shoved a glass of red wine under Yale's nose.

The smell of the wine made Yale taste bile. "Uh, no thanks." Yale took off his coat, making sure that his gun was visible. If Tartaglia developed doubts about Yale being on The Job, the Smith & Wesson would quash them. "We may go over some stuff you already told other

183

detectives, but I just caught the case, so bear with me, okay?"

"Yeah, sure. Hey, you know, I liked Mr. Zoltag. He did shit was a little hairy," he held out a pudgy hand, palm down, and turned it from side to side, "but he was always good to me. Very good with a buck." He rubbed his first three fingers of his right hand together.

Yale smiled. "Like what kind of hairy shit, Bruno…can I call you Bruno?"

"Yeah, sure, but don't yank my crank. You guys already know about the drug thing. The last dick talked to me about it."

"We've discounted a drug connection, so it's gotta be something else." Yale could smell the pungent odor of the wine, and it was making his stomach cramp.

"Well, whatever the fuck it was, I'm glad to be alive. This broad, the one he picked up that night—not the kid, the other one, the one they think clipped him—she coulda done me, but she let me alone 'cause I was sleepin'."

"You were lucky."

"Fuckin' A." Tartaglia burped.

"I want to start from when you picked up Mr. Zoltag that night. Tell me what happened."

Tartaglia described Zoltag's routine when he was looking for women, the bar hopping, inducing females with drugs and promises of a good time.

"How long was he in the bar where he met the two women?"

"Maybe an hour. He come out with the two broads."

"Describe them."

He sighed and moved the cigar to the other side of his mouth. "Lemme think…the younger broad, as I recall, was really fucked up. Mr. Zoltag had his arm around her waist to help her walk. She was maybe eighteen, nineteen."

"The other one?"

"Yeah, she looked straighter than the kid and maybe a little older, say twenny-three, twenny-four. I jumped outta the car and opened the door. The older one was the first in the car. I says hello, but she didn't even look at me. Snotty bitch."

She probably didn't want you to hear her voice, Yale thought. "How was she dressed?"

"All's I remember was the short skirt. Great legs. She had on shades, but lots of those Village types wear 'em all the time. Night don't mean shit. They think they look cool."

"What about her hair?"

"Long, down to about here." He turned his head and touched his shoulder with the cigar. "Dark. Black, I think."

Yale placed Leah Porter's pictures on the coffee table in front of Tartaglia. "She look familiar?"

Tartaglia picked up the photos and examined them intently. "Lemme get my glasses" He left briefly and came back with a pair of half-glasses perched on his nose. He picked up the pictures and stared at them for a minute. "Man, I'm not sure. Hair's all wrong. It was dark, you know, and a long time ago."

"Take your time. Think."

Tartaglia squinted and concentrated. Finally, he shook his head. "Can't say, man. This the broad done the shootin'? 'Cause if it is, say the word and I'll ID her."

"It doesn't work that way, but thanks anyway." Yale put the pictures back in his pocket. "Okay, so they're in the car, what happened then?"

"I start drivin' back to his apartment on Bank Street, like always. I

185

didn't have to ask him where to go 'cause every time he picked up a broad, it was back to the apartment. This time, though, he lowers the partition and tells me to go to Flushin' Meadow Park."

"Ever take him there before?"

"Are you kiddin'?" Tartaglia laughed. "This guy thought Queens was another country."

"So why do you think he wanted to go to the park?"

"No fuckin' idea. He tells me where to go, I go."

"How'd you know where to go?" Yale asked. "Anybody give you directions?"

"Mr. Zoltag did. Every cupla miles or so the partition goes down and I get told 'Turn right here,' 'Turn left there.'"

"How do you think he knew the directions to the park?"

"Ain't it obvious? The broad, the one that did the killin', had to be tellin' him. Then he'd tell me."

"Why couldn't it have been the other girl? She lived in Queens, you know."

He removed the cigar from his mouth and wiped some spittle from his lip with the back of his hand. "You kiddin'? That poor kid couldn't give directions to the front seat. She was fucked up. Bad."

"You didn't hear the older one's voice at all?"

"Not really."

"What's that mean?"

"Well, when the glass went down, I heard her mumble a few things."

"What kind of things? Did you catch any words?" Yale leaned forward. He realized he was sweating, and his legs were sticking to the plastic seat covers.

"Well, I remember bein' a little worried we'd get made by the cops.

I mean, Mr. Zoltag, he probably had a load of blow back there, and I didn't wanna get busted. So this time I lower the glass and says somethin' about the cops. I hear the broad say somethin', and I figure somebody's gonna be sick back there."

"What makes you say that?"

"Well, she said somethin' about heavin'."

"Heaving?"

"Yeah, like gettin' sick. It happens in this business all the time. I remember once…"

While Bruno Tartaglia reminisced about vomit, Yale thought that the word 'heave' had another meaning. It was police jargon for a place to goof off.

"…and then wham, all over my fuckin' seat. What a mess." And with that, Tartaglia concluded his fascinating story of the Hollywood starlet who had projectile up-chucked in his new stretch limo.

"Did you ever tell the investigating detectives what you just told me?"

"You mean about the heavin'? Nah, nobody asked me, and I thought it was a kind of stupid thing to bring up—hey, that's a joke—bring up, get it?"

Yale smiled, but inside he was seething. If the detectives who had originally questioned Tartaglia had been a little more thorough, they might have zeroed in on a cop being involved in the crime, and he might not be here now trying to solve a couple of homicides that should have been cleared years ago.

Tartaglia went on to describe waking up after three in the morning and not feeling any motion from the back of the car. After a few minutes, he made his grisly discovery and used the car phone to call the police.

Yale was still in search of a motive. "Tell me about your boss, Mr.

187

Zoltag. Something other than what happened that night."

"Like what?" Tartaglia poured himself another glass of wine.

"Like his business. He was a photographer, right?"

"Yeah, and a damn good one. Did you know that he was one of the first guys to use video? He had a real good business in the late seventies, early eighties takin' videos of weddin's and bar mitzvahs, things like that. He was doin' that before it caught on. Made him a pile of dough."

Yale was formulating a motive for murder. "You say he used to bring these young girls back to his apartment? All the time?"

"If they'd go with him, every time."

"Do you think he videoed girls in the apartment?"

Tartaglia spat out some wet tobacco from the soggy end of the cigar. "I don't know what went on in his place. Alls I know is that he treated me okay."

Yale remembered Mike Sheehan had told him that Zoltag's place had been thoroughly searched. Could the killer have been looking for a videotape or pictures, he wondered? Was this whole thing about blackmail? Could Zoltag have picked up a married woman, videotaped her performing sexual acts, and then extorted money from her? Was Porter a hired killer? Blackmail was a good motive and it was a lot better than any explanation he currently had.

Yale got up to leave. "Thanks a lot, Bruno, you've been a big help."

"No problem."

"Can you answer one more question? Are you gonna smoke that thing?" The cigar was still stuck in Tartaglia's mouth, unlit.

"This here?" He removed the wet stogie from his mouth and rolled it lovingly between his fingers. "My doctor says these fuckn' things'll kill me. That's not how I wanna go. I plan on dying peacefully in bed when I'm ninety."

"Don't we all," Yale said, wistfully, thinking about Charlie Wright. "Don't we all."

Chapter Eighteen

The weekend weather was too blustery and unsettled for Yale to use Nieves' Super Bug on a rooftop anywhere near the windswept Hudson River. An early winter storm had dumped a few inches of snow on the metropolitan area early Saturday morning, so Yale decided to use the down time to become proficient with his new toy.

He set up the device in his living room, aiming it at a third-floor apartment in a six-story co-op building across the street. He had a straight shot at an uncovered window, and he was able to pick up a clear conversation between an adult male and female, even though he was unable to see them. The building blocked most of the wind noise, and the conversation, while not crystal clear, was understandable. He switched off the Bug once he was sure he knew how to use it.

He had called Wright late Friday, bringing him up to speed on his interview with the chauffeur. Yale told him his theory about blackmail being a possible motive for the two murders, and Wright agreed that it could be a valid reason for homicide, but Yale was relying on the "death ray" to provide something a little more solid. He spent the rest of the weekend catching up on paperwork and visiting the gym.

By Sunday night, he realized that he hadn't heard from Wright since the late Friday night phone call. He told himself that if he didn't hear from Wright by Monday night, he would beep him. He was just as concerned about the former detective's ability to stay sober as he was about his health.

Monday was bright, sunny and cold, but the wind had diminished to a gusting breeze, and the forecast promised higher temperatures. Perfect spying weather, Yale thought, as he lugged the duffle bag packed with equipment to his car. In the black nylon shoulder bag, he had a thermos of hot soup, three tuna sandwiches, a windproof blanket, gloves, a compact flashlight and a cellular phone with extra batteries. He wore a black surplus SAS parka and pants and a knit watch cap, an outfit he'd used on more than one cold-weather surveillance. He still had his Knapp weather-proof boots from his days on the Tactical Patrol Force more than twenty years ago and slipped into them with no effort. The boots'll outlast me, he thought, as he threaded his way through rush-hour traffic to Manhattan's West Side.

He parked the Lexus in a garage two blocks from Porter's brownstone. When he stepped out of the car and got a strange look from the parking attendant, he realized that he looked like O.J. Simpson going to visit his ex-wife. He didn't want to attract attention, so he stopped in a men's clothing store on Broadway and bought a cheap, oversized raincoat, which adequately concealed his military appearance. He stuffed the knit cap into his pocket.

He mounted the stairs to the building directly opposite Porter's brownstone and pressed the bell marked "Super." A middle-aged man answered the door carrying a mop. Yale felt the direct approach was best, so he waved two hundred-dollar bills under the superintendent's nose and told him he needed his roof to take pictures of migrating Peregrine hawks that had been mating in New York City building cornices. The beer-bellied super told him that for a double C-note, Yale could take pictures of him and his missus mating. He personally led Yale to the roof, even helping carry the equipment.

There was a thin layer of ice on the roof. Yale guessed it had to be fifteen degrees, taking into consideration the wind chill coming from the Hudson River. Still, he felt comfortable in his insulated clothing. He went to the parapet, which jutted out about three feet into 69th Street's airspace. The distance between where he stood and Porter's window looked a lot shorter than the original seventy-five feet he had estimated. The angle was almost straight, and he realized that he would have to remain prone behind the Bug not to be seen.

He got on his knees and began unloading his equipment, spreading the tripod as much as possible to reduce the angle to Porter's window. It took him ten minutes to set up the Bug and connect it to its external battery supply.

Leah Porter's window had a row of raised blinds. He didn't see any movement in the apartment. The window itself was one large pane—not unlike this goddamn surveillance, Yale thought, chuckling at his own pun. He had been hanging around Charlie Wright too long.

The Super Bug was assembled and ready to go. He aimed the laser in the general direction of the window and switched it on, greatly relieved when the old brownstone didn't explode. He could see a red dot just to the right of the window on the building's façade and goosed the tripod a bit to get the laser situated on the glass. Once he had the laser where he wanted it, he turned it off.

He lay on his stomach and retrieved the binoculars from the bag, got to his knees, and looked into his subject's apartment. He flipped the toggle switch to the IR beam and rolled over on his back. He waited thirty seconds and then peered over the edge of the roof with the glasses. No movement in the apartment.

He moved a short distance from the edge, wrapped himself in his blanket, and put on the earphones. Okay, he said to himself, start incriminating yourself, you homicidal bitch.

He looked at his watch. It was 10 a.m.

At two-thirty, there was still no movement from across the street. One battery had died in the cold, and Yale's numb hands replaced it. He felt much colder than he had just a few hours ago. He had watched the sun disappear behind an endless bank of clouds. What was it the Weather Channel said? The arrival of a warming trend? Sunny and pleasant? He didn't know whether he wanted to use his cellular phone to have a fifty-five gallon drum of coffee sent to the roof so he could sit in it, or to call the Weather Channel and curse out the incompetent help. When he flared his nostrils, he thought he heard his frozen nose hairs crack. His gloves were becoming useless, and he felt himself begin to shiver.

He shoved the thermos into the front of his pants for added heat. *Are you happy to see me or is that a thermos in your pants?* When he laughed at his own joke, his face hurt. His Knapp boots, the policeman's friend, were performing superbly. It felt like warm puppies were snuggled around his feet. Yale tried to recall what his training officer had told him when he was a rookie. Oh, yeah, he remembered: a good cop never gets cold, hungry, or wet. Well, one out of three ain't bad, he thought, as he stuffed three frozen tuna sandwiches back into his duffle bag.

Three-thirty.

Still no movement or sound. Yale decided to give it until four o'clock. After that, he would pack up his frozen carcass and look forward to tomorrow when he would do it all over again. He wondered if Nieves had a long distance Super Bug that had a range from, say, the Caribbean.

He was lying on his back like a frozen carp when his earphones

193

picked up the sound of a door slamming. He struggled to roll over and looked into Porter's window with the binoculars. Adrenaline surged through him when he saw Leah Porter, or at least a female with long blond hair, pass the window. He shifted to his back and checked the time.

Three fifty-six.

For the next two hours, he heard no voices. Occasionally, he heard sounds, though unidentifiable, indicating she was still in the apartment. It was almost dark, but Yale dared not look back into the apartment until the sun had totally set. He was getting a bird's eye view of a winter sunset. His admiration for the beauty of nightfall gave way to the realization that it certainly wasn't going to get any warmer now that the sun was somewhere over Nebraska.

Yale was jarred to attention when he heard a female voice through his earphones. He checked his watch. Five-thirty.

"Can I speak to him, please," he heard, loud and clear, before about fifteen seconds of silence. He peered over the parapet. He saw Porter walk past the window holding a cordless phone. He rolled over on his back.

Then he heard, "Tell him it's his stock broker, would you, dear?" More silence. He was obviously listening to Porter's side of a telephone conversation.

"It's me. Coming over?"

Pause.

"A little after five."

Pause.

"I wanted you to be rested. I've got plans for you that require a fully charged battery."

Yale thought he heard her laugh.

"Me."

Pause.

"I'll call Lenge. They deliver. See you what, about seven?"

Then he heard Porter make a call and order Japanese food. That was it. He tapped the headset, not knowing whether the power died or Porter had hung up. He guessed the latter.

He had positively identified her when she passed by the window at least a dozen times while she talked on the phone.

"Stockbroker" was an obvious codeword. Porter was probably seeing a married man. Could this be how her bills were being paid, Yale wondered.

At six fifty-five, he leaned precariously over the roof's edge, camcorder at the ready, and awaited Porter's boyfriend, his thoughts focused on getting some good pictures and then going home to a hot meal and a warm bed.

At seven oh-three, a silver stretch limousine turned left off Central Park West onto 69th Street. Yale began videotaping the car as it slowed in front of Porter's brownstone. The car resumed speed, and Yale turned the camera off. He watched as it continued toward the corner and pulled into the curb next to a fire hydrant adjacent to a phone kiosk. There was a man in the kiosk.

Yale brought the camera up and zoomed to the tenth power, targeting the phone.

The man was Tony Cippolone.

After about a minute, Yale saw a tall man get out of the back of the car and walk toward Porter's building. Cippolone craned his head around the kiosk and watched the tall man walk away. Yale suddenly wished he was the comedian Marty Feldman with eyes on both sides of his head so he could watch both subjects, but he had to make a choice. He chose the tall guy. The limo pulled away as Yale tracked its passenger up the block

195

with the video camera.

Yale followed the man as he walked, head down, large Stetson pulled low over his eyes. If he walked past the brownstone, Yale was resigned to wait until someone else came into the block and double back to Cippolone, if he was still by the phone.

Yale's headset picked up a ringing phone.

#

I hope Wolf's not calling to tell me he'll be late, Porter thought, as she picked up her phone.

"Leah, it's Tony,"

She didn't recognize the voice. "Tony?"

The man on the other end sounded aggravated. "Yeah, Tony, Tony Cippolone."

She didn't recall the voice because he sounded sober. Why the hell was he calling her now, she wondered. Wolf would be walking through the door any minute.

"What is it, Tony?" She looked at the front door and strained to hear the sound of her man's footsteps.

"Listen, I wanna apologize for the other night. I was a little wasted, ya know?"

"Tony, I'd like to talk, but I've got something in the oven. My parents are coming over. I really gotta go."

"That's okay, I understand. Can I come by later?"

Leah was infinitely sorry she had ever mercy-fucked the guy. Any favor she had asked of him over the years, he was more than happy to do for a short roll in the sack. If Wolf ever found out....

"Look, Tony, you really can't. I've got a boyfriend, you know how

196

it is. In a few weeks, he'll be out of town, and we can get together." She distinctly heard Wolf's size fourteens on the top landing, and she broke into a sweat.

"When you want me to do your dirty work, it's call Tony, no problem," Cippolone said. "I thought we were friends. C'mon, twenny lousy minutes."

Tumblers were turning in the lock. "Look, Tony, call me tomorrow, okay?"

"You can bet on it."

He hung up.

Wolf breezed through the door and brought the cold air in with him. He had on his trademark John Lennon sunglasses, but his shoulder-length hair was tucked under a felt cowboy hat. He tossed his canvas duster and hat on the polished wood floor and scooped Leah into his arms. He had to bend his gangly frame to grab her ass and bury his face in her hair.

Her body was hard and tense. "Something wrong?" he asked, eyeing her with suspicion.

She avoided eye contact. "Uh, no, just a little headachy."

Slowly, she regained her composure. She smiled. "See, as soon as you show up, I feel better." She led him into the bedroom by the hand, turned, and began unbuckling his belt.

He ran his hands through her hair. "Apparently, I've got the cure."

The phone rang. She ignored it. She reached a warm hand into his underwear. This will make him think everything is normal, she thought.

Wolf seemed distracted. "Aren't you going to answer that before...you know, we get started?"

She leered at him. "Let the machine—" She suddenly remembered that she had put the speaker on high when she went to the shower, and if

197

it were Cippolone again, his voice would fill the room. The machine picked up.

"You have reached Leah Porter. I'm not home right now, if you leave a—"

"You're right," he said and turned his full attention to his lover.

"No, I'd better get it," she said, giving him a peck on the lips and a quick smile. The closest phone was by her bed, and she could easily make it before the outgoing message ended. When she turned, Wolf grabbed her arm.

"No, you were right the first time. This is no time for a conversation. Get the fucking thing later." He pulled her back to him and guided her hand back into his pants. She tried to pull away, but he was too strong for her.

"—message at the sound of the beep. I'll get back to you."

An annoying tone sounded, and Tony Cippolone's voice boomed through the room. After clearing his throat, he said, "I hate these fucking things. Listen, Leah, this is Tony again. I know you're up there with your friend, and I know who he is. I called you from the corner before. I got good eyes. You treat me like shit, you'll pay for it. Save some for me."

He hung up.

Leah felt Wolf's grip tighten. He slapped her hard with his free hand. Her head snapped back, and a spray of blood flew from her mouth. She lost her footing and staggered into the wall, her head making contact with a dull thud. She saw bright flashes of light, and the room went dark for a second. Nausea swept over her as she sank to the floor.

Steiner was on her in a second. He bent down and picked her head up by her hair. "He knows who I am?" He punched her. The blow landed just under her left eye and sent her tumbling over the bed. She tried to crawl under it, but Steiner was too quick. He grabbed her by an ankle and

198

dragged her to the center of the room.

My God, she thought, how vivid her recollection was of when her father used to beat her. She would crawl under her bed, and her father would drag her out. He would grab her by her ankles and then he would....

"You fucking cunt!" Wolf bellowed. She had never seen him such a mountain of rage and uncontrolled fury. As she lay before him on the floor, he pulled back a weighty engineer boot to kick her in the head. She moved at the last second. She watched him lose his balance and fall to the floor.

Seeing a chance to escape his wrath, she got up and ran for the front door. She sensed Wolf right behind her as she reached the foyer. He got a fistful of her denim pants and threw her sideways into the living room. She slid on her chest and face across the polished wood and came to rest in front of the stereo. She flipped over on her back and drew her legs tightly to her breasts.

Wolf grabbed a pewter candle stick from a small table. He was sweating, and his breath came in big gulps. He raised the weapon and advanced on her. She crossed her arms in front of her face, resigned to the fact he was about to crush her skull. Then he paused as he passed the bare living-room window.

"Stupid bitch!" He lunged at the window, violently yanking the cord that lowered the mini-blinds.

Porter stared at him through blood and sweat and watched Steiner as he turned on her once again. But she saw his rage was now spent, and he dropped the candlestick and fell to his knees, seemingly exhausted.

She felt no pain. In fact, she rather liked the way the blood mixed with her sweat in a rivulet cascading between her breasts. She remembered her father had liked it, too. She waited a few minutes, watching Wolf gulp lungfuls of air, before she slowly rose and whispered, "I'll make us some drinks."

#

Yale shook, and it wasn't from the cold. He thought he had been witnessing Leah Porter being beaten to death by her boyfriend. Years of police training almost had him racing downstairs and into Porter's building to stop the homicidal assault, but thoughts of Katherine Carpenter and her violent death changed his mind. *I'm not a cop anymore*, he had to remind himself, *I'm on a mission to catch a killer.* He had continued to record the assault until it ended.

The boyfriend, whoever he was, was incensed at being recognized by Tony Cippolone. That much Yale knew from listening to his end of the conversations. *Who was this guy?*

Yale rolled over on his back and pressed "rewind." As he looked through the eyepiece at the exposed tape, he saw a clear shot of the limo, but the boyfriend, backlit by the living room light, was a blotch of black. He cursed his luck and put the earphones back on, positioning himself back on the edge of the roof, binoculars fixed on the window. He heard no sound for the next six minutes. Out of sheer boredom, he checked out the block, beginning with the end closest to Columbus Avenue.

He saw a young Japanese male walking down the block carrying two large brown paper bags. Yale remembered that Porter had ordered Japanese food, and he figured he was looking at the delivery boy. He yanked the headphones off and ran to the roof door as fast as his stiff legs could carry him. He bounded down the four flights of stairs and arrived in front of Porter's building breathing heavily, beating the delivery boy by seconds. He stood blocking the stairs.

"Scuse me," the kid said. He looked about seventeen.

"You from Lenge?" Yale asked, remembering the name of the restaurant Porter had mentioned, trying to speak normally and gulp air at the same time.

The kid eyed him suspiciously. "Yeah, what of it?"

Yale reached into his pants pocket. "I'll take it up, save you a trip. How much?"

"Who're you? I'm supposed to bring this to the third floor."

"I'm her boyfriend. I placed the order. How much?"

"Oh, yeah? What's in it then?"

Yale remembered every last detail of Porter's order because he was so hungry. He hadn't eaten all day and almost chipped a tooth on one of the frozen tuna sandwiches.

"Well, okay," the kid said and handed the bags to Yale while accepting the cash, which included a generous tip. "Hey, thanks!"

Yale watched the delivery boy trot up the block. He figured that Porter would be in no shape to answer the door, and this would be a perfect opportunity to get a look at her boyfriend and maybe get an I.D.

He rang the bell, announced a delivery, and was buzzed in. He knocked on Porter's door and said, "Lenge, delivery."

Yale heard movement inside. A muffled male voice said, "One moment." Yale waited less than a minute. The door opened and Yale, at six feet tall, had to look up to see the man's face, at least what he could see of it.

The guy standing there was wearing sunglasses and a cowboy hat that slanted over his face. Yale guessed he was six-four or five. He was clean shaven with an angular face. Yale thought that he had a lot more hair than was showing tucked under the hat. It was hard to pinpoint his age, but Yale figured him to be about thirty-five. He held a wad of cash in a trembling right hand.

"How much?" The voice was deep and resonant.

Yale had his thermos under his left armpit and faked a look at the bill, which was stapled to the top of one of the bags. The thermos began to slip.

"Hey, man, could you do me a favor?" Yale said. "Grab the thermos, would ya?" He turned his side to the man. The metal bottle began to fall. The man grabbed it.

"Hey, thanks," Yale said. "I been runnin' around all night deliverin' this stuff, and the only thing keeps me warm is the joe in the thermos." He was doing his best to sound like John Malkovich playing Lenny in *Of Mice and Men*. If the giant in front of him was suspicious, he didn't show it. The man grunted, looked at the total circled in red at the bottom of the bill, and exchanged the thermos for the bags. He shoved a bill in Yale's breast pocket.

"Thanks," the man said, and he stepped back and slammed the door.

Yale carefully handled the shiny metal thermos bottle by the cap and placed it in his right jacket pocket. Thanks for the fingerprints, asshole, he thought. He went back across the street, got the super to let him back in, and retrieved his gear from the roof. Tomorrow, he would call Mike Sheehan and have him run the prints.

#

What he wanted to do was throw her out the window, but there were two good reasons for not doing that. The first was the delivery guy. He had seen him, and while he doubted he could identify him, the cops would know that there was someone else in the apartment about the time she took a header out the window. The second reason was that he needed her to kill Tony Cippolone.

He sat across the living room from Leah, who was on the couch playing with a stuffed animal like nothing had happened. He chewed quietly on a piece of shrimp tempura and sipped a Saporo beer. When he saw her look at him, he put the food down and sat beside her.

She looked up at him through a closed left eye and smiled. "I love you," she said weakly.

Steiner took two deep breaths, trying to control his temper. "How many times did you fuck him?"

She covered her head. "Three times."

He didn't touch her. Quietly he said, "Why?"

She began to sob softly. "He helped me. He helped me to help you."

Steiner felt his temper rising. "What?"

"He drove me from the park, you know that," she said, meekly. "He also helped me flake Danny Doremus. I didn't have the connections to get the kiddie porn, he did. He didn't want money; he wanted me. I went to Doremus' apartment myself, I swear. He didn't know."

"Jesus Christ," Steiner said. "You said three times. What was the third time?"

She sat up and held her head. "That Tavlin guy."

Steiner grabbed her by the hair and jerked her head back. "He was there when you whacked him?"

"No, no," she squealed, "he found him for me. I didn't know where to begin to look. Tony never knew I killed him. Please let go."

Steiner pushed her head aside. "He knows who I am?"

"But he'll never make the connection."

"Don't bet on it." He didn't know whether he was angrier at her or

Cippolone. "I want you to kill your friend Tony. Kill him dead. Understand?"

"Yes."

"And do it soon."

"Yes." She looked up into his eyes. "Fuck me, Daddy."

"What?" Sick bitch. I've gotta watch my back around this one, he thought. She's off the deep end.

"I said fuck me, Daddy." She smiled. Her one good eye was unfocused, and it scared Steiner. "You could hit me first if you want to." She began to cry and started to unzip her jumpsuit.

Steiner wondered if her father did it to her that way. He tucked his hair beneath the cowboy hat, put on his coat, and sat down beside her. The top half of her jumpsuit was down around her waist. She unsnapped her bra and let it fall to the floor. She appeared to be in a world of her own, paying little or no attention to Steiner. He cupped her left nipple and squeezed. Give her a little more of what she's used to. "You kill that little weasel, and things will get back to normal. Got it?"

She nodded.

He turned and left the apartment without another word.

## Chapter Nineteen

Yale tried beeping Charlie Wright four times before 11 a.m. the next morning. There was no answer. Shortly after the last call, he threw on the same clothes he had on the night before and started for Wright's apartment. It had been four days since he heard from Wright, and he was worried.

The second snowstorm in less than a week was raging as he fought Manhattan-bound traffic. He estimated at least six inches on the ground, and the city was entering its paralysis mode, with traffic practically at a standstill. After an hour of dodging stranded motorists, Yale turned into East 96th Street, drove the two blocks to Wright's building, and parked in front of the closest fire hydrant. He transferred the duffle bag full of surveillance equipment he still had in the back of the car to the trunk and hoped he wasn't being watched by the neighborhood junkies. The deserted street allayed his fears: too nasty out for junkies or ticket-writing cops.

He took the steps to Wright's tenement two at a time and entered the lobby. He punched Wright's bell. When he got no response, he wondered if any of the damn things worked. The bell marked "Super" yielded the same results, so he tested the door to the interior foyer with his shoulder. Strong door, weak jamb. Two body slams and he was inside.

A radiator just beyond the entrance was encased in ice. It felt colder inside the building than outside, and he wondered what had happened to all the warm dry air he had encountered during his first visit. He was up the three flights of stairs in less than twenty seconds and felt his heart pounding, not from the exercise but from what he was afraid he would find inside Wright's hovel.

He rapped on the door three times. A feeling of dread came over him, and the sounds of his own labored breathing and the sight of exhaled air vapor inside the small hallway was all that greeted him.

He put his nose along the edge of the door, sniffing for the tell-tale odor of a dead body. Nothing. He banged on the door, harder this time. After getting no answer, he went down the stairs to the first floor, using the bannister for support all the way. His legs felt weak and rubbery.

There were two apartments on the first floor. Yale figured the one in the rear belonged to the superintendent. He knocked loudly and heard shuffling sounds.

"Yeah?" a voice said.

"Police, open up!" You want results, you bullshit big time. He waited for the assortment of locks to be opened.

Armand, aka Moldy, was still wearing the same shorts and T-shirt Yale had seen him in last week.

"Remember me?" Yale said.

Moldy squinted. "Oh, yeah, the cop's friend. What's goin' on?"

Yale felt a warm blanket of heat envelope him. "How come you got heat?"

"I'm the super. Super's always got heat. You come here to ask about the fuckin' heat? The fuckin' boiler's busted. It'll be fixed tomorrow...maybe. I called the plumb—"

"You seen Wright lately?"

206

Moldy scratched his chin. "I don't think for a cupla days. Maybe three days."

"You got keys to his apartment?"

"Yeah, but I ain't goin' up there. I wouldn't go if I was you, neither. The fuckin' guy's nuts. He's liable to shoot us both."

Yale stuck out his hand. "He won't shoot me. Hand 'em over."

"You think somethin's wrong with him? He don't look so good lately."

A classic understatement, Yale thought. "Yeah, he's real sick. C'mon, the keys." He wiggled his fingers.

"Okay, okay, wait here." He left the door open and disappeared into the shadows. The warm air felt good against Yale's face. Moldy was back in seconds, holding a ring of keys. "I guess I gotta go with ya. All these keys are mixed up." He led the way, with Yale wondering why he wasn't freezing in his skimpy attire.

Yale banged on Wright's door again but didn't wait for an answer. He turned to Moldy, said "Go for it," and stepped aside.

The super fumbled with the keys, finally getting through both locks. He stepped back to the bannister. "You first," he said. "He's your friend."

Yale's heart pounded like a piston as he reached into the small of his back and unsnapped his holster. "Wait here until I call you," he said. Moldy nodded vigorously.

The apartment was dark. No surprise there, Yale thought. "Charlie, it's Ray Yale." He stood motionless just inside the door, waiting for an answer that never came.

The warm sweat sunning down his back became cold. His eyes adjusted to the blackness. He began to make out familiar shapes. The Christmas tree was still up, but the lights were off. No one had re-arranged the furniture. He moved further into the apartment, his shoes scraping the grit that blanketed the wood floor. He heard only the sounds of his own breathing and the distant wail of a police siren. He turned to his right and saw a stream of bluish light seeping from beneath a doorway. He sidled up to the door, turning sideways to avoid a surprise bullet or that unwelcome kick to the groin that could ruin his afternoon. He put his ear to the door and his nose to the jamb. No sound, no odor.

"Charlie!" He thought he heard a moan.

Yale crouched low and barreled into the door, splintering the rotted wood and sailing into Charlie Wright's bedroom. He hit the door with such force that, if it hadn't been for the bed that stopped his forward trajectory, he might have crashed through the window. He wound up on his side, next to the bed, staring at the chipped woodwork.

He got to his knees. The faint light was coming from a portable black and white television on a flimsy metal stand in front of the bed. There was a picture but no sound.

Charlie Wright lay on his back, bundled in a soiled white robe under a torn, worn wool blanket. One arm extended from beneath the cover. A battered paperback book lay on the floor next to the bed.

Yale leaped up, holstered his gun, and hit the wall light switch. The room flooded with light from a naked bulb dangling from a loose connection in the ceiling. He looked into Wright's eyes. They were wide and staring, pupils fixed but not dilated. Yale grabbed Wright's limp wrist, which was ice cold, and felt for a pulse. He didn't feel one and began to gently shake the frail man.

"Charlie, wake up. You okay?"

Wright's eyes focused, then blinked. He reached for Yale's arm. "Ray," he croaked. His arm fell back to his side. He was saying something that Yale couldn't make out. Yale put his ear to Wright's lips.

208

"I'm sick," Wright said, barely audible.

"No shit." Wright's skin was a translucent shade of gray, and his face was hard to the touch. Yale sighed and saw his breath. "Moldy!" He started rubbing his hands up and down on Wright's decrepit arm, trying to warm him. The super came in on a run, stopping abruptly when he saw Wright.

"My God! Is he...dead?"

Yale felt a dichotomy of anger and pity: a violent fury at the superintendent for not having heat in the building and a profound sadness at the helpless human being in the bed. "He's alive! Get a fucking ambulance! Tell nine-one-one a retired member of the force is sick, and it's an emergency." Moldy began backing out of the room and Yale added, "And get an ETA!"

Moldy was almost out the bedroom door when he stopped. "What's an ETA?"

Yale screamed, "Estimated-time-of-fucking-arrival! Now move!"

When the super was gone, Yale went to the window and yanked down two heavy blankets. The snow was heavier and swirling now, and it reminded Yale of the glass domes he would get as a kid at Christmas, the kind that when shaken sent fake snow cascading around a plastic snow man. He covered the frail ex-detective with both blankets, then stumbled into the kitchen and turned on what he thought to be the hot-water faucet, only to be greeted by a gush of frigid water. I've got to remember to seriously hurt Moldy, he said to himself, and raced back to the bedroom.

Wright was trying to talk but was having difficulty. He was swallowing hard and coughing a dry sandpaper rasp. Yale asked him when he ate last and was met with a stare. He wondered if the blankets were doing any good and felt Wright's forehead. Colder than the police commissioner's heart. He lifted the sick man by the shoulders and cradled him, hoping to transfer some of his body heat. By this time, Yale was sweating profusely, and he thought he had enough body heat to cook a turkey. Where the hell is that bus, he thought. No, ambulance. God, he thought, I'll be using cop-talk until the day I die.

He rocked the desperately ill Wright like a baby. Yale saw a chipped nightstand next to the bed that had an open shoebox with enough medication to stock a pharmacy. The letters AZT he recognized, but he was looking at an array of orange plastic bottles with words he had never heard of: Biaxin, Pentacarinate, Neutrexin, Zeret and a bottle hand lettered "3TC."

There were about a dozen paper-wrapped syringes in the box.

Moldy ran into the room gasping for breath. "I called from my apartment. They're on the way."

"ETA?"

"Huh? Oh, yeah. The broad said about ten minutes."

"You told her it was a former cop?"

"Yeah, she didn't seem too impressed. Ten minutes. She said that's the best she could do."

"Not good enough." Yale knew ten minutes was probably more like fifteen or twenty. He stood, scooping up Wright effortlessly. It was like holding a bag of coat hangers. Yale thought he couldn't weigh more than a hundred and forty pounds. "Hold open the doors, we're going to your apartment." The blankets dragged on the floor. Hold on, buddy, he silently prayed. Yale felt tears welling in his eyes.

Moldy looked bewildered. "We are?"

Yale shot him a look to convince Moldy to buy both of them round-trip tickets to Tahiti if that was Yale's pleasure.

During the wait for the ambulance, Yale danced around the super's questions about Wright's illness.

210

Blood Shot Eyes

"Ever hear of Arterial Monochromia?"

Moldy shook his head stupidly. "Uh, I don't think so."

"Look it up."

The ambulance arrived in twenty minutes. By that time, Wright had begun to respond to the heat in the downstairs apartment; Yale saw that he was getting some color back in his face, and his skin was warmer to the touch.

Yale followed the ambulance in his own car to the Emergency Room in Metropolitan Hospital. He talked to a doctor and advised him on Wright's condition, and they discussed the results of some preliminary lab tests. The doctor, young, dedicated, and overworked, was compassionate and friendly. He thanked Yale for remembering to bring Wright's medication and said that his friend's T-cell count was 355, the norm being about 500, and not bad for a person in Wright's condition. The doctor said Wright apparently had a bad reaction to the AZT, which was common, and in conjunction with the cold in the apartment, it had put him precariously close to pneumonia. He was also malnourished and would be in the hospital for at least two days for observation, at which time if the pneumonia didn't develop, he would be released after a nutritional workup.

Wright had been attached to an IV and was beginning to communicate, albeit incoherently. Before Yale left his friend, he saw a trace of tears in the sick man's eyes. He leaned over Wright's bed. "Get some rest. You're gonna be okay." He squeezed Wright's boney shoulder and thought he saw him smile thinly before dropping off to sleep.

Yale filled out the necessary paperwork and listed himself as next of kin. He talked with the ambulance personnel, who by that time had made several trips back to the ER with other patients. One harried EMT apologized for the delay in reaching Wright. Yale knew they tried their best

211

and had little in the way of support. Welcome to New York, he thought; getting sick in Bosnia would have brought a faster response. Yale got the name of a private ambulance service and called them, leaving his American Express card number as a deposit to deliver Wright to his house in Queens when he was released. He had a vacant apartment downstairs, sparsely furnished, but it was Trump Tower compared to Wright's crumbling digs. Wright took enough hard knocks in his life, Yale thought. He deserves a little help.

Yale got home after midnight. He was too tired to lug the duffle bag of surveillance equipment up two flights of stairs and trusted the locks on his garage door to keep it safe. He took a hot shower, walked to his bed on automatic pilot, and pulled back the covers. He remembered the money Porter's boyfriend had stuffed into his pocket the night before. He retrieved it from his parka and held a crisp hundred-dollar bill up to the light. Yale tossed it on the end table. He dove into bed, and his last conscious thought was that he was in the wrong business.

*Blood Shot Eyes*

Chapter Twenty

Yale rose early and called Metropolitan Hospital. He was worried about Wright and had slept fitfully. The phone in Wright's room rang ten times before it was picked up.

"Hello," Charlie Wright said, hoarsely.

"It's Ray, Charlie. How're you doing?"

"Better. That AZT kicked my ass. It happens sometimes, but this was a bad one."

"Lack of heat didn't help," Yale said. "I felt like laying out that shithead Moldy, but he wasn't worth the effort."

"It's really not his fault." His voice was weak but steady. "The owner of the building, some slumlord in Scarsdale, doesn't give a rat's ass about the place. Doesn't give Moldy any money to maintain the place. Moldy's a nosey son of a bitch, but he's okay. Listen, I wanna thank you for what you did. If you hadn't showed, I'd be a popsicle by now. I understand you carried me to the ambulance."

"I lugged you as far as Moldy's apartment. You needed thawing. EMS carried you the rest of the way."

"Most people knew what I had wouldn't even shake my hand."

"Forget it," Yale said.

213

"Well, the doc says my T-cells are on the way up again and there's no pneumonia. My lungs are okay, so maybe tomorrow I'll get out of here. He told me you did the paperwork. He also said something about me getting a private ambulance outta here. What's that all about?"

Yale told him what he had done and that he was putting him up at his house in the downstairs apartment.

"Ray, I really appreciate all you've done, but I can go home. It's okay, really."

"Humor me and take the apartment, okay? It's vacant anyway. What happens if the heat goes again in your place? No, no way, you're staying in Queens."

"But—"

"No buts. Look at it this way: I've got an investment in you. You're a better detective than I'll ever be, and between the two of us, we're breaking this case. Stay at least until you're feeling better, okay?"

Wright laughed. "That may never come, but okay, I appreciate it."

"No problem. Now let me tell you what happened while you were laying around your apartment living the good life." Yale gave him a detailed account of his adventure on the roof.

"And I thought I was cold."

"I froze my ass off, but it was worth it. Without the Super Bug, we'd be right where we were last week." He started to explain how the device worked.

"Hold on, buddy," Wright said. "You're talking to a guy who got confused when they changed Beckys on *Roseanne*. I have no idea what the hell you're talking about. Tell me more about the boyfriend."

"Don't know any more. Porter didn't use his name on the phone. The thermos should give us a positive ID though. And I think he's involved. What do you think we should do next?"

The line went quiet.

"Let me think about," Wright said. "You gonna be home?"

"For a while anyway. I want to get the thermos to a friend of mine to lift the boyfriend's prints." He felt mentioning Sheehan's name on the phone would be unwise. "If you should get here and I'm not around, the key'll be in the garage on a hook. I'll leave the garage door unlocked. You'll see it."

"Okay, but I'm not taking any ambulance. If I'm well enough to leave here, I'm well enough to take a cab."

"Just get here," Yale said. "I'll have the juice turned on down there and stick some food in the refrigerator. Bon appetit." He hung up.

Yale used a piece of cardboard to fingerprint himself. The process, known as "elimination printing," would differentiate his prints from those of the unknown boyfriend on the thermos. Lacking regulation fingerprint ink, he used a stamp pad in its place. Sheehan, he knew, would get the idea.

Yale wrapped the thermos in a large paper bag, secured it with string, and put his prints in a manila envelope. He put on a sweater and leather bomber jacket, and as a last thought, he shoved his service revolver in a holster and threaded it through his belt. He was getting used to being armed again, and now it felt strange to go outside without the clumsy gun. He dropped the package at a Dunkin' Donuts on Northern Boulevard.

Sheehan had told him via payphone that he would do him the favor of processing the prints, but he couldn't afford to be seen with him. Yale filled him in on his progress in the case, leaving out the blatantly illegal eavesdropping and the unauthorized computer work. If anything came of the investigation, he would let Sheehan have the glory. A fair deal all the way around. He drove on to Manhattan and returned the Super Bug to Ralph Nieves, who didn't ask how the device had performed. A true professional, Yale thought, the less he knew, the better.

215

Yale tried calling Arnold Carpenter when he returned to his house. No answer and no answering machine. He liked the old man and thought he would be pleased to know that there was some movement in the case. He typed the case reports, indicating his progress to date, leaving out his methods and concentrating on results. He was on edge all afternoon thinking about Porter's boyfriend and his reaction to Cippolone's phone call. Surely, a man with such a violent temper could be capable of being involved in murder. He lacked any certain connection between the mystery man and the park killings; hell, he really had nothing on Porter either, other than some circumstantial evidence. What he had was a cop's instinct, an instinct that told him the odd couple on 69th Street was almost certainly in on the murders together.

He looked at his watch: 5:50 p.m. He had expected a phone call from Sheehan about the fingerprints by this time. As if on cue, the phone rang.

"Yale Investigations."

"Ray, it's Charlie. I'm signing myself the hell out of here. Be there in about two hours. Gotta stop at my place and get some clothes."

"Hey, hold on, I thought you said tomorrow."

Wright complained about everything from hospital food to doctors who didn't speak English. "I'm okay enough to leave here. Just wanted to see if you were there. See ya." He hung up before Yale could respond.

Wright arrived via gypsy cab at eight o'clock. Yale told him to stretch out on the recliner in his living room while he carted his gear to the downstairs apartment. Yale was carrying an armload of clothes up the outside stairs when Wright called out from the apartment.

"Yo, Ray, phone call. Some guy named Abdul."

Yale bounded up the stairs. That's gotta be Sheehan, he thought. He grabbed the phone from Wright. "Yale."

"Abdul, here." It was Sheehan talking in a coarse whisper. "We got bad news. No hit on the package you gave me."

Yale's heart sank. "Whaddaya mean, 'no hit.' I gave you five clean ones," he said referring to the five fingers Porter's boyfriend wrapped around the thermos. He heard Wright in the kitchen singing, "Someday My Prints Will Come."

"Oh, yeah? Well, three were smudged. We need five good ones, you know that. Two's okay if you got something to compare them with. I'm not McGarrett, and this ain't *Hawaii 5-0*. You got something else?"

Yale thought for a second. "I've got a videotape, but all you can see is shades and a cowboy hat."

"Well, I tried," Sheehan said. "For a while there, I thought we had something. What're you gonna do now?"

Yale felt tired. "Don't know."

"If you come up with anything else, let me know," Sheehan said. "We still haven't got shit." There was a few seconds of silence. "Say, Ray, you're not holding anything back on me, are you?"

"No," Yale lied, "you have everything." He wasn't about to tell him about Porter and have some rookie detective screw things up.

Yale stared at the dead phone and considered his options. He could approach Cippolone and try to scare him into telling him the truth, but what would that accomplish? He still couldn't prove anything. He couldn't place Porter or Cippolone at the scene independently, which he would have to do to satisfy a prosecuting DA. He got a sudden chill at the thought of borrowing the Super Bug again and spending any more time on the roof.

Wright came in from the kitchen holding a steaming cup of coffee. "I heard your end. No good on the prints?"

Yale shook his head and told him what Sheehan had reported.

Wright sat on the couch and sipped the coffee. "I have an idea."

Yale felt a glimmer of hope. "What?"

"Let's go to the videotape, sports fans."

Yale got the video camera and connected it to the television. "I don't know why we're doing this. I've looked at the damn tape twenty times. The boyfriend's face is a big black blotch. Too much light behind him when he came to the window."

Wright smiled. "Maybe he's a black guy."

"Very amusing."

Wright sat cross-legged in front of the television. "I wanna see it any way."

I might as well humor him, Yale thought, as he turned on the power and went to the kitchen to make tea. I've seen the tape enough times, let Wright play detective if he wants.

"Hey," Wright called from the living room, "come in here a minute."

Yale went to the living room and stood in front of the television. The tape was in freeze frame. It showed the tall man getting out of the limo. He was still unrecognizable. "Yeah, so?"

"See," Wright said, "you got a shot of the back of the car, too."

Yale knelt on the carpet. The back end of the limousine was a blur of gray. He shrugged. "So?"

"Can't we get his enlarged or something? Maybe we'd see a plate."

Yale shook his head. "See how grainy the picture is? We enlarge that, it'll look like a snowball. No good."

"I can't believe that. You're the techno-nut, the computer guy. Hasn't somebody invented something to make sense of this shit?"

"Nah, forget about it. Want some more coffee?"

Wright got up. "Fuck the coffee. You're giving up, I can see it.

218

You're the one who kept telling me to shape up, now I'm telling you. We got a case here. Let's do something with it."

Yale knew he was right. He rubbed his temples. "Let me think for a second."

"We need a computer nerd," Wright said, "or a—"

Yale snapped his fingers. "I've got it! Nick Abrutti has the latest in computers, and I know he's got a resident genius on staff."

"It's worth a shot. Call him."

Yale hurried to the phone. Abrutti was in and would wait for them. Yale came out of his office and grabbed Wright's arm. "Let's go. Bring the camera."

#

Nick met them on the threshold of his office. He hugged Yale. "Who's your friend?" he said, staring at Wright.

"Don't you recognize Charlie Wright?"

Wright smiled, tight-lipped. "Hiya, Nicky." He stuck out his hand.

Nick eyed the former detective and shook his hand warily. "Uh-huh." He waved them into his office, all the time staring at the emaciated Wright. He removed his black silk jacket and carefully folded it inside out and laid it across a vacant chair. "Now, what do you need?"

"We got a videotape," Yale said. "We want to see if you can make out a license plate. It's too grainy now, we need something to enlarge—"

"Enhance," Wright said.

Yale shot him a look. "Yeah, enhance a piece of videotape."

Abrutti screamed for his secretary. "Tina! Is Marty Burke in the back?"

"Christ, Nick, can't you use the intercom?" Yale said.

219

Abrutti shrugged. "I don't trust anything I gotta talk into. Can't help it."

The secretary's sweet voice floated through the intercom. "He's in his office, Nick. Want me to get him?"

"No, we'll go back there."

They followed Abrutti through a series of partitioned cubicles containing ex-cops trying to look busy. Everyone was dressed in suits, the uniform of mobsters. They entered a small enclosure in back of a spacious office. It was windowless and coffin-like and was loaded with computer equipment. Hanging like tentacles from assorted electronic equipment was enough wire, Yale thought, to provide power to Yankee Stadium. Huddled over the keyboard was a bear of a man who made the twenty-inch monitor beside him look like a hand-held slide viewer.

"Guys," Abrutti said, "this is Marty Burke, the best computer guy in the business." He leaned toward Yale and whispered, "He's very hackadacious."

Yale was about to ask what "hackadacious" meant but assumed Burke was a hacker. Abrutti had a language all his own.

Burke rose, and it seemed like he kept on rising. He was at least six-four, maybe a little more than 300 pounds. Yale thought he looked a little like the actor John Goodman, only bigger. He had the map of Ireland on his face, complete with freckles and a shock of unruly red hair.

Burke looked over the top of his glasses and said with a brogue as thick as his thighs, "Pleased to meet you." The big man shook hands all around with a snowshoe-sized paw.

"You don't have to shake my hand, Marty, you work for me." Abrutti said. "Let me tell you guys somethin'…this fuckin' guy's a genius. He can break into any computer in the world. He's proved it dozens of times. I handle more cases right from this room than I do on the street. I buy this guy any equipment he wants, and he sits back here for sometimes fourteen hours a day and plays with the stuff. I offered him two large a week, and he says he'd take a grand if I just leave him alone. The fuckin' guy may be strange, but he's a whiz. Me and him are like brothers. He'll do anything for me. We're like this." He intertwined two fingers.

Burke smiled. "Now, what is it I can do for you gentlemen?"

Yale told him. "Can you help us?"

Burke gestured with club-like fingers. "Give it here." The camera looked like a miniature 35mm in his large hands, but he handled it with dexterity and care. He put his eye to the view finder. "Piece of cake."

"See," Nick said, beaming, "he's a fuckin' genius."

Burke connected the camera to his computer using three cables.

"Explain to the guys what you're doin', Marty," Abrutti said.

The redhead went into a two-minute dissertation on how he planned to enhance the tape, leaving Yale confused and Wright scratching his head.

Abrutti, however, grinned like he had written the script. He pointed to a computer. "How much that thing cost me?"

"The entire setup?" Burke said. "About nine thousand."

Abrutti gave Yale a jab in the ribs with his elbow. "See? Only the best for my man Marty."

"To make the connection," Burke said, "you need this RCA plug jack—"

"Of course," Abrutti said.

Yale rolled his eyes.

"—and you apply these key strokes." He demonstrated. "See, your picture comes up on the monitor." The tape was running on the monitor as it would on a television screen. They saw the tall man get out of the car and begin to walk. Burke froze the portion of the tape that showed the back of the limousine.

"Can you do something with that?" Wright asked.

Burke framed the rear of the car with a mouse and hit more keys until the back end of the car enlarged, but the quality was very grainy. He continued to press keys, and the picture became gradually clearer. In three minutes, they could see the license plate, but it was unreadable.

"See this printer?" Burke said, caressing a piece of equipment. "It'll give me forty-eight hundred DPI. Very sharp imaging." He activated the printer, and a picture came out in seconds. Yale grabbed it.

It was a New York plate that read: WROK.

"What's WROK?" Wright asked, looking over his shoulder. "A Chinese restaurant?"

"No, it's a radio station," Abrutti said. "That tall guy has to be The Wolfmeister...Wolfgang Steiner."

"Who's the Wolfmeister?" Wright asked.

"He's on the radio," Yale said. "I'll explain later."

They left Burke to his high-tech toys and went back to Nick's office. Abrutti sat behind his enormous desk while Yale studied the enhanced picture of the license plate and Wright counted the photos of movie stars on the walls. Yale wondered what other surprises he was going to get on this case.

"Steiner involved in the park murders?" Abrutti asked.

Yale folded the computer copy and put it in his pocket. "I don't know, Nick."

"C'mon, Ray, don't jerk me around. He's involved, ain't he?"

Yale knew Abrutti was chomping at the bit to get included in a high-profile case. There's nothing Nicky liked better than getting his picture in the paper for a million dollars' worth of free publicity.

"I know the guy," Abrutti said. "I can help you."

Yale looked around at Abrutti's framed pictures of celebrities on the walls. Nick's definition of "knowing someone" usually meant being able to nod at a celebrity while standing at adjoining urinals. Still, it couldn't hurt to ask. "How well do you know him?"

Abrutti shifted in his leather chair. "Well, uh, I sort of ran into him at a party once. But we bullshitted for an hour—"

"At least," Wright said.

"—or so. I could probably get a source at his radio station. C'mon, lemme know what's goin' on."

Regardless of his ability to self-promote, Yale thought, Nick was a damn good investigator and probably could come up with someone who would talk to them at WROK. On the other hand, what if it all appeared on *Hardcopy* before they had a chance to nail everybody involved?

"Nick, listen, I'll be straight with you," Yale said. "We really don't know what we've got at the moment. Yeah, we think Steiner's involved. We also have that psycho policewoman close to the scene of the murders, plus one other guy. What we don't have is motive. We don't need another finger in the pie. It's too late for that."

Abrutti held up a hand. "Okay, I get the message, but I tell ya, I could get us on every TV talk show in the country, not to mention big bucks from the supermarket shit-sheets. You're sittin' on a MOW here."

Wright lifted himself from his chair and looked down. "I am?"

"Movie of the Week, Charlie," Yale said. He had enough experience with the term when his wife was sick and some production companies wanted to bring her story to the screen. In the end, they had decided against doing a movie; they wanted to keep their lives private "Publicity isn't my thing, Nick. I just want to do the case and get on with my life."

Abrutti looked to Wright. "You too?"

"Yeah, me too."

"Hey, I tried." Abrutti got up and came around his desk. "If you need any help, I'm here. I won't say anything, no problem."

Nick had the last word. "Charlie, you take care. You don't look so good." The three ex-cops shook hands.

He knows about the AIDS, Yale thought. He's too sharp not to. Wright either ignored it or didn't get Abrutti's implication. Yale guessed the former. During the short walk to the car, Wright kept firing questions at him.

"So who's this Steiner guy?"

It took Yale a few minutes to tell him all he knew about the Emperor of the Airwaves. Wright took it all in without comment. "Let's talk about the case. We have to decide what's next."

"I give up, what's next?"

"First thing I gotta do is call the client, Carpenter. I tried him yesterday. No answer. I think he'll be happy with the progress we're making. And I want to get some more money out of him. The hours are adding up, and I don't wanna hit him all of a sudden at the end of this thing." If there was an end to it, he thought.

"What's the second thing we gotta do?"

"I came up with the first thing. Your turn."

"I think we should roust Cippolone," Wright said. "We'll double team him and force a confession out of him."

"What've we got to bargain with?"

"We could threaten him with a parole violation. Maybe he'll talk."

"And maybe he won't. You wanna take that chance? Look, he decides to warn Porter, we're screwed. Maybe he's a stand-up guy and takes a blast of five and keeps his mouth shut. We don't know the guy. Uh-uh, no good."

224

"So what do you suggest?"

"I suggest we eat." They stopped at a Chinese take-out place about three blocks from Yale's house and dined sitting on his living room floor, contemplating strategy.

"I've got an idea," Wright said.

"What?"

"I think we should break into Porter's apartment."

"Why?"

Wright chewed on a sparerib. "I think the place deserves a toss. Women save things. Maybe she's got something up there worth looking at."

"Like what? A diary, maybe? This girl's nuts, but I wouldn't be expecting her to write down every thought about her involvement in a double murder."

"We have to find out about Steiner's connection to the killings. He's gotta be connected some way. Why the hell would he get involved with a nutso lady cop and whack two people? From what you tell me, this guy's got the world by the balls. It makes no sense. I think it's worth a shot. There could be something up there."

"What I know about him I read in the papers," Yale said. "Look, I specifically tried to stay out of that apartment when I bugged the place."

"Why?"

"For one, I'm not a burglar. I'd probably get caught. Two, I wouldn't know how to break into the place."

Wright tossed a bone into a paper bag. "I would."

Yale's eyebrows shot up. "You would?"

"Spent three years in Safe and Loft. Learned a lot." He searched through the maze of cartons and bags. "We got more ribs?"

Yale handed him a carton. "You can get into the apartment?"

225

"No problem. I've got enough tools at my apartment to unlock the Federal Reserve Bank." He had a rib in each hand and was alternating like a harmonica player on speed. Yale was glad to see he had an appetite.

"I'll do it," Yale said "Show me how, and I'll go in."

Wright wiped his hands on a paper bag and took a long pull on a can of Diet Coke. "How come Chinese food always makes you thirsty?" He shook his head. "I don't think you should go. I'll do it."

"It's my case."

"But unlike you, my friend, if I'm caught, I've got nothing to lose. If I get locked up for burglary, it's no big deal. Hell, look on the bright side, I'll probably die before I can come to trial. Let me do this, okay? I wanna nail those bastards worse than you do."

Yale pondered the suggestion. "Okay, if you wanna do it, be my guest. I think before you go in we should find out a little more about Steiner and see if we can get more evidence on Cippolone. He's the weak link here. We get him positively involved, and can prove it, he'll flip...guaranteed."

"And how do you propose to do that, Sherlock?" Wright poked through the ruins. "Got any mustard?"

Yale tossed him a plastic packet of hot Chinese mustard. "Maybe you could re-interview the cop from the One-Ten. It could be he saw something he forgot to tell you."

"Moran? You gotta be kidding! It takes that asshole an hour and a half to watch *60 Minutes*. Believe me, I got outta him all I'm gonna get. What we should do is go to the street where Moran and his partner cooped that night, you know, the broad's house where they conked out, see if we can find anyone remembers seeing anything."

"I'll do that," Yale said.

They agreed that no matter what happened with their inquiries, they would hit Porter's apartment within the next few days. After they cleaned up their dinner mess, Wright excused himself and went downstairs complaining that his stomach bothered him. No kidding, Yale thought, you just deprived a Chinese family of four their week's rations.

Yale showered, put on a robe, and padded to his office. He thumbed through his address book and called the person who would know plenty about Wolfgang Steiner. The same person who had gone out of his way to treat he and his wife with dignity during her illness. He hadn't see Jason Davis since his wife's death, but Yale knew he could depend on the local reporter to know the background, dirt and all, of most New York celebrities. Crime might be Davis' beat, but he made it his business to be on top of gossip, too.

The pleasant female voice said, "Good evening, NBC. How may I direct your call?"

"Jason Davis, please."

## Chapter Twenty-One

Leah Porter examined her puffy face in the bathroom mirror when she got up the next morning. Her right cheekbone was a sickly hue of yellow, orange, and black, swollen and grotesquely misshapen. She tenderly touched her split bottom lip. Blood had congealed in the corner of her mouth while she slept. Leah's nose hurt, and she prayed it wasn't broken. Her body ached from the furious abuse inflected by her lover.

She would stay inside today and hoped she's look better tomorrow. Solitude was also needed to plot the impending demise of Tony Cippolone. What happened last night was all his fault. There was no way I'm going to lose Daddy, er Wolf, over that piece of shit, she promised herself.

She soaked in a tub for what seemed like hours, constantly running warm water as she attempted to wash away her pain. The soothing warmth made her feel better, and after thirty minutes of stretching on her living-room floor, most of the joint pain had vanished.

She busied herself rearranging her stuffed animal collection. You could cuddle them and they wouldn't hurt you, unlike her father and the other men in her life; they were lovable and there for her, just like Wolf could be at times. She favored life-sized animals, which comprised much of her collection.

Satisfied with the way her animals looked against a living-room wall, Porter took a pile of magazines she hadn't had the time to read to the window seat overlooking 69th Street. One periodical was *Spring 3100*, the official NYPD publication. She had three back issues.

She smirked. Once a cop, always a cop, particularly when it came to *Spring*, as cops on The Job called it. You could be suspended, locked up, or accused of shooting the mayor; as long as you renewed your subscription, the magazines would come quarterly until the day you died.

Porter liked to keep current on the inner workings of the NYPD. As much as she disliked The Job for the trouble it had caused her, she still missed it occasionally. She thought most ex-cops felt the same way.

She was thumbing through the pages of the oldest issue first, trying to spot exploits about former colleagues, when a story caught her eye.

A glossy white page was ringed in black, and the story dealt with a female police officer who had recently passed away from cancer. The cop's name was Vivian Yale. Porter didn't know her. The story told of her valiant fight against the disease and her battle to get The Job to change retirement rules regarding long-term sick cops. Porter stroked her bruised face. And I thought I had problems, she mused.

There was a picture of the cop in uniform at an award ceremony. Pretty, Porter thought. What a shame she should die so young. She didn't look more than thirty. The man standing in civilian clothes next to her was identified as her husband. She thought they made a nice couple and wondered if she and Wolf could ever have their picture taken together.

Porter's back tightened. An icy finger began a slow journey from the base of her neck to her waist.

The man in the picture was the same guy who she had spotted across the street from her house last week. She was almost sure of it.

She slanted the magazine into the sunlight. *Jesus Christ!* It was definitely him. She needed time to think. She needed to know what this—she glanced at the captioned picture—Ray Yale was doing now.

The cops! The ones who had given Yale a ride that day in front of her building! She was on the telephone to the 20th Precinct in seconds, impersonating a clerk from the Department of Personnel. Within minutes, she had the names of the cops who had the sector the day she spotted Yale. They worked steady days, she was told, and they were on their last tour before a three-day "swing."

She caught one of them on the phone when the tour ended and the day platoon was lining up to sign out. She had gotten a brief glance at the driver of the radio car that day and knew him to be a young officer. Young cops are scared to death of losing their jobs, she knew, particularly those on probation.

She was going to scare the hell out of this one.

After identifying herself as a detective from the Internal Affairs Bureau, she said that a civilian named Yale had alleged that he had lost his wallet in their radio car (she recited the number of the car she got with her first phone call) and that it was never returned. If she wasn't so nervous herself, she would have found some humor in the panicked reaction from the young cop. He stuttered and stammered, professing no knowledge of a wallet, but he gave her most of the information she needed. She now knew Yale was a private investigator on a surveillance that day, subject unknown. Yale hadn't imparted that information. Neither had she gotten Yale's address from the cop, something he should have noted in his memo book, but hadn't. She told the cop to thoroughly search the radio car, and if they came up with the wallet, to call her at IAB, but she thought the case would be closed as "unfounded." Hell, she said cheerily, wallets could be lost anywhere. The cop was relieved. She invented a phone number and hung

230

up.

Porter grabbed her giant Panda and sat on the floor facing a blank television screen. She thought better with her favorite stuffed toy.

After several minutes, she called telephone information and had them search the five boroughs for Yale's home or office number. No home number, but his office was listed. She dialed.

*Shit!* An answering service. She cursed cops and their paranoia. She'd get his address some other way. She speculated as to why Yale would be watching her. Wolf's wife? Had she found out about their relationship? Porter doubted it. Wolf was extremely careful, and from what he had said, his wife wasn't that bright. Zoltag? Did Yale know about Zoltag? About the others? She ticked off in her mind every illegal act she could remember, no matter how trivial. All she succeeded in doing was making herself crazed.

Damage control, she thought. Eliminate mistakes and loose ends. If Yale was close to the truth about Zoltag or the others that meant Tony Cippolone was helping him. She knew that feeble excuse for a man would fold after ten minutes of interrogation. She also realized that if the PI had talked to Cippolone, she would be in jail by now. It was only a matter of time. She should have listened to Wolf when he had said Tony couldn't be trusted. Wolf knew everything; that's why he was where he is today, she concluded. She could take care of her problems without Wolf ever finding out about the PI.

Tony first. Then Yale.

Porter went to the kitchen, poured a glass of mineral water, and got comfortable on her bed. She thumbed through her phonebook and then dialed Tony Cippolone.

"Hello."

One word and she knew he was high. His voice was high-pitched and breathless, a symptom of too much cocaine. "It's Leah, Tony."

There was a momentary silence. "I thought you were pissed off at me. You know, from the other night."

Porter laughed. She wanted to sound relaxed to put him at ease. She hoped she sounded convincing. "If I was pissed off, you'd know it. I was expecting company when you called. I'm sure you understand." She changed hands with the phone and picked up her glass of water.

"Listen," Cippolone said, "I'll forget who I saw going into your building, okay? Your friends are your business."

He'll probably say anything to get laid, she thought. "You didn't tell anybody you saw him come into the building, did you, Tony?"

"Who the hell am I going to tell? You know I can keep my mouth shut. I don't wanna know nothin'."

"It's just that my friend likes his privacy."

"Yeah, yeah, sure. Hey, can I come over? Or do you wanna come over here? We could meet someplace if you want or maybe you want a cupla drinks or somethin' else first…."

He rambled on for another minute, talking so fast that Porter had trouble understanding what he was saying. Junkie diction, she called it. The more coke they do, the less sense they make. She thought of the young blonde in the car with Zoltag. "Slow down, sweetheart. Sounds like you've been partying."

"A little, you know. Say, maybe we should make it tomorrow? I just remembered something I gotta do tonight."

"I thought you were anxious to see me." She wanted to get this over with. Another day might have that Yale guy closer to him.

"Um, well, could you…uh…."

Shit, she thought, his dick must be like a dead puppy from the coke, and there's no way he can admit it. She tried to convince him to see her tonight. No amount of cajoling worked. "Okay, then," she said, exasperation creeping into her voice, "tomorrow. And don't tell anyone I'm coming over, okay?"

"Yeah, sure. Tomorrow night, right?"

"Yeah, I'll call you first. Good—"

He hung up.

## Chapter Twenty-Two

Yale drove to Manhattan on a freshly fallen thin blanket of snow for his meeting with Jason Davis. He smiled as he recalled Davis peppering him on the phone with questions as to why Yale needed information on Wolfgang Steiner's background. Davis would have to wait for a face-to-face meeting. Yale felt the subject too hot to discuss over the telephone. If Yale could bug an apartment, anyone could. Besides, it would give Davis time to do a little research.

He crept along in traffic toward the Midtown Tunnel and noted the sound-numbing quality that virgin snow offered a noisy city. Within hours, the silence of rubber on a cushion of white would yield to the annoying sound of slush and rock salt slamming against windshields and grills. For now, however, the quiet was welcome because it gave him time to think and to try and get insight into the mind of Wolfgang Steiner.

Yale spent thirty minutes listening to WROK, hanging onto every word Steiner uttered in a vain attempt to read between the lines of what invariably proved to be a mindless radio show. There was nothing in Steiner's ridiculous, obscene patter that would indicate a propensity toward violence or his involvement in two murders. Yale figured he was mercifully saved from more dick jokes when his car entered the tunnel and the radio signal was lost.

Traffic inside the tunnel was like his rotund Uncle Alphonse, heavy but moving. Yale hit a wall of creeping cars when he emerged from the tunnel and decided to try his client again from the cell phone.

"Hello," Arnold Carpenter said, his voice sounding weary.

"Ray Yale, Mr. Carpenter."

Yale heard the old man's voice perk up at the sound of his name. "Mr. Yale. How are you? Good news perhaps?"

"Perhaps." Yale recounted his progress so far, omitting any illegal acts performed for anyone that might be listening and to spare his client co-conspirator status.

"So, you think this Steiner person could be involved? I've read things about him in the papers, most of them not flattering. It's difficult to imagine my Katherine being involved with such a person. Why would he do such a thing?"

"The one thing we don't have, Mr. Carpenter," Yale said, "is a motive. We're continuing to make progress, and you and I will talk more in person."

"Once again, you've given me hope, Mr. Yale. May God bless you and your efforts."

I'm gonna need all the help I can get, Yale thought. "I'll be in touch." He put the phone in the glove compartment just as he swung into East 58th Street. He parked in a garage located next to the restaurant where he was meeting Davis.

The up-scale Italian trattoria was packed when Yale arrived. He was ten minutes late, and the lunch rush was in full swing, consisting mostly of the "ladies who lunch," taking a breather from spending their husbands' money at Bloomingdale's. Yale scanned the crowd for Davis but didn't see him. For once, he had arrived first to a meeting.

235

Yale had been to the restaurant twice with Davis, the last time well over a year ago, and was surprised when he was recognized by the owner, a small, dapper Italian named Giovanni who rushed from behind the bar to greet him.

"Mr. Yale, buongiorno. Welcome to Tre Scalini. You come maybe to meet Mr. Davis?"

"Si." That was the extent of Yale's Italian, other than a slew of swear words he had picked up from his father.

"He's not here yet, but his table is always ready in the back. Come." The restauranteur weaved his way through the narrowly spaced tables to a small alcove behind the main dining room. Davis' favorite table was located adjacent to the kitchen. Likely considered "Siberia" by those trying to make an impression, the location was perfect for the reporter because it was far away from prying ears.

Yale seated himself and looked over the top of his menu. He saw Davis working his way toward the back, stopping at tables to shake hands with fans and admirers. Everyone wants to be on television, Yale thought, except me.

"Sorry I'm late. Traffic." Davis draped the obligatory newsman's Burberry trench coat across an empty chair. They shook hands.

Yale considered telling him he had been waiting for a while. He looked at his watch. What the hell, he thought, a little dig couldn't hurt "That's okay. Been here twenty minutes, though."

Davis laughed, pinched the creases in his pants and sat down. "Who're you kidding? You've never been on time a day in your life." He was wearing a three-button, charcoal gray Brooks Brothers suit with a white button-down shirt and a rep tie. His curly dirty-blonde hair was in its usual disarray, and his unlined face belied his age. He smiled broadly. "So, how are you, Raymond?" Davis spoke slowly and deliberately, the way he did when reporting a story on television. Yale knew him to be a Brooklyn native who had actively worked at losing his New York accent. It was gone now, thanks to a highly paid speech therapist, replaced by something that sounded to Yale like a Bostonian college professor on Quaaludes.

"Good, Jason, yourself?" They exchanged pleasantries until the waiter took their drink orders and departed.

Davis got to the point first. "Tell me why you want to know about Steiner."

"You first. What've you got?"

Without referring to notes, Davis dove into a recitation. "Wolfgang Steiner, the Wolfmeister, the Emperor of the Airwaves, born 1955 in a small town in upstate New York. Raised Jewish, not religious. Moved to Yonkers with his parents in 1974. Average student, two years of college, both parents deceased—"

"How'd they die?"

Davis looked at him strangely. "Mother, breast cancer. Father, heart attack. Why?"

Yale wouldn't put anything past Steiner. "Nothing, just curious."

"He broke into broadcasting when he was twenty-four, worked in some small towns in the Midwest. He had a well-deserved reputation as an in-your-face kind of jock before some New York radio exec picked him up, and the rest, as they say, is history."

"Married?"

"One wife, supposedly brain dead, and three kids living in Connecticut spending his money. Married when he was twenty-five."

"He's a family man?"

"Depends on how you define the term. Yes, he's got a family, but he's involved in so many different projects, he's rarely home. I understand his wife doesn't care too much, just as long as he brings home the money, which, by the way, will be about ten million this year."

Yale let out a soft whistle.

"He's at the pinnacle of his career," David said. "From what I hear, he's got three movie deals in the works, plus a pay-per-view special on New Year's eve. His biography was the hottest selling book out of the gate in publishing history. The guy's got the world by the proverbial testicles."

"Enemies?"

"Bound to have them, wouldn't you think? There's plenty of jealousy in show biz. The more successful you are, the more people can't wait for you to take a fall. Comes with the territory." Davis made an elaborate production of removing a cigar from a silver case, cutting the end, and lighting it. He puffed with apparent pleasure and smiled. Yale declined an offered stogie.

The tuxedo-clad waiter wheeled up a cart and put dishes laden with food on the table. They each got a plate of fragrant carpaccio smothered with Parmesan cheese and olive oil. He put a basket of hard-crusted bread in the center of the table. Davis put aside his cigar and began to dig in.

"We didn't order any of this," Yale said.

"I never order anything here. Giovanni brings me what he's having. I think that's a pretty good testimonial, don't you?"

Yale tasted a piece of thinly sliced raw beef. "Good stuff," he said. He looked forward to the rest of the meal. "What I meant was, any enemies in particular?"

"The line forms to the left. The guy offends everybody. Don't you ever listen to the show?"

"Not if I can help it," Yale said. "I appreciate the biography, but what I need is the dirt. Stuff about his background, not generally known."

"Quid pro quo, Raymond, my man." Davis' eyes bore into his.

238

Yale examined the man who had saved his wife's job and consequently his own. Davis had publicized Vivian's case with zeal, thereby getting a change in ancient department rules that would have forced her out. Also, without the reporter's influence in city politics, Yale would certainly have been fired for insubordination. He owed him a lot. But deep inside, he was still a cop with a cop's distrust of the media. The Job had taught him to be wary of media-types because they were only out for themselves. Yale wondered if Davis could be trusted with a potentially career-making story. I've got to get rid of that cop mindset, he told himself. The man sitting opposite him might be the best friend he ever had. Their relationship transcended the cop-reporter thing, and it was about time he let his guard down.

"I've got a story to tell you, Jason, a story you're not going to believe." Yale spent the next half hour relating events as they unfolded, beginning with the meeting in Flushing Meadow Park with Arnold Carpenter, which now seemed so long ago. Davis sat with rapt attention as Yale graphically laid out every detail of the investigation. He left nothing out. When Yale concluded, he had an overwhelming urge for another Scotch.

"Jesus Christ," Davis said, "that's a helluva story. Got any proof?"

"That's why I wanted to see you. I need motive. It's evident to me that Steiner's got Leah Porter doing his dirty work. Her motivation is probably greed and a warped sense of love. But what's his? What made him get involved in killing Zoltag? I know he was the target, not Katherine Carpenter. I need a connection." Yale leaned back in his chair. "Maybe there's something in his background that can give me a better idea of who I'm dealing with. Maybe even come up with a motive for murder."

"I've heard he's supposed to have a woman on the side. From what you tell me, it's undoubtedly this Porter person."

The waiter appeared with their main courses They scooped up medallions of veal, chicken swimming in a light cream sauce, and three different kinds of pasta from a platter in the center of the table.

"He's got a rather nasty background," Davis said.

"Arrests?"

Davis raised a finger, his mouth stuffed with veal marsala. He chewed slowly, savoring the milk-fed meat, and then dabbed his mouth with a linen napkin. "Arrests would have been made public by this time. No, he was just a mean bastard." He went into his jacket pocket and pulled out a small notebook. "What I'm going to tell you came from notes prepared by a reporter who was going to do a story on Steiner for one of our tabloid shows. It got killed at the last minute because the network thought there weren't enough sources to back it up."

Yale was getting those familiar knots in his stomach again.

Davis looked at the notebook briefly, cleared his throat, and began. "Steiner was a wild child. A natural born leader-type, but a bully and a braggart. He was always in trouble in school, or I should say schools. He was disciplined or suspected of being involved in some serious pranks right through high school."

"Such as?"

Davis flipped a page. "Such as getting a hooker to bed his high school principal and getting him fired. It was never proven that he did it, but he supposedly mailed pictures of the principal and the hooker together to the local paper, and there was quite a scandal."

"Why'd he do something like that? The principal make him stay after school or something?"

Davis shrugged. "That's the odd thing, Raymond. There was no problem between them. At least the reporter doing this research couldn't come up with any reason."

240

"Why then?"

"Thrills. Our Mr. Steiner is a thrill seeker. At least he was as a youth. Unfortunately, at other people's expense, it seems to me."

Yale rubbed his chin. "What else?"

"The reporter talked to a high school friend of the feral Mr. Steiner. He told him that Steiner got aggravated with his neighbor in..." Davis checked his notes. "...Yonkers and killed his dog. A rather large German shepherd. Hung the dead canine from the neighbor's porch. The story couldn't be backed up with a second source, though."

"But you believe it?"

Davis nodded, took a sip of his drink, and said, "Oh, yes, Raymond. He and a gaggle of his knuckle-dragging buddies were involved in a lot of these mean-spirited pranks. Most of the facts of other disreputable deeds are obscured by the passage of time. That's why the network couldn't go with them for the story." He returned the notebook to his jacket pocket.

"He also thinks he's smarter than everyone else," Davis said. "I think that's evident from listening to his show. It's not an act, Raymond. He believes his distorted image of being an emperor."

Yale was getting a good picture of the personality of Wolfgang Steiner. While it might not provide a motive for murder, it still might help solve the case. Yale learned a long time ago as a rookie detective that if you can get into the brain of a suspect, you can defeat him by understanding how he thought. "Anything else?"

"Oh, yes. I've noticed that the breaks seem to come his way too often."

"How so?" Yale pushed away most of the cream sauce from the chicken with his fork.

"A while back, a guy named Marvin Tavlin was taking him to task about obscenity. No one paid much attention to him at first, but the fellow's campaign heated up, and sponsors started to drop Steiner. It was beginning to hurt his ratings. Then, all of a sudden, Tavlin turns up dead. Cops called it a mugging. End of problem for Steiner."

Yale was interested. "What did you call it?"

"At the time? The same thing. Then came the Danny Doremus fiasco."

"That one I read about," Yale said, "Doremus was sort of a wild man himself, wasn't he?"

"Wild, yes. A pedophile and a drug addict, no."

"I thought he had a drug problem?"

"That's the operative word, Raymond, had. He cleaned up his act long before he was arrested for the cocaine and pornographic pictures of little boys. I knew the man. There was no way he was using again, and as for the pedophile thing, that's ridiculous. Once he got rid of the drug and alcohol problem, he tightened up his show and was closing the ratings gap with Steiner. Doremus had talent. Not much shock value at the end, just good writing and great on-air personalities. I think he was set up."

"By Steiner?"

He nodded. "Or a crazed fan. When Danny got rid of his demons, Steiner sent him a quart of vodka. Said it was a congratulations present for kicking booze and drugs. That's the way the fellow thinks. He was hoping to get Danny drinking again. A real madman, if you ask me. The point is, once the scandal broke, Danny was ruined. He was tossed off the air, and Steiner's ratings went through the roof. Lucky break for him, don't you think?"

Yeah, real lucky, Yale thought.

"I'll see what I can find out about Zoltag for you," Davis said. "Who has the case?"

Yale waved his hand. "Forget the police. I've got more than they do. Hit your show biz and druggie sources. Find out more about Zoltag's background. There's got to be some kind of connection between him and Steiner." He was beginning to believe that Steiner was also behind the killing of Tavlin and the framing of Doremus. He wanted Davis' opinion.

"Sure, sounds reasonable. But if he did those things, we know why he did them. With those two out of the way, his career had no limits. But that doesn't tell us why Zoltag was killed. You know I want this story when and if we get something solid, correct?" He pushed his plate away and re-lit the cigar.

"Goes without saying. Just leave me out of it. Give the credit to Mike Sheehan, One-Ten Squad."

"Certainly. Well, Raymond, I must make some stops."

"Where?"

Davis smiled. "I never reveal my sources." He checked the time. "I'll give you a call tonight."

"I've been working on this case for weeks and you're going to come up with something useful in a few hours?"

Davis grinned and signaled for the waiter. "Power of the Press, Raymond. Stick with me, perhaps you'll learn something."

And we're never too old for that, Yale thought, are we?

Chapter Twenty-Three

The following morning, Yale stood shivering on the corner of
111th Street and 55th Avenue in Corona. According to Wright's notes, this
street was where the cops from the One-Ten were cooping the night of
the park killings. There were at least thirty homes on the block. Who
would possibly remember seeing Leah Porter on that street nine years ago,
he wondered. Still, he needed someone to corroborate Moran's
identification, only he didn't know where to start looking. He checked the
time. Eleven-thirty. Even if he talked to everyone who was home, he
would still have to come back and catch the afterwork crowd. This was a
middle-class neighborhood; most people had jobs and were already gone.
He was staring at shoveled driveways and clean streets when an idea hit
him.

When in doubt, ask the local sector cops.

He called the One-Ten precinct from his cell phone, stating he was
a retired member of the service and needed some assistance, no
emergency. Within ten minutes, a radio car rolled up to where Yale stood.
Two young women officers—Yale thought both their ages added together
wouldn't equal his jacket size—smiled after he showed them his retired
member's ID card.

"Ladies, I'm a private investigator working on an old homicide." He offered a business card to each. "I'm looking for the block yenta, someone who makes it their business to know everything that happens on this street."

They were new to the sector, the driver explained. In fact, most of the precinct consisted of cops who had less than ten years on The Job. They were sorry they couldn't help him, but they knew someone who might know.

He was directed to an Italian deli two blocks away. There, for the price of a nine-inch, cholesterol-laden, fat-festooned sandwich, Yale was able to get the name of a local widow who had resided on 111th Street for the past forty years and knew everyone. Yale would recognize the house, he was told, because it had a pink plastic flamingo on the front lawn. He stuck the sandwich inside his trench coat and went back to the block.

He knocked on the door of an old, but well-maintained, red brick home in the middle of the street. An old woman, who Yale figured to be in her seventies, answered the door.

"Mrs. Caccavale?"

"Yes?" she said, eyeing Yale suspiciously. She was wearing the uniform of the Italian widow: black dress covered with a heavy cardigan sweater, also black, and what looked like a ten-pound silver crucifix dangling from a thick chain around her neck. Her hair was in the requisite bun, and she had the hangdog expression of a woman who was still in deep mourning. Yale knew that tradition dictated she would grieve for her dead husband until she passed away.

He decided to be straight with her. After he showed her his private investigator's license and told her he was investigating the park murders, he was led into an immaculate living room adorned with religious artifacts and pictures of Connie Caccavale's deceased husband. He expressed his condolences and inquired as to her health. He politely refused an espresso.

They talked about her children and grandchildren for a while, and when the prerequisite pleasantries were dispensed with, Yale got right to the night of the murders.

"Of course I remember that night," she said. "How many double murders happen around here? Not many, I can tell you that. The last two killings I remember around here was Little Augie Piasano and his girlfriend back in fifty-seven, or maybe fifty-eight. They got it in his car, by the old Traveler's Hotel. Shotgun." She pointed a finger at Yale. "Bang."

Yale was impressed. "You remember that? It was a long time ago."

She smiled and sipped her espresso. "My Angelo, he knew Augie. They were in the same business."

Which to Yale meant mob business. Mob wives embraced violent death as an everyday fact of life. "Do you remember anything unusual about that night?"

"What do you mean, unusual?"

"What I need to know is if you saw a pretty lady walking on the block, someone that didn't belong. She had long dark hair."

"What time?"

"Late, maybe around two-thirty in the morning."

Connie Caccavale laughed. "Two-thirty in the morning? You gotta be fooling. I never used to make Johnny Carson. Two-thirty? Not me, I was long asleep."

He knew it was a long shot. "Well, thanks anyway." He got up to leave.

"When you say unusual, I remember one thing that was strange, but it happened much earlier."

He sat back down. "What happened?"

"I called the cops on a man, about ten o'clock."

"A man? What man?"

She shrugged. "A man. He was sitting in a car in front of my house. For hours, he was sitting there, smoking cigarettes. I thought maybe he was waiting for my Angelo, you know, to do something bad. I always remember Little Augie. I get scared and call the cops."

"What did the man look like?"

She smiled. "Ah, mister, it was so long ago. All I remember is the burning cigarette. So I called the cops."

"And they came?"

"Yeah, they came. Took them an hour, but they came."

"And...."

"And they took the man outta the car, and he put his hands on the roof." She stretched her arms out in front of her. "Like this. They searched him."

"What happened then?"

"Dunno. I saw the cops talking to him for maybe five minutes, then they let him go."

"Did he go?"

"No. He got back in the car and sat there. I went to bed about an hour later."

Yale questioned her about the make of the car and the man's clothes, walking her through a physical description menu: did he have facial hair, a hat, glasses? And on it went, but she didn't remember anything. It was so long ago.

Yale thanked her for her cooperation and left. He stood in front of her house momentarily and tried to crawl further into his trench coat to ward off the cold. He had an idea. Yale drove the half mile to the One-Ten Precinct station house.

The desk officer on duty remembered Yale from the publicity

surrounding his wife and said he would help in any way he could with his investigation. Anything for a retired member. Thank God, Yale thought, he was dealing with a rank-and-file cop and not a boss. He directed Yale to the stairway and said, "The archives are downstairs. The room's supposed to be locked, but the lock's busted. Just give it a good yank."

Yale soon found himself in a cramped room the size of his living room that had been set aside to store old forms and reports.

All commands, he remembered, were required to store copies of completed forms in an orderly and neat manner. Whoever was in charge of this room, Yale thought, forgot to read the Patrol Guide. The place was a filthy mess, with cardboard boxes piled on top of each other and an overpowering smell of dry rot. He took off his jacket and began to shuffle through the history of the One-Ten Precinct. Three hours later, he found what he was looking for.

The New York City Police Department Patrol Guide required that any officer who stops and questions an individual must fill out a "Stop and Frisk Report" if the person is not subsequently arrested. Yale recalled it was a three-page, snap-out form. Two copies were sent "downtown," wherever the hell that was, Yale mused, and the third copy was to stay in the precinct archives until an order came down to destroy old files. Yale prayed that the order had not been implemented for Stop and Frisk Reports, and for once a higher being granted his wish.

His dirt-streaked, paper-cut fingers held a Stop and Frisk Report dated October 29, 1986. The time read 2205 hours, and the reporting officer stated that he had stopped a suspicious man on 55th Avenue, between 111th and 112th Streets, after being dispatched by Communications, who had received an anonymous call. The unknown female caller stated that a male had been sitting in a parked car on that block and hadn't moved for hours. The officers established the man's identity and stated he told them he was waiting for a friend. The male was searched, found to be clean, and released.

The name on the report was Douglas Lindberg, known to Yale as Anthony Cippolone. The listed address was Cippolone's old apartment building.

Yale knelt on the grimy floor, staring at the important evidence. Finally, he had something concrete to place Cippolone near the scene of the homicide.

He went directly home and found a note taped to his apartment door. It said: Gone to the doctor. Later-W. Yale scribbled "upstairs" on the paper, left the door unlocked, stripped quickly, and took a fast shower.

He sat down in front of his computer, still in his robe, and began to probe the life of Wolfgang Steiner. Jason Davis, he knew, would get the street gossip on Steiner, but Yale wanted the facts, no matter how insignificant and obscure. Know your adversary.

His eyes were burning from staring at the monitor for too long. He glanced at the clock. He had spent the last three hours running Wolfgang Steiner's name through every database he could think of and had drawn a blank. Steiner had excellent credit, wasn't being sued, drove like the proverbial little old lady, and had no judgments or liens against him. His family also provided mundane information. He ran a criminal check on his wife, with negative results. His kids were too young to exist on paper, and Yale even found an uncle in New Hampshire who led the life of a monk.

Yale was still leaning toward the blackmail angle, but could find nothing in Steiner's past, at least through computer databases, that would provide him with a stepping stone.

He cradled his head in both hands and rubbed his eyes. There was a time not too long ago when he could sit in front of a computer screen for an entire day without his eyesight failing. Another sign of approaching old age, he thought. First his blood was turning to mud, now his eyes were going. What next? Wright's voice coming from the hallway saved him from total meltdown.

"Ray, it's me."

"In the office."

Wright took off his fatigue jacket and pulled up a chair.

Yale turned off the computer. "I went to Corona today."

"Congratulations."

"You'll be congratulating me all-to-hell in a minute, wise ass." He told Wright about the stop and Frisk Report. He handed him a photocopy.

Wright read it carefully. "Jesus. We've got him." He turned it over. "Where's the original?"

"We'll subpoena that when the time comes, buddy. We don't wanna be tampering with evidence, do we?"

"Makes sense. The cop still on The Job who made this out?"

"Retired in eighty-eight. Lives in Detroit. Want to go there to interview him?"

"I bet if he retired to Spain you'd wanna go."

"There's no need to talk to him. The form was prepared concisely enough so we don't have to interview him. He wouldn't remember one Stop and Frisk Report anyway, not after nine years." The officer described Cippolone accurately, even going so far as to write down "Doug Lindberg's" driver's license number. "The description fits Cippolone perfectly."

"Like a condom."

"I think it's time we paid him a visit. What do you think?"

"Now?" Wright asked. "I'm kinda tired. You think he's gonna bolt?"

"He hasn't gone anywhere in nine years, so I don't think so, but I want to move on this now. I can go alone if you don't feel up to it. We can both go to Porter's place tomorrow when you feel better." He took the form from Wright and put it in his pocket.

"Don't want to miss this, I'm coming." Wright picked his coat off the floor. "What do we do when we get there?"

'I think we should just wave the Stop and Frisk in his face and lay it all out. I think we can make a deal with him now. The choice is his. We tape his statement and take him to the One-Ten Squad."

"What about his rights?"

"We're civilians now, Charlie, we don't have to read anybody their rights." Yale went to the file cabinet and took out a micro-cassette tape recorder. He handed it to Wright. "There's a blank tape in there, and the batteries are new." He went to the bedroom, got dressed, and returned to his office to get his revolver.

"Let's stop at the diner on the way for something to go," Wright said. "I'm starved. You?"

Yale whipped out the Italian hero from the inside pocket of his trench coat. He flipped it to Wright. "Want mayo?"

"What's this, your off-duty sandwich?"

"It's a long story. Enjoy."

When they reached the bottom landing, the phone rang. Yale bounded back up the stairs two at a time. He got to the phone on the fourth ring. It was Jason Davis.

"Raymond? I was all set to hang up. What kept you?"

"I was counting my money." Yale heard the sounds of traffic in the background. "What've you got?"

"Something weird is going on. I'm in Yonkers."

"That's really odd. I was in Scarsdale once, talk about weird."

"Very amusing." Davis said. "I'm in Yonkers checking on Zoltag."

Yale sat down. "Why Yonkers?"

"Because he lived here at one time, Raymond, at about the same time Steiner did. I would have assumed you ran the late Mr. Zoltag on your computer."

"He's been dead for nine years. There was nothing to run. His credit isn't very good these days. What made you go up there?"

Wright came upstairs. "What's going on?"

Yale waved him to a chair.

"I checked our morgue. It seems we ran a story on the late Mr. Zoltag in seventy-five. A feature on photographers, weddings a specialty. The piece called Mr. Zoltag 'a Yonker's native.' Ergo, here I am."

"Were they friends?"

"They lived three blocks apart and went to the same high school."

"Jason," Yale said, "you're worth every cent of that ridiculously large salary your job pays you."

"You've got your connection, my friend. I assume my exclusive is imminent?"

Yale laughed. "Any day now." *If I don't get locked up for my next felony.* He hung up and turned to Wright. "We're getting closer." He summarized the conversation he just had with Davis. They did an adolescent high-five and tripped over each other going down the stairs.

## Chapter Twenty-Four

The object was to completely change her appearance so that she couldn't be identified on the closed-circuit television tapes at Tony Cippolone's hotel but without alarming him to the point where he suspected something was wrong. She figured that if she dressed sexy enough, Cippolone would be concentrating on her outfit, not her face. She was under the opinion that most men thought with their little heads, not their big ones.

She shimmied into black pantyhose, electing not to wear panties. The tight, black wool skirt she chose came to an abrupt halt eight inches above her knees, and a matching jacket, pinched at her waist, accentuated her curves. The jacket was single-breasted with gold buttons and a neckline that formed a V below her breast bone. It was made to be worn with a bra, but she vetoed the idea. Three-inch black leather heels completed the upwardly mobile hooker look. She doused herself liberally with Opium perfume, knowing a healthy amount was needed to make an impression on Cippolone's cocaine-decimated nose. She examined herself in a full-length mirror. *If he even glances at my face in this outfit, he needs a dick transplant.*

She applied a cream bronzer to her face to darken her features and conceal the freckles. To further confuse any would-be Dick Traceys, she slipped on a pair of wire-frame glasses that contained ordinary glass instead of prescription lenses. Her angular face concerned her, and she experimented with cotton balls stuffed into her cheeks to fill out her most striking feature. One piece of cotton in each cheek did the trick nicely; subtle enough to make a difference, but not drastic enough to make her look like Donna Corleone. Bright red lipstick drew attention to her lips and away from the rest of her face. She gathered her blonde hair and fastened it to the top of her head with bobby pins and put on a black wig.

Porter chose a shoulder bag large enough to conceal a High Standard .22 caliber semi-automatic pistol, a knife, and four sets of handcuffs. She put on a long black leather coat and left her apartment. A brisk walk would get her to Tony's hotel in fifteen minutes, she figured; she couldn't risk a taxi. She looked at her watch. It was 8:45. She didn't call him as promised to let him know she was on the way. No sense having a record of a phone call to his hotel on her phone bill on the night he was going to die.

The night air was frigid, but exhilarating, and she sensed the thrill of the hunt. She clutched the shoulder bag close to her side, lifted the collar on her coat, and buried her chin against her chest. Two men made comments about her legs when she turned onto Columbus Avenue. She didn't look up. The only person she intended on making eye contact with tonight was Tony Cippolone.

Porter walked into the Wilshire Hotel and straight to the double elevators adjacent to the reception desk. The lobby was empty except for a lone clerk reading a concealed magazine. She ignored him and waited for the elevator.

"Excuse me…miss?" the clerk said, waving her to the desk.

She opened her coat as she walked the short distance to the desk and made sure he got an eyeful. So much for him being distracted by sex magazines. I'll have to provide the distraction, she thought.

"Yes?" she said, sweetly.

The man's bow tie bobbed up and down. "All visitors must be announced," he explained to her breasts.

She smiled and slowly licked her lips. "So announce me. Lindberg, room nine-oh-four. He knows I'm...coming."

The clerk turned beet red. "Er...your name, miss?"

"Just tell him his date is downstairs."

He busied himself with the phone and spoke in hushed tones. After several seconds, he hung up. "Yes, go right up, Mr. Lindberg is expecting you."

She smiled and walked to the elevator. The less talk the better. Don't give them too much of your voice to remember you by, she thought.

She stood in the elevator with her back to the camera. Her heart pounded as she walked down the ninth-floor corridor, aware that there was a possibility that her every move was being recorded on videotape. She knocked on the door to room 904 with her right hand and removed her glasses with her left. As she passed the glasses in front of her face, she spat both wads of cotton into her hand and deposited everything in her bag. Just then, the door swung open.

Tony Cippolone was wearing a multi-colored robe that stopped at the knee. With her heels on, she was at least four inches taller than him. She wondered if he might be naked beneath the robe. She smiled. He leaned forward to kiss her and she gave him her cheek.

"Hey, you look great," he said. He was staring directly at her chest.

"So do you," she lied. "Better than the last time I saw you." She looked over his shoulder. "Don't I get to come in?"

He was gawking at her legs and didn't hear the question. She rolled

255

her eyes, pushed by him, and shut the door. The room was a large studio with a kitchen nook off to the left. The bedroom area was tiny and separated from the rest of the apartment by a folding partition. She saw that the bed was neatly made. She counted two closets. If he was making money with his con games, he certainly wasn't spending it on material things. The room was sparsely furnished, and the television was an old portable. She figured he was shoving his profits up his nose.

There was a small fabric-covered couch against a wall, and she draped her coat over a cushion, sat down, and crossed her legs with an elaborate movement. She made sure he got a glimpse of crotch. She had him totally off guard.

"Can I get a drink?" she asked.

He gulped. "Yeah, sure. What do you want?"

She moved her bag closer to her thigh. "What've you got?"

"Uh, Scotch…and um, vodka." He was breathing hard.

"Scotch and water would be nice. Three cubes."

Cippolone went to the refrigerator. "Coming right up."

He had his back to her, digging inside the tiny freezer. She was behind him in less than two seconds. Porter raised the heavy automatic and brought the butt down on top of his head. He collapsed to his knees, incredibly still conscious. He began to turn, mouthing a sound that she didn't hear. She brought the pistol broadside against his cheekbone. Cippolone went down with a thud and lay still. He was bleeding profusely from both wounds. She returned the pistol to the bag.

Porter backed up and began to remove her clothes. First kicking off her shoes, followed by her pantyhose. Next, she unbuttoned her top and let it fall to the floor. The skirt soon followed, joining the jacket in a heap at her feet. The striptease was her way of making certain she would leave the hotel minus any blood on her clothes from the massacre that she knew was only minutes away.

Porter straddled him, naked, and lifted him from beneath his arm pits. Dead weight and all, she figured he couldn't weigh more than a hundred and thirty pounds. She easily rolled him onto his bed, face up, robe spread, and went into her bag for the handcuffs. She manacled both his wrists to the brass bed posts while astride his chest. Pirouetting on his stomach, she clamped both remaining cuffs on his ankles and spread his legs wide enough to anchor them to opposite sides of the bedframe

Porter rummaged through the kitchen cabinet until she found a pitcher. She filled it with cold water and brought it and her bag back to the bed. Cippolone was still unconscious. Not for long.

Porter sat, legs splayed, across his chest and dumped the water on his head. He came around with a start. He blinked away the cascading bloody water.

"Wha...Leah?" He stared at her with confusion. His moussed black hair, now flat and wet, looked like an oil slick from the Exxon Valdez.

She rummaged through her bag. "Could I ask you a question?" *Cool and calm. Let him think he's going to live.* She felt the smooth titanium-handled knife.

"Yeah, yeah, anything," he said hoarsely, trying to sit up in bed, the handcuffs forcing him back down. "What the fuck?"

"You never said anything to anybody about the night you picked me up from the park, did you?"

It took him several seconds to focus. "Huh? Hell, no. What's goin' on?" She could see the unwelcome feeling of panic beginning to grip him. *He knows me better than anybody, even Wolf.*

"You sure?"

"Yeah, I'm sure. What the fuck're you talkin' about?"

"How's Ray Yale?"

"Who?"

"Ray Yale." She couldn't tell if he recognized the name.

"Don't know no Ray Yale." He squinted. "Why the fuck'd you slug me? My head, man." He tossed his bloody head from side to side.

She removed her hand from the bag and showed him a Microtech push-button, front-opening knife. She pressed the slightly recessed button, and a four-inch, bead-blasted, stainless steel blade snapped into place with the sound of a shotgun going into full register. "We have to talk." The sheets beneath his ass became wet with urine.

"What're you gonna do?" He licked his lips and recoiled at the taste of his own blood. Fear widened his eyes. "Oh, God!"

She smiled. "Nothing is going to happen to you if you tell me about Ray Yale."

"I never heard of Ray Yale. Leah, please, let me up." He shot glances around the room. The water mixed with the congealing blood and washed his face with a pink silt.

There's no one here to help you my friend, she thought. She dismounted him and sat on the edge of the bed. "I don't know if I believe you." She repeatedly opened and closed the knife. "I guess there's only one way to find out." She grasped his deflated penis with her left hand, pulled it straight up like she was stretching taffy, and raised the hungry double-edged blade with the other. His eyes went wide with terror as she swooped the knife downward in an arc, and in a flashing second, passed the blade a fraction of an inch over his stretched member. He screamed.

She jumped off the bed. "Now I believe you." Cippolone began to cry softly. She grabbed her pantyhose and began shoving it in his mouth. He shook his head wildly and tried to speak. Porter thought she heard the word "money." She put the blade to his left eye and yanked out the nylon.

258

"Speak when spoken to, and softly I might add." He swallowed hard and nodded. "Did you say 'money'?"

"Yes," he gasped. "In the closet. I got lots of money. You can have half." He was tugging at his restraints. "Please, get the money. Half is yours...really."

Porter looked at him with dead eyes. "In the closet?"

His head, resting in a pillow of blood, craned toward the closet to his left. "In there. Go ahead, see for yourself."

There were a few hanging sport jackets that Porter thought he must have stolen from John Travolta's wardrobe for *Saturday Night Fever*. She dragged a heavy battered suitcase to the foot of the bed and turned to Cippolone. "Here?"

He raised his head as far as it would go. "Yeah, yeah, in there. Half is yours...go ahead."

She easily popped the two flimsy locks with her switchblade. The suitcase was crammed with money, all neatly stacked bills banded in four-inch high piles and secured with rubber bands. Porter counted thirty-five piles. She smiled. *My lucky day.*

"How much is in here?"

"Hundred and sixty kay. Take half, it's okay."

She smirked, amused to see him bargaining for his life. She stood up, dropped the money, and stared into Anthony Cippolone's desperate face. "Why don't I just take it all?"

At that moment, she suspected, Cippolone knew he was going to die. He began to scream, but Porter shoved the pantyhose into his mouth. He thrashed like a wild animal, and Porter was concerned the bed might fall apart before she did what she had to do.

Her naked body glistened with nervous sweat. Reaching into her bag, she removed the High Standard pistol.

"I can't trust you anymore, you stupid bastard. You should have gotten out of my life when I told you to." She felt an unexpected tear glide down her cheek, but it wasn't for her victim. "I can't lose him," she said and placed the barrel of the pistol against Cippolone's left eye.

Tony Cippolone howled unintelligible pleas. He yanked at his restraints so hard that his wrists began bleeding.

Porter wrenched the bloody pillow from beneath his head, wrapped it around the gun to silence the report, and fired.

He stopped fighting. His body gave one convulsive jerk and settled in a heap. Porter rolled off the bed and backed up. She surveyed her handiwork. Cippolone lay naked with the pillow over his face. Better this way, she thought. She didn't want to look at him. Guilt? She shrugged the feeling off as out of character. She had done what she had to do.

The handcuffs, pistol, and knife were back in her bag in seconds. The gun, cuffs, and wig would be in a sewer shortly. The knife she didn't want to part with. No use getting rid of it until she used it. Someday, she knew, it too would be history. She quickly dressed and ran a bath towel over the few items she touched. As an afterthought, she put her hand beneath the pillow and yanked her pantyhose from Cippolone's dead mouth. They also went into the bag. She was concerned about the stray pubic hairs. The cops didn't have DNA testing nine years ago, but they've got it now. She reminded herself to push the elevator button with her elbow. The money was an extra added bonus. The fool had probably been hoarding the cash for years. Whatever he didn't ram up his nose must be in that suitcase, she thought. All he had to show for his miserable life was a shitty hotel room, a bad coke habit, and a pile of money he would never spend. She smirked. *What an asshole.*

One quick look in a mirror to make certain the wig was on straight. Her glasses on, she picked up the suitcase and let herself out quietly. The

260

perfect exit.

The hallway was empty and quiet. She waited for the elevator, the stillness unnerving. The door slid open. Empty. Porter kept her head low to avoid the surveillance cameras.

The digital floor indicator blinked "Lobby." Porter took a deep breath and stepped out of the elevator.

## Chapter Twenty-Five

Yale and Wright strode into the Wilshire Hotel and were immediately challenged by the desk clerk.

Yale flashed his replica shield. "Police. We're going upstairs." The clerk mumbled something and went back to his magazine.

Yale and Wright entered the elevator, moving to the rear wall and facing the door. As they stood there waiting for the doors to close, Yale heard the adjacent elevator doors opening. A woman, who looked to Yale like a prostitute, passed them walking into the lobby. She was struggling against the weight of a heavy suitcase. She glanced over her shoulder and looked directly into the face of Ray Yale. Her eyes widened, but Yale thought she caught herself. As the doors glided shut, the hooker turned back and resumed her slow walk to the front door.

"A pro goin' to work," Yale said.

They got off on the ninth floor, and Wright followed Yale to room 904. Yale knocked. They waited a moment, then they both pounded on the door. Yale tried the knob. Locked.

"Let's go talk to the clerk," he said.

The desk clerk had his head buried in a copy of Penthouse. Yale had to rap on the desk to get his attention. "Hi," he said, "remember us?"

The clerk discreetly closed the magazine and cleared his throat. He was about fifty and balding and looked to Yale as if he had spent his whole life at the desk of the Wilshire Hotel. "Yes, of course."

"We're looking for Douglas Lindberg. What time does he usually come in?"

The clerk looked confused. "Oh, well, sir, he's in now."

Wright said, "You're sure?"

"Oh, yes, sir. That, ahem, lady that just left was up there. Did you see her when you got into the elevator? The woman in black? Carrying a suitcase?"

Yale remembered the eyes, even with the glasses; deader than a day-old corpse. He had thought the thousand-mile stare was an affliction also suffered by hookers. Now, he could add Leah Porter to the list. "Jesus Christ!" He ran outside and scanned the street. She was gone.

When Yale returned, Wright said, "What the hell's going on?"

"Back upstairs," Yale said. He pointed at the clerk. "You too. And bring a key to nine-oh-four."

"You see the woman with the black coat when we got into the elevator?" Yale said to Wright, who held the door open for the clerk to trot in behind them carrying a ring of keys.

"Yeah."

"Leah Porter." The door slid shut, and Charlie Wright drew a sharp breath.

"Oh, man," he said. "Are you sure?"

"I am now." Yale's gut tightened in dreaded anticipation of what he would find in Cippolone's room. He raced from the elevator, dragging the clerk by the arm. Both Yale and Wright flanked Cippolone's door and drew their guns. The clerk gasped.

Yale rapped on the door. "Tony, open up. You okay?" He barely

263

waited for a response before ordering the frightened clerk to open the door. With trembling hands, the clerk opened two locks and nodded at Yale.

Wright grabbed the clerk by the shirt collar and pulled him from the door. He crouched low and grabbed the knob, nodding at Yale, who was standing to his right. Yale nodded. Wright turned the knob and pushed.

With his gun extended, Yale charged into the room, followed by Wright, who came in at a crouch. They both swept the room with their guns. Yale spotted blood seeping from behind a partition. He knocked it over with a sweep of his arm.

Cippolone was spread-eagle on the bed, arms stretched above him. Yale carefully lifted the pillow covering his face. There was always the chance, however slight, that he was still alive. Wrong. Cippolone's head was tilted slightly to the right, one eye staring, lifelessly. There was an empty, oozing socket where the other eye had been. Yale recalled how Zoltag and Katherine Carpenter had died. Porter's trademark, it seemed.

Yale pointed to the deep gashes in the victim's ankles and wrists. "Restraints." Wright didn't respond. The room stunk with urine.

"Well," Wright said as he holstered his Glock, "he won't be doing any more cons anytime soon."

Yale stepped gingerly around the bed, careful not to walk in any splattered blood, and examined the corpse carefully. He looked over his shoulder at Wright standing in the alcove next to the stove.

There was a thud behind them. Both men whirled to see the desk clerk lying on the floor, flat on his back.

"Grab his shoulder," Wright said. They picked him up and carried him into the hallway, placing him gently on the carpeted floor. Yale and Wright knew that keeping him in the apartment could contaminate the crime scene.

Wright lit a cigarette. "Now what?"

"Now," Yale said, "you take off. I'm calling the cops."

"Why can't I stay?"

"What's the point? You're tired, and it's going to be a long night. If Rip Van Winkle here," he gestured to the unconscious clerk, "mentions there were two of us, I'll square it with the cops. This is Manhattan. I know everybody. We've got a tough day ahead of us tomorrow. I need you fresh."

"What're we doing?"

"We're gonna hit Porter's apartment. I want to know what was in that suitcase she carried out of here."

"You gonna tell the cops it was her you saw here?"

Yale shook his head. "What am I gonna say? I recognized her dead eyes? You were standing next to me; did you have any idea who it was?"

"Nope."

"Without the makeup and the wig, she looks nothing like what you saw, believe me. It would be my word against hers. I don't think the clerk'll be any good; she was disguised too well. Besides, I don't want her to know I recognized her. She could spook and warn Steiner." He reached into his pocket and gave Wright the keys to the Lexus. "And here, take these."

Wright pocketed the keys.

The clerk started to moan.

"You okay?" Yale asked.

"Oh, God!" The clerk turned his head and threw up.

"I guess that answers that question," Wright said. "Let me try." Wright helped the man to a sitting position against the wall. "What's your name?"

"Malcolm...Malcolm Pierce." He held his head with both hands.

"How awful."

"Not a pretty sight, Malcolm," Wright said. "The suitcase the woman was carrying…did she have it on the way in?"

He thought for a second. "Er…no. She had a big purse, but no suitcase." He coughed. "I'm okay. Could I get some water?"

"Yeah, sure," Yale said, "I'll go with you. Lead me to a phone." He turned to Wright. "Take off, Charlie. I'll get a cab."

Within twenty minutes, the hotel was infested with cops. Manhattan North Homicide assigned uniformed officers to search the building and knock on doors. Yale told them Cippolone was wanted for questioning in a double homicide and that he had been hired by the family of one of the victims to track him down. He had been tipped that Cippolone was living in the hotel under an assumed name, and when he came to check, he found the body.

The desk clerk told his story but couldn't remember much about the woman visitor's appearance. He told the detectives that he thought she was a hooker. The assigned detective, who once worked for Yale, attempted to expedite his questioning, but Yale still wasn't cut loose until three-thirty the following morning. He caught a cab to Queens and made a brief stop at the local diner for a tuna sandwich to go. He wanted something without sauce.

He gobbled the sandwich seated at the edge of his bed. He thought about always getting close to solving the case and then something happening to set him back. First, it was not being able to identify the fingerprints on the thermos. Now, Cippolone's murder. Had he been five minutes earlier, he would have grabbed Porter in the act. He was almost back to where he had started.

## Chapter Twenty-Six

Leah Porter luxuriated under a stream of hot water, and the shower washed away the aura of death. She felt relieved that Cippolone was out of the way, but Ray Yale's presence in the hotel bothered her. She was convinced that Tony had been telling the truth when he said he that didn't know Yale and that he hadn't told anyone about the night of the park killings. No man would lie when his cock was at stake.

She wondered if Y:ale had recognized her. Even if he had, she knew it was his word against hers. His buddy had paid no attention to her, and the desk clerk's identification would only be valid if her tits stood in a lineup.

She had tried putting the cash in her small safe, but it wouldn't fit. For now, it remained in the suitcase in the back of her closet. She would treat Wolf to the best vacation he ever had, hoping he could escape for a week. That would be nice. She couldn't wait to tell him that Cippolone was no longer a problem. Killing Yale would be her little secret; Wolf would never even need to know he existed.

She stepped from the shower and stood naked in front of a mist-covered mirror. She wiped away the moisture and ran a finger down her face, pleased to see that the bruises were healing nicely.

Helga was retired for now and would be resurrected another day. Another day real soon.

Chapter Twenty-Seven

Yale awoke to Charlie Wright banging on his door and calling his name. Glancing at his watch, Yale slipped into his robe and staggered downstairs to let him in.

"Why the hell didn't you use the key?" he asked Wright, as the former detective breezed past him.

"Why? So you could come out of a dead sleep and think I was that Porter dame and shoot my ass? I'm no fool." He was dressed in his uniform of jeans and fatigue jacket.

Yale went to the bathroom and flipped on the light. He had gotten some decent sleep, albeit only four hours of it. The ghost of Tony Cippolone hadn't invaded his dreams. He showered, shaved, and joined Wright in the kitchen, where the gaunt man was cooking breakfast.

"Real eggs for me," Wright said, "and this powdered shit for you, okay?"

"Whatever." Yale put on a pot of water for tea.

"Fill me in."

Yale explained the familiar cadence of a police homicide investigation and the story he had told the detectives.

"Sounds reasonable," Wright said. "Did they want to know about

269

me?"

"They didn't ask. I didn't say."

"What about the desk clerk?"

"Poor guy was so confused, he probably thought he was seeing double." Yale checked the time. "Stuff those eggs." He was hungry, but the case was paramount. "We should get to Porter's apartment before eleven. I want to catch her coming out the door for her morning jog or wherever the hell she's going."

"You think she'll go running? I think she got enough exercise last night, don't you?"

"She was on her way for a run the first time I saw her. I think she's the type that would work out on her deathbed. By the time she gets to the Central Park track, or wherever she goes, does maybe two or three miles and gets back to her place, it should be about an hour at least. That enough time for you to get in and out of there without getting busted?"

"It is with my handy-dandy pick gun." Wright reached into his jacket on the back of a kitchen chair and removed a cylindrical black metal tube about seven inches long. "You think you got the corner on high-tech gear? Bullshit." He went into his shirt pocket, took out a small cloth bag, and emptied its contents on the table. Three thin metal picks spilled across the Formica.

"Looks like a vibrator," Yale said.

"In a way, it is. You insert one of these two raking tools or this tension bar into the end of the tube, hit this switch, and stick it into the lock. The pick gun vibrates a few thousand times a minute and wham-o, the tumblers fall into place. It takes seconds. Hopefully." He handed it to Yale.

"Batteries?"

"Rechargeable."

"The Job taught you how to use this thing?" He stuck a raking tool or a tension bar—he didn't know which—in the opening at the end of the cylinder and hit the button. The attachment vibrated in a small arc like the wings of a hummingbird.

"Hell, no," Wright said. "I took this off a perp. He had an instruction manual on him, too. Bought the thing through the mail, all perfectly legal. Bet you didn't know these things are for entertainment purposes only."

"Why else would anyone want one?"

"Anyway, I practiced with it on my own locks, and in twenty minutes, I was a burglar."

"You've got a criminal mind, Charlie."

Wright disassembled the pick. "What's that supposed to mean?"

Yale sipped his tea. "You're out for a day in the country and you come across a beautiful wooded stretch of deserted farmland. What's your first thought?"

Wright shrugged and smiled. "It's a great place to hide a body."

"I rest my case. Gather your equipment and let's get moving. Traffic's gonna be a bitch." He was already clearing Wright's dishes. "We're picking up a rental car. Mine stands out, and she'll be looking for a tail after last night. We have to be careful."

They switched cars at the airport rental agency, picking up an unobtrusive Ford Thunderbird, which didn't have the four-door look of a department unmarked car. Forty minutes later, they were sitting on the Queensborough Bridge, stuck in the middle of the morning rush hour.

"Think she leaves this early?" Wright asked.

"Maybe not this early, but if we're not there in thirty minutes or so, I'm going to start worrying. While we're sitting here, let's go through the game plan. Go into my attaché case; there's a cell phone in there." Wright

271

popped open the case and got the phone. He turned it on, and the annoying sound of generating power blared in the small car.

"What do I do with this," Wright asked, "reach out and touch someone?"

"The first thing you do is turn it off. The book says the battery has about four hours of standby power, but it's been lying around without being turned on for about a year, so I have no idea how much juice you have left. I had it in the charger overnight, but you never know with an old battery. Don't turn it on until you're actually in the apartment. It goes dead, you're screwed. I'll call you when she's on the way back. Hopefully you'll be long gone by then."

"Gotcha."

"You're looking for that suitcase. If she's smart, though, it'll be gone by now, but the contents may still be in the apartment somewhere."

"It'll only be gone if it can be directly linked to Cippolone. I'll toss the place good. I might find other interesting stuff, you never know."

"Just be conscious of the time. Assume you've got forty-five minutes, no more. If you two pass in the hallway, and she recognizes you from last night, she'll kill you in a second. It's better to leave emptyhanded than chance getting bagged. We can always go back."

The traffic was beginning to move, and they were on the exit ramp making pretty good time. Yale estimated they would be on the West Side in about fifteen minutes.

"No problem." Wright took a black plastic object that looked like a remote control on steroids from the attaché case. "What's this?"

"That's a portable copier," Yale said. "You find any documents of interest, don't steal them. Run the copier over any paper, and it makes pretty legible copies, just as long as it's less than three inches wide. If it's wider than that keep running it over the page 'till you get it all in. There's

272

enough thermal paper in there to copy about five pages. We can alert the cops where to look when they get a warrant, if it comes to that. Us burglars don't need warrants." Yale reached into his pocket and handed Wright a Minox-B miniature camera.

Wright turned it over a few times. "Don't I feel like James Bond. You want some wallet-sized pictures of her pad?"

"This may be our only shot. We should preserve it for posterity. If you should miss anything or think something is unimportant, we could examine the pictures after you get outta there." He explained the intricacies of the tiny Minox to Wright.

Yale pulled into 69th Street and backed into a space by a fire hydrant near Porter's building, west of the brownstone. He assumed Porter would be heading east, into the park for her run.

Yale suggested they take turns craning their necks behind them to keep the building under continuous surveillance. The street was quiet now, most people already at their jobs. Those Yale did see had their heads bowed against the bitter wind whistling off the Hudson River. No one paid any attention to them. They were in place thirty-five minutes when Porter came out of the building dressed in gray sweats, leg warmers, sneakers, knit hat, a quilted parka, and gloves. She carried a large canvas bag.

Wright gave Yale a nudge. "She's out of the building." They both lowered themselves in their seats and watched Porter as she stood at the top of the stairs, surveying the street.

"She did that the last time," Yale said. "Checks out the block."

"She always carry a bag with her when she runs?" Wright said with a touch of sarcasm. "She could be goin' around the corner to do her friggin' laundry for all we know. How am I supposed to know if I'll have enough time?"

"Want to abort?"

273

"Aw…fuck it. We're here, let's do it. Just stay on her real good and give me a buzz when you have even the remotest notion she's getting homesick."

"You got it," Yale said. "Look at that psycho bitch. Last night she kills a guy, and today she looks like she stayed home and baked cookies." She was still on the top landing, just beginning to do her warm-up stretches. She gave a few short jabs at an imaginary opponent and started down the stairs.

"Oh shit!" Wright said, "She's coming this way!" Instead of heading east toward the park, Porter was walking west and would be passing their car in about twenty seconds. Even allowing for Wright's lack of bulk, there wasn't enough room to collectively cram themselves into the front foot well. "We shoulda got a fuckin' Cadillac." Wright moved fast and said, "Bye." He was out of the car walking west, his back to Porter, about six seconds ahead of her. With more room to work in, Yale was able to stretch across the floor and push himself under the dashboard. He closed his eyes and prayed.

In about a minute, Wright was banging on the door. "Ray, move your ass! She just turned uptown on Columbus."

Yale reached up, opened the door and crawled out of the car on all fours. He stood up and started to run toward Columbus Avenue. He hollered over his shoulder, "She make you?"

Wright shook his head, turned, and sprinted to the brownstone.

Yale raced to the corner and stopped, peering cautiously around the building line. He saw Porter walking at a good clip, apparently unaware of a tail. He crossed to the opposite side of the street and followed at a discreet distance, watching her turn occasionally or stop and look in a shop window. Yale thought she was checking for a tail, but there were enough people on the street to allow him to close the gap between them without

274

fear of being seen.

She walked straight on Columbus, turned left on 110th Street, and entered a high-rise building on the corner of Broadway. The second floor had floor-to-ceiling windows and a sign that read: Body Builder Gym. The woman had just walked forty-one blocks, Yale thought, now she's gonna work out? This was, he had to admit, to their advantage. He figured it would take her about fifty minutes to walk back, plus the workout time. He backed into a doorway and dialed Wright's cell phone. His eyes immediately returned to the front of the building. Wright picked up on the second ring. "Burglars R Us, good morning."

"Let me ask you a question," Yale said. "Do you find yuks in everything?"

"I stop laughing, I die," he said, seriously. "What's shakin'?"

"Me, it's freezing out here." He explained the time element. "I think you got at least an hour and a quarter more. How long you been inside?"

"Just got in. The goddamn place has three locks, plus the one on the door downstairs. The pick worked good, I just had to play with it a while."

"I'll call you when she leaves the gym. After that, you've got forty, maybe forty-five minutes."

Please let this go right, Yale prayed, as he huddled against the cold in the doorway.

#

Wright took a pair of rubber surgical gloves from his jeans and snapped them into place. He took a deep breath and examined the apartment with an expert's eye, dividing the floor and walls into imaginary

275

grids and perusing each square foot carefully. When he was sure he knew the layout, he began a slow and deliberate walk around the apartment.

He was in a one-bedroom apartment that was sparsely but expensively furnished. He guessed it would be called a minimalist look. An expensive stereo system in the living room had two large speakers Wright thought big enough to push together and seat four comfortable for dinner. The number of stuffed animals amazed him because of the sheer size of the collection; it took up an entire wall, floor to ceiling, and because Porter didn't seem like the stuffed-animal type. He always thought people who liked them were kind and gentle. Come to think of it, he remembered reading somewhere that Hitler liked dogs. Go figure. The collection rated the first picture of the day.

He resisted the temptation to hurry through the apartment and look for the suitcase. Good searches were conducted with deliberation. He might find other incriminating items besides the suitcase. Perhaps he didn't have all the time he needed, but he was damned if he was going to miss anything because of sloppy procedure.

He took off his jacket and placed it on the couch, careful not to spill anything from the pockets between the cushions. He took a portable power screwdriver from his jacket pocket, removed the rear of the speakers, and examined the interior with a pocket Mag-Lite. He found nothing but electrical components. He did the same to a television with the same results. He lifted a throw rug, checked behind hanging pictures, unzipped seat cushions, and looked for new stitching. He opened over twenty plastic CD cases, admiring Porter's taste in music. He slipped a Natalie Cole disc into the music system and listened to Nat's little girl do her thing. He kept the volume low; no need to alert nosey neighbors.

He moved on to the kitchen and took a picture before entering. He shook every can and checked for false bottoms, with negative results. He checked the time. He had been in the apartment for thirty-six minutes. Plenty of time left. The hallway closet came next. No suitcase but plenty of clothes. He squeezed every garment and checked for hollow wooden hangers. Nothing out of the ordinary. The bedroom was last. He had just started to crawl under the bed when the cell phone rang. It rang four times before he got to it.

He had to speak above the music. "Yeah?"

"Having a party?" Yale asked.

"That's music to rip-off by. I'm in the last room. Haven't found shit."

"Well, she just left the gym. We're approaching Amsterdam Avenue on 110th Street. She's in no hurry, probably a little worn out. You've got about an hour before she sticks her key in the door. Be out in forty-five minutes, okay?"

"What? You say forty-five minutes? The battery's going." Wright smacked the phone against his knee. "Fucking Japanese, they're getting back at us for The Bomb."

"Yeah, forty-five minutes, out the door. Copy?"

"Roger, oh, Captain Video," Wright said, doing an Ed Norton impression. He turned off the phone and looked around the bedroom, then he went back under the bed and checked between the springs and mattress. Finding nothing, he rolled out and checked the pillow cases. He thought she needed to change her sheets, but he found no contraband. All that remained was the closet. He had plenty of time.

#

Yale and Porter were still on 110th Street when she passed Columbus Avenue. A brief moment of panic seized Yale. Why didn't she make the right on Columbus? He thought about it and figured that Central Park West was the more scenic route. Her brownstone was halfway between Columbus and Central Park West, allowing her to use either street. He cursed himself for being so paranoid.

Sure enough, he saw her turning on CPW, and he pursued her at a leisurely pace. He rounded the corner from the opposite side of the street and nonchalantly looked south to see his quarry approaching 109th Street. She looked back, but Yale was standing in a bus shelter and out of her line of vision. It was then that he realized she wasn't checking for a tail.

She was looking for a cab.

His heart dropped into his scrotum as he watched Porter step into the street and hail a taxi. The first yellow cab passed her by, but a second pulled to the curb. She was inside in an instant as Yale stood by helplessly, searching for an unoccupied taxi that wasn't there. He fumbled for the cell phone and carefully punched in Wright's number. This wasn't the time to mis-dial. He heard the call connect. The relief that swept over him was short-lived.

A recording said: The cellular customer you are calling is either away from the phone or out of our network. Please try again later.

Yale was gripped by panic as Porter's cab pulled into traffic and headed downtown.

#

Wright found the suitcase in the bedroom closet. It had a chain secured with a combination lock around it to prevent it from being opened. The end of the chain was looped around a pipe with a padlock. The chain, as well as the pipe, were made of heavy-gauge steel, but the padlock was easily picked. He dragged the suitcase into the bedroom and went back to the closet. A large padlocked duffle bag lay on its side in the rear of the closet. He lifted the heavy bag and saw the safe.

It was small, about a foot square and bolted to the floor. A combination lock in the center of the door stared at him like a cyclops. He jiggled the handle. Locked. He knew from his days in the Safe and Loft Squad that most people who had safes with combination locks didn't spin the dial after closing the door. They usually left the combination one number away from opening to save time when going back into the safe. The practice was called "day locking," and every professional burglar checked for this before trying to force a safe door.

He knew that practically all small safes had three number combinations, and most commenced with turning the dial to the right. Consequently, the last number could be found by rotating the dial in that direction. He had at least twenty-five minutes before he had to vacate the premises, so he slowly began moving the dial one click at a time and trying the handle after every turn. On the tenth try he leaned on the handle, and the door swung open. The safe was empty except for one item resting alone on a shelf toward the back.

It was a video cassette in a colorful Winnie the Pooh sleeve. Funny, he thought, when I was a kid, I loved Pooh, but I'll be damned if I was crazy enough about him to give him a hundred-pound, tempered-steel condominium. He put the tape inside his shirt.

#

Yale watched the taxi pull from the curb and get caught at a red light on 108th Street. He searched frantically for a cab or a precinct radio car but saw neither. He called Wright's cell phone again and got the same recording. When he looked up, he saw the traffic light turn green, and the cab slowly accelerated. He considered trying to outrun the taxi, and he thought he might beat it to 69th Street because the cab had to stop for lights and the traffic was slightly heavy. But that idea would have him passing Porter, at a run no less, and she would surely notice him. In the midst of his dilemma, he felt a rumbling beneath his feet.

A subway.

There was a subway entrance across the street. He dodged traffic to the stairs, flying down three at a time and getting to the token booth in time to see the downtown local pull into the station at a crawl. He fished for change and started to shove the money through the slot in the clerk's cage. A CLOSED sign stared back at him. Screw it, he'd hop the turnstile.

It was a revolving gate turnstile, completely sealed, allowing no one without a token to gain entrance. With no cashier on duty, you either had a token or you walked. He dug his hand into his pocket and pulled out all his change.

The train was now at a full stop, and he knew he had maybe ten seconds to board.

It took him a second to focus on his money in the station's dim light. He had been taught by his training officer on The Job to always carry a token. Was he a good student?

Despite the cold, sweat ran from his face and into his eyes, blurring his vision. He discarded pennies to the ground because they resembled tokens. There it was, a tarnished New York City transit Authority subway token! He wondered how long he had been carrying it as he fed the token into the turnstile slot and pushed his way to the train.

The doors began to close, and he still had fifteen feet to go. He leapt the remaining distance and jammed his arm between the closing doors. They flew open, and he stumbled into the car, tripping and falling on his side as the doors closed securely behind him. The car was moderately crowded, but no one looked at the prostrate Yale on the floor. Welcome to New York, home of the disinterested citizen. The train began its journey downtown.

There were two stops before his 72nd Street destination. If Porter's cab didn't catch the lights and managed to hit a little traffic, Yale could be able to beat her to her brownstone and warn Wright. The subway system was known for its unreliability, and unscheduled stops in the middle of tunnels was the norm. "Please God," he said out loud, "make this iron horse travel with the speed of light." *Christ, I'm talking out loud to God and no one is paying the slightest bit of attention.* He looked around at the crowd and realized there were at least five other people talking to themselves. He latched onto a pole and began muttering. He fit in nicely.

After what seemed like an hour, the train came to a creeping halt at his stop. The moment the doors opened, Yale flew out, knocking an old lady to the ground and pushing two men aside as he ran for the stairs.

He emerged from the underground as if he were hurled out, running with every ounce of energy he had, not bothering to look back to see if there was a cab behind him. He knew if he turned into 69th Street and saw a taxi in front of the brownstone, it would be too late.

He rounded Porter's corner like a man being pursued by a lynch mob.

No cab!

He silently thanked a God he vowed he would no longer neglect.

Yale took the stairs to Porter's stoop three at a time and began punching her bell like a pecking chicken. He looked down the block.

A cab was pulling into the street.

He jabbed at the bell furiously, his face pressed against the glass door. He saw Charlie Wright walking down the stairs like he didn't have a care in the world. Wright pointed to a suitcase in his right hand. Yale waved to him insanely. Wright smiled and opened the door.

Wright said, "What's the prob—"

Yale shoved him violently backward just as the taxi pulled in front of the building. "Move your ass back upstairs! Quick!"

Wright glanced over his boss's shoulder and saw Porter getting out of the cab. "Oh, shit!" They scrambled up the stairs with Wright in the lead. They passed her top-floor landing and collapsed in a heap in front of the roof door. They dared not open it for fear of making too much noise. Wright was breathing heavily, clutching the suitcase so tightly that his fingers were white.

Yale was certain his pounding heart could be heard on Broadway. He took short breaths, controlling his breathing, and slowly reached for his revolver. He put a finger to his lips and poked Wright, signaling him to remain still.

The sound of keys turning tumblers was a song to Yale's ears. When they heard Porter's door shut behind her, Yale and Wright made their way quietly downstairs and into the street. They soundlessly got into the ticketed rented car and drove toward Columbus Avenue and out of harm's way.

Wright, sweating profusely, broke the silence. "What the fuck was that all about?"

Yale told him about the great chase. "I tried to call you, but I think I was in a dead area."

"Well, not exactly," Wright said, sheepishly. "The battery was almost DOA, so I turned the phone off. Hey, you told me I had at least thirty minutes. I didn't think I needed it anymore." He shrugged. "Who knew the exercise nut would take a cab back? Lazy bitch."

Yale turned to chew him out but began laughing instead. It was the nervous, mirthless laughter of the greatly relieved. Wright joined in, uncharacteristically displaying a mouthful of bad teeth.

When the hysterics subsided, Yale said, "You didn't leave anything up there, did you?"

Wright checked his pockets and gave Yale the tiny Minox camera. "Nope, got everything." He reached over to the back seat. "I got the suitcase, but my pick doesn't work on combination locks." He balanced the leather suitcase on his knees. "She had a duffle bag full of weapons up there. I didn't examine everything, but there was a gas gun in there which probably killed Zoltag and the girl. No sense taking it; no ballistics on those things. Man, she had knives, two sawed-off shotguns, a MAC-11 sub-machinegun, all kinds of shit. I put it all back where I found it." He told Yale about the stuffed animals.

"A kinder, gentler psycho," Yale said and put his hand on the suitcase. "Maybe there's something worth looking at in here. She probably knows it's gone already."

"Only if she looks in the closet. I couldn't very well leave it. Oh, I got something else." He dug into his shirt and showed Yale the videotape. "Remember the blackmail theory? This was the only thing in a small safe she had in the back of her bedroom closet. It's gotta be something good; why hide it otherwise?"

"You broke into a safe?" He was developing a new admiration for Wright's abilities.

"Silly bitch had it day-locked, no problem."

"She sees the suitcase gone, she may go for the safe to check on the tape."

"I left the cardboard sleeve in there."

Yale grunted and turned onto the entrance ramp of the Queensborough Bridge. "I hope this turns into something. I'm about fresh out of ideas. You?"

"Me, too."

They were at the car rental office in less than twenty minutes. Yale tossed Wright the keys to the Lexus and went to the office to return the Ford. He paid for the car, and the summons he got for parking in front of a fire hydrant, with a credit card. His line-of-duty ticket would be passed on to the client. Wright was in front of the office, Lexus motor purring, when he emerged.

Yale slid behind the wheel. "We'll be at the house in five minutes."

## Chapter Twenty-Eight

That's odd, Leah Porter thought, as she opened her front door. She thought she had double-locked the bottom lock on the way out, and now it took only one turn to open. Perhaps she forgot to turn the cylinder twice in her haste to get to the gym. She dropped her workout paraphernalia in the small foyer, went directly to the phone, and went through her stockbroker charade with a meddling receptionist before she got Wolf.

"Good morning," he said. "I read the paper. I take it that was you." His voice was upbeat and friendly.

"Are you referring to our friend's accident?" she said, coyly.

"That's right."

"Only for you, my love. Are we back on track?"

"We were never off." He made no mention of the beating he had given her. "We just needed to get a few things taken care of, and that's been done. Can I see you tonight?"

"Can't you come over now? I just got back from the gym, but it'll only take me a few minutes to shower. I miss you. I need you." She stood in front of the full-length mirror in the hallway and ran a hand over her bruised cheekbone. It was still a little painful, but the mark was hardly visible.

"Can't, sweetheart. I've got a one o'clock with my agent at his office, which will probably include lunch, and a five o'clock with some Hollywood types in my attorney's office downtown. I should be out of there about nine-thirty. Kind of late. I'll see you tomorrow. I'll be able to stay. Sound okay?"

She hesitated. She had planned on tailing Yale tomorrow to get his routine down, but she could do that today instead. "Yeah, sure. Could you bring a bottle of DP with you?"

"Dom Perignon? You don't drink."

She laughed. "I don't drink much. I think we have something to celebrate."

"Okay."

"I love you," she said, but he had already hung up. She was grinning to herself as she walked by her CD player, but her smile faded when she noticed something out of place. Her compact discs were normally stacked neatly against the wall like a mini-office building, but she saw that the plastic case on top of the pile was slightly askew. She picked it up, and Natalie Cole smiled back at her. She hadn't played that particular disc in months and knew it should be somewhere near the middle of the pile.

She sprang to attention like a panther spotting a lounging antelope. She was motionless for a second before whirling around and scrutinizing the living room.

Someone's been here, she thought. First the lock, now this. She broke for the bedroom and flung open the closet door. The suitcase was gone! "Sonofabitch!" She shoved the duffle bag aside, searching for the missing suitcase in the tiny closet much in the same manner she would look for the family station wagon in a single-car garage after discovering it

286

stolen.

Her mind raced with murderous thoughts. Fucking burglars, she thought. They picked my locks and took the money. She sat on her bed and buried her face in her hands. Within minutes, the rage subsided, and she began to think more rationally. Why did they only take the suitcase and not the stereo? What about the duffle bag? It was still locked, but someone could have hauled it away. A thought struck her. What kind of a burglar knows how to pick locks these days, anyway? The average rip-off artist usually knocks on your door, and if no one answers, he takes it down with a sledge hammer. Crackheads don't have much finesse. She began to suspect more than a run-of-the-mill burglary. She went back to the closet and checked the safe, jiggling the handle. Locked.

She tried to open the steel door by using her day-lock method, but it didn't budge. Her body started to shake.

"God, no," she whimpered and turned the combination dial. She took a deep breath and leaned on the handle. The door swung wide, and she saw the carboard sleeve. She sighed with relief, but when she picked it up, she realized the tape was gone.

*Fucking Ray Yale. The sonofabitch was turning up everywhere.*

She went to her bed and tried to think. Okay, if he and his emaciated friend have the tape, they may still not know what they've got. She knew she wasn't out of the apartment that long, which meant they probably got to wherever they were going within the last few minutes. She cursed herself for not getting Yale's office and home address sooner.

An idea struck her like a bolt of lightning.

Porter knew that every reported crime had to be documented within the precinct of occurrence. In this case, Cippolone's murder was recorded in the Mid-Town North Precinct on a Complaint Report, which listed all witnesses along with their home and business addresses and

287

phone numbers. She ran to the phone, punched directory assistance, and got the number she wanted. The phone rang at least fifteen times before the line was picked up. It was a recording.

"This is the Mid-Town North Precinct. If you have a touch-tone phone and wish to speak to the Community Relations Officer, please press one…" and on the message went until she had the extension for the clerical office.

A bored female voice said, "One-Twenty Four Room, PAA Chilzer speaking."

Good, Porter thought, she's bored; bored is good when you're trying to get information out of one of these bureaucrats. She tried to sound equally as bored. "This is Detective Louise Anderson, Manhattan North Homicide. Listen, I was wondering if you can help me. We assisted in a homicide investigation at a hotel last night in your command, and my copy of the Complaint Report ain't too clear. What I need is the address of one of the witnesses." She rumpled a piece of paper. "Looks like the name's Yale…can't really make out the first name."

The weary civilian said, "You got a Complaint number?"

More crackling paper. "Nope. Not really. This copy's piss-poor. It happened around twenty one-thirty last night." She gave the woman the address and heard her sigh.

"Yeah, hold on a bit." The clerk came back in a few minutes with Yale's home and business addresses. "There's a note here says the business address is one of those mail drops. Contact at the residence. Want the number?"

"Yeah." Short and sweet. Porter scribbled the information on the front page of yesterday's newspaper. "Thanks." She dragged her duffle bag to the foot of the bed and opened the lock. It took her less than five minutes to choose her weapon and to conceal it under a loose-fitting raincoat. She pulled her hair tightly into a bun, tucked it under a baseball cap, grabbed a pair of lightly tinted sunglasses, and went to her phone and punched in Yale's number.

## Chapter Twenty-Nine

Yale and Wright were in Yale's living room. The videotape was temporarily forgotten on the couch, as Yale took a hammer to the combination lock that secured the chain around Porter's suitcase. It popped open on the second bang. He flipped back the lid. It was stuffed with money.

"Jesus Christ!" Wright said.

"Man, look at all that money." Yale sat back on his haunches and stared at the stacks of bound bills. He lifted the suitcase and set it down on the carpet in the living room, then looked at Wright.

Wright was propped up against the couch. "Thrifty sonofabitch, wasn't he?"

"Cippolone was a con man and drug dealer." He emptied the contents onto the carpet. "What we've got here are the fruits of his labor."

"How much fruit do you suppose is there?"

"I dunno, maybe a couple hundred grand. The question is, what to do with it."

"Maybe we should call Porter and return it," Wright said, with a wry smile.

Yale barely heard him. Cops spent their entire careers dreaming about situations like this. He'd often wondered what he would do if he ever came upon a treasure like the one spread out in front of him now. Police officers were obligated to voucher found property and contraband, but would he have the fortitude to return this kind of money? Would anybody? He looked at Wright, who had a puzzled expression on his face.

They were civilians now, and while they still had the moral obligation to turn in what wasn't rightfully theirs, the spiritual aura of the badge wasn't there to jab at their consciences. After all, this was dirty money, wasn't it? It didn't belong to the church, did it? Yale wondered if he was acquiring a greed demon to sit alongside his others.

"I don't believe I'm saying this, but I got half a mind to turn this shit over to the cops," Yale said.

Wright looked at him incredulously. "Then I suggest you reason with the half of your mind that's sane."

"There's too much death associated with this dough." Yale was silent a moment. "We keep it, what do you do with your end? Half's yours, you know."

"Well, thank you John Beresford Tipton." The frail former cop scratched his head. "What the hell could I do with it? Can't make any long-term investments." He laughed without a hint of amusement.

"Don't you owe any medical bills?"

"Some, but not many. Insurance. I'll pay off what I owe and give the rest to Sloan Kettering. It's a good hospital; they're keeping me alive. All I wanna do with the time I got left is to make sure that fuckin' Steiner and Porter get theirs. What would you do with your end?"

Before he had a chance to reply, the phone in the office rang. He went to answer it while Wright began to count the stacks of money. When he got back, Wright was nearly finished.

"Hang-up call," Yale said. He turned his attention to the money.

"You count all of it already?"

"They look to be all equal stacks. One hundred and sixty large. Even."

Yale was staring at the money when he remembered the tape. "Let's check out the videotape. Leave the money where it is."

"We can't leave this kind of dough laying around." Wright grinned. "Someone might steal it."

They put the money back in the suitcase, but without the chain securing it, it wouldn't stay shut. Yale took the suitcase to the foyer closet. He dumped the money on the floor and began kicking stacks of bills inside with the side of his shoe. "Damn maid, always leaves the house a mess."

Wright had inserted the videotape into the VCR in the living room by the time Yale had finished with the money. Yale sat on the couch, and Wright hit the play button.

A darkened residential street appeared immediately. A date stamp in the corner of the picture said: Mar/8/77. The camera panned to a street sign. Momentarily out of focus, it slowly became sharp: Continental Avenue. The tape was in black and white, no sound. The camera zoomed back to a wider angle and swept over both sides of a tree-lined street. Yale saw apartment houses and a few private homes in the distance.

"What's that look like to you?" Wright asked.

"There's a Continental Avenue in Forest Hills. What do you make of it?"

"That's Forest Hills, alright. I was assigned to Queens for a few years, remember?"

The screen went black.

"Boy, that was worth killing three people for," Wright said. "Call *Hard Copy*."

The picture came back to life. The camera angle had changed, but

292

it was the same block. An occasional car drove slowly down the street. From the new camera position, bright lights could be seen in the distance.

"What are those lights in the back?" Yale asked.

Wright got off the couch and squatted in front of the television.

"That'll help," Yale mumbled.

"Looks like a wide street, wiseguy, probably Queens Boulevard. See the subway station?"

The camera moved slowly to the right and zoomed in on the stairs leading from the subway. Within fifteen seconds, a woman, carrying what looked to Yale like an armful of books, walked into the street from the underground station.

The camera pulled back, and Yale saw the woman entering the picture from the right. She was the only person on the darkened street. For the first time, Yale noticed a street lamp as the woman strolled beneath it. She became distinguishable to Yale: tall, slim, long dark hair. He couldn't tell how old she was. She held her books against her chest.

Once again, the camera pulled back and panned further to the left. A tall man was on the other end of the block. He was wearing a watch cap and a dark sweater. He was walking toward the woman.

"Can you make him out?" Wright asked.

"Nope. Too dark. What's he got in his hand?"

"Looks like a paper bag."

The tall man waved at the camera.

"What are we watching here, home movies?" Wright said.

Yale felt the now all-too-familiar knot in his stomach. "Somehow, I don't think so."

The two figures converged. The camera zoomed in as they approached each other. The man stopped under a street light. From this distance, he was unrecognizable. Yale saw his right hand inside the paper bag.

"Why'd he stop?" Wright asked.

Yale kept his eyes on the television.

The woman tried to walk around the man. He shifted to his left and blocked her way. She tried again. This time, he pushed her backwards with his free hand, at the same time raising his arm and pointing the bag at her head. The woman raised her books in front of her face.

Yale winced as the bag exploded into a fireball. "Jesus Christ! He shot her!"

The woman took one step back and fell to the ground, the books at her feet. Yale caught the glimpse of a gun as the man shoved the tattered bag into his pocket. He straddled the victim and bent down.

The camera jiggled.

The shooter got up, looked behind him, and ran toward the camera. A blur shot past the camera lens.

"Wha…?"

"I think it's a truck door, Charlie. Or maybe a van door. It slid, it didn't open out."

The shooter was coming closer. He slowed down as he crossed the street. Yale guessed he was walking eastbound across Continental Avenue. The killer was suddenly out of focus. The picture became sharper as he neared what Yale thought was a vehicle.

Yale gripped Wright's arm. "Charlie! The shooter's Wolfgang Steiner."

Wright's eyes were wide. "You're sure?"

Steiner was smiling.

The camera fell back, and Yale got a fast glimpse of the inside of the suspected vehicle. It was a van, just as he thought. Steiner raised one leg inside and hoisted himself up. He came in so fast that he bumped his head against the camera.

The picture went dark.

Yale nodded vigorously. "Sure, I'm sure. I delivered Japanese food to him, remember? Besides, I've seen him on television." He kept on looking at the television but expected Wright to say something. When he got no response, he turned and saw Wright staring open-mouthed at the set. "Charlie?"

Wright gaped at the blank screen. He shook his head briefly and turned to Yale. "Ray, I had that case."

"What?"

"The shooting. I had the case. It just hit me. March eighth, seventy-seven. And the books. Shot through the face right through her school books. I caught that homicide." He was shaking his head slowly, as if trying to remember. "Young Columbia University student." He snapped his fingers. "Voskerician! Virginia Voskerician!"

"Jesus, Charlie, are you sure?"

He was nodding, slowly. "Oh yeah, I'm sure. I've handled two hundred homicides, but that one I remember. That was the sixth Son of Same killing. Remember the case?"

Who hadn't, Yale thought. During 1976 and '77, David Berkowitz gripped New York in a reign of terror as he slaughtered and maimed young people throughout the city. "Sure, but what does this shooting have to do with the Son of Sam?"

Wright pointed to the television. "This killing, the Voskerician murder, was blamed on Berkowitz. Same M.O. Young woman, long dark hair, shot with a forty-four caliber handgun." He smiled ruefully at Yale. "But, ya know, he always denied it. He confessed to all the others, but he denied this one."

Yale was trying to digest the information. "But Berkowitz

295

confessed. Didn't they find the gun? He got life, right?"

"They locked him up for something like three hundred years. He adamantly denied he had anything to do with this one. Of course, no one believed him. Or maybe The Job just wanted to close out all the murders with his arrest.. The Job never did say the bullet recovered from Voskerician's body matched the forty-four they found in Berkowitz's car." He smirked. "They had themselves a confessed killer. The good citizens of New York were crying for a conviction. Berkowitz went to jail with no trial. End of case." He brushed his two hands together. "Finito. What I don't get is Steiner's connection to the Son of Sam killings. Could he have been involved with that nut Berkowitz?"

Yale was beginning to understand. "This was, what did you say, the sixth shooting?" He didn't wait for an answer. He told Wright about his meeting with Jason Davis. "Davis told me Steiner was a wild man when he was younger." He related the stories Davis told him about Steiner. "I think he did it for a thrill. He's that kind of person"

"A thrill? A fucking thrill? You mean a copy-cat killing?"

"That's exactly what I mean." Yale began to pace. "Everybody who lived in New York knew who the Son of Sam was by the fifth shooting. Berkowitz, the psycho, was sending letters to the newspapers. Did everything but sign his name. It was easy to jump in there and do a shooting and have the Son of Same blamed for it. The ultimate thrill." Yale sat next to Wright on the couch. "And Zoltag taped it for posterity. His chauffeur told me he started getting into video in the late seventies to record weddings and things."

Wright rubbed his forehead. "I need a cigarette. I'm going outside." He started to get up.

Yale grabbed his arm. "Have it here. I wouldn't go outside with Porter still loose." Wright lit up and seemed deep in thought. Neither man spoke. Yale let the tape run a few more minutes, but the screen remained dark. He turned the power off but continued to stare at the dead screen.

Wright ran his hand through what remained of his hair.

"Who knows how many times they watched that tape? That was probably their biggest thrill. The shooting lasts a second; a videotape is around forever. There's your blackmail angle. A few years go by, they grow up, nobody wants to play anymore. Steiner goes on to fame and fortune, and Zoltag wanted a piece."

"So when Steiner ordered the hit on Zoltag," Yale said, picking up on Wright's lead, "Porter tortured him into revealing the location of the tape." He snapped his fingers. "That's why Zoltag's apartment was tossed. I'm sure Steiner got a copy, which he probably immediately destroyed, and Porter either made a copy for herself or there were two to begin with. Steiner can't know this one exists."

"So this was like her insurance policy?"

"Could be. Maybe she wanted it for an ace in the hole should Steiner ever decide to boogie."

"Rewind it," Wright said, "and let's get it to Sheehan at the One-Ten."

Yale shook his head. "First, we need insurance." He rewound and ejected the tape. "This is the only copy we've got. There's enough evidence right here to put Steiner away for life. You know he'll take Porter along with him. Let's get this over to Jason at NBC and make a copy and let him do the story on the news. Then we'll get it to Sheehan. It's not that I don't trust Mike, but this is opening up a can of worms. The city closed this case out almost twenty years ago. Would you want to be the Police Commissioner who says, 'Oops, we made a mistake'? Or worse, 'Maybe my predecessor concealed evidence.' People could go to jail over this. The press'll crucify The Job. Before you know it, they'll bring into question

297

every major case from the last fifty years." He wanted Wright to tell him he was doing the correct thing. The former detective had been by his side through the entire investigation, and Yale felt part of the decision was his.

"Do it."

Yale tossed him the cassette and hurried to his office. He called Davis. The reporter was editing his stories for the six o'clock news. Yale told him what he had.

"Jesus Christ, Raymond! The story of a lifetime. Can you get the tape here for the six?"

Yale laid the ground rules. "Okay, but my name isn't to be mentioned."

"Still publicity shy?"

"I've had enough to last a lifetime. Lt. Mike Sheehan, One-Ten Squad, broke the case as far as you're concerned. And he didn't give you the tape. I don't want to get him jammed up. Cite your usual unnamed source."

"A deal, Raymond. You had better leave now, the Christmas tree-lighting ceremony in Rockefeller Center commences at five fifty-five. The crowds will be daunting. It doesn't leave you with much time. I'll meet you by the police barricade next to the skating rink on the Fiftieth Street side. I'll be able to get you through our security."

Yale's memory drifted back to when he and his wife would attend the Christmas tree-lighting ceremony. The event unofficially kicked off the holiday season in New York and put them both in the Christmas spirit despite her health problems. He looked at his watch. Four o'clock. They had plenty of time. "See you then." After hanging up, he made one more call to the local precinct to have a sector car give his house special attention. He wanted the house watched in case Porter came for her property. Yale emptied half a box of ammunition into his overcoat pocket.

Expect the unexpected. He met Wright at the head of the stairs. "Let's go."

The street was quiet. It was beginning to get dark, and snow had started falling. "You got the tape?"

Wright's hand emerged from his coat pocket with the cassette. "Got a death grip on it."

Yale didn't spot anything out of the ordinary on the street. As they walked down the sloping driveway, a radio car pulled up. Yale identified himself to the two uniformed officers, who told him they would check on his house frequently.

Yale and Wright piled into the Lexus and backed out of the garage. Yale watched as the police officers popped the plastic lids off their steaming cups of coffee.

He felt strangely serene, despite the moment's intensity. Everything was finally working out. They would make it to NBC with plenty of time to spare, and Sheehan would have a copy of the tape within hours. All the evidence they needed to put Wolfgang Steiner away forever was resting comfortably in Wright's pocket. Coward that Steiner was, Yale knew, he would take Porter down with him. For once, nothing could go wrong.

Chapter Thirty

Leah Porter heard a man answer Yale's phone. She hung up gently.
Within fifteen minutes, she had rented a low-profile Buick from an agency
on Broadway and was on her way to Queens. She had no time to devise a
safe operation. It was obvious to her that chances would have to be taken.
Her immediate plan was to park a short distance away from Yale's house
and wait a reasonable length of time for him to come out. She would
accost him on the street and demand the tape. If he had it with him, she
would take it and execute him on the spot. If it was in his house, she
would bring him back at gunpoint, retrieve the tape, then shoot him.
Anyone with him would suffer the same fate.

Using a map supplied by the rental agency, she was on Yale's street
within thirty minutes. She parked about half a block from Yale's house,
which afforded her a clear view.

She checked the time. Two o'clock. She would give Yale until four
to emerge before moving to Plan Two: a frontal assault on the house. Leah
Porter sunk in the front seat of the rental car as the One-Fifteen Precinct
unit passed her and came to a stop in front of Yale's house. What now, she
wondered. In her lap, she cradled a Glock nine-millimeter semi-automatic
pistol. It contained a fifteen-round magazine, and she had two spares in

300

her bag.

She had parked far enough down the block to be carefully hidden from view. With the approaching darkness, she had assured herself that she could be on top of her quarry before he knew what hit him. The door to Yale's house swung open. She recognized the skinny one from last night. Yale, the bastard, was the second one out. She saw something in the skinny one's hand. Her lips clenched, and her eyes blazed. "My fucking tape!" she screamed, her fury muffled by the confinement of her rented car.

She gripped the pistol tightly. *Should I drive by or walk right up now and let them have it?* She resisted temptation and waited patiently for the police car to leave, fingers drumming on the steering wheel. She saw Yale and his friend drive off in a Lexus. The radio car remained behind. She knew she had to follow Yale and wait for an opportune time to open fire.

They would be looking for a tail, but she had darkness on her side. If she stayed a few car lengths back, they wouldn't be able to spot her headlights from the rest of the traffic. Besides, she thought, the Lexus stood out. She doubted she would lose it. Maybe, after she killed them, she would even have enough time to go back to Yale's house and look for her money.

Porter felt the familiar adrenaline rush, similar to the one she had experienced when she killed the two in the park. She knew she would be in Wolf's arms soon, and next to retrieving her tape, that's all she cared about.

Chapter Thirty-One

The snow was falling harder now. The outbound rush bogged traffic going toward the Triborough Bridge on the FDR Drive. The southbound lane Yale was in was almost as heavy due to the snow. Yale rode the brakes on the Lexus and resigned himself to a frustrating drive. The luminescent dial of the dashboard clock gave him more bad news. It was 5:05.

"I'm getting off at Seventy-Third Street," Yale said. "We stay on here, we won't make it to NBC by seven o'clock let alone six."

Traffic had built to a steady crawl on a side street. They made slow but steady progress Yale stopped for a light on 66th Street and Fifth Avenue. He turned on the radio to a local news station to get a better read on the traffic. Yale checked the time. It was 5:20.

"Oh, we're screwed," Yale said. Traffic, the radio commentator said, was stopped dead from 55th Street south. "The goddamn Christmas tree lighting. The crowds are always bad, but this sounds impossible."

"Never been to one," Wright said. "Bah, humbug."

Yale thought it unwise to bring up the good times he and his wife had at the ceremonies they had attended; it might start Wright thinking about his wife. Yale figured Wright had enough things to get depressed about. "Sonofabitch!" Yale banged a clenched fist against the dashboard. "I don't think we're gonna make it."

"I say we abandon ship and haul ass on foot." Wright said. "We can't walk six or seven blocks in thirty minutes? What are we, crippled?"

The traffic light changed to green, and Yale proceeded at a snail's pace. "You've never been to one of these Christmas tree things. Every New Yorker and his goddamn brother shows up. We'll be elbowing our way through a mass of humanity for those seven blocks."

"So what if we don't make it at the stroke of six? The news goes for thirty minutes, doesn't it?"

"I just don't like carrying around the world's only copy of that tape you have in your pocket any longer than we have to." Yale sighed. "Fuck it, if we're late, we're late."

"Very profound."

Yale turned to survey the traffic behind them.

"What do you see?" Wright said.

"Cars. Lots of cars." Headlights glared back at him, and he realized it was a waste of time to look for a tail. He turned back. "Look," he said, hope springing into his voice, "I've got an idea. There's a few garages on Fifty-Sixth Street east of Fifth. Let's park this pig and make feet for the studio. It'll save us time."

"Couldn't have come up with a better plan myself."

The streets were mobbed with pedestrians, most carrying packages. Yale passed beneath a giant illuminated snowflake strung across Fifth Avenue. There were a group of carolers on the street belting out a rap version of "Little Drummer Boy." Isn't anything sacred, Yale thought. He turned left onto 56th Street. In contrast to Fifth Avenue, 56th Street was almost deserted. The immense crowd behind them was pushing south down the avenue.

He pulled into the first garage he saw, ignoring a sign that read "Full." Yale bounded out of the car with a fifty-dollar bill clutched in his hand. The attendant took the bill and the car.

"Okay, we've got twenty-five minutes to show time," Yale said. "Let's move out." They walked quickly to the corner, turned left, and were immediately swept into a surging crowd of humanity that pushed them along like twigs in a slow-moving stream.

#

Porter had stayed at least ten car lengths behind the Lexus for most of the trip. As she turned onto Fifth Avenue, she said aloud, "Where the fuck are you going?"

The turn onto 56th Street did not come entirely as a surprise. Traffic had come to a virtual standstill, and she figured Yale would ditch his car as soon as possible. Passing the Lexus at precisely the time it stopped at the top of the garage's ramp, she pulled into a second garage down the street before either Yale or his friend had a chance to get out and the check the block. By the time she got her claim ticket, she almost missed the two men turn into Fifth Avenue. Once they were caught up in that crowd, she knew, they might as well be swallowed up by quicksand. She ran for the corner, keeping her right hand at her side, resting against the high-powered pistol secured comfortably in her waistband.

She was about thirty feet behind them when she turned the corner and almost lost sight of them. The crowd was growing. She figured at least a hundred thousand people were packed into Fifth Avenue between building lines.

Porter was pushed, pulled, and goosed to within seven feet of Yale's back, separated by a buffer of four people. She figured they were

304

moving about a block every five minutes. Every few seconds a body would push in front of her, and she would elbow the person out of the way.

There were uniformed cops everywhere. She wondered how many plain-clothes detectives were assigned to mingle with the crowd to nab pickpockets. The temptation to open fire to clear away the people between her and Yale and his buddy was almost irresistible. Like parting the Red Sea, only the sea would be blood. Porter vetoed the idea. Cops would be all over her like flies on shit. She took a deep breath. No use getting the tape if I gotta die for it. She hoped they would turn into a less crowded side street where escape would be easier.

She had walked three blocks and was exhausted from pushing against the surging crowd. Because of the crush of bodies, the cold weather was no longer a discomfort. The mass of people buffered the wind and created enough body heat to cause her to sweat. Every so often, she would walk through a blast of warm air from a chestnut vendor's cart. The roasting nuts smelled good and briefly propelled her back to the Christmases of her childhood. The aroma had comforted her as a child. Now her comfort lay in the nine-millimeter nestled against her abdomen.

## Chapter Thirty-Two

Yale marveled at the sheer size of the crowd. It somehow reminded him of the throngs of tourists who flocked to the San Genero Festival on the narrow streets of Little Italy to feast on sausage highjacked by the mob, play rigged games of chance, and have their pockets picked. He remembered his father leading him by the hand through the festival's thick crowds, recalling that it would sometimes take them one hour to walk four blocks. The only difference between the two events was the smell of roasting chestnuts replacing the aroma of zeppoles floating in vats of boiling oil. He knew that only the 10,000 people crammed into 49th and 50th Streets would actually see the switch thrown that would illuminate the huge tree. The rest would have to be satisfied with filling the void in front of the tree after the people with vantage points got bored and went home. This was definitely an all-night event.

Wright was beginning to look a little peaked, and Yale saw that he was breathing heavily to fuel his fragile lungs. *Hell, even I'm tired, I can imagine how Charlie must feel.* Yale was about to ask Wright if he needed to stop for a rest when he spotted a female cop on horseback. She was passing through the 50th Street intersection and appeared to be heading up the block toward the tree. He tapped Wright on the shoulder. "We're

306

going for the mounted cop," he said, raising his voice to be heard above the crowd. Before Wright had a chance to respond, Yale assumed the lead. They jostled their way on an angle, the going getting tougher because it seemed everyone on Fifth Avenue was trying to squeeze into the same street. Yale caught up with rider as she was about to enter the block. He tapped her on the knee with his phony shield.

Flakes of snow blurred his vision when he looked up. "Listen, we're trying to get to the rink on official business." He waved the tin in her face. "Could you run interference for us?"

The policewoman leaned over as far as she could. She smiled at him. "How?"

He got as close to her as he thought safe. He had seen too many Black Beauty and Flicka movies as a kid and thought the gigantic horse might kick him if it sensed its rider was in danger. "Cut through the crowd, we'll follow," he said. Wright was practically riding him piggy-back, the crush of the crowd so intense. "Just as far as the rink, we'll take it from there."

The policewoman pulled the horse back and yelled, "Yes, sir!" She guided the animal's head to the right, into the crowd. The multitude began to part.

"I never thought I'd be breaking my first case as a PI by following a horse's ass," Wright said, inches away from Yale's ear.

"Better than being a horse's ass!" Yale screamed over his shoulder. He grabbed Wright's arm and pulled him closer. "I suppose it's a little late to ask, but I trust you still have the tape?"

"Right here." He patted his pocket and tested the snap. He took a deep breath.

"You okay?"

"Just ducky. Lead on."

#

Porter started cursing out loud when Yale and his buddy began turning toward 50<sup>th</sup> Street before reaching the corner. She knew that if she opened fire now, an escape from mid-block would be difficult. She plowed headlong after them, hanging a few feet behind as she watched Yale talk to a horse cop. At least 2,000 people stood between her and the safety of the east side of Fifth Avenue. She had to get the tape but searching two dead bodies in the midst of a panic-stricken crowd could get her trampled to death, apprehended, or at the very least injured bad enough to prevent her escape. Besides, she still had no idea where they were going. Any minute now, they could wind up in an empty building lobby where Porter could shoot them down with ease.

As the mounted cop pushed through the crowd, Porter realized that she was acting as an escort. The cop was now part of the equation. If she stayed with them, Porter would have no choice but to add her to the list of victims. She couldn't turn her back on an armed police officer. What was one more body?

She fell in behind her quarry. She slid her hand under her coat and gripped the gun. The pistol's metal skin felt oddly warm. She slid her finger into the trigger guard, still hoping they would get off the crowded street and into an area that afforded her a means of escape.

That's when she saw the reporter.

She had seen him, a hot-shot crime reporter, numerous times on television. He was frantically waving his arms, standing behind a barrier directly in front of the ice-skating rink and about twenty feet from Yale. *Is he signaling to Yale?* The cop on horseback stopped and moved her mount slowly to the right, affording Yale a good view of the reporter. Yale waved

308

back. The mounted cop blended into the crowd, waving farewell to Yale.

*Jesus fucking Christ! He's gonna give my tape to the goddamn reporter!* She looked up at the majestic building that was Thirty Rockefeller Plaza.

The home of NBC.

*It's going to be on the news!* She pushed her way through the crowd, moving in for the kill.

#

Yale nudged Wright. "There's Jason!" He pointed to the gesturing reporter. Davis was standing by a police barricade that separated the crowd from the ice-skating rink twenty feet below street level. Yale recognized an old timer from his tenure in the Mid-Town North Detective command standing beside the wooden barricade. Probably volunteered for this ceremony, Yale thought. This was one of the few details cops actually liked. Families out looking to have a good time. Nice break from the normal stress-filled tour.

About half the size of a football field, the rink was situated between 49th and 50th Streets, accommodating about eight skaters. It was dwarfed by the two buildings on either side of it. Yale figured that Davis would lead them across the rink and into the building to the right that housed the NBC studios.

The ninety-five-foot Christmas tree was mounted on a pedestal on the east end of the rink. The Douglas fir was dark now, at nine minutes to six, its multi-colored bulbs concealed by rich, green branches so blessed after 110 years of growing in the wild. Yale new he would be in the NBC studios in a few minutes and miss the sighs of amazement as the switch was thrown, illuminating the thousands of lights. He'd catch it on the eleven o'clock news at home.

Yale saw that Davis was already talking to the uniformed cop. The reporter helped the officer move the barrier that prevented unauthorized persons from spilling down into the rink area. Yale pushed through the spectators lucky enough to get a ring-side view of the festivities and shook Davis' hand. Yale smiled at the uniformed cop.

"Let's go," Davis said and waved Yale and Wright around the stanchion.

It was 5:52.

Yale was the first past the barrier. He walked down several marble steps, with Wright an arm's length behind him. Peripherally, he saw the mounted policewoman, who had blazed the trail for them, flailing her arms wildly in the center of the crowd on 50ᵗʰ Street. He stopped suddenly and turned. Wright crashed into his back.

"What the fu—?" Wright said, bumping his nose on the back of Yale's skull.

Yale grabbed his arm and spun him around. The horse cop pointed toward the crowd.

Puzzled, Yale watched as the female officer drew her gun and extended it toward the brass railing that separated the on-lookers from a perilous drop onto the ice. The only person who seemed to be agitated was the cop. Everyone else was smiling and looking at the tree, which was still dark. The deafening roar of thousands of festive people drowned out whatever the cop was shouting.

Yale spotted the barrel of a pistol jutting through the mob's fringes, then the crowd swallowed up the weapon and whoever was wielding it.

"Gun!" he yelled and pointed to the crowd. Davis still had both hands on the wooden barrier and was helping the cop return it to its secured position. When he heard Yale, his face crumbled in confusion and

310

fear. He looked for cover and dove under one of the hedges that ringed the ice.

Yale saw the policewoman's mount whirl suddenly. She fired two shots in the air, violating department policy against warning shots. Yale immediately thought she used good judgment in not firing into a crowd at the person wielding the gun. Her horse reared slightly but stood his ground. The spectators in the cop's immediate area stopped gaping at the unlit tree and looked in her direction. Yale wondered if they thought the cop was part of the festivities.

Yale drew his revolver and pointed it impotently at the horde. Wright was to his left in a combat crouch, his Glock sweeping the railing line.

"Where? Where?" Wright hollered.

Yale pointed with his pistol. "The cop. She was trying to warn us. I saw the barrel of a gun. Can't see who's got it."

Wright moved closer to Yale. "Where is it now?"

"Don't know." The people ringing the edge of the promenade began pushing back at the sight of the drawn guns. Yale watched as the mounted officer guided her horse through the onlookers, her pistol hanging at her side. Yale saw her move further to his right, and that's when he spotted Leah Porter.

Porter turned her attention to the horse and swung her pistol toward the animal. The mounted cop leveled her revolver at Porter and dug her heels into the horse's sides. The animal lowered his head slightly and advanced on Porter, knocking pedestrians to the ground as he moved forward, quickly, with deliberation. Yale watched, unable to fire for fear of hitting civilians, and marveled at the guts of the female cop as she charged Porter with her shooting arm extended like a knight in a jousting match.

Porter opened fire from the hip. The horse took three shots in the

311

chest and neck and crumpled to the cold pavement, face first, and rolled over, pinning the brave policewoman to the ground. Yale watched as the spectators within fifty feet of the mayhem began to push outward away from the downed horse and rider, toward the railing and the opposite building line. Before Yale could react, three children, too short to grasp the railing, were prodded under the brass stanchion and fell about five feet to a level of shrubs, which cushioned their fall.

Yale and Wright raced up the marble steps leading from the rink in time to see two less fortunate victims who didn't have a concrete wall to stop their movement thrown through windows of tall plate glass. Yale recoiled as they were truncated by showering guillotine-like shards of transparent death.

Yale and Wright held their fire; they still didn't have clear shots. The uniformed cop who had let them through the wooden barrier brushed by Yale and ran for the downed horse and pinned cop, who was struggling to get her legs from beneath the dead animal. The cop drew his pistol and was immediately cut down by two shots from Porter's gun. He collapsed next to the prostrate policewoman, who strained to reach for her pistol on the pavement next to her.

Yale was torn between intellect and instinct. His brain sent messages to his shooting arm. *Hold your fire. Civilians too close to target.* Instinctually, he knew that if he didn't fire, Porter would undoubtedly shoot some innocent spectators herself. As if he willed them to move, the crowd parted in a desperate bid to escape, giving Yale an opportunity to fire. He crouched behind the brass rail and raised his weapon.

Porter, however, now had room to maneuver. She stepped to the railing and fired at Yale, who was about thirty feet away. The weapon bucked, and the rounds went wild. Yale ducked and fell backwards, slipping on a thick blanket of snow, knocking Wright to the ground as he too sought cover behind the rail.

Yale recovered and emptied his six-shot revolver at a kneeling Porter. He was amazed at the loud report of the .38 as the sound bounced off the concrete and glass buildings. Panic gripped Yale as he saw Porter stand and advance on him. He had missed. She was grinning. Her movements were deliberate. No panic. No wasted movement. Cool and calculated. Watching her robot-like motion frightened Yale more than the thought of impending death. She looked crazed.

He reached into his overcoat pocket and struggled with a handful of loose bullets, numb fingers dropping rounds to the street. Yale broke open the cylinder and dumped six shell casings to the pavement. Porter raised her pistol, now not more than twenty feet from Yale. He fell to both knees, disregarding the sharp pain that tore up his legs. He managed to get two bullets into the cylinder before flipping it shut. In the split second that he thought remained in his life, he wondered if he lined the cylinder up correctly. Smith & Wesson cylinders spin clockwise, Colt's spin counterclockwise. Or was it the other way around? He was forever getting it wrong during practice at the range when he was on The Job. He extended his arm, elbow locked, and fired.

Click.

*Oh, shit.*

He felt a sudden impact to his right shoulder and fell over on his side. Oddly, there was no pain. *Am I shot?* Charlie Wright, he saw, was crouching above him, shielding him with his body. He realized that Wright had knocked him over; he wasn't hit. Yale scrambled to his feet as Wright fired seven rounds from his Glock a fraction of a second after Porter had opened up with her pistol. The shots came so fast and close together that they sounded like one big boom to Yale.

Wright went down, clutching his side.

Yale swung open the cylinder and tried to place the first bullet where it would be struck by the firing pin when he pulled the trigger, but he knew it was too late. His hands shook from cold and fear.

Porter stood five feet from him, the same sardonic smile on her face. Spectators were still running and screaming, but she paid them no attention. With glacial calmness, she raised the weapon to the center of Yale's chest.

Yale knew he was going to die. In the nanosecond he figured he had left to live, he looked her straight in the face. *She won, the bitch, but I'll be fucked if I'm gonna beg for my life.* Thoughts of his wife raced through his mind. He felt the tears coming. *Maybe this won't be too bad after all.*

The Christmas tree lights blazed on like a Fourth of July fireworks display.

Yale saw Porter flinch, instantly distracted. She looked up for a fragmentary second at the tree which was now a myriad of twinkling, shimmering colored lights overlooking a Christmas celebration gone mad.

At that moment, an arm enclosed Yale's waist. Wright yanked him backwards down the stairs leading to the rink. Yale vaguely remembered the buildings spinning and seeing Charlie Wright grinning while hovering above him, blood soaking the front of his jacket. Yale struck his head many times on the hard marble before coming to an abrupt stop at the bottom. He felt the revolver fly from his hands. Falling snow obscured his vision.

Wright smiled through blood-stained teeth. He threw his upper torso on top of Yale's chest. The din of the crowd vanished. Yale heard nothing but the sound of Wright's voice. It came in a whisper. "Everything's gonna be okay, Ray." There were tears in his eyes.

Before Yale could reply, Wright limped to an erect position and started up the stairs. Yale saw Porter in a combat crouch at the top of the

314

stairs. Wright placed himself between Yale and Porter and opened fire with his automatic. She leveled her nine at Wright and fired at the same time, standing her ground, cursing.

"Noooo!" Yale yelled. He saw his friend struck in the head, chest, and stomach, his body spinning in a deadly pirouette. Wright tumbled backwards down the marble steps like a toboggan and lay still next to Yale.

Yale got to one knee and charged Porter as she advanced down the stairs. His head throbbed, and he felt a warm trickle of blood run down his neck.

Porter was frantically trying to reload her Glock. Rage exploded in Yale's chest. He lunged for Porter's gun, just as she sent a new magazine home and raised the automatic at him. Yale jammed his thumb in the ejection port just as she pulled the trigger, preventing the gun from discharging.

Yale wailed in pain, his thumb broken. He yanked his hand away, causing Porter to lose the grip on her pistol. It clattered down the stairs with the sound of a dozen castanets.

"Motherfucker!" she bellowed, kicking him in the chest and sending him the rest of the way down the remaining stairs.

Yale flipped over on his stomach and started to low-crawl to Wright's body, intending to snatch the nine that Wright still clutched in his hand. It was then he heard the blessed sound of sirens and the familiar shouts of his police saviors, as more than one cop yelled, "Police, don't move!" At least twelve uniformed cops lined the perimeter of the skating rink.

Porter, cursing wildly, ran around Yale, apparently deciding that escape was more desirable than sticking around to do battle with a dozen cops. She paused long enough, however, to drive the heel of her boot into the side of Yale's head and to reach into Wright's coat pocket and snatch

315

the videotape. She also grabbed Wright's gun before Yale could reach it and ran up the stairs and onto 50<sup>th</sup> Street.

Two uniformed officers stumbled onto the stairway. They had fallen over the dead body of their comrade, the officer who had left his house that morning for a quiet day of barrier duty.

Yale watched as they turned their attention momentarily to the prostrate police officer. Yale felt himself being lifted up from behind by his arm pits.

Jason Davis had a large scrape across his face. A thin stream of blood ran from his forehead. He hoisted Yale to a standing position. "You okay, Raymond?"

Yale was already halfway up the stairs. He hollered over his shoulder, "I'm goin' after the bitch!"

He heard Davis scream "Get that motherfucker!" at his back as he turned down 50<sup>th</sup> Street. His first thought was that Davis' speech therapist would be pissed at that kind of talk.

The two cops who had stopped to examine their fallen comrade were now joined by the others from the skating rink.

"What the fuck's goin' on?" a beefy young officer yelled, his gun pointed at Yale.

Yale groped for his phony shield. "On The Job!" he screamed as he frantically waved the badge in the cop's face. Better to call himself a cop, he thought, then try yelling "Private investigator, formerly on The Job and currently engaged in a to-the-death shootout with a crazed former policewoman!" He stooped down and snatched the service revolver from the dead cop's warm fist. Pain shot up his arm due to his broken thumb. "Girl, blond, thirties, long hair, gun!" he shouted, as he ran toward Sixth Avenue, confused cops in pursuit.

Uniformed cops poured onto 50<sup>th</sup> Street. They seemed to Yale to be coming from everywhere. At least ten officers in various stages of dress knocked against each other as they exited Hurley's, a bar on the corner. A marked radio-car, siren wailing, spun into a blocking position at the intersection of 50th Street and Sixth Avenue.

The block was now almost deserted. As Yale ran toward Sixth Avenue, he saw about a dozen people that had been injured in the rush to escape the shooting lying in the street like broken toys.

Yale had tunnel vision. The injured didn't concern him; he raced for the intersection with only one thought in mind.

*Get Porter.*

The crowd on Sixth Avenue was being held back by still more police officers. Yale's forward movement was slowed as he waded into the mob. Cops screamed orders, shouted questions, and pointed weapons in every direction imaginable.

Yale stopped. He felt weak. I haven't got the faintest goddamn idea where I'm going, he thought. He had at least twenty cops following him, and he had no clue as to where Porter had gone. He scanned the crowd. Too many people on Sixth Avenue to facilitate a fast escape, he thought. Yale grabbed the nearest uniformed cop.

"Up Fiftieth Street!" he shouted, as he led a phalanx of confused but determined cops.

The block west of Sixth was almost totally deserted. Maybe a dozen people were leaving office buildings. The business day was over. Manhattan was locking down. All the action was confined to the ceremony on the street behind Yale. He slowed to a trot and began examining building lobbies. He cursed silently. *Midtown Manhattan. There had to be twenty-five office buildings on this one block.*

Cops fanned to both sides of the street, peering carefully around archways. A voice cried out from across the street. Yale whirled and saw a policewoman frantically pointing into a darkened lobby.

Yale reached the building as numerous cops converged at the entrance. A body of a man in uniform was just inside the plate glass. The doors swung out, but Yale couldn't open them because of the weight of the army in blue behind him.

"Back off!" he yelled, stinging sweat pouring into his eyes.

The cops pushed back, allowing Yale to open the door.

The dead man was a security guard. A bullet hole had punctured the area between his eyes. Yale wondered if the man had ever been a cop.

"Anybody see anything?" Yale asked of no one in particular.

"I think I saw someone come in here when we hit the street," a young cop said.

Immediately, guns waved in all directions. Some cops started for the stairs, while others punched the same elevator button numerous times. Curses were the means of communication.

Yale grabbed the young cop as he went for the stairs. "Hold it! What exactly did you see?"

The cop tugged at his sleeve. "She's in here, man! She could only go up." He looked toward the ceiling.

Another cop said, "What about the basement?" There was a chorus of agreement. Cops split into groups and began an aimless, disorganized search of the building.

Yale stood by the body and watched them go. A mob mentality, he thought. The cop believed he had seen someone enter the building. The damn building was almost on Seventh Avenue. There were people, legitimate people, on the street as they poured onto the block down on Sixth. How could this one cop see anyone enter this building from almost a block away?

He knelt by the dead man. No gun. An unarmed guard. Why

would Porter shoot an unarmed man and have someone possible hear the report of a gun? The guy had to be seventy years old, Yale observed.

She could have given him a swift kick and he'd be sleeping until New Year's day.

He stood, realizing what Porter had one. *It's a diversion. The conniving bitch. She's got a platoon of cops combing this building, and she ain't in it.* He turned and charged from the building.

He looked back to Sixth Avenue. She couldn't have doubled back there; he would have seen her. Another building? Yale doubted it. Another building was a trap. Why would she confine herself to a building?

*Think.* No one else seemed to be doing it. What's the quickest way out of the area, he asked himself. He suddenly felt guilty for not moving. Moving anywhere. He resisted the temptation to pursue a wild hunch as the cops bumping into each other in the building behind him were undoubtedly doing.

*The subway!*

Yale moved now, arms pumping, gun in his waistband. He crossed Seventh Avenue, weaving his way through people on their way home after a hard day at the office. The next block was short; Seventh Avenue and Broadway converged three blocks south. Traffic surged down Broadway as he disregarded the red light and snaked his way to the other side of the street. Police cars, sirens screeching, turned down 50th Street. Yale didn't see any uniforms. Rockefeller Center must be a crowd-control nightmare by this time, he thought. Every available foot cop in the area must be over there. Or searching an empty building, he thought wryly.

He grabbed a sidewalk Santa Claus by the arm. "Where's the nearest subway?" I've lived in this town all my life, he thought, I should know where the goddamn subway stations are, especially in midtown.

"Up the corner," Santa said, pointing toward Eighth Avenue.

319

"Merry Christmas!"

*Yeah, right.*

Yale broke into a run. Pedestrians paid no attention to him. The pain in his thumb was excruciating. He knew he would have to shoot with his weak hand if it came to that, because he sure as hell couldn't grip a pistol with his strong one.

He tripped and stumbled down the subway steps. For no particular reason, other than it was the closest entrance, he chose the uptown side. Now people were paying attention to him. Typically, they avoided his eyes and moved as far away from him as they could get. His overcoat was filthy with street grime, and his shirt was covered with Charlie Wright's blood. He briefly wondered what his face looked like as he pushed a well-dressed man out of the way and hopped a turnstile. No time to look for tokens now.

There were about seventy people waiting for the uptown train. Yale slowed his pace. He wanted to blend. Carefully, he transferred the .38 to his right coat pocket and began the walk down the platform. He was breathing like a locomotive and thought everyone on the platform could hear him. No one even glanced in his direction.

There was a concrete pillar every twenty feet or so. He approached those with care. An easy place to hide. Within a minute, he had walked the entire platform. No Porter. Now what?

Dejected, he walked toward the exit. Porter wasn't escaping by train. He was wrong. Wouldn't be the first time. As the headlights of an approaching uptown train began illuminating the tunnel, Yale looked across to the downtown side of the station, which was almost empty.

He caught a wisp of blond hair from behind a pillar. Who the hell would stand behind a pillar if they had the whole platform to wait on?

He looked at the uptown tracks. The train was screeching into the

320

station. Time to make a decision. Go across the tracks or go back to the street and down the other stairs. The decision was made for him when he heard a downtown train in the distance. No time to go the long way.

Yale leapt onto the tracks. Those around him reacted. Some screamed, others turned away. Yale made it between the north and southbound tracks as the uptown train passed behind him. He hugged a filthy cement pillar, swallowed hard, and gingerly stepped over the electrified third rail and onto the downtown side.

The screams from those who saw Yale's jump onto the tracks had to have alerted the person standing on the downtown side. Yale saw Leah Porter poke her head around the pillar. Her eyes went wide. Yale went clumsily for his gun. Porter drew hers in an instant and started firing.

Bullets danced against metal. Sparks flew. The echo of people screaming was magnified in the enclosed area. Yale managed to get the gun in his weak hand and fire a shot. It went wild.

Porter crouched and fired numerous rounds at Yale, who threw himself flat behind the third rail in two inches of dirty water. Once again, he had the feeling he was going to die: either by Porter's bullets or the downtown train, which Yale could hear rapidly approaching.

There were more shots. Nothing ricocheted around Yale. He raised his head cautiously. Two uniformed cops were on the stairs on Porter's side of the station pegging shots at her. She had moved behind a metal garbage can for cover, momentarily giving Yale an opportunity to seek better concealment.

Yale jumped to his feet and ran down the tracks toward the approaching train. If he could mount the platform at the other end of the station, Porter would be boxed in between him and the cops. He had seconds to spare.

Yale jumped sideways across the tracks as the train exited the

321

tunnel, whistle blaring loudly in warning. He rolled onto the platform. He came to rest behind a pillar, breathing heavily, as the train pulled into the station.

Porter began firing at Yale. He crouched low, bullets bouncing all around him.

Yale realized that the conductor, or whoever the hell drove trains, had the good sense to keep the doors closed. The cars slowly began moving out of the station. Within a minute, the train had vanished into the tunnel.

Yale peeked around the pillar. Porter had dragged another garbage can between her and Yale. He counted about ten people hiding behind pillars and soda machines or just lying flat on the ground.

"Don't anybody move!" he yelled. One of the two cops on the stairs challenged him from the opposite end of the platform. Once again he became a cop. "On The Job!" he screamed, frantically waving his bogus shield.

Cops started streaming onto the platform. Two uniforms joined him behind the pillar. Others came down the opposite stairway. Porter opened up with a furious volley of shots. Bullets flew everywhere, and for the first time, Yale worried about getting shot by the growing number of rounds coming in his direction from friendly fire. Where the hell did they get that term from, he thought.

Yale heard another downtown train approaching. He turned to the petrified cops huddling next to him. "Anybody think to stop the goddamn trains!"

Both cops looked stupidly at each other. One grabbed his radio and began screaming to his dispatcher. "Stop the fucking downtown E train coming into five-oh!"

The train kept right on coming. More people are gonna get hurt,

Yale thought.

He heard someone calling his name.

"Yale!"

It was Porter.

"What?" He couldn't think of anything else to say.

"I'm coming out! Don't shoot!"

Even she had the sense to know she was trapped. "Throw out the gun, Leah." Jesus, he sounded like Pat O'Brien coaxing Jimmy Cagney out of a surrounded building in *Angels With Dirty Faces*. To his surprise, Wright's automatic clattered onto the platform. Yale came from behind the pillar. He noticed the slide on Wright's gun was back. *Christ, she's out of ammo.* "Hands on top of your head. Come to the middle of the platform." He leveled his gun at her chest.

The approaching train made a high-pitched wail as it rounded a final turn and came barreling into the station. Porter stood up, hands clasped on top of her head. She walked slowly toward the center of the platform.

Yale saw the videotape gripped on top of her head. She kept walking to the edge of the platform. She glanced at the approaching train, smiling.

"Oh, shit," Yale said. He broke into a sprint toward Porter. He saw cops beginning to get from behind their cover and look at him in amazement.

Yale was at least forty feet from Porter when she pressed the videotape against her chest. She blew Yale a kiss with her other hand.

Then she tumbled in front of the train as it thundered into the station.

## Chapter Thirty-Three

Yale was released from the hospital at 8:00 p.m. Afterward, he withstood three hours of questioning by the police. *The police.* How strange that he referred to them in his mind as something foreign, as if he had never been a part of them. He couldn't even remember when he felt a part of them. They were the enemy. His thumb throbbed in sync as he told one lie after another.

It was past midnight and Porter's body, or what was left of it, still had not been identified. Yale's story was that he and his friend Charlie Wright were on their way to see the Christmas tree-lighting ceremony when the shooting began. With his buddy killed, Yale pursued the shooter until she killed herself by jumping in front of a downtown express. A Deputy Inspector from headquarters told Yale that police witnesses had said he and the shooter called each other by name. Yale told him the cops were mistaken. He had no idea who the woman was or why she did what she did.

Porter was dead, but Steiner was still loose. For Yale to identify Porter would certainly have alerted Steiner. Yale had no idea what became of the videotape. Without that tape, he had no case. He desperately racked his aching brain for a way to trap Steiner. Before leaving the Midtown

North Precinct, Yale called Lt. Mike Sheehan, his one friend on The Job. He caught him just as he was leaving the One-Ten Precinct after his tour.

"For a guy who likes to avoid publicity," Sheehan said, "you sure got your share of it tonight. It's all over the tube." He lowered his voice. "Hey, I'm sorry about Wright."

Yale felt his stomach heave. Tears came to his eyes. He didn't wipe them away. He was exhausted, and it was an effort for him to speak. "Mike, I need a favor."

There was a moment of silence. "Sure."

"I'm on a precinct phone. I'll tell you what all this is about," Yale looked at his watch, "in about a half hour."

"Meet me in my office. I'm the only one here. It's okay."

Yale hung up. He left his car in the garage and took a cab to Queens. He didn't trust himself behind the wheel.

Sheehan was behind his desk, sleeves rolled up, when Yale arrived. The squad room was empty.

Sheehan reached into his desk and took out a bottle of Scotch and two plastic cups. He poured two drinks and handed one to Yale. "You look like you need this."

Yale took the drink with his good hand and sat in a wooden chair opposite his friend. He wondered if the drink would put him into a stupor. At this point, he didn't care.

Yale felt he owed Sheehan an explanation. "It's about the park killings."

Sheehan took a sip of his drink. "I figured as much. Soon as I heard about tonight, I made some calls."

Yale told Sheehan the whole story. He left nothing out. It was a cathartic experience, but he didn't feel much better when it was over.

"Jesus," Sheehan said, "Wolfgang Steiner? Hard to believe. Wait

325

until the press finds out Porter was the dame from last night. An ex-cop. Sweet Jesus."

Yale looked at Sheehan. "Tell me the videotape is intact."

The lieutenant shook his head. "Melted like a plastic ashtray in a blast furnace. The shooter—Porter-was dragged over a hundred feet by the train, then eleven cars passed over her body. The cassette was found jammed between her body and the third rail. Six hundred volts melted most of her and the tape. Sorry, buddy."

Yale's heart sank. Almost inaudibly, he said. "Anything else on her?"

Sheehan shook his head. "Not on her. I just got these pictures faxed to me from the lab." He passed a contact sheet of photographs across the desk. "There was a roll of Minox film in Charlie's pocket. The lab developed them. Thought maybe they might be some sort of evidence. I called for them when you phoned me. Thought you might be interested."

Yale looked at the pictures. It was the roll Wright had shot inside Porter's apartment. "Can I keep these?"

Sheehan shrugged. "Sure. Why not?" He took another sip of the Scotch. "We've got nothing, you know. Steiner walks." His voice was hard and bitter.

Yale continued to stare at the pictures. He straightened in his chair. "Mike, could you work a miracle and keep Porter's name out of the press and stay away from her apartment after she's identified?"

Sheehan looked over the rim of his cup. "Why?"

"There's still got to be a way to get Steiner." Yale chewed on a knuckle. "If he knows about Porter we'll never nail him."

"What makes you think he didn't send her after the tape?"

Yale explained his theory about Porter keeping a copy of the tape for insurance. "I'm almost certain Steiner knows nothing about it."

326

Sheehan stared at his friend. Yale knew Sheehan's career was flashing through his mind. "Ray, I could get seriously screwed for this."

"It might mean an arrest, Mike. You can take the credit."

Sheehan smirked. "Credit? I'd be happy to keep my fucking job." His head bobbed, lips pressed together like he was trying to resist a career-damaging decision. "Aw, shit. Okay." He waved a finger at Yale. "But listen up, you've got twelve hours. That's it. The M.E. will probably take another six hours or so to ID her. After that, I can stall for another six hours. When the time's up, her name gets released. What the hell makes you think you can trip Steiner up?"

Yale stood. His legs felt rubbery. He smiled thinly. "Because I know the enemy."

#

Yale was home within the hour. He formulated what he considered to be a half-assed plan. He phoned Ralph Nieves. At first, Nieves balked at being awakened at 4:00 a.m., he but calmed down after Yale explained what had transpired and that he needed to borrow Nieves' jacket that contained the hidden camera and recorder. He would try to get a confession out of Steiner, either by tricking him or coercing it out of him if he had to. He knew the plan was weak, but with less than twelve hours until Porter's name was plastered in every newspaper in town, he was reaching for anything.

Yale figured he could use a five-minute shower before his next call. A blast of cold water gave him a second wind. He ran his fingers through his damp hair and went to his desk for his address book. Yale checked the time: 5:10 a.m. He called his answering service.

"Ray Yale Investigations, may I help you?"

327

"Jackie? Ray Yale."

"Well, excuse me! I must have over twenty calls for you, most within the last two hours. You a star or somethin', honey?"

He guessed every news organization in the country was trying to reach him. "How long you been working, Jackie?"

"Since midnight, honey...work 'til noon today. Why, you want to ask me out on a date?" She chuckled. "I don't date white men. They all look alike to me." She laughed heartily.

She must not have seen a television or listened to a radio, Yale thought. "It's a long story, and believe me, you haven't got the time to hear it all. I'll fill you in later, okay?"

"Whatever you say. How'm I gonna get messages to you? You got a fax?"

"Forget the messages for now, Jackie. I need a favor."

"Do I gotta get naked?"

He chuckled. It felt good. "No."

"Okay, I'll do it. What it is I gotta do?"

"Make a phone call." He told her to call Steiner's office at the radio station at exactly 2:00 p.m. "I want you to say you're his stock broker." After a little coaching, Yale was satisfied she could handle the assignment.

"That's cool. I gotta go."

"No, hold up a minute, Jackie. When's your next vacation?"

"I get two weeks in July. Why?"

"Going anywhere?"

"Me? You gotta be kiddin'. I got two kids and no man. Where am I gonna go?" There was a brief moment of silence. "What's this, like *Queen For a Day*? If I could, I'd like to go see my mother in South Carolina. It's been seven years since I've been there. Why you askin'?"

"Writing a book about po' black folks."

She laughed. "Hey, hold it. There's another call comin' in on your line." Randall clicked off. While she was gone, Yale put the phone on speaker. He went to the closet and took $3000 of Cippolone's money and put it in a Federal Express envelope. Jackie Randall would get to see her mother. He was addressing the envelope care of the answering service when she broke back in. "You know a guy named Sal?"

Yale didn't immediately make the connection. "Who?"

"Some guy named Sal. Says he works out with you at the gym."

Yale sighed. Sal Bertuna. "What's he want?"

"Says he's lookin' for work."

Chapter Thirty-Four

The phone rang in the back of the limousine. Wolfgang Steiner yanked it from its cradle.

"Yeah?"

"Mr. Steiner?" a woman's voice asked.

"Who the hell else would be answering this phone?"

"Yes, sir, I'm sorry. This is Charity, in reception."

He sighed deeply. "Yes, Charity in reception." *Where does the station get these brain-damaged kids?*

"Well, sir, Mr. Steiner, sir, your broker just called, and she said it's important she see you at her office as soon as possible."

*Leah?* "What time did she call?"

"About five minutes ago, sir."

"Thank you." He hung up. He expected to see Leah a little later in the afternoon, as usual. He looked at his watch. He had an appointment with his agent in twenty minutes. What the hell, he was horny. He lowered the partition. "Lonnie, head back uptown and drop me off on Sixty-Ninth Street. The usual place."

"You're not goin' to the meeting?" the driver said.

"Not unless it moved. Go for a ride or something for two hours, then come back and get me." Screw my agent, Steiner thought, he makes enough money off me. He can wait.

"You got it, boss." The glass slowly slid closed.

The limo pulled over on Columbus Avenue. Steiner lowered his baseball cap over his eyes and walked with a slight stoop to disguise his height. The block was quiet—several hours to go until the Friday-night rush home. He reached into his jacket pocket and felt for Porter's keys.

He took the three flights of stairs two steps at a time. He inserted the key into the top lock of the apartment door. His heart quickened. He was beginning to feel movement in his jeans and expected Leah to be waiting for him on the other side of the door completely naked or close to it.

He was a little surprised that she wasn't there to greet him when he stepped into the apartment. He double-locked the front door. The apartment was neat and orderly. This pleased him. At least he wasn't footing the bill for a slob. He called her name. No answer.

Steiner went to the window and lowered the blinds. Idiot, he thought, she'll never learn. Steiner looked around for a note but didn't see one. *Where the hell could she be?*

Steiner took off his studded leather jacket and tossed it on the mountain of stuffed animals. He shook his head. the woman has enough blood lust to make Dracula look anemic, and she's got a cuddle complex. Look at the fucking things, he said to himself as he gave a life-sized panda a nudge with his boot. *Nut.*

That's when he saw the gun.

A revolver was sticking out from under the couch, barrel first. Steiner left the stuffed toys and slowly walked to the couch. He bent and picked up the gun.

A Charter Arms .44 caliber. A thin line of sweat ran down his back.

The same type of gun David Berkowitz had used in the Son of Sam killings. The same type of gun he had used to kill that college kid in Queens years ago. He licked his lips and broke open the cylinder. Loaded. Leah was into weapons, but it wasn't like her to leave a loaded gun lying around. And he didn't know she had a .44. At least she had never mentioned it, and she liked to talk about her weapons.

Something's wrong. He gripped the gun tightly and got down on his knees. He looked under the couch. Nothing but dust bunnies. He got up and went into the kitchen, sweeping the pistol in front of him as he went. He checked the lower cabinets. Empty. He went into the bedroom and looked under the bed and in the closet. Satisfied that there was no one in the apartment, he went back to the living room.

He heard a humming noise coming from the front door. It wasn't the sound of a key. He saw the door knob move. He backed into the kitchen and waited.

## Chapter Thirty-Five

Yale inserted the pick gun into the top lock of Porter's apartment door. He flipped the power switch and heard the tumblers fall into place almost immediately. One more to go. The bottom lock was a little tougher. Sweat ran into his eyes. He wiped it away and checked his watch. He took a deep breath and tried again. In less than a minute, the lock gave up the fight. He tried the door knob. It turned.

Yale closed the door gently behind him and stepped into the living room. He removed a tape recorder and a roll of packing tape from his jacket pocket. He looked around the room, walked to a set of stereo speakers, and wrapped some tape around the recorder. He hit the record button. As he was securing the recorder in back of a speaker, he sensed movement behind him.

"Turn that fucking thing off!" Steiner said from the kitchen alcove.

Yale whirled and reached for his waistband.

Steiner cocked the revolver. "Uh-uh."

Yale slowly let his hand fall to his side. "Don't shoot." He hit the stop button on the recorder.

Steiner gestured with his gun. "Two fingers. Gun on the floor. Kick it and the recorder over here. Now!"

Yale did as he was told. Steiner bent down quickly, picked up Yale's .38, and shoved it in his waistband. He stomped on the tape recorder with a massive engineer boot. The sound of plastic cracking make Yale think of a skull being crushed. He swallowed hard.

Both men faced each other from across the room. Steiner ordered Yale to his knees. Yale winced as he went down and was reminded of the pounding his knees had taken at the skating rink. It seemed like such a long time ago.

Steiner moved a little closer but still kept a respectable distance. He looked at Yale quizzically. "Don't I know you?"

"I delivered your Japanese food, remember?"

Steiner's eyes narrowed. "Who are you? What're you doing here?"

Yale smiled. "I eat sushi, I get the urge to burglarize apartments." Steiner was across the room in a second. He kicked Yale in the chest. "Try again."

Yale felt like he had been by a truck. He fell over backwards and rolled onto his stomach. He couldn't draw a breath. His meager breakfast began to back up. The feeling passed quickly, but it took him a few seconds to get air. He gasped, "Fuck you."

Steiner was on him again. Yale shielded his head as Steiner's boot heel connected with his ear. Yale screamed in pain. The room went temporarily dark, and Yale struggled to remain conscious. He waved a hand. "No more. No more."

Steiner backed away, grinning. "Sit up!"

Yale slid on his buttocks to the couch. It felt good to rest against a solid object. Blood streamed down the side of his face. He touched his ear: still attached, but terribly cut. "I'm a private investigator. Name's Yale." The room spun. God, don't let me pass out, he thought.

Steiner pushed the smashed recorder with his foot. "What's with this?"

Yale shook his head.

One long step and Steiner was inches from Yale. He brought back his boot. Yale yelled, "No!"

"Then tell me what the fuck's going on!"

"Okay, okay. I was hired by the father of the woman Porter killed in Flushing Meadow Park. A videotape she had implicated you. I came here to trap you into a confession."

Steiner smirked. "A little fucking late, aren't you? I beat you here. Dumb fuck." He frowned. "What videotape?"

Yale wanted to buy time. He told Steiner about the video tape.

"Jesus Christ! The stupid bitch had a copy?" He moved to where Yale sat and stuck the .44 in his damaged ear. "Where is it?"

Yale gritted his teeth against the pain. "Destroyed." Through shooting stars, he told Steiner about the gun battle in Rockefeller Center.

"She was the one in Rockefeller Center?" He mumbled to himself, "What the fuck was she doing behind my back?" Yale saw no sorrow, no feeling of loss at the news of his lover's death. Steiner stared at Yale intently. "How do I know you're telling me the truth?"

Before Yale could answer, Steiner backhanded him across the cheekbone with the pistol. Yale thought now he knew what it must feel like to get shot in the head. Sound and motion ceased. His head flopped back against the seat cushion as a fine spray of blood stained the white leather couch. He thought he passed out for a brief moment. When he was able to focus, he saw Steiner pacing in front of him.

"So let me see if I have this straight." He turned like a caged animal. "You're a private eye. Somebody hires you to solve their daughter's murder, and you're bright enough to figure that out but too stupid to beat me up here on time to plant a recorder. Is that right?"

Yale's left eye was closing. His lips were swollen, and he had
trouble talking. "I was going to beat a confession out of you if I had to."
He gestured weakly to the crushed tape recorder. "The recorder."

Steiner appeared to be soaking all of it in. "I don't buy it." He hit
Yale on the back of the head with the gun. "On your stomach!"

Yale was on his way there anyway. The blow to the head wasn't as
painful as the previous clouts, but it was enough to flip him over on his
belly. Steiner began to pat him down.

"Hold everything," Steiner said as his hand stopped on the
recorder secreted in Ralph Nieves' jacket. "What have we here?" He
backed away. "Take off that coat."

Every muscle in Yale's body ached. He got to his haunches and
took off the jacket. Steiner took a cautious step forward and snatched it.
He squeezed it. Within seconds, he found the recorder and the miniature
camera.

Steiner began to chuckle. He backed to a chair and sat down. The
camera and the recorder lay side by side on the polished wooden floor in
front of him. Three rapid blows with his boot reduced them to so much
high-tech rubble.

In addition to all this abuse, Yale thought, now I owe Ralph for the
equipment. It would appear not to be his day.

Steiner stopped laughing. "You think you could outsmart me? You
gotta be fucking kidding! That first recorder was a ruse, wasn't it? I see you
plant it, you've got a backup I'm not supposed to know about, and I talk
myself into jail, right?"

Yale didn't answer. He had to tilt his head back to see Steiner
clearly. The nausea was returning.

Steiner leaned forward. "Let me tell you something, asshole. What
the fuck do you think my voice on tape would get you? I've been recorded

for years, for God's sake!" He bent his dead down and looked in Yale's good eye. "I'm on the fucking radio, dickhead! You could make a tape of me confessing to killing President Kennedy, for Christ's sake, just by piecing together recorded syllables I've said on my radio show over the last fifteen years!" He got up and took a step toward Yale but stopped. He crouched down. "How fucking stupid are you? I'm smarter than some asshole private eye! I'm fucking smarter than everybody! I'm the Emperor of the fucking Airwaves!"

Steiner's melodious radio voice was replaced by the screech of a beyond-the-fringe psychopath. What a perfect match, Yale thought: Porter and Steiner, two lunatics. That conclusion, however, didn't ease the pain, which increased with each passing second. "The cops are on the way, you know."

Steiner appeared to think for a brief moment. "Bullshit! It's you and me. If they had anything, they'd be here by now."

"You killed that girl in Forest Hills. I saw it on the tape."

"Voskerichian? You know it, and I know it. The cops nailed Berkowitz for that one, just like we figured. If the cops knew about it, I'd be in jail by now." He sat back down and glared at Yale. "We were fucking kids, for Christ's sake! Me and Zoltag. Two assholes. I admit it. We were looking for the ultimate kick."

"So you killed her. Then you had that psycho Porter kill Zoltag when he tried to blackmail you. The girl Zoltag picked up that night was in the wrong place at the wrong time."

"I had Zoltag killed to stay out of jail." He got up and moved toward Yale. "What would you have done? Huh? Answer me!"

Yale held up a hand. "You want me to justify murder? You were a kid? That's an excuse? What about Tavlin?"

Steiner's eyes went wide. "You know about him?" Yale saw

Steiner's knuckles get white as he gripped the pistol tighter.

"Yeah, I know about him. It was all about the ratings. Fucking ratings. You weren't a kid then." Yale actually felt himself chuckle. "Some fucking excuse. How smart was that?" He watched Steiner's face get red.

"How smart was it? I'll tell you how smart, wiseguy." Steiner walked to the window and turned. "I'm where I am because I took chances. Tavlin thought he was smarter than me. Than me! Can you imagine? He had to go." He was laughing in short bursts of a mirthless cackle. He came to where Yale was sitting and crouched before him. "And what about Danny Doremus, the jackass? He tried fucking with me, too. Look where it got him. Now he's entertaining some jerkwater farmers in Arkansas somewhere."

"Georgia." Yale could feel Steiner's breath on his face, hot and angry.

Steiner got up. "Oh, Georgia, is it?" He kneed Yale in the ribs. Yale winced, air rushing from his lungs. Steiner's radio voice returned. "You know, my friend, I think you know a little too much." He raised the pistol.

Yale's chest was on fire. He was certain the last kick had fractured a couple of ribs. He looked Steiner in the face. "You gonna shoot me?" It came out almost as a whisper. The blood in his mouth tasted sweet.

The gun waivered for an instant. Yale saw Steiner swallow, then square his shoulders. "Leah's not here to do it for me. I've got no choice." He took a deep breath. All Yale saw was the gaping hole in the barrel of the powerful pistol.

Yale looked past Steiner. He saw the stuffed panda move.

Out from under the pile of stuffed animals, the man who Yale had teasingly called the dwarf, Sal Bertuna, silently struggled to his feet. He was carrying a tire iron in his right hand. Steiner whirled, Yale supposed, because he had followed the PI's gaze.

Yale saw a split second of confusion on Steiner's face. He recovered quickly and thrust the gun at Bertuna. He pulled the trigger. *Click.*

As Steiner momentarily looked at the gun, two things happened. With Steiner's back now toward him, Yale swept his outstretched legs in a wide arc, catching Steiner on the ankle, toppling him. The big man fell on his back with a terrific thud. The .44 went flying.

Bertuna, who looked more insane to Yale than Steiner had during his worst moment, lunged at the prostrate Steiner and the raised the tire iron.

Yale rolled to Steiner and threw his body on top of the taller man, who was struggling to get up. "No!" Yale screamed. He held up a hand. "No, Sal!" Yale was fighting the smaller man and having a difficult time.

Steiner pushed away from Yale and grabbed Yale's .38 from his waistband. He pulled the trigger just as Yale knocked the tire iron from Bertuna's hand. Yale heard a click. Both he and Bertuna stopped tussling and turned into the bewildered stare of Wolfgang Steiner, who was gawking at yet another useless gun. He dropped the pistol and buried his face in his hands.

Yale stood in front of the couch. "Gimme the recorder," he said to Bertuna.

The little man was staring daggers at the fallen giant in front of him. Bertuna lifted his shirt and removed a small tape recorder from his waistband. Bertuna passed it over his shoulder, never taking his eyes off Steiner. "Here. I hope the motherfucker gets put to sleep."

"Lethal injection?" Yale said. "Him? Nah. He's too smart." His legs gave way and he sank onto the couch. "Sal, do me a favor? Call Lt. Mike Sheehan." He rattled off a phone number. "I'm too tired."

*Blood Shot Eyes*

## Chapter Thirty-Six

Yale huddled against the cold on a park bench in Flushing Meadow Park. He had been up for thirty-six hours, but it felt more like three days.

In fifteen more minutes, it would be totally dark. He wondered if the lampposts that stood over the poorly maintained pathways actually worked. He tried to remember the last time he was in the park with Arnold Carpenter.

He heard Sal Bertuna before he saw him. The sound of boots against the frozen snow carried a great distance over the open terrain.

Bertuna sat down next to him and buried his hands in his jacket pocket. "Jesus, Ray. You look like shit. You took a helluva beating."

Yale's eyes were bloodshot and supported deep bags. He hadn't shaved in a while either. His five o'clock shadow looked like it had originated in another time zone. He glanced at his bandaged thumb and touched a hand to his gauze-wrapped head. Must look like a homeless mummy, he thought.

Yale had taken a bad battering. He didn't need anyone to remind him. But wounds heal, scars fade. Charlie Wright wouldn't be on the mend any time too soon. Neither would Katherine Carpenter, Herman Zoltag, nor Marvin Tavlin. Yale briefly thought of the horse that was cut down by Porter's bullets. NYPD horses are named for cops killed in the line of duty, he recalled. Whomever that horse was named after gave his life twice

340

for the City of New York.

"I had to, Sal. Steiner had to think he had the upper hand. I couldn't risk him knowing the trap was in place. He had to think I was a bumbling idiot." It hurt to talk. "At least I couldn't get shot. It took me two hours to pull the .44 slugs from the shell casings and dump the powder. I never bothered loading my gun."

"It was takin' a helluva chance, you ask me. How'd you know he'd fall for it?" The little man turned to Yale. "I mean, how'd you know for sure you'd take a beatin' to test your theory?"

Yale smiled. That hurt, too. "Because I know the enemy, Sal. Steiner thought he was smarter than everyone else. I set out to convince him he was right."

Bertuna had his coat pulled over his ears, and the bulk of his parka made him look like Jabba the Hut. "I coulda come out sooner, ya know. Every time he clocked you, I got more pissed off."

"The more the better. We got all we needed for a few more shots. After a while, I got numb. Didn't feel a thing." He lied.

"Why'd you need to sneak me in there for anyway? Just a recorder woulda done it. Why'd you need me?"

Yale looked at the little man he owed so much. "What Steiner said was right, or at least could have been. A smart lawyer could have convinced a jury the tape was a fake. Steiner's rich. He'd get the best forensic experts in the world to twist the evidence. Money buys justice, Sal. Remember O.J.?"

Sal smirked. "Yeah."

"Well, now what we got is an ear and eyewitness—you—in addition to the tape."

Bertuna studied Yale's face. "Why'd you ask me to do it? Ain't you got any cop friends?"

Yale squeezed Bertuna's arm. "Two reasons. One, you're small—"

Bertuna snorted. "I am?"

"You were able to fit snuggly under that pile of stuffed animals. Two, I thought you were tough enough to do it." For a second, Yale was swept back to Vietnam. The two of them sitting here, survivors. "I was right."

"Thanks, Ray." Yale thought he heard the little man choke up. Bertuna looked around. "Why are we here? I'm freezin' my ass off."

Yale kicked a battered suitcase under the bench. "The press is all over me. I figured it would be quiet here. When are you going back to work?"

Bertuna looked at him and smiled. Yale didn't recall him ever doing that. "Who keeps track of time anymore? I think I gotta be back at Bellevue tomorrow at seven in the a.m." He dug for a cigarette and lit up. He laughed. "Ya know, when I started smokin'? Six years ago. I was thirty-seven fuckin' years old. By that time most people are quittin'."

"The job?" Yale asked.

"Yeah," he said bitterly, "the fuckin' job."

Yale pulled the briefcase from beneath the bench and rested it on his knees. "I guess you're still looking to get out of Bellevue, right?"

Bertuna came to life. He sat up straight and his head emerged from his jacket like a turtle in heat. "You got some work for me, Ray?"

"You like dogs?"

Bertuna looked at his friend and squinted. "Yeah, I like dogs. I got me one, a Bulldog. Some people say I look like him. His name's Westmoreland."

"I know a guy who owns a dog health food store. He's looking for a partner, can't handle the business by himself." He explained Bob Zanichelli's operation. "I spoke to him a little while ago. He's willing to take you on as a partner."

Bertuna shook his head, his enthusiasm waning. "It sounds like a pretty big operation. What kind of green is he lookin' for?"

"Fifty large for twenty-five percent, plus a salary. You'd probably triple what you're making now. It's a bargain."

The little man sighed. "I ain't got that kind of bread, man. I could scrape together maybe ten grand. For that, I couldn't buy a fuckin' dog biscuit, from what you're tellin' me."

Yale withdrew a sealed manila envelope from the briefcase. He placed it in the short man's lap. "You got it now."

Bertuna tore open the envelope. His eyes got wide. "How much is in here?"

"Fifty grand. It's yours."

The little man jammed the envelope in Yale's jacket. "I can't take this, man. I could never pay it back."

Yale took out the envelope and held it against Bertuna's chest. "It's not a loan, Sal, it's a gift. Take the money and have a good life."

The burned-out veteran gingerly grasped the envelope and stared at it for a full minute. He turned to Yale with tears in his eyes. His voice cracked. "I did what I did for you 'cause you're a decent guy. You're the only person talks to me in the gym. What I did, I did 'cause I consider you my friend; I didn't do it for no money." The cash began a return trip. Yale stopped it in mid-flight, placing a hand on Bertuna's forearm.

"Sal," he said gently, barely audible over the increasing wind, "you helped me end an eighteen-year tragedy. This money is intended to make things right for a lot of people, including me. Take it and start over." Bertuna's eyes shifted between Yale and the money. "Go on, take it." Yale carefully pushed the money back to his friend's lap.

"Thanks, man." The tears flowed freely, and he wiped away years of pain with the back of his hand.

Yale got up. Every muscle in his body ached. "I don't want to rush you," he said, smiling, "but your new partner wants to see you tomorrow at noon. You think the city will mind?"

"Fuck the city," Sal said through sniffles. "I just quit." They both laughed. "C'mon let's get outta here."

"You got wheels?" Yale asked.

"No, I trained it."

"I'll give you a ride. My car's underneath the expressway."

"Think it's still there?"

He fingered the Lexus' keys in his pocket. He really didn't care. "The way my week's been going, I wouldn't be surprised if it's not."

They walked together around a bunch of naked shrubs and trees, on the twisting, broken path, avoiding the shorter route because it would take them through tall weeds. They suffered from the same demons. Yale grabbed Bertuna's arm as they were passing two flagpoles. "Check this out." He pointed straight up.

The moon had come to rest directly behind the Nazi swastikas, silhouetting them against the cloudless winter sky.

Bertuna craned his neck upward. "Jesus Christ! Swastikas."

Yale looked at the hated icons and thought about what had transpired since he had last seen them. "Frightening, huh?"

"Amazin', man," Bertuna said, unable to take his eyes off them. "Right here in New York. And I always thought the VC were motherfuckers." He gestured with his hand. "Those bastards had to be the most evil sonsabitches that ever lived."

Yale blinked and fought off tears. "We never get away from evil, Sal. We just deal with different degrees of it."

*Blood Shot Eyes*

# Epilogue

Yale and Arnold Carpenter stood silent beside each other in front of the unmarked grave. Each man had his head lowered, lost in separate shrouds of grief. Carpenter broke the silence.

"This Mr. Wright, he must have been a good friend."

Yale smiled thinly. "He saved my life." It was a brutally cold mid-December morning, though Yale hardly felt the penetrating frigid chill. Two weeks had passed since Wright had been murdered, and Yale still felt numb.

Carpenter squinted against the sun. "This then is the gentleman I read about in the newspaper? The man who was killed by the woman who killed my daughter?"

"Yes. Leah Porter."

"A friend like this comes along once in a lifetime, Mr. Yale. My family had such a friend during the war. He is why I stand here now." He sighed. "Ah, but that is ancient history." He gripped Yale's arm. "I'm very indebted to you for solving Katherine's murder. She can rest now. So can my wife."

Yale looked at the old man. "I'm sorry, sir, for not calling you sooner. I needed some time to heal." He wasn't necessarily talking about

345

his broken ribs and battered face. Solitude was his way of grieving. Yale had stayed in his apartment for almost two weeks. Right or wrong, he had done the same thing after his wife had died, perhaps for too long, now that he thought about it in retrospect. He found himself going through the same process for Charlie Wright.

Carpenter nodded. "I understand."

Yale looked at the freshly packed earth on the grave. "I couldn't find Charlie's family. He told me once about a sister in Pennsylvania, but I couldn't locate her." Yale had searched every computer database imaginable to no avail. Women marry, change their names; he had given up after a week and bought a plot for his friend. "The headstone'll be ready in about three months," he said, uneasy at Wright being in an unmarked grave. He pointed to a hill. "My wife is over there."

"You are a kind man."

Kind of what, Yale thought, taking a page from Wright's book of puns. *I paid for his funeral and interment with money I ripped off from a drug dealer and con man.* Somehow, Yale thought, Wright would have appreciated the irony. He did some quick calculating in his head. Of the hundred and sixty thousand dollars they took from Porter's apartment, fifty had gone to Sal Bertuna, three to Jackie Randall, and ten each to the mounted cop who was paralyzed as a result of her dead horse pinning her and to the family of the old-timer cop who was killed at Rockefeller Center. All money was donated anonymously. In addition, Yale gave twenty-five thousand to Sloan Kettering Memorial Hospital in Wright's name. He had about sixty large left. Yale was going to keep the money. He felt he deserved it.

Carpenter cleared his throat. "So tell me, Mr. Yale, what is to become of this man Steiner?"

"He's trying to cop a plea...er, plead guilty to a reduced charge."

"A reduced charge!" His face reddened. "He will go free soon?"

346

Yale shook his head. "No, sir. The district attorney has a case, but its circumstantial." He explained to his client about the absence of videotape. "There are two witnesses to his confession, however, me and a colleague. The confession was also recorded. There's also the forty-four caliber pistol he had with him. The same type of gun, maybe the same guy, he used to kill that college student in Forest Hills twenty years ago—"

"Yes, I read about that." Carpenter interrupted. He seemed perplexed. "Why could he keep the same gun for all that time?"

*Why indeed.* Yale had gotten the .44 from Ralph Nieves for two reasons. One was to get Steiner confused and unnerved, to have him dwell on the crime that had started it all. Second, Yale didn't think it would help Steiner's defense to be caught with a similar gun that was used in the Son of Sam killings. The Voskerician murder was committed twenty years ago. David Berkowitz pleaded guilty. Voskerician was killed with a head shot. The bullet was more than likely too damaged for comparison purposes. Another nail in Steiner's coffin.

Yale shrugged. "Who knows? I think he won't risk a trial and will take fifteen to twenty years rather than lose and do twenty-five to life. He'll do fifteen."

Carpenter's eyes narrowed. "You don't think he will survive in prison, do you, Mr. Yale?"

The old man's sharp, Yale thought. Every thug in the joint will want to be the guy who sticks Wolfgang Steiner. An instant reputation maker. "It's a violent world inside." He wanted to change the subject. "Do you listen to the radio, Mr. Carpenter?"

"Mostly classical music, some jazz. I did, however, listen to Steiner's show after you phoned me about him. I thought I would get some insight into the man. I assumed his colleagues would be talking about him."

347

Yale smirked. The day after Steiner's arrest, his show took a one day "hiatus" and was back the next day with Danny Doremus at the helm, the rival Steiner had run out of New York with planted evidence. Fame is fleeting in the Big Apple. Or a better cliché, Yale thought, would be, "what goes around, comes around."

"More justice, Mr. Carpenter." He explained what Steiner had done to Doremus.

"I'm glad for Mr. Doremus." He reached into his pocket. "Now, there's a matter of your payment, Mr. Yale."

They politely argued about that for a few minutes before Carpenter relented and put his check back in his pocket. "I told you that you were a kind man."

Yale picked up the collar on his coat. It was the first day without his gauze turban, and he wished he had worn a hat. "Thank you, but I'm also a cold man." He gestured gallantly to a path. "Shall we?"

Yale dropped Carpenter in front of his apartment building and begged off an invitation to dinner. He still wanted to be alone.

He recalled that when he was a kid, his father would occasionally take a day off from the restaurant, and they would go uptown to Times Square and watch cowboy movies in the twenty-four hour theaters that dotted the neighborhood back then. Yale wanted to be a kid again, at least for a few hours. He knew the westerns and all-night cinemas were a thing of the past, but there were still a few theaters that opened early in that area. While the new movie heroes were no match for Lash LaRue, they would have to do.

As long as the bad guys lost and the good guys didn't die, he would consider it time well spent.

## About the Author

Patrick Picciarelli is a retired NYPD Lt., licensed private investigator, and multi-published author in the crime genre.

Made in the USA
Middletown, DE
18 December 2020